Ohio River Dialogues

Books by William Zink

The Hole
Isle of Man
Torrid Blue
Ballad of the Confessor
Homage: Sonnets from the Husband
Riffs from New Id

Ohio River Dialogues

William Zink

Sugar Loaf Press
granville

ISBN: 978-0-9700702-3-4
Library of Congress Control Number: 2007903427

Sugar Loaf Press
343 North Pearl Street
Granville, Ohio 43023

Printed in the USA

The Players.

Doans, *eldest brother*

Hector, *middle brother*

Emanuel, *youngest brother*

Gabriel, *brother-in-law*

Narrator, *Oedipus, Jesus, & Rodin*

Scene: *Muskingum River, Ohio, summer of 2002*

~ PART ONE ~

The Jabbering Spray

In the sky, one flies. On the ground, the other, brother-in-law as it were, putters against the slippery river's banks, winding through growth and regrowth after man's caustic loogey of timbering and strip mining has succumbed to the earth's cyclic and never-failing healing womb. To a cabin, they go. The cabin of men without moats around their souls. The state is Ohio. The old barb wire river, The Muskingum.

Gabriel   If he—Leonardo—could see me now! If he could have actually built his flying machine! . . . What if someone did? Flying, when everyone else knew only horses, chariots, or their own two feet. To even imagine it—that in itself was a leap. But to have actually done it. . . There must have been leaps like that, anomalies of such a magnitude that. . . But *I'm* not an anomaly. . . Well, yes I am, sort of. But I'm neither a great dreamer, nor dinosaur. I've been pushed to the sky by the very opposite—a completely normal, uneventful life. A life without surprise, a life without risk, a life without self-determination. . . *This* is risk! Doansy wouldn't dream of doing it. He thinks I'm crazy. Abby thinks I'm crazy. Her folks think I'm crazy. Which is why I'm doing it. Which is why even if the fear gets to me, I have to keep doing it. I have to be a little crazy. I have to throw them off the trail. I have to feel something. I can't go back now. . .

Doans   If you crash, Gabe-man, can I have your keyboard? . . .

No, don't crash. You know I'm just a kiddin'. But if you do—an'
I'm not sayin' I want you to—can I have your air compressor?
Abby don't need it. She wouldn't even know how to turn it on. If
you crash, all your things'll be wasted. I'd hate to have to ask
Abby on the ride back from the cemetery. Maybe we could put
little tags on things; let's do it now before anything unfortunate
happens. How can I ask you about a thing like that? I'm not tryin'
to be an opportunist, it's just that nobody thinks a these things
until after, an' then people who have maybe two air compressors
already, or some dope who don't need or want one, they end up
gettin' it, when somebody like me, who's droolin' for one, who
could use the shit out of it—why, it could be the thing that changes
my whole life dynamic—I get screwed Casino Royale, an' I won't
even be able to borrow it. . . Gabe, you are one crazy lunatic. I
hope you know what you're doin', 'cause I sure don't.
Gabriel . . . *Oh, fuck.* . . You forgot to mow the backyard. . .
Shit. . . She's going to be pissed. Why did you forget. You had it
on the list. You did everything on the list, except that. That makes
it worse. Oh well, she'll have to do it herself. . . Why didn't you
do it Wednesday night when you had the chance. You could have
done it after dinner. But you went down in the basement instead.
You didn't do much of anything down there. Fiddled around with
some gears. Tried to find that AM station Doansy told you about.
Watched that centipede in the spider web for an hour—those
fucking bastards deserve worse than that. . . and now the lawn
isn't mowed, and you'll be thinking of that for the next three days.
No, don't think about it. It's too late. She'll just have to get over it.
Doans This truck don't sound too good. You think we got that
chain on right? A whole week spent fiddlin' with that timin' chain,
an' it still sounds sloppy. We should a had Crosby come down.
Yeah, but Crosby wanted to tow it back up to his place. He said he
didn't like people watchin' 'em work. That's cool. Okay, I can dig
that. But I couldn't let 'em take the truck. . . Crosby, man, like I
need the truck to-*day*-ee. . . I trust you, Gabe. You're a chip off the
old man's cloth; too bad you ain't his own flesh an' blood. . .
Come on, beat-mobile. . . Hang in there. . .

Gabriel   —Where's Doansy? Where's the road? I can't see it.
The trees are in the way. . . where'd he go? . . . How many men
have followed a river the way I'm following this one? Maybe
nobody's followed this one. Maybe I'm doing something nobody
in the world has done before. . . There you are, Doansy. Good
man. Stay where I can see you. . . The trees look like stars. The
river is flat and gray; the muddy waters of the Muskingum. I've
never even swimmed it, yet here I am following its scoliosis spine
toward the great Ohio. Some day I'll follow *it*, all the way to the
great Mississippi. I'll pass the Missouri, oh Lewis, oh Clark, oh
uphill battle, set out in the days of dusty conquest, past Hannibal,
birth of Huckleberry Finn and racial consciousness and shadowy
antebellum tales of guiltless fratricide—the collision of sanity and
inertia. . . through the long arms of bayou country that no man
should ever tame, lest he drain the whole primeval soup, the way
he's drained the patience of alabaster angels once prodigious in
these fields and plains; finally to the silts of New Orleans itself!—
distributor of all loose feet and stolen properties, fingers fanning in
glorious native maze of sea sustenance! Up here, I can dream! I
know what they can't know! I've cast off my unexamined,
unfulfilled, assembly line life!

Doans   A little somethin' to loosen the load. . . okay, where'd I
put it?—*fumbling, groping in lascivious panic*—Oh hoochie-
coochie bag, where are you? . . . Why, you little Rasputin; you
were in my shirt pocket all the time. You little devil, you. You
Smokey da Bear Band-*dee*-toe. . . Two days with no rabbit snare
horse shit bobbin' for apples tryin' to protect my hiney from
those—yes, you—whorish, philanthropic an' tasteless voyeurs a
any aesthetic awareness, lemming stampedes deaf to anything but
reproductions a Van Gogh sunflowers 'cause some crow at the pop
machine told 'em that's the real deal, McQueen, the thing you
should have, the canvas you oughtta sail, the way it should be. . .
Senator, where's your baby boy? Whose trumpet playin' are you
tryin' to copy? What you all be sayin' the Pledge of Allegiance on
those sacred steps for? . . . yeah. . . hmmmmm. . . whatever you
say, Sergeant Carter. Aye, aye, Skipper. . . I pledge allegiance to

the flag a the United States of America, an' to the Republic for
which it stands. . . to the *Republic*, Socrates. To the *Republic*. You
hear that? Why, it's only a *word*. . . Ho-*hoooooooo!* Not cloth an'
dye an' symbol, Gomer, but the Reee-pub-lic; beautiful, sacred
holiness that it is. To the Republic for which it stands; an' who be
that, Ace? What's this Republic so duly deservin' a our high
reverence? What *is* it? . . . Irony! . . Tragedy! . . . All the whilst
you fat cats be layin' off workers like maybe your job depended
on it; sellin' out the people, senators, a.k.a. the Republic, to Me-
hee-koe, China, Indonesia, the Philippines, Korea, India, an' the
communist papa bear formerly known as The Soviet Union. Any
American-hatin' plebe who'll slave an' sweat for a ha' penny will
do, yes we have no bananas, though we gots plenty a flesh over
there on yon shanty hill. In them ghettoes a rice. In them flesh-pots
a ready-made warriors—'cause where else they gonna be one a the
few, the proud, the come an' take *that*, serpent in the garden. . .
Congress. Wall Street. One an' the same. Brothers-with-charms.
Whore an' John. Ying an' Yang. Double-barrel. . . Oh, so *that's*
how it works! That's what's goosin' my flip-side. Sellin' out the
Republic to the lowest bidder! For sale! Over here, you grubby,
grovelin' mass a Morlock-flesh! Don't give us your tired, your
feeble, yo' blistered a feet; we'll come to *you*. . . Hush-hush, leetle
bambino, don't be a slob, Uncle Georgie's gonna give you Mister
Johnson's job. America: not from sea to shinin' sea no mo'—
that's ancient history, a memory to bore our progeny—but from
global portfolio to portfolio. No taxation without representation—
remember! . . . *Remember?* . . . Why? . . . What does it mean? . . .
Chew on it, Billy. . . It means we don't have no sovereignty with
you red-coated folks pokin' them muskets in our hollow bellies,
takin' your cut a the choicest meat, leavin' us the bones. You don't
give us no *say*. You say—shut up, Yank, er we'll blow ye to itsy-
bitsy pieces. Well, well. . . what goes around, comes around. It
ain't the taxation robbin' us blind—it's pullin' jobs, wages, dinero
en mi pock-*ee*-toe, the individual's right to sell his bananas on the
corner, or shoes, or corn, or *music*, God help us, without the potato
head brigade forcin' us to goose-step in line; an' then when we

do—*poof!*—Made in China! . . . *Fuck,* man, like I'm gonna end up
bein' a greeter at Wal-Mart, an' I'll be glad for the op-poor-tune-
it-eeeee. China ain't gonna send no bombs over here, man. Who's
gonna buy all their *shit*?

Gabriel   . . . Did I bring my harmonicas? When I got to
Doansy's, I left the stuff in the car. . . We went into the studio. . .
we came out, went inside the house. . . had a cup of coffee. . .
looked at Doansy's guitar. . . went back outside and into the
studio. Then we started loading up the truck. Amps and cases first.
I don't remember putting the harmonicas in. . .

Doans   A fireworks display. . . Shootin' stars galore. . . Starry
starry night. . . Think about it, Gabe; there oughtta be some
glorious illuminations tonight. Tonight—or tomorrow? Now,
which night is it. . . Tonight's the night, it's gonna be all right. . .
Me an' my brothers, an' Ol' Man River, an' Lucy in the Sky, an'
September Morn'—oh blushin' virginal bride-offerin' for these
vagabond, hobo-mojo misrepresented eyes. . .

Gabriel   What'll I do without my harmonicas? I can't play
guitar. I can't sing. All I know how to do is play harmonica. I'll go
into town and buy one. Any cheapie harmonica, it doesn't matter,
but I gotta have one. This is worse than forgetting to mow the
lawn. . . What's that? . . . Is that a plane? I'm one of them now.
I'm with the buzzards and hawks and airplanes. I'm with wild
men—real dreamers. Harmonica sky. Harmonica jet. Harmonicas
showing me their open notes; I can feel them against my tongue
and lips. . . *harmonica*. . . It's not that I don't love her. It's
necessary for every man to want to get away now and then.
Without her, there would be no getting away—freedom would
surround me day and night—this would be nothing special—a
habit, not an enterprise. It's because I'm not free that freedom
lures me with her seductiveness—false though it might be. Would
I want to be without her forever, not as an idea which I would then
use to further my night's fantasies, but really, permanently? I can't
ever leave her. I love her. . . What am I thinking about this for?
The idea of being free is powerful. It erodes my self-discipline. It
comes from the monotony, but now I'm flying, I'm crazy, it's

risky, I've ripped through the membrane. . . I hope the truck is all right. The tension on the timing chain isn't right. Too loose is better than too tight. . . Tonight I'll sleep under the stars. I'll think of Abby, when we were young. When her hair was long, when she smoked with us. When she begged me for rides on the Triumph. Michigan and camping on those big dunes. The Indian blanket, coffee and sunrises, moons through tree branches, my beard and her body; the whole time-explosion of those years when I was looking forward, driving fast, unafraid, confident we would make it. . . There's Doansy. He'll never know, really, what Abby is all about. He's the older brother. He's the piper, the band leader, the scribe. He doesn't see what I see, he doesn't know the person I know. . . Why didn't I put just one harmonica in my pocket?

Fallow Towns As Landscape

On a different route along the same river, two more, brothers-in-anguish, brothers-falsely-condemned, brothers-in-blood ride the back pages of the say-hey-day of internal combustion's magic carpet ride to wherever the asphalt spat from invention-sloth takes them—the beast of hard-wired ease and comfort—the black snake catalyst of unanswered fears from familial sediment. These two swordless warriors, in youth comrades against the massah, cannibals at first chance, lovers of the escape found in a smooth, tanned thigh.
Emanuel You talk to mom an' dad lately?—*the boy is a natural born cuckoo. Lays them eggs sos others can scramble and fry, come what may.*
Hector No, man. Have you?—*and he, four years the elder. Ten pounds at birth, a raging hurricane lashing the sedated coastline of status quo. Wit, cynic, eyes wide as The Whale's mouth.*
Emanuel Me an' Mazz went up last Sunday. Aw, you know.

They're doin' about the same.

Hector   Mom have her check-up?

Emanuel   Two weeks ago. The aneurysm's about the same size. She's gettin' thin, man. She's frail. So frail she can't hug you; she just leans in a little an' pats you on the back. *Elbow out the window, hand somersaulting in the wind, he sees the greens and silverfish flashes of unrelenting sunshine, and neither his mother's failing health nor the forgotten towns with their gutted downtowns and prideless outskirts of sameness and fastfood crass could beat that freely-given and graciously-taken optimism. His eyes pop from landscape, to brother, to the blank abyss of memory through the windshield.*

Hector   Well, she won't eat! All they eat's toast, an' ham sandwiches. An' God damn maybe Taco Smell. *He sees only the carcasses of small town Midwest America tossed aside in the cattle drive South and West and even across the globe. It smolders within him continuously to light fuses of helplessness winding back to those he loved and those he wept for from afar.*

Emanuel   She's smokin' about like she used to.

Hector   Well, she knows the score. Doctor Fuck-Dick told her—one a the few times he's been straight with her. I figure she's gonna do what she wants. What else is there for her, when you really stop an' think about it?

Emanuel ·   She told me once, when she was just startin' back up again, that cigarettes were like a friend to her. *His eyes remain on his brother's as he tries to find a hope or an answer or magic from their youth years ago. . .* With all us kids, an' takin' care a dad, they were like some real live person she could confide in. She said nobody understood that. If she just had half a cigarette four times a day, maybe it wouldn't be too bad.

Hector   You can't blame her, except it's killin' dad. He spends half the day down in the basement to get away from the smoke. Me an' Sid won't stay over anymore. It's fucked up. We stay in that shit-hole motel—*that shit-hole motel being located across the highway, what used to be a swamp, where they used to tromp looking for frogs and snakes.*

Emanuel Sometimes I wonder if. . . *Their eyes meet and lock, each knowing the terrible thoughts of the other.*
Hector Don't. . .
Emanuel It sounds crazy, but . . .
Hector Like she's tryin' to smoke 'em out.
Emanuel Like she's tryin' to *kill* 'em.
Hector I know, man. I've thought about it.
Emanuel She knows that if she goes first—what'll he do? I'm not sayin' she's doin' it consciously, but she knows what'll happen if she dies first.
Hector Part of her might feel relieved.
Emanuel She's spent her whole life takin' care a people. First, her mom dies in high school. Grandpa made her the surrogate mom. Says stay home, girl, an take the reins, while everybody else—the girls, I mean—was either goin' to college or nursin' school. A real live Cinderella. After the war she marries dad, has what?—four, five kids—bing, bing, bing, bing, *clunk*—an' then he gets polio. Then six more. *Shit, man*. . . Think about it. . . She resents 'em, you know? An' he feels guilty. All she's ever done is look after people.
Hector I wish she could a had more. We always talk about dad 'cause he was in the wheel chair. Mom can be cold as hell. But look what she did! I just wanna do somethin' for 'em. But there's nothin' we can do, Manny. There's not a fuckin' thing we can do.
Emanuel Visit when we can.
Hector I wanna change it all. I wanna go back to 1952—I wanna steer 'em away. . . Where'd he get it? . . . From a pool? He was workin' two jobs—he didn't have time to go swimmin', man.
Emanuel His resistance was down. It gets children, an' adults whose resistance is down. *The words not his, repeated from the skipping requiem of unblossomed familial happiness.*
Hector Think about it, man. We remember it in abstractions; but there was a single moment when he came in contact with it. With that fuckin' dirty bastard bug. It happened in a specific place an' time. . . His resistance was down. . . workin two jobs. . . providin' for his American Dream family. . .

Emanuel   He's had some life.

Hector   He's an amazing guy. He didn't drown any of us, or take a two-by-four to our heads.

Emanuel   Just the belt every Sunday night.

Hector   Yeah, but he could a done a lot worse.

Emanuel   I know, man.

Hector   Really. He could a fucked us up real bad. I've seen guys fall apart 'cause the toilet's clogged an' the Roto-Rooter dude's under the haystack fast asleep with the wife.

Emanuel   What the hell's that supposed to mean?—*laughing suddenly and easily.*

Hector   *Shrugging*—people're weak, man—*fingers rolling atop the steering wheel.* Dad's got bull balls all the way.

Emanuel   Hey—what time are Doansy an' Gabe comin' down?

Hector   Two.

Emanuel   You been to Doansy's lately?

Hector   Mm. . . the last time me an' you went was the last time I saw 'em.

Emanuel   He left the wax original out in the sun.

Hector   What wax? Wolfy?

Emanuel   Guess you didn't hear.

Hector   *Fuck.*

Emanuel   It's all right, man, don't worry. He said he put it out to dry 'cause he was gettin' ready to make the mold, an' it basically turned into butter.

Hector   Oh, *Fuck.*

Emanuel   He thinks he can rework it. I asked 'em if he could make a wax outta the first mold, but he said it's too old, he's made too many changes to the wax original. He said it'd take less work to fix the original. You guys work out the bubble problem with the resin?

Hector   No, man—*still in the oil slick of best-laid-plans, he shakes his head and makes acrid faces.* He said he made another test with just a cube, an' there weren't any bubbles. But we haven't made any more from the mold. It's gotta be done in air conditioning, man. The guy at the art store told me. He said you can't have any humidity. I might take it home an' do it myself.

Emanuel   Maybe Gabe can figure somethin' out. Give 'em time an' Gabe can figure anything out.

Hector   Yeah, I hope that timing chain's on right.

Emanuel   He said it was. Doansy doesn't wanna let go a that truck.

Hector   You offer 'em yours?

Emanuel   I was gonna, but Mazzy didn't seem too keen on the idea, if you know what I mean. That's our commuter vehicle. I said—what about the Jeep?—but that's our low mileage vehicle. Besides, she likes havin' the top down for the summer. But that's not why I didn't give 'em the truck, man. I mean, how do you do somethin' like that? He's had that truck for almost twenty years. He doesn't *want* another vehicle. My truck's only five years old, an' I don't wanna think about gettin' another one either. It's got trips in it. Me an' Mazz went out West in that thing. It's my horse, man, you know? He doesn't need it really; I just thought I'd help 'em out before his truck finally dies.

Hector   He might not take it.

Emanuel   I don't wanna put 'em in the position a lookin' like he's not providin' for Chelsea. The way I see it, not everybody's born to be a drone, man. Some people got things to give an' they can't give it if they have to be drones like you an' me.

Hector   You mean like artists?

Emanuel   Sure, man. Artists, writers, musicians.

Hector   Yeah, well, dad always said Doansy should get a job teachin', an' do his art on the side.

Emanuel   Dad. Yeah, okay. It's not a hobby, man.

Hector   No, but you gotta eat. You gotta make money somehow.

Emanuel   Look, man, you don't get it either.

Hector   Hey, no—I get it, man.

Emanuel   You said you gotta eat somehow, right? For Doansy, paintin' is like eatin' for you an' me. That ain't simile. That ain't hyperbole. That's a fact.

Hector   Man, I understand.

Emanuel   Yeah, well, okay—*acquiescing, to avoid the clash, but unconvinced.*

Hector   Hey, man, don't get mad.

Emanuel   I ain't mad, man. But you tell me you get it, but everything comin' outta your mouth tells me you don't.

Hector   *When he appeases, he is all sloped eyebrows and raised shoulders.* All I'm saying is, Doansy's fifty years old. The way I see it, he's got no money saved, no retirement, nothin' big on the horizon in the way a projects to set 'em up financially. Where's he gonna be in fifteen years?

Emanuel   Maybe livin' in some shelter in Kent. So what?

Hector   Hey, I'm just worried about 'em.

Emanuel   You're scared. I'm scared too. But if he can handle it, I can handle it. He's not stupid.

Hector   He's not stupid, just maybe not prudent.

Emanuel   He's an artist—don't you know what that means by now?

Hector   But he's a middle-aged guy, just like you an' me.

Emanuel   Look—he's not a bohemian. He's not playin' some role, man. Maybe he was—yeah, probably—twenty years ago, but he's just an artist now. Art—the need to express the slappin' a God's hands on the bare ass a some across-the-tracks goddess—runs through his veins.

Hector   It's hard to see somebody you care about struggle, man.

Emanuel   Sure, it is.

Hector   Well. . .

Emanuel   Well, nothin'.

Hector   I just don't wanna see 'em fade away.

Emanuel   You're not gonna stop it, if it's in the cards, man.

Hector   *He knows it's true. He says nothing, watching the blur of summer leaf and trunk just out the window.*

Zeitgeist Folly Coming In For A Landing

Doans . . . **The jurisdiction a intellectual pursuits,** as seen
from the perspective a man, capital M, Mankind, may fall from the
tar-spittin' mouths a locust regurgitations a the enlightened an'
elite, to those livin' in doughnut holes a simplistic, blissful,
regressive pods that we, the current hay-makers a the grandiose
empire, have spawned; but said pod-dwellers desire nothin' from
the froth—in fact, spit back in the face a intellectual achieve-
ment—as though *it* were the acid-cloak rainin' down on lamb's
wool, an' so determines the resultin' conclusion thusly stated:
There can be little consideration given to neo-Neanderthal, when
he demonstrates a real an' viable threat to the intellectual pursuits
a Man's onward march toward more an' better understandin' a his
environments, aims, an' existence on planet Earth. History lies
with its reference to this assault an' battery conquest tragedy as
havin' a head like a dragon an' a snake's slitherin' form, when it's
more a loose, indigestible cloud-mass a disjointed object-events,
bein' *moved*, not *movin'*, *by*, an' not *toward* the great mystery
known by a thousand names, over ten thousand years, whispered
by all the souls of all the lands of all the systems of all the ships
ever known by the name capital M, Man. What pursuit is worth
pursuin', when the object in question is an illusion, a shape a
misrepresentation, an' the truth lies beyond the scope of a bird's
eye, in the individual, infinitesimal water drops that throb
exponentially in the logarithmic off-the-charts curve, shot-gunnin'
through all the stories a the tallest fables, today's Babel piercin'
the sky with caustic, anonymous crassness an' utilitarian chest-
thumpin'? Intellectualism may be dead. If so, then accept the new
truth-rainbow a blindin' ignorance, the quest for socio-economic
equalizin' by the forfeiture a intellect-banks to intellect-robbers,
who only wish to make a witch's brew an' seduce the world with
their lungfish desires an' amphibious croaks a neo-nationalistic,
Orwellian fall-in-line goose-steps an' corporate-communism.
Accept, an' do not cry against, if this reveals itself to be the true
color, the final comin', the diagnosis of all separate parts collected

into one single, vaguely-identifiable cloud a symbolic duck-doo, capital M, Mankind, whatever that means. . .

Gabriel   Now, for the descent! . . . Big Beaver Island. . . there's the dam. . . and there's the bridge. From up here, oh, what a slow-moving, washed-out scene! Only treetops and dull slate roofs, and the meager small-pond erections of bank buildings, barbers, bars, diners, and dollar stores—the dying remnants of a spent allowance, too fast, not enough rationing. If I could take a picture in Koda-chrome and trade places and live the picture and not the leeward reality. . . live the picture and not the reality. . . Abby, above and below. Abby, with her long brown hair and sweet-smelling skin. Abby, you are my one and only love, even if I did hesitate when our first chance sped past, because youth is sometimes full of itself and bumps the best of show from the wedding cart. I loved you no less then. I love you with as much drag racing full-throttle to-hell-with-tomorrow. . . It's all for you, this sheer madness! It's all for you, my heart split diagonally in two. . . Big Beaver Island, labyrinth of the Minotaur, Atlantis in this holy sea of corn. . .

Doans   Easy, mojo-man. You gots plenty a room, now don't be greedy an' try an' put on a show for ol' Doansy. Nice wide ball field. All you gotta watch are those telephone poles, an' that billboard at the end a the street. . . From this creosote guardrail on this island surrounded by the dark blood a farmers—the pisser of all industrial arrogance—you look like you're outta control, my friend. Still uncertain a how that contraption is to be maneuvered through the clouds an' high flyin' birds. So, take it easy, will you. No hurry. Doansy ain't goin' nowhere. He'll prop his flat butt against this smelly old log, strike a match, an' appear calm as can be, the Winston Churchill a Big Beaver Island, waitin' for the daylight bomber's return from factories of our ancestors, Celtic interlopers, Rome-bashers, Holy Roman bastion a the Vatican Elite, target a some celestial alignment where the Son a God somehow got hog-tied an' fell asleep. Gabe, Gabe, Gabe. . . lookin' good. . . Who would a thought two years ago you'd be flyin' free, man? Who would a believed you'd disappear into the wild blue yonder an' emerge like Icharus, only without the meltdown? I, for one, saw you on one pasty plane, subverted only by our time fiddlin' on cars, puttin' up drywall, or wigglin' wires on my Fender amps. You're stoic, Gabe, a real quiet man, a frieze on the Parthenon. Why, there's more to your Cheshire grin than meets the eye. . . Come on now, get over those trees. Lookin' a bit low for my likin'. No need to get fancy. Just stay up till you're clear, an' then bring her down without no chain bracelet rattle. White bread landin' is what we want, sos we can enjoy the weekend without hospital visits an' callin' hours. Forget what I said about the air compressor. I don't wanna jinx you. . .

Trapped By A Smoldering Heart

The coals burning black at his heart's core, a single note of past discord, fan up into shredding claws of rage. He can't let go, this one. His seared heart—in youth a bouquet of all the countryside's variance and chance—finds reassurance in the stake-pounding of those vampires of yesterday—oh, they will not die!—pound though he will!—sprayed with the hot blood of madness and manslaughter!—attacking his future, the very clone of what he despises— thus, guaranteeing his recycling of half-dead bitterness.

Hector   You don't know what it's like to have your daughter livin' with a complete nutcase like her. I mean, Moondog is a *nut*.
Emanuel   They're in South Carolina now?
Hector   Every year they go to Kiawah Island. Lurch has a timeshare down there. She sits by the pool all day. They drive twelve hours to the ocean so she can sit by a pool. *He bangs the steering wheel with a hard palm.* God, what a fuckin' nut. She won't let Corrie in the ocean without her an' Lurch. And since all they do is plop their fat asses on lounge chairs beside the pool, guess what? Corrie has to sit there too. Isn't that a real blast for a twelve-year-old girl? . . . Corrie just bought a $70 swimsuit.

Emanuel   Corrie did?

Hector   Moondog paid half, which means I paid half. A rhinestone swimsuit. What the hell does a twelve-year-old need a rhinestone swimsuit for? She wouldn't let Corrie take it to White Rock. You know, not in that dirty lake—*sarcasm, as thick as cold honey.* Not with her *dad.*

Emanuel   Man, that really sucks.

Hector   You know what she's doin' now? She's been handin' me these notes. She won't talk face-to-face. So the last time I went to pick up Corrie, she tried to hand me one a her notes an' I tore it up right in front of her. I said—look, Moon, why're you handin' me these notes? What're you up to now? You got laryngitis or somethin'? She can't be civil about anything. She tells Corrie there's sharks in the ocean, an' killer whales, an' jellyfish. All kinds a shit that'll mess you up. She's gonna make Corrie afraid a life the way she is.

Emanuel   Jesus.

Hector   She's such a feeble, mousy, scared bitch—*again, the steering wheel.* I wish she'd let the kid be normal. But she can't, 'cause she's so fucked up.

Emanuel   I know it doesn't help much now, man, but in six years you won't have to deal with her anymore. That'll be the end of it.

Hector   I know, man. It's fuckin' hard though. I wanna enjoy these years with Corrie. I don't wanna wish 'em away. . . *He recalls the times in the back yard of the old house by the railroad tracks, the house he bought after the divorce, of Corrie swinging in the back, alone, and he, peeking from the kitchen window, dying from the distance between them. . . But I do—he nearly whispers.*

Winged Victory, Hallowed Ground

Unstrapped, grounded, a Red Baron hero with only the yawning waterfall spray of hazy summer trees and dusty ball fields alive with spinning cyclones; friend approaches friend in silence as centuries of Adena spirits bang their drums and stomp their feet and make commotions. . . Why? Because it is what men do!

Doans   Superman! Superman Gabe!

Gabriel   Hey, Doansy. *Goggles up, revealing the Better Boy sheen of fruition. . .* Whew—*beginning to tug at the fingers of his gloves.* . . I made it.

Doans   You had me a disbeliever at times, ol' Gabe, but you came through like a reg-*u*-lar superhero. Three cheers for the flyin' ace a Dover. . . How was the air up there?

Gabriel   Nice. Real calm. A perfect day for flying.

Doans   Nice an' clear an' perfect, eh?

Gabriel   Yeah, man. Could have been clearer, but for this thing, flying so low, it was fine. How's the truck running?

Doans   She's purrin' like a midnight wench, Gabe. I think she's better than ever.

Gabriel   No slippage?

Doans   Only a little. Nothin' at all.

Gabriel   I was worried about you. I kept looking down for the truck, and when I didn't see it I thought maybe you broke down.

Doans   *You* were worried about *me*? . . . Ha! Now that's a laugh. No, no, *neeeeeew.* . . Those Japs know how to build shit. She's a trooper. . . Oh—so that's why you circled. I thought you dropped somethin'. I even stopped an' looked for it in a hump a weeds I swear looked like a nat-*u*-ral place for gorillas to be hidin' in. Then you took off again, so poof!—I was gone, man!

Gabriel   It's a lot hotter down here.

Doans   I bet it is. No wind down here, an' more atmosphere. Gabe, some time you're gonna have to strap your video camera on your head. I wanna see what it's all about.

Gabriel   Take it up some time.

Doans   Oh, no. . . No, no. . . not me, Gabe. I do travelin', but not a the kind you've attached yourself to. *No.* . .

Gabriel   Anybody else here yet?

Doans   Nobody.

Gabriel   I thought maybe you'd pass 'em on the road.

Doans   Yeah, I don't know what kind a car Hector drives.
Gabriel   I think it's a Toyota. . . A Forerunner maybe. . .
Doans   Yeah, you might be right, Gabe-a-roon. *Noticing the
sweat still moving down the side of his face like candle wax—*Bet
you could use somethin' wet on the back a the ol' throat.
Gabriel   A beer!
Doans   Gabe-man, you got the whole weekend, my friend, an'
nobody lookin' over your shoulder, bless Abby's heart.
Gabriel   I want a beer, damn it!
Doans   An' you shall have it, Mr. Lindbergh. Break out the
champagne. Where're the dancin' girls?—*yeeeeeee-ha!* The key to
the city is yours, say we, the citizens a Munchkin Land.
*Among the shacks rooted deep along the river's widemouth banks,
the ghosts of ancestral friend and foe open their waiting arms so
that the new-name, sure-of-thought, sure-of-right has its moment
in time's spotlight. What floods and winter's twisting ice has not
sent down river stands on gangly bones, fleshless, the arthritic
metatarsals propping up what yesterday's glory demands—its sole
demand—to merely exist and wait for the finality of this eye-
blinking chapter of infinity. These two comrades arrive at the gate,
give their tickets to the boatman, and, finding Hades—the
ramshackle castle of warps, creaks, and turbulence withstood, a
snug, neat perch above the fray—all of the island opens up to them
as if they were sitting in Robinson Crusoe's tree house. They drop
off their bags inside, tarry in the kitchen wiping sweat from brow,
and then, as if pulled there, head out and descend down the long
stairway to immerse themselves in the saturated banks of mud and
afternoon sun.*

*The other two are not far behind. They make the final winding
miles silently, each contemplating his own life's chaos with gritty
resignation. They stop in front of the shack where the skimmed
grass meets dried mud. Ignition off, they sit listening to the somber
tides of the river smacking faintly against the arid stone temples of
Christ's cavalier children. It's a moment neither wishes to break,
but then break they must. As they dismount, shutting the car doors,*

all is pastel chlorophyll brilliance and hazed mystery. Like the two before, they enter the shack, look around, and then head toward water.

A gaggle of jumping beans, they shake hands and embrace and pat shoulders and squeeze arms of lean, wiry middle-age. Gradually, jumps turn into nervous shuffles and the four back away from each other to form an adolescent back alley huddle.

Doans   Wow. Like, it's really great to see you guys.

Emanuel   When you get here?

Doans   No more than—what—twenty minutes ago, Gabe?

Gabriel   *To the lazy eye, the bird now landed moves and speaks as the sloth; that is to say, with John Entwistle restraint.* Yeah, I guess so. I'd say twenty minutes. Maybe a half hour.

Hector   Gabe, you really fly down?

Gabriel   All the way.

Hector   Any problems?

Gabriel   Nope. Smooth as can be.

Hector   How'd the truck do, Doansy?—*his eyes, as if marveling at a history book with arms and legs, roam.*

Doans   Perfect-o. Not a glitch.

Gabriel   You guys come down route 60? Thought we'd see you.

Doans   Yeah! Like, I was lookin' for you guys, but I forgot what sorta internal combustion beast you were ridin'.

Hector   This place is great!—*the water flowing, the mud, the debris, the rudimentary giraffe-dwellings.*

Doans   Ain't it like Shangri-La in mud?

Hector   How long's Eddie had it?

Doans   Mmm. . . how long, Gabe? What'd Eddie say—five years?

Gabriel   Something like that. Five, maybe six or seven.

Doans   Six or seven, yeah. More like eight or nine. Yeah, he's been comin' down on weekends an' workin' on it. Those steps are brand new, man. The guy just finished 'em two days ago.

Hector   Those are some serious-lookin' steps, man!

Doans   Yeah, they are! There's some real lumber in that piece!

Hector   Gotta be strong enough for when the floods come.
Doans   I know. No such thing as overkill around here.
Hector   How high's the water get?
Doans   See the line on the basement wall?—*he points, moving his finger horizontally.* See that?
Hector   No fuck.
Doans   Yeah! Yeah, fuck! That's how high this bad boy gets.
Hector   I don't think I'd be sleepin' up there when the river gets that high.
Doans   Oh, it's solid. This place has been here for years. Look at the shacks on either side, man. They look like they could go with the next sprinkle. But, they won't. Naw—Eddie's place ain't goin' nowhere.
Emanuel   You guys bring your poles?
Doans   Why, sho', Homer. They're still up in the back a the truck.
Emanuel   Doansy, you gonna do some fishin'?
Doans   Maybe.
Emanuel   You haven't been fishin' probably since the Mogadore days with dad.
Doans   Man, like I can't remember the last time I actually had my own pole in my hands. . . Yeah, probably at Mogadore.
Hector   Well, tonight my brothers, we're gonna catch some fish!
Doans   All right!
Hector   Yeee————aaahhh!
Emanuel   A————oooh!
Gabriel   Owww!
Figuratively, the peace pipe goes round. Meat is taken from the spit and offered—lubricant to individuality grinding against individuality. Gifts are given and received. None, and yet all, of these rituals are performed in the modern equivalent—a chest filled with ice and beer.
Emanuel   Want one, Doansy?—*standing over the ice chest, he pulls one out.*
Doans   No, thanks. I got my tea—*he says, lifting his mug.*

Emanuel   Gabe?

Gabriel   Maybe in a little while. I'm still working on this one.

Emanuel   I know me an' Hector aren't shy.

Hector   Shut the cooler, man.

Emanuel   Doansy, you wanna sit on the cooler? You look kinda compressed squattin' on that log.

Doans   I'm cool, man. Thanks, bro'. You take it.

Emanuel   I'm all right on this cinder block. Gabe?

Gabriel   Me? I'm okay.

Emanuel   Hector, I guess it's all yours then.

Hector   Take it, man.

Emanuel   You sure?

Hector   Take it.

Emanuel   Okay. Can't let a perfectly good cooler go to waste.

Hector   Make sure it closes all the way.

Emanuel   It's closed, man. Don't worry about it.

Hector   Doansy, you try any more casts with the mold?

Doans   No, man.

Hector   Maybe I can take it home and try it.

Emanuel   Gabe, what time's Jules comin'?—*talking amongst themselves, as the business partners go about their business.*

Gabriel   I think he said, what, Doans—about seven o'clock?

Doans   Yeah, take it. You might have better luck at your place.

Hector   The guy at the art store said there couldn't be any humidity in the air. He made a point about it.

Doans   Sure. He's gotta know what he's talkin' about.

Hector   I haven't gone to any galleries yet. Maybe this week.

Doans   Groovy, man.

Hector   We gotta get a good cast first. We can't take one that has bubbles in it. It's gotta be good, know what I mean?

Emanuel   The river's wider than I thought it would be.

Gabriel   It joins the Ohio just down the road.

Doans   Yeah, but don't tell Jules it's not the Ohio—*suddenly turning his head, chiming in.* He said he's never fished along the Ohio.

Emanuel   Don't you think he'll figure it out? He's from

Zanesville, for Christ's sake.

Doans   Naw, he won't know the difference. Just pretend it's the Ohio. Don't burst his bubble.

Emanuel   He'll know. Jules ain't stupid.

Doans   No, man. It's cool. Like, he won't know any difference. Look at it. Don't that look like the Ohio to you?

Emanuel   Sure, man. But all you gotta do is look at the map. We're ten miles up from Marietta. A ten-year-old could figure that out.

Doans   Naw, man, he won't know the difference. Just play along.

Emanuel   I'll play along. Sure—I mean, if you wanna play this make-believe game. The Muskingum runs *through* Zanesville, you know—*a cock-eyed glance.*

Doans   I appreciate it, bro'.

Emanuel   Don't hold it against me if I let it slip out later on when I'm drunk. That's gonna be a hard thing to remember.

Doans   If it comes out, I won't hold it against you. Naw, man. Just pretend it's the Ohio to yourself, an' then you won't even have to make-believe. That's what me an' Gabe are doin'.

Emanuel   He finish his painting?

Doans   Which one?

Emanuel   The one with his ol' lady an' their kid.

Doans   He's still workin' on it, man. You like that one?

Emanuel   That one, an' some a the ones with the guys playin' music.

Doans   Yeah, those are pretty good.

Emanuel   I like his stuff. I like his studio. I like his attitude. Shit—I just like the dude.

Doans   He's the real deal, man. The best thing that sleepy river town's got.

Hector   You talk to dad lately?

Doans   We were up about a week ago.

Hector   How'd they seem to you?

Doans   Good.

Hector   Really?

Doans   Yeah. They seemed real good. Mom had lots a energy. Me an' dad worked on my guitar.

Hector   I worry about 'em.

Doans   Don't worry about 'em.

Hector   I do.

Doans   What for, man? They're doin' fine.

Hector   Mom can hardly get around. She's frail, man. She's gotta be under ninety pounds. . . What're they gonna do in a few years?

Doans   They'll get by. They always do.

Hector   They won't let anybody help 'em.

Doans   Would you?

Hector   Yeah. If I was in dad's position, an' my wife was still smokin' like a chimney, an' she had an aneurysm, an' she was down to ninety pounds. An' now I got the beginnin's a emphysema. Yeah. I'd take any help I could get.

Doans   Naw, they're all right.

Hector   They're like children.

Doans   They're tough.

Hector   It gets to a point where you have to treat 'em like children because that's, in a way, what they are.

Emanuel   Dad won't let anybody get that close.

Hector   Yeah, well fuck him.

Doans   Hey, man. It's cool.

Hector   It's not just about him.

Doans   Mom's the one who don't want us knowin' diddly-squat about her condition. It ain't dad.

Hector   He can't ignore the situation.

Doans   He's not ignorin' the situation, man. He's tryin' to hold onto his pride. Wait till you're pushin' eighty. See how fast you ask for help.

Hector   It's better than dyin' before you have to.

Emanuel   He's selfish. He always has been.

Doans   Selfish with his own life? Bravo for him.

Emanuel   Well, there's degrees. When you pump out a fuck-load a kids, don't you think you owe 'em somethin'? I mean, his big thing is he doesn't wanna *bother* anybody.

Doans   Not many like 'em left. The guy's a saint.

Emanuel   Sure, we all know he's a saint. But the thing is, if he really didn't wanna bother anybody, he'd let us help.

Doans   He owes nobody nothin'. No-theeng, amigo.

Hector   I don't know, man. . .

Doans   You gotta let 'em go the way they wanna go.

Hector   It's like watchin' a ship goin' down real slow.

Doans   Naw, man. Those two are on their way to heaven.

Hector   If there is one, they'll part the waters to let 'em through. But they're not there yet. They're still alive, man.

Doans   An' still livin'.

Hector   Are they? . . . Are they, man? . . .

Doans   There's more life in those old bones than there is in all four of us put together.

Hector   I think about 'em every night before I go to sleep. *Fear is fear is fear; is pain also so lumped? The big one, the champion-at-heart, chained to his rage, feels it deeper than the rest. Where they keep the beast offshore, he wades out to greet it for regular whippings.*

Doans   That's good, man.

Hector   I think about mom an' how she's already gone. How she's not part a my life anymore. She won't talk on the phone. When you go up to see 'em, she watches TV. She blares it so loud you have to leave the room with dad. He gets pissed, but won't say anything. It's just sad. I want 'em to be part a my life. I want Corrie to know her grandparents. I want 'em to know her. . . But we're all strangers. . . They're fadin'. . . There's nothin' I can do.

Doans   She loves it when you come visit, man. She's always been on the peripheral. She's just recedin' back into the place she's most comfortable.

Hector   I know—*he reflects softly.* But we used to be able to talk. We don't talk anymore. It's like she's already gone.

Emanuel   Me an' Hector were talkin' on the way down—*he lights, hopeful at the prospect of confronting the undefeatable with constructive effort*—why don't we build 'em a ranch? One story, no steps. No elevator for mom to trip over. We could all take turns stayin' with 'em. I could do it a couple nights a week. Hector said he could come up one. Abby could manage one or two. Between the rest of us, we could have the whole week covered. It's not lookin' good for mom, Doansy. That's a fact. I don't want dad endin' up in some nursin' home. That's bullshit. If mom goes first, somebody's gonna have to stay with dad.

Doans   They don't wanna move outta that house—*he offers the simply-stated fact.*

Emanuel   They'll have to sooner or later—*but the boy, still tethered, rouses at the specter of passivity.* Mom shouldn't be goin' up an' down those steps.

Doans   She's fine.

Emanuel   Yeah, well, you stay with her next time she falls an' breaks her hip, man. I understand what you mean about it bein' their lives an' all—but who helps out when shit like that happens? If you don't, then it's easy to say let 'em go, it's their lives. I stayed after mom fell, an' I stayed after dad fell outta his wheel chair an' broke his knee.

Doans   You want a pat on the back? Here—*reaching out, dangerously*—let me give you a pat on the back.

Emanuel   Fuck off, man—*pulling his arm back.*

Hector   Come on, man. Take it easy.

Emanuel   Tell *him.* Tell *him*, come on, man. All I'm trying to tell 'em is that it's easy to sit back an' not worry when you've got no involvement. When you don't intend to involve yourself. You're outside, Doansy. That's your prerogative, but then don't be tellin' me—who's inside—what I should or shouldn't be doin'.

Doans   Look, man, I don't mean nothin' by it—you dig? I don't mean *nothin'.* I ain't tryin' to loosen your bumper, man. I know. I know—it's tough. It sucks. That's what I'm sayin'. It sucks with a capital S. . . I'm so bad about these things, I go crazy inside too. I just, fuck, try an' funnel it into somethin' I can deal with. That's all, man. I'm a coward. I know it!

Emanuel   You ain't a coward, man.

Doans   But I am. I can't take it head on like you an' Hector an'

Abby. Me, I have to look at it with mirrors, if I look at it at all. I follow the footprints—that's as heavy as I can get. . . I'm there, man. I'm just around the corner.

Talk Is Over-Rated

The foursome, split in two by the wedge of unresolved fratricide ambush and counter-defense, smoothed over over the years, almost hiccupped, then driven back down with the unfulfilled expectation of peer acceptance—smack! The hammer of ailing parents, weary days, and blissless matrimony, the young one trots off to the dam. Behind him, without knowledge, Doans nods to Gabe—Go on, man. See what you can do. He's hurtin' real bad these days. See what you can do, my brother. Hector, mechanism of pure pain and pleasure, grimaces, a thousand miles and dreams away, his own hurricane roaring in fast.

Hector   Moondog pulled the classic bait-an-switch. Soon as we got married everything changed.

Doans   It always does, man. Can't be helped.

Hector   Manny doesn't mean anything. You know that.

Doans   I know.

Hector   We're all just scared.

Doans   Yeah, I know. . .

Hector   Moondog? Yeah, she's always let her fears run things.

Doans   What's the big plan now?

Hector   Don't know, man. I'm tired a sales. With the dot-com bust, things aren't lookin' so good, even if I wanted to stay in.

Doans   How's Sid takin' it?

Hector   Sid's cool with it, man. She doesn't care what I do. She doesn't want me to do somethin' I don't like anymore.

Doans   That's a good woman you got.

Hector   I thought about maybe gettin' a house inspector's license. That wouldn't be too bad. I could work the hours I wanted. Take in as little or as much business as I wanted.

Doans   That'd be cool, man. That's right up your alley.

Hector   It's just an idea.

Doans   Why not stay home an' read all day, man?

Hector   Sure—*tipping his beer casually*. Maybe I will.

Doans   Learn to play the guitar. Man, like I'll loan you one. I loaned Manny one. It'd be groovy.

Hector   I gotta do somethin'. I can't sit at home very much longer.

Doans   That's a good thing.

Hector   I hate to think I'll end up where I was, back in sales. But I don't know what else to do.

Doans   Why don't you hang on till Corrie graduates, then take off an head back to Montana, man? Spain was the place to go when I was young. Everybody I knew wanted to go to Spain. . . Man, like why're you laughin'?

Hector   I was thinkin' about your letter.

Doans   What letter?

Hector   Your letter to dad. The one where you told 'em thanks for teachin' us how to be a janitor.

Doans   Oh. Yeah, that was some piece.

Hector   That's funny as shit.

Doans   Poor guy. He tried, I guess. Janitors was a nice way a puttin' it.

Hector   *Vavoom—into his vaudevillian parody on a stage of frayed roots and mud. Orson Wells' brooding Hamlet mug with Robin Williams at the wheel.* Hector, come here. I got somethin' for you to do. *Come here. . .* Hold this pipe. Not like that—here, like *this. . .* Steady now. . . Don't let go! . . . Here—wrap your hands around it. . . *like this. . .* No, not like *that*. Like *this*. You got it? . . . Hey. Don't look out that window. What do you think this is—recess? This ain't recess, boy. Pay attention. . . No, you can't do the sawin'. You da boy, I'm da boss. . . Fun? You think this is supposed to be *fun*? This ain't fun, Hector, this is work. Work is hell. Work is shit. . . It's slippin'. . . God damn it, anyway. . . *Back off stage now*—What the fuck's wrong with bein' a janitor? But no—we're too good for that. He pushed us into college. Told us to get an education. *He squats gorilla-like, cocks his head, and peers down at his brethren with sarcasm heaped upon sarcasm.* Said never to work with your hands like him, 'cause you might end up on your back just like him, an' *then* what are you gonna do? Use your *mind*, he said. *His thick, pole vaulter's finger stabbing at the side of his temple; brute collard greens anger boiled in buffoonery.* Use your *mind*? Why? You know? . . . Why? Soooooooooo. . . you trained us how to be janitors, but now you tell us to go out an' ed-u-crate ourselves. Okay. Sure, dad. Sounds like a real plan you got there. Even though you worked with your hands your whole life, half of it from a fuckin' wheel chair—I'll steer clear a *that* formula for success, an' try this here booby trap theory you seem to got a hardon for. *He shrugs his shoulders in limp, gorilla surrender.* So we all bought into it. Not you, but most of us did.

Doans	Me too, brother. I bought it hook, line, an' sinker.
Hector	If that's not a recipe for one fucked up life. . .
Doans	You're hurtin' me, man. Cut it out. I'm gonna die laughin'.
Hector	Well, it's true—*even he can't hold back the laughter now.*
Doans	I know it's true, man. That's why I'm gonna cry. Poor dad. . .
Hector	*He sits, not defeated, but resigned. Lights a cigarette, gripping it between fingertips, awkwardly. He picked up weekend smoking from the ex-wife before they were exed. The prop befits his squared-off John Wayne stance and rough-hewn machismo. To the mud he stares. Doans observes, and thinks, and considers, but then he need not—the champion unrolls the carpet—out jumps Cleo-patria, the seducer of honest, bread-and-butter men.* He bred a bunch a malcontents. It sucks, man.
Doans	You?
Hector	You're not?
Doans	*His own armor—quick wit, a reservoir of hypotheses, an even more robust reservoir of experience—the web of authority woven tightly around the fly—responds immediately.* Naw, man. I

ain't no malcontent—I's just malnourished.

Hector   I think you are—*greasing the gears of friction with a chuckle.*

Doans   Yeah? Hm. . .

Hector   We all are.

Doans   Yeah, like what are you malcontent about?

Hector   Myself. My life. I don't know; just generally, you know, not happy about things.

Doans   You think that's a reaction to dad's good cop/bad cop shtick, or just followin' the blazed path?

Hector   *He drags the cigarette with winced, blood-shot eyes.* Fuck, man, I don't know. Probably both.

Doans   Yeah, probably both.

Hector   It's pathetic, man.

Doans   *He, poet in youth, sponge of the counterculture, refuser to judge the tragedies of others, holds aloft his own cigarette with impartiality and the expressionless stillness of religious listening.* It is what it is.

Hector   It's hard to break the chain, man.

Doans   Sure it is.

Hector   It's hard when it's so—fuck, man—ingrained inside you.

Doans   I don't even worry about it. But I don't have kids. Maybe I would, then. I sorta quit that game after I figured out— hey, here I am, product B not responsible for content or effect if swallowed. Write to the old man if you have any complaints or suggestions, otherwise just keep it to yourself an' smile.

Hector   Is that what you tell Chelsea?

Doans   No. I don't have to tell her. She knows.

Hector   Talk is overrated.

Doans   Talk is overrated. Right on. Where'd you hear that?

Hector   From you.

Doans   Yeah? . . . From me?

Hector   *He flicks an ash, then the cigarette itself after a final hit.* She doin' all right?

Doans   She's doin' great.

Hector   That's great, man. How's her sculpture?
Doans   Pretty good.
Hector   Yeah?
Doans   Yeah. She's workin' like thirty hours a week. Too much, but she finds time to get out in the studio.
Hector   Hey—it's steady cash, man.
Doans   Oh, I know. Yeah—gotta have that influx greater than the reflux—right, dad? I know. She's great. Chelsea's a real saint, bless her. Some days I wanna call up her ex an' thank 'em for bein' such a pig.

Where'd Everybody Go?

If Hector's bane is bottled pain, expressed as anger as reaction to or mimicking of; Emanuel's constant companion, from his position as janitor #7, from a knee-jerk venom inborn spat in the eyes of friends and family alike, is laid-bare infantile self-absorption. If Hector believes the world is on the prowl to get him, Emanuel believes it already has. . . Where the water meets the sun—there you'll find 10-year-old dreams caged in middle age's own cage of too much sleeping with one eye open. . . Skipping stones, Gabriel and the boy quickly forget all but technique and the day's current political storm.
Emanuel   I do. I think they should line 'em up an' shoot 'em—*he says, sending another stone across the water.* Hey, nice one. Six?
Gabriel   Five.
Emanuel   So you got seven so far—*pointing to Gabriel*—an' I got six—*swinging the same finger back to thud his chest.* Not too many flat ones lyin' around. *Standing ankle-deep in the river. Dripping forearms and squints against the glare. They trudge like lungfish in search of the arsenal.*
Gabriel   There's more over here by the dock—*he calls over. The game continues here where the internal combustion of the*

river had, over time, dumped a relative goldmine of small, flat stones.

Emanuel   Now these are some real skippin' stones—*he sends one stuttering across the water.*

Gabriel   I haven't skipped stones since I was in the Army.

Emanuel   *Nice.*

Gabriel   Good one!

Emanuel   Shoot 'em, hang 'em—do whatever you want. Those guys, however you wanna do it, should be exterminated.

Gabriel   They're bad apples, that's for sure.

Emanuel   You know what's gonna happen to 'em? Not a fuckin' thing. They ruin the lives a their own workers. They ruin the lives a shareholders. They send the country into a tailspin. There's no good reason not to line 'em all up, give 'em their cigarette, an' fire away. Instead, they'll keep their money. So they get roasted by Congress? So what? Do you think Congress really wants to see those dudes fry?

Gabriel   A few of 'em might.

Emanuel   A few—hey, was that like ten or somethin'?

Gabriel   I didn't count—*he grins salamander-like.*

Emanuel   But most of 'em got shit so far up their arms they're like walkin' fudge cicles. They're doin' what they always do. They're puttin' on this facade, like they really care, like they have *ethics.* They'll roast those fuckers on C-Span for all the country to see. The president'll sign some new let's-get-tough-on-corporate-America jerk-off bill. . . an' life will go on. . . Do you know anybody who actually believes in those people anymore?

Gabriel   *His silence is Damon to his words, Pythias.*

Emanuel   I mean anybody who thinks outside the bullshit the media feeds 'em?

Gabriel   Some.

Emanuel   Why?

Gabriel   Why what?

Emanuel   Why do they still believe?

Gabriel   *A tough question to chew on, and he did, answering in a contemplative calm.* Oh, the same reason they believe in God, I guess. The idea of not believing is too much.

Emanuel   You're not a believer, Gabe?

Gabriel   I don't know what I believe. I don't think there's a big brother up there. It seems like there's got to be something, but I can't believe whatever it is is too involved with us. But that's the thing people have to have more than anything; they have to think somebody with real power is looking out for them.

Emanuel   Nobody *is* looking out for 'em. *He pauses, stone in hand, and continues the dialogue watching his brother-in-law, who carries on.*

Gabriel   We're coasting.

Emanuel   Coasting?

Gabriel   That's why they believe. We're not the same as we were before. *They're* not the same as they were before. We're just rolling down that big empire hill. Everybody thinks it's power, when it's really just momentum.

Emanuel   Capitalism, now in the homestretch, is the aphid feeding on its own past glory, an' our children's future. . .

Gabriel   Something like that.

Emanuel   You ever feel like somebody died?

Gabriel   Yeah. But you'll get used to it.

Emanuel   Do you?

Gabriel   You have to—*he grins again.*

Emanuel   When did it happen for you?

Gabriel   *He stops himself before a toss and stares into a void a few feet from his eyes.* Man, it's not like it's one thing—you know? It's just like the aging of the body; you can't see it from day-to-day. It's happening all the time—you just don't notice it.

Emanuel   I was a freshman in college—*he says without having to think too hard.* I was in the dorm listenin' to Joni Mitchell. In comes The Three Little Pigs, my roommates. I'm lyin' in my bed, but the tape deck was in the main room. I hear some talkin', then cussin', then the one who made his house outta straw says—Fuck this Joni Mitchell shit—pops out Joni an' stuffs in probably Rush or Journey—I can't remember exactly—but you get the idea. . . In Hector's class, just four years before me, it seemed like everybody you talked to was goin' into social work. The girls in my class couldn't tell you what social work *was*. It was all business. Everybody went into business or computers. . .

Gabriel   You can't blame 'em. I mean, look at us. *Gabriel, proud of his work as a techno-geek, stood in contrast to Emanuel, who wore the cloak like Hester Pryne's A. Gabriel separated the worlds of work and ideal, whereas to Emanuel they were seamless.*

Emanuel   He let the stone, through lack of any remaining desire to hold it, slip through his fingers. It plopped into the river. Was everybody just followin' some fad? . . . Is that what it was?—Is that what's burned inside a my soul, Gabe—is the fuckin' root a my moral pole been some kinda pop culture joke?. . . I mean, where'd everybody go? . . .

Gabriel   *Always steady, never unhinged—a soothing balm for the scorched dreamer, he answers as the river—without feeling either way to the humanity scrum all around.* Some died. Some disappeared. Most are still around, Manny, it's just that you don't recognize 'em.

Emanuel   It's like all my friends, all my heroes, all the champions a everything I believed in have been shot off. . . *Shivering, beer-sticky floors of regrettable aftermath coated his veins.* Where the hell did everybody go?

I Dream Because I'm Stuck

A thousand years ago, or fifty, or a mere thirty, he, Doans, punching bag of North Hill, runt, wordsmith, exploded in one summer's flourish at the crossroads, became receptor and amplifier, experimenter and dedicated student, lover of the overloaded fuse that was his generation's providence, lover of a woman's form, lover of the truths unfolding, changing before him and all his fellow witnesses. He bought Dylan's reinterpretation of Bible America. He trusted no one over thirty—especially cripples

*and maidens in distress. He allowed himself to flow where the
rivers took him, and cared not when floods spilled over and
brought chaos on the orderly descent. His greatest gift—and gifts
he had many—was supreme empathy. Valid was the individual.
Worthy was the strife, struggle, and anguish of every soul. Of man
and woman there was innate equality. The land was an organ
keyboard to be played and heard.*

Hector   Manny's a dreamer.

Doans   We're all dreamers.

Hector   He's a romantic. He gets too caught up in how he'd
like things to be.

Doans   Yeah, he's a real sucker for a nice rack an' a husky
voice.

Hector   I dream, but I keep 'em close to home, you know?—
eyes dart over for immediate covering of he-man tracks. Manny's
got no limitations on his dreams. They're way out there—most of
'em are broken before he starts.

Doans   It's a beautiful thing—*absently, sweetly. His mind is
absorbed in the thousand-breasts-in-the-sky mural from which he
takes his work, as a traveler takes water from a spring. New
Orleans busting, lusting, cramming, and orging—too much for his
winding-down id—too fruitful for an artist's one life. Thus, the
perpetual bathing in and gazing at, more safely, from the outside.*

Hector   Yeah, but it drives 'em into one drama after another.

Doans   May you live in interesting times, or somethin' like
that.

Hector   *The probe was hitting thin air, he pauses, then backs
away from the point.* Yeah, shit, what the fuck. . . It's just fucked
up, man. You shouldn't have to see your mom an' dad suffer like
that.

Doans   Naw, man. Why do you think I only come up for the
holidays.

Hector   For the fights?

Doans   Hey, man—like I haven't gotten into a fight at
Christmas for twenty years.

Hector   I'm proud a you, son—*he slaps him on the back.* No

politics, religion, or sex talk for comin' on near a generation.
Nothin' but pie, the penny game, an' the same old stories about
kids you hated then, but love to talk about now.

Doans   Heyuh-heyuh-heyuh. . . I don't even wrap fuck you's
in Santy Claus paper anymore to give to you guys as a token a my
love an' fealty.

Hector   No, I'll have to say, we've all mellowed. We don't
even have to sneak beer anymore. Nobody drinks an' now we just
don't talk!—*he slaps his brother's knee.*

Doans   Nothin' wrong with that. I like peace, man. Especially
with my brothers—*wrapping his hands around the husky one's
neck, in strangle mode.*

Hector   *The pain for this clan is never far off.* . . I can't say that
I can handle it any better than Manny. It's just fucked up. . . *He
sees the image of his father lying on his side. Agony in limbs, in
muscles, even in thought. He could not bear to think of his father's
shins with their burns that never healed, or the times they were
bumped by an errant pass with the football. But the more he
blocks these specters out, the more they hammer on the door for
entrance into his bare soul. Why'd he try an' do that?*

Doans   *Remembering back to a Christmas long ago when his
art was a bud and the future a horizon of bountiful seasons, when
poverty was his rite of passage and not a permanent condition,
when recognition was just around the corner. The swords
exchanged over Vietnam, and the ensuing smashing of Norman
Rockwell gatherings that never did really exist, except in the
desperate hopes of the believers of fairy tales.*

Hector   He could barely lift that arm over his head, let alone
throw a football.

Doans   You mean dad?

Hector   I didn't wanna do it, but he'd insist. Jesus Christ,
Doans. He'd try so hard sittin' in that chair. You know that look
when he was tryin' to smile for you, but the pain did somethin' to
his face an' it made you wanna cry?

Doans   Me an' the old man never tossed the football, man. But
then I never tossed a football in my life, I don't think. But I've

seen that look enough. Like maybe in the evenin' when he'd sit an' help somebody with homework.

Hector   There we were, a father an' son tossin' a football. Me, shit, I was probably eleven or twelve, an' I'd have to stand fifteen feet away. He couldn't throw it any farther. All I was thinkin' about was not hittin' 'em in the legs.

Doans   An' a course you did.

Hector   *That wound. . . flesh that would not heal, but remained permanently scabbed, pink and tender, baiting the harpies of daily existence to ravage mercilessly, while the children, mere observers, bled black tears and prayed without answer for an end.* God, it was fucked up. . . God, I hated it.

Doans   Why'd he do it, man? Cause—he wanted you to have a normal dad.

Hector   I know.

Doans   It still bug you, man?

Hector   Yeah, it bugs me.

Doans   Why's it bug you?

Hector   'Cause it's not over.

Doans   Man, it ain't gonna be over till he dies.

Hector   Yeah. Man, that's just fucked up.

They watch as two squirrels—not in play—race past over the brittle, muddied leaves and into the brush. A line had been crossed, and the pursuer was out to do real damage.

Doans   How's Manny's baby?

Hector   He says fine.

Doans   He's a natural daddy.

Hector   She looks nothin' like 'em, except when she smiles you can see his chin an' mouth. She has blue eyes an' blonde hair.

Doans   I hear he's playin' John Lennon; how's that goin'?

Hector   Okay, I guess.

Doans   I gave 'em one a my guitars so he can practice an' maybe join our band.

Hector   I don't know how much time he has for a guitar, man. I think she's got the leash pretty tight—*a lift of the brow and a swig.*

Doans   He got any new contracts lined up?

Hector   Don't think he wants to do it anymore. Burnt out, like me. Says he doesn't care if he ever goes back to work.

Doans   What's Mazzy think a that?

Hector   I don't know, man. He says she's cool with it, but I don't know if she is or if he's just puttin' a spin on it so he doesn't have to answer any questions.

Doans   Man, like he don't have to answer up to nobody.

Hector   *Though he knew their younger brother better than anyone, he often didn't know cover-up from sincerity. He shrugs.* You'd have to ask him.

Doans   So what's he dreamin' about these days?

Hector   Dreamin'?

Doans   The big dreamer. What's he dreamin' about?

Hector   Ireland.

Doans   Ireland? That's an old dream. He still hooked on Ireland?

Hector   Says he wants to make the move.

Doans   I hope he does. *In a very poor Irish brogue*—I envy the young lad!

Hector   Yeah, but it ain't gonna happen now with a kid. He's toast. *Envy, yes. The snickering—a botched attempt at veiling his competitive satisfaction.*

Doans   Ireland's a small country, man. I dig why he'd wanna plant his feet over there.

Hector   Doesn't it rain a lot there?

Doans   I don't know, man. . . I guess it does. Isn't it pretty much like England an' Scotland? . . . Isn't it on the same parallel as England? *With raised hands, a demonstration, accompanied by a squint.*

Hector   Yeah—*swig of beer, and some cockeyed confidence.* They're right next to each other.

Doans   Well, then. I suppose that answers it. England's pretty much like Seattle, an' it rains all the fuckin' time in Seattle. What's the matter, man, don't you like rain?

Hector   Not every day.

Doans   Well, yeah, who likes it every day.

Hector   Didn't it rain a lot in Portland?

Doans   *Suddenly, playfully, nodding in the affirmative and blinking his eyes like they hurt*—Oh, yeah. It sho' did rain a bunch in Poatlan'. Maybe not as much as Seattle, but enough so you had moss growin' inside the door a yo' automobile.

Hector   You like it there?

Doans   Naw, man. Well—yeah, it was cool. I mean, sorta. I guess it was all right. For six months it was all right.

Hector   What were you doin' up there?

Doans   Murals.

Hector   On buildings?

Doans   *He sucks his cigarette and then holds it. Nodding, exhaling, constipated release*—Yeah, man.

Hector   You just have one job up there?

Doans   I only wanted one job up there.

Hector   I thought you said you liked it.

Doans   I didn't say I liked it. I said it didn't kill me to live there for six months. Isn't that what I said?

Hector   I don't know, man.

Doans   Yeah, I'm pretty sure that's what I said.

Hector   He sure does whine a lot.

Doans   Who—dad?

Hector   Manny.

Doans   Oh, yeah, Manny. You think he whines a lot?

Hector   Pretty much. *With another cigarette planted in his lips, his indifference is only a sham. The constant cud-chewing, hypothesis-spitting—a product of a vagabond mind.*

Doans   He did come outta the chute screamin', as I do recall.

Hector   God, he used to bug the fuck outta Levon. I mean, he would not let *up*.

Doans   Yeah?

Hector   Maybe he was hyperactive. Really. Fuck—the guy couldn't sit still, man. Remember the noises he used to make?

Doans   *He'd left home after his final crew cut—adios, get me outta this cannery row right now—and knew these two as holiday idolizers. But he remembers the Brownian Motion that was his youngest brother, the fly that would not die, the nail dad used to hammer down with each night's lickin'.* He probably was. Man, I used to wonder when dad was gonna lose it an' like strangle 'em with his belt.

Hector   You ever wonder what it would a been like to be born in another family?

Doans   Man, you're talkin' 'bout my nightly prayer down in the basement.

Hector   You didn't like sleepin' with your brother?

Doans   Sure, man. I loved havin' Adam's prick pokin' me in the back every night. Almost as much as the centipedes.

Hector   At least you were away from the long arm a dad's law.

Doans   You ain't a kiddin', bro'.

Hector   Sometimes I wonder how Manny would a turned out somewhere else.

Doans   Man, like there's nothin' to think about. He would a been a semi-sane, not-so-paranoid fine contributor to the society a mankind; like us all.

Hector   He teased the shit outta Levon, but Jessie. . . he slapped *him* around pretty bad. I mean he'd hit 'em so hard Manny'd go flyin' across the floor. . . *fuck*. . .

Doans   Familial abuse, man, is the one constant we can all count on.

Hector   I honestly didn't think he was gonna make it. I thought either dad or Jessie was gonna kill 'em.

Loosening The Noose

Retired to the cement slab, *a crudely constructed rhombus attached to the serenely overflowing dam like a boil, crystalline water with green witch strands of algae waving underneath, they gaze out across the river, diagonally, to the far shore of haze and the billboard of dreams. The man-boy remembers his mother as* *she was, before her failing health. Being the youngest boy, she had felt a special fondness for him. His untamed mania toward the butcher shop carnival of life reminded her of his father. But where he saw a disjointed antagonist, she saw an unpolished brazen-heart. . . In the pastel riverside he could see her standing on the front porch, her hand beckoning him for a walk. The love he felt for his mother was matched only by that which he felt for Hector. They were his two lifelines on a gored, bleeding vessel.*

Emanuel Your mom doin' all right? *At the edge of the slab they sit, feet dangling, kicking, palms burning from the pressure of arms and torsos as they alternately lean back and slouch forward. Small eddies swirl past, the river carrying them away like lost chicks to a feeding.*

Gabriel She's not bad.

Emanuel That's good. That's real good, man.

Gabriel She's been lucky. No big problems like your mom's had. . . There's a lot of us around to keep an eye on her. We're not as spread out as you guys.

Emanuel She's just fadin' away, Gabe. She barely knows who I am.

Gabriel She does seem to be deteriorating pretty fast.

Emanuel You noticed?

Gabriel She keeps asking who that boy out in California is.

Emanuel Maybe if Jessie came home once in a while, she'd know.

Gabriel Doansy talks to him sometimes. I think Hector does too.

Emanuel He better come home soon if he wants to see 'em. . . *He gazes into the sky away from the trees as Gabriel allows him, patiently, to go wherever his mind wants.* Eleven children, Gabe. Eleven children an' married to a guy in a wheel chair. The diapers alone'd send my wife to the nut house.

Gabriel Jeez, that's a lot of dirty diapers.

Emanuel You think we're fucked up, Gabe?

Gabriel *Pausing to think, he responds evenly.* Not really.

Emanuel No?

Gabriel   You guys are just your typical Catholic family, except you got the added Cracker Jack surprise of having your dad in a wheel chair.

Emanuel   You didn't answer my question.

Gabriel   You're not much different from us.

Emanuel   I don't know how to take that, Gabe.

Gabriel   I'm trying to give you comfort.

Emanuel   Oh yeah?—*tossing a crumbled hunk of concrete as far as he could.* How come it doesn't make me feel any better?

Gabriel   Sorry—*he lifts his werewolf eyebrows in a smile.*

Emanuel   There's other stuff, Gabe. Stuff maybe Doansy's told you about; maybe not. *He almost tells him, but then refrains for reasons he did not understand himself. . .* Yeah, we probably are pretty typical, an' ain't that a real sucker punch in the face?

Gabriel   Nothing you can do. Just roll with the punches.

Emanuel   I wish I could. My problem is, I can't.

Gabriel   It's hard sometimes.

Emanuel   How come you left the seminary, Gabe?

Gabriel   I don't know. I wasn't cut out for it.

Emanuel   How long were you in?

Gabriel   Three years.

Emanuel   Three years? Is that right. . . You like it?

Gabriel   It was all right.

Emanuel   Doansy said he liked it.

Gabriel   Yeah, it was good. I mean, it was pretty much like any boarding school. The priests were cool, most of them.

Emanuel   Over in Ireland, the Catholic church is bein' vacated like the confessionals all got herpes or somethin'.

Gabriel   Yeah?

Emanuel   So I heard. Same with Latin America. They're all goin' Evangelical.

Gabriel   Sheez. Well, I don't blame 'em.

Emanuel   No, you really can't blame 'em.

Gabriel   I guess the last refuge is Italy, then.

Emanuel   I guess it is. . . Is that a good thing, Gabe?

Gabriel   The exodus?

Emanuel   Yeah. I mean, I'm not a church-goer myself. I'm not mournin' the beginnin' a the demise; but what's out there in the meantime?

Gabriel   *Scratching his rough chin—already a creeping shadow from only a day's growth—he gives an answer, like he'd had it all mulled over already. Truth was, he had.* How about if everybody shut their ears to anybody with an agenda, and opened their eyes to the world around them?

Emanuel   That'd be a breath a fresh air.

Gabriel   I think it's great how the church is sticking to its guns. Keep it up. More people might wake up.

Emanuel   From what, exactly?

Gabriel   From a long, long fall down the rabbit hole.

Emanuel   Okay, then *to* what?

Gabriel   Who knows?

Emanuel   You more scared about the *from* than the *to*?

Gabriel   A lot more scared.

Emanuel   Things can always be worse.

Gabriel   Things could be a lot better.

Emanuel   Yeah, things *could* be better. . .

Gabriel   Or worse.

Emanuel   *Leaning forward, unconsciously clenching his hands together, tensing his legs—*But, what's the alternative, Gabe? Where's the moral flagpole, the town well, the light you need to keep you from jumpin' off a bridge when your life's comin' apart at the seams? What fills that great big void?

Gabriel   *Unmoved, he remains leaned back on his hands.* For a while, chaos, brute rule. After the reality sandwiches have a while to digest, Jesus comes down from that cross an' walks among us, like He should have been doing all along. . . There's the flagpole, the light anybody could ever want.

Emanuel   People need superheroes, Gabe—*he leans back himself.*

Gabriel   Yeah, well, even Superman had kryptonite to take him out.

Emanuel   We ain't Europe. No immortality's too big a sandwich for this country to sink its teeth into.

Gabriel   Give it time.

Emanuel   Yeah, but the thing is, the hole's gonna be filled with somethin' meanwhile. There's no such thing as treadin' water in world history. What're we gonna worship in the wait?

Gabriel   You worshipping now?

Emanuel   I'm sorta flutterin' around this ledge with a broken wing an' a pusy eye.

Gabriel   But are you worshipping now?

Emanuel   I want to, Gabe. I really want to.

Gabriel   Yeah, but *are* you? . . .

Emanuel   No.

Gabriel   *He shrugs in his slouch.*

Emanuel   I wanna belong to somethin' way up there in the stars without the scowls. Without the guilt. Without the fear. . . I want the soul a Man, not the pornography a the church.

Gabriel   *He leans forward dropping his eyes to the fluid green-gray of the river's daydreaming. Of the four men, he alone was truly content. His life had purpose, mainly in his work, but also in the near-constant nagging and picking from his wife—for who would nag and pick at something without value or necessity?* Well, the church sort of invented pornography, didn't it. . .

Emanuel   Pretty much.

Gabriel   Maybe some day some new religion will wrap a poison blanket around crying, or laughter, love even? . . .

Emanuel   How about eatin', Gabe? Eatin' oughtta be a sin.

Gabriel   Breathin'. Why not breathin'?

Emanuel   Existin'. . . . *They look at each and slowly break into grins.* . . Oh yeah. They already got that covered.

Gabriel   There are worse religions.

Emanuel   An' better.

Gabriel   It all went sour when the afterlife came into it.

Emanuel   It all went sour, man, when monotheism reared its ugly head.

Gabriel   It really went south when not just a few laws got chiseled into stone, but when that big black cookbook for success got sold to the masses.

Emanuel   Things got too serious. All the horseplay got squeezed out.

Gabriel   All the aberrations got rubbed out.

Emanuel   Some things *are* sins, though—*he offers.*

Gabriel   Yeah, I guess.

Emanuel   *He crosses his legs and, squinting, asks*—What's a real sin, Gabe?

Gabriel   A real sin? . . .

Emanuel   Yeah. What's the worst thing you can do in this world?

Gabriel   Kill somebody, I guess.

Emanuel   Kill somebody—sure. . . Maybe not, though. . .

Gabriel   Rape.

Emanuel   I don't know, man. . . You know what I think it is?

Gabriel   *He shakes his head and waits.*

Emanuel   I think lyin' is the worst sin there is. Just plain' lyin'.

Gabriel   Yeah? . . . Yeah, lying's pretty bad.

Emanuel   It's the worst—*he says bitterly.* I think any time you got truth in the palm a your hand an' you crush it, I think that's worse than just about anything. . . Aw—fuck—murder's way worse in terms a the result. But in terms a fuckin' yourself, your own soul, lyin's got 'em all beat by a mile.

Gabriel   Yeah? . . .

Emanuel   You lie to somebody else, you're lyin' to yourself. An' when you do that, you got nothin'. You got nothin' left.

The Right To Exist As Others Don't See You

Hector and Gabriel set off on a quest for food, *smoldering asphalt crumbling at their feet, the sun branding their shoulders, stripped bare of cloth. Behind, in the denizen of mud and roots, a workingman's Eden, the other two sit toward the river and its ghosts of prize-fighter pioneers past, its women of wood limbs and*

cherry blossom hopes, its children made to forfeit school yard
games for Darwin's natural selection at the tenderest age.
Beneath a mammoth witness tree sits the elder one, accustomed to
Texas heat, preferring not to boast about it. The younger, with an
Aztec heart, in full sun-worshipping mode, pays homage with a
tilted chin and morning crocodile sprawl. Cast with casual hope, a
line, and on the end of the line a hook, and skewered to the hook a
worm whose poor luck at being plucked from beneath suburban
mulch gives warning to all those with a tenuous grip on happiness.

Emanuel   Doans, you want a beer yet?—*lifting his head from his*
lazy recline.

Doans   Naw, man. I got my iced tea—*he too, in recline,*
cradled in the bare toes of the trunk.

Emanuel   How's the shade?

Doans   Oh, it's fan-tast-ico. How's the fishin'?

Emanuel   Nothin' yet. I'm just tossin' out my line. Why the hell
not.

Doans   You never know when the white whale is gonna come
along an' give you more than you bargained for.

Emanuel   I should a told Hector to get some beef jerky.

Doans   Give 'em a yell, man. They can't be too far down the
road.

Emanuel   Aw, what the hell. . . Gabe really gonna show 'em the
flyin' machine?

Doans   That seems to be the plan.

Emanuel   He better not take it up.

Doans   Gabe ain't stupid.

Emanuel   Yeah, but Hector can be persuasive. Especially after a
few.

Doans   I think he just wants to see the prop go round.

Emanuel   I'm tellin' you—Gabe better keep it locked up tonight.

Doans   Hector ain't got no suicide wishes, does he, man?

Emanuel   Not suicide exactly. I think the war with Moondog an'
her keepin' Corrie away's turned 'em sorta militant nutso. He's
got no fear.

Doans   You're barely sweatin'. How come I'm sweatin'

underneath this porch, an' you ain't sweatin' at-tall.

Emanuel Beats me.

Doans Global warmin' is just some fiction conjured by enviro-quacks sos they can get on the *cover a the Rooooow—lin Stooooowne.* That's all anybody wants, when you boil away the fat.

Emanuel Yes, mein furor. I believe.

Doans Yeah, you better believe it.

Emanuel Doans.

Doans Yeah, man?

Emanuel I didn't mean what I said last time on the phone. Just ignore it.

Doans Hey, I'm just glad your gears are workin', man. Everybody else is on strike.

Emanuel I agree. I agree with you a hundred percent that nothin' outside a bein' directly attacked yourself justifies hittin' those two towers. That's not what I meant. All I'm saying is, when you got the United States pourin' billions a dollars into Israel, when hundreds a thousands a Palestinians are livin' in refugee camps after bein' booted off their land; after *we* created the situation a bein' dependent on foreign oil, sold Iraq a big chunk a their weapons, then go in an' play pinball with their tanks in the sand, killin' a hundred thousand soldiers; I'm just sayin', you gotta be blind to be totally surprised at what happened.

Doans Israel's got a right to exist.

Emanuel Hey, man—I know. *Quick to avoid another butting of hard-heads, but unwilling to move aside in deference.* But what they did to the Palestinians is the same thing we did to the Indians. It's the same kind a arrogance. It's the same kind a man-made mess.

Doans Look, man, we don't need to hash it out again. You made yourself clear. I made myself clear. We don't need to do it all over again.

Emanuel Okay. I don't wanna be called an anti-Semite. I'll stop. Yeah, okay.

Doans Nobody called you an anti-Semite.

Emanuel By definition, I am. I don't buy the Promised Land bullshit. I don't happen to think that shovin' a group a people off their land 'cause *I've* been shit on is a very nice thing to do. I'm *sorry* about the Holocaust. But it don't give you carte blanche for oppression.

Doans Watch what you say, man.

Emanuel I know—*quickly, then gulping with head tossed back.*

Doans Really. You don't know who's listenin'.

Emanuel I know. . . *Ghoulish eyes, plotting hands grinding together, he whispers*—I might be the next terrorist.

Doans It ain't safe to talk about it, especially when you hold such an unpopular view.

Emanuel Unpopular view in *this* country.

Doans Sure, in this country. What country you think you're in?

Emanuel I know what country I'm in. But go to any country *but* this country an' you ain't gonna find Israel so untouchable. *The personal wounds of being shit-on, of being ignored, of being bullied, of being janitor-trained, finds natural empathy with the Palestinians. This empathy has wings, takes flight as the embittered kicking back of the cornered rat.* Look, I don't support bombin' people to get your message across, understand? Listen to what I'm sayin'—*sitting up, raising his hands wide, bellowing the proclamation:* I don't condone killin' innocent people. Under no circumstances do I support killin' innocent people to get your point across or to promote your agenda. . . I empathize with their *position—that's* all I'm sayin'.

Doans I'm tellin' you, man, Washington's got ears in trees. Even in these parts. They don't need much reason to pick you up off the sidewalk these days.

Emanuel I believe it! Now we got ourselves a real do-gooder. The penis is out. The cheerleader is *in*, man!

Doans Rah!-Rah!-Rah!

Emanuel Two hundred an' whatever million people to choose from, an' we end up with . . . *him*? . . . It's the *system*.

Doans That was our battle cry, man. It's the system, stupid.

Emanuel You know, Doans, sometimes I go weeks without

turnin' on the news or readin' the paper. I can't take it. I find it hard to care. How do you care about somethin' you know you can't change—a make-believe, upside-down fantasy world run by dishonest, greedy assholes? *He gets up, hands stuffed in jeans pockets, arms stiff.*

Doans   You gotta find a shell that fits an' back yourself into it, man.

Emanuel   I have trouble sleepin'—*manically sliding a foot against the ground.*

Doans   Don't do *that.*

Emanuel   Man, like—I have nightmares! The good apple gone bad.

Doans   The good apple gone bad? What do you mean?

Emanuel   I mean *us.* This country. We ain't the good guys anymore, man.

Doans   Uhhh. . . we never were, man.

Emanuel   As empires go, we weren't too bad.

Doans   Empires end up as archeological digs.

Emanuel   Almost every major international stance we've taken in the past twenty years has been the wrong one.

Doans   You talkin' morality now? Governments can't be judged on their morality—'cause they don't function as moral engines.

Emanuel   I'm embarrassed. I'm ashamed.

Doans   Too much guilt. Let it go, man. Up-chuck that core. You didn't set this li'l ol' mousetrap.

Emanuel   I wanna shout across the ocean—*Help!*

Doans   Too far. Nobody but the seagulls an' crabs to hear you.

Emanuel   I wanna tell 'em I'm not with *them.* It's not *me*—it's this Lone Star Aristocracy. It's treason! It's—

Doans   Look, man, what're you so whacked out for? You livin' in some kind a Mother Goose story? You think this is *new?* You think *this* is oppression? This ain't oppression, man. This is Disneyland.

Emanuel   It's a fallen champion.

Doans   Easy Street, milk an' honey.

Emanuel What once was, an' what could a been.

Doans What never was, an' just be glad you ain't in Afghanistan.

Emanuel It's tragic! Colossal! Epic!

Doans As the world turns. Hey—quit lookin' beyond your own private garden.

Emanuel Doans. . . *Shuffling forward, toward the one soul on this earth he trusts not to laugh, not to belittle, to hear and—at least momentarily—to consider. . .*

Doans I hear you, man. . .

Emanuel *You, witness to Kent State. You, of communes an' acid trips an' rap sessions. You, ooohh-weeee, ridin' me high. You, art in the maelstrom a Mrs. Robinson's Lonely Hearts Club Band. You, paintin' in the rain. You, the Mardi Gras countdown in a post-modern mush. You, grape harvested from the school a peace an' love an' dig this an' groovy that. You, my own personal Dylan.* You haven't given up. . . have you? Have you, Doans?

Doans *Untouched, yet not so calloused by time to trample the naked soul laid across the tracks.* Man, I never got *in*. What do you want from me, man? Like, what do you want me to *say*?

Emanuel I want you to *Scream*! I want you to *Howl*! I want—at least in words—*never say die!—I've yet begun to fight!*

Doans Fight? Fight who, an' what for?

Emanuel Fight *them*, for. . . for somethin' worthwhile. Remember Pearl Harbor! . . . Remember I Have a Dream! . . . Remember Enron!

Doans You been to Ireland one too many times, man. Molly McGuire done left for the coast with the roadie from Neil Diamond's Vegas act.

Emanuel Look, man, this ain't the fall a Rome. It ain't the sun settin' on the British Empire. It's not Atlantis bein' swallowed by the sea, or Vikings burnin' monasteries. . . This is the Walkin' Liberty bein' fucked across the pool table. It's the Buffalo Nickel bein' turned into beef jerky. It's the Wheat Penny bein' crossed with the DNA a maybe, shit, I don't know, fuckin' Pee Wee Herman—It's—It's the chiselin' a the greatest ideals ever gathered together under one banner, the highest imperfect collective point mankind has ever known, an' sellin' the shards for a new fuckin' leather couch! It's the end of a dreamer's possibilities—turnin' our backs on hungry mouths—the denial a Common Sense!

Doans　　*He leaps up himself, hopping in place, the pain of blind stabs hitting close to the heart.* Man, step outta that light!—your head be swimmin' with too many gall stones.

Emanuel　　Doans. . . *you*—I thought *you* were the bugler. I thought you were one a the few who knew the score—who wouldn't join ranks with those *things*. . .

Doans　　Man, you gots it all *wrong*. You seen too many Spielberg cartoons, watched Jesus Christ Superstar without a wink-wink, mistook that times are a changin', give peace a chance, joy to the world pop-music fad as somethin' this species could really chew up an' live by. There ain't no Santy Claus or Easter Bunny neither, little brother.

Emanuel　　*A gruesome expression of disbelief rises on the boy's face.* . . No, man. I know what's in your heart. I've heard you rail against it. Are you *you*, or just the body a somebody I used to know?

Doans　　I'm more me than I ever was, man. Sorry you don't like the new fenders.

Emanuel　　Where did *you* go? Jesus Christ, Doans. . . where'd you go? . . . *Drifting along the shore, clutching his thick crop of hair, eyes burning, he bumps into the wall at the dead end alley of his broken hope, and for the first time in his life he does not attempt to scale it, or even to run out the way he came, but sits down in the piss puddles and puke and weeps, a lament for the death of something too big to describe with mere words.*

Looking Back

Doans　　**Standing on the shore, looking out,** *surveying rafts*

and crude waste whose final destination must be the vast sea itself,
he fumes, flicks a switch against the very trunk previously giving
him support. The young one, he sucker punches with sour truth.
His aim, though sometimes off, dislodges sturdy jaws and thick
heads wherever it falls. The elder, having spent half a century in
the construction of his cocoon, once spun with revolution, most
recently closed in with bricks of Republican babble easily
withstanding the most ferocious huffing and puffing. . . and yet, his
brother incites rioting within. What the hell? You want me to piss
on your shoes, instead a these old tree roots? Why don't you put
yo' head down there where the water meets the bark, an' I'll whet
your whistle, feed your appetite, an' suit you in pinstripes all in
one fell *swoosh!* Piss. . . on. . . *you*, Manny. Here's what I think a
your moanin' an' groanin'. . . *He swipes his Tom-Cat spray across*
the ancient roots. Here's to the hope that there's no more like you,
an' that your offspring's a better handler a gift horses in glass
houses. . . Why're you tryin' to pigeonhole me? Ride somebody
else for a while. *Old*, you say? Naw, man, I ain't old. I'm who I
always was. Cleaned up, shed my adolescent hormones, mellowed
out. So you be a gallopin' down the backstretch, while I'm
roundin' for home. You got fresh legs, an' I got this torch ridin'
the back a my neck. You an' me, we'd be singin' in Beach Boys
harmony if the Chinese calendar didn't drop us down in different
zoos. Look man, all my old friends, your so-called long-haired
heroes, are sellin' porn on the Internet, humpin' three jobs to keep
up with their third ex's child support, or buryin' treasure before
the third quarter earnings adjustment. Well, yeah, some are still
tripped out, an' some were snakes all along. . . *Old*, you say?
Naw, man, I ain't old. I'm just readjustin' my expectations is all,
like any Johnny who's ever got his gun. I see it from this hill over
yonder, the same flood, the same mess. Looks a lot bigger over
here, an' besides, these broken bones from the last salmon run got
my little head a thinkin'; it's thinkin' that's bought me these
khaki's an' a new cellular phone. . . You don't get it, man! I ain't
throwin' in no towel; but how am I gonna go against the sledgehammer now, when the voice a villages has been de-amplified, so

to speak? What's the point in martyrdom when there ain't nobody there to see you bleed? Everybody's got one big push, an' mine came out somewhere in a long jet stream between Kent an' the French Quarter. You wanna push now? Be my guest. I'll not try an' turn you from your task. Just be warned: The dogs roam in bigger packs than before. They've got all the bases covered, all the escape holes plugged. McCarthy Redux signed a contract with Big Brother, an' then they swung by an' kidnapped Jesus—their official spokesman with a .45 pointed to His head. . . Watch what you say, man. Speech ain't free no more.

Birth Of Vaudeville

Hector stands near drunk, having pounded beers from the moment of hello to now, the moment of fishing. In Rome, he would have been first lieutenant, and given his life for Caesar. In Camelot, the unsung workhorse of both king and king's betrayer, Lancelot. Under Custer, silent dissenter weeping tears for the other side. He has nothing heroic to which he might apply himself and so, as a multitude of men now do, each for his own reason, he drinks himself drunk while away from wife and home, a lung fish, this world's soon-to-be appendix. His stance nevertheless is proud, unconcerned, and strong. The others, behind him, have lines baited and ready for the pot luck cast of the ever-hopeful.

Gabriel   Maybe Jules got lost.

Doans   He ain't lost, man.

Emanuel   Then he'll figure out this isn't the Ohio—*his eyes on Gabriel, who surveys the water for a cast, the boy works a hook for Doans on the perch of his lap. He points enthusiastically to the shade of the giant tree.* Here Gabe, toss it out right over there by the point a the dock. Bet there's a mama catfish waitin' for you.

Doans   The only way to fish; havin' your little brother bait your hook.

Emanuel   I'm only doin' it 'cause we're not usin' maggots.

Doans   Even I know you don't use maggots for catfish.

Emanuel   That's what I mean. Be glad we ain't fishin' for somethin' else.

Gabriel   Maybe he got the weeks wrong.

Doans   Naw, man. I talked to 'em this week. He's comin'.

Hector   *Without looking, holding his pole in hand instead of leaning it into the Y of a stick, he calls back*—Doans, tell me about the three-tailed cat.

Doans   Who told you about that? Gabe. . . you spill the beans?

Gabriel   We ran out of things to talk about on the way back from the store. *Nobody but Emanuel sees his mischievous, Boris Karloff grin.*

Doans   Yeah, hmm. . . the three-tailed cat. Or somethin'. . . Man, I don't know what the fuck it was. He came into the yard the other day—in broad daylight. I was in the studio listenin' to Art Bell, or maybe Rush Limbaugh; one a those two. Anyhow, I was passin' between the studio an' the house when I saw somethin' movin' in the yard. . . I walked up to it. . . It looked like a monkey.

Hector   A *monkey*?

Doans   Yeah, man. I wondered, how the hell did a monkey get into my front yard?

Hector   What kind a monkey, man? *Christ.*

Doans   I don't know. Just, you know, a regular monkey. I don't know what kind a monkey. It looked like it had about five arms. Man, it looked like it was moltin'!

Hector   Moltin'?

Doans   Yeah, man! Not like a buffalo; more like a crab or somethin'—like it was comin' outta its own *skin*! That's why maybe it looked like it had so many legs.

Hector   You sure it wasn't a raccoon, or a turtle? Snappin' turtles'll come outta the water, an' they can get pretty fuckin' big.

Doans   Man, I know what a raccoon looks like. It was a cat. It just went round in circles. It looked like it had a broken back, man. So I hit it with a shovel.

Hector   *He tries to maintain the interrogator's discretion, but everyone hears the chuckle in his voice.* You killed it?

Doans   Fuck yeah, I killed it!

Hector   What for?

·Doans   Man, that thing wasn't right! Didn't you listen to what I just said? Like, I didn't want it messin' around with my cat.

Hector   What'd you do with it?

Doans   I fuckin' buried that thing.

Gabriel   Well, not at first.

Doans   Yeah; oh yeah. That's right. First, I stuck it in a trash bag an' put it in the trashcan, but then Chelsea said she could smell it. Man, I didn't want the neighbor lady to come nosin' around an' smell her dead cat, an' then lift up the lid an' see it halfway stickin' outta the garbage bag along with some coffee grounds an' egg shells.

Hector   It was her cat?

Doans   I don't know. I don't know whose cat it was.

The four fishermen cast and reel, cast and reel, wait and drink, watch and think, think and regret, regret and breathe deep with new hope pulled from the ether of nothing. Hector, drinking at twice the pace as the others, is now dead drunk.

Hector   *His large, tubular frame swaying, he turns with a defenseless, puffy-eyed frown.* You sure it wasn't a groundhog, man? *The three look silently to one another, mouthing and grimacing.*

Doans   I wish it was, man.

Hector   Why'd you have to whack it?

Doans   It scared me.

Hector   Yeah, I know, but why'd you have to whack it to death just 'cause it scared you?

Doans   It was somethin' from another dimension, man. You had to see it.

Hector   Where'd you bury it?

Gabriel   Down in the gully on the other side a the studio.

Hector   Let's go dig it up—*reeling in his line, quickly, then turning toward the cabin-on-stilts.*

Doans   I don't wanna dig that thing up, man. You crazy?

Hector Come on—*tapping Doans on the back as he moves past. The others stop, jaws unhinged.*

Doans You mean now?

Hector Yeah. Come on. It's only two hours to your house.

Doans Two *hours*? Man, are you outta your mind! I just drove all the way down here.

Hector But, a three-tailed cat!—*rummaging through the cooler, in a squat, wavering.* We'll be back in no time. It'll take two minutes to dig it up. I'll hold it on the way back. *Upright again, a bottle of cold beer in each mitt, dripping. He wonders why they all are so sluggish. He fears their immovability, and ponders death.*

Doans That cat's stayin' in the ground, man. That's an evil beast.

Hector I'll go.

Emanuel Hector!—*he shoots up, knowing peril when he sees it.* Man, you're in no shape to be drivin' anywhere. Come here!—*he hands Gabriel his pole and takes after his big brother.*

Doans Manny—don't let 'em go. He'll kill himself.

Emanuel Hector!

Hector *In the bleach white of daylight, he is lost. His sycamore-limb arms go out. Like a blind man, he is.* Shit! Who moved those stairs? Those stairs were on the other side a the house before—*and up that mammoth structure of treated lumber he climbs, in a jog, as though running steps for football practice. A fall backward will break his neck.*

Emanuel *In full chase, he calls out to his brother*—Hector, you want me to drive? I'll drive you there, man. We can look at the three-legged cat. Come on. Slow down.

Doans Hector! Why don't you guys stay here! I think somebody's got a tiger shark on the line! Hey! What does it mean when the end a the pole touches the ground! . . . Hector!

Hector *Bouncing off the shrubbery, then against his vehicle and back to the shrubs again that clutch him like a witch's glove. Head in circles, he spots the door, thrusts it open, and throws himself in, crunching his shoulder, chin, and knee. A memory*

*blast—they come to him while sober or soused—this one, a
recurring time tunnel to the back hallways of high school,
February, those first days of track practice, doing fiver repeats
until legs melted in liquid fire that blew up the ribcage and burned
the lungs clean out. In his mind, music. Always, the music. Never a
moment without the music sending him off to heroic lands where
brute strength, brute honor, and brute love rule with poetic fist. . .*
Emanuel *Seated beside his brother, an orb of low modulation.*
Hector, get outta the driver's seat. Let me drive.
Hector I'm okay. Really, man. . . *Suddenly awakened—*
Manny, I gotta see it! I gotta see the three-tailed cat! The monkey-
cat!
Emanuel But Hector, we'll never find it. How you think we're
gonna find it without Doans or Gabe to show us where it is?
Hector Chelsea's there.
Emanuel Yeah, Hector, an' we don't wanna scare Chelsea just
'cause we heard about some three-tailed monkey-cat. They got a
shotgun—remember?
Hector So?
Emanuel So, maybe Chelsea'll think we're somebody breakin'
in. She might just fill us both with lead.
Hector We'll honk outside the house. Fuck, man, she knows
my car.
Emanuel Still—*showing grave concern.* It's kinda risky, man.
Hector I'm worried about her.
Emanuel Chelsea?
Hector With that dead an' buried three-tailed cat hangin'
around. We gotta save her, Manny! We got to!—*he tries for the
ignition, but finds Manny's hands. He pulls back, not angry,
disappointed, a boy who asks and does not receive.*
Emanuel Give me the keys, Hector.
Hector I'm okay. Come on. Let's go.
Emanuel Sorry, man, but you ain't drivin' anywhere.
Hector Okay. I'll let you drive. I'm okay, but you drive if you
want. Here you go—*and he hands over the keys without the need
for police brutality.*

Emanuel   Let's think about it.

Hector   Wow! A three-tailed cat!

Emanuel   It's a long way up to Doansy's house. We gotta think about it real good before we just go barrelin' up there an' scare Chelsea half to death.

Hector   You know, Manny, it might be a missin' link! It might a escaped from a lab where the government's doin' some really nasty cross-pollinatin' research shit! Maybe it's a new kind a apple picker! You know—you can never get to the very top a the trees, even with ladders. Maybe the Mexicans don't wanna climb that high!

Emanuel   Yeah, man. Maybe.

Hector   The Mexicans are *everywhere*. Where'd they all come from?

Emanuel   *He shrugs and shakes his head dead quiet.*

Hector   They're *everywhere*. Landscapers, roofers. . . in orchards. . . McDonald's. . . Wendy's. . . They're *everywhere*, Manny—you see 'em?

Emanuel   Sure, I've seen 'em. Hey, man. If you're tired, just close your eyes an' go to sleep. We'll be at Doansy's in no time.

Hector   But the car's not runnin'.

Emanuel   I'm thinkin'. Don't worry. We'll go just as soon as I'm done thinkin'.

Hector   Who's watchin' the border? How'd they get here? My neighbor had a pack of 'em livin' in the attic of his garage. A whole family of 'em were livin' up there. He didn't even know it! Burnt a hole in his roof—that's how he found out! They snuck in at night, an' snuck out before the sun came up. . . Mexicans! They're everywhere!—*whip-lashed forward—terrorized with fright—his head on the wheel, eyes out in surreal madness.*

Emanuel   *He leans, straining, between his brother's back and the seat—*Here, man. Push the lever. The seat goes all the way back.

Hector   We at McDonald's yet? I'm *starvin'*. When we get there, order me a Big Mac, fries, an' a chocolate milk shake. Fuck—they still got cherry pies? Man, I love their cherry pies. 'Cept they'll fuckin' burn the shit outta your mouth. . . Man, what's takin' so long?

Emanuel   We'll get there. Just as soon as I'm through thinkin',
Hector.

Hector   Yeah, okay. Hurry up, will you. I'm really hungry.

Emanuel   You want any ketchup?

Hector   On my Whopper? Special orders don't upset us, at
McDonald's. . .

Emanuel   With your fries.

Hector   Biggie Size it. I want the Biggie Size.

Emanuel   Okay, man. I'll let you know when we get there. Just
as soon as I'm done thinkin'.

Hector   Manny!—*bolting upright, eyes on fire* . . . Where are
we?

Emanuel   Here, man. Sittin' in the car.

Hector   What country are we in?

Emanuel   Still in the U.S., man.

Hector   The United States? . . . Are you *sure*?

Emanuel   We haven't gone anywhere. I'm still thinkin'.

Hector   Where's Jules?

Emanuel   He ain't here yet.

Hector   Did we go to Doansy's yet?

Emanuel   No, man. I'm still thinkin'.

Hector   Why're you thinkin'?

Emanuel   Then we'll be ready to go. We'll go when I'm done
thinkin'.

Hector   God, can you believe it? That's fuckin' wild!

Emanuel   Believe what?

Hector   Frogs with extra legs growin' outta their backs! Frogs
with extra legs!—they're everywhere, man! That's fuckin' wild!

Emanuel   I know, man.

Hector   What's up with *that*? How'd you like to have an extra
arm pokin' outta *your* back! . . . How do you deal with somethin'
like that—frogs with extra legs? Where'd God go, man? Poof!—
He's gone! All my life, I've been lookin' for 'Em. All my life!
An' you know what? He ain't said *boo*! He ain't said
booooooooooooooooo. . . Frogs with extra legs, Manny! How much

worse can things get than frogs with extra legs!

Emanuel   It's fucked up, man.

Hector   Why doesn't He give dad some extra legs? Why
doesn't He do that? Even frog legs. You think dad cares what kind
a legs he has? He wears pants all day long anyway; you're never
gonna see his frog legs. . . *Polio*. . . What kind a diabolical shit is
that? Where'd that come from? Why'd it have to hit our dad?
Think a the odds. . .

Emanuel   Whenever I do, that's when I lose all faith. I've been
tryin' to become a believer again.

Hector   Polio fucked up our lives. It fucked him up, an' it
fucked us up. Now it's workin' on Corrie. . . Frogs with extra legs,
an' nobody cares. We're livin' in the Twilight Zone, man! Now
they're givin' guns to pilots! Are they outta their minds! *Pilots.*
Why not bus drivers, or cabbies? Why not teachers? Guns in the
hands a people flyin' our fuckin' *planes*! An' they're givin' tax
breaks to people who buy *Hummers*! An' they're drillin' in the
Alaskan wilderness! An' pretty soon we're gonna go start another
war over *oil*! An' millions a people are dyin' a AIDS in Africa
every year, an' we're supposed to believe it's about *helpin'
people*! An' they're fuckin' with the DNA a *life*, Manny, *life*! . . .
Why're Americans so fat? 'Cause we stuff our fuckin' faces with
crap an' drive two blocks to buy a gallon a *milk*, that's why! It's
insane! . . . Nobody's in control! A *thing's* in control! *Polio's* in
control! Eunuchs in the *Vatican*! Big Brother on the *street corner*!
Bradbury's fire chief's in the *White House—*in the *White House*! .
. . The anti-Christ is *born*! . . . Chaos! . . . The Flood's about to
come again! . . . Manny! *Collapsing, fingers digging into the
steering wheel, the mental assault is too much. A torch suddenly
exhausted of its fuel, he flickers.*

Emanuel   *He rubs his brother's shoulders, the brother who saved
his life from the hyenas of his youth.* Go to sleep, Hector.

Hector   *He curls, tucking his hands beneath his head.* . . . I think
I will. Let me know when you wanna go to Doansy's. We're still
goin', aren't we?

Emanuel   Oh, sure. Just as soon as I'm done thinkin'.

Hector   Okay. Don't leave without me.
Emanuel   I wouldn't do that, Hector.
Hector   I wanna see that three-legged monkey-cat. We could make millions. . . *sshhhh*. . .

Scotch-Irish Horse-Thievin' Mojo Train

You think I hyperbolize. Saved his life? No? And what do you know about such crimes—the stealing of youth, the pinching of delicate tendrils, the smashing of self-esteem beyond any remote chance of repair? Would you recognize a personal savior in the guise of an inebriated tinder box if you saw him? . . . The young one stands at the top of the new stairs and glances back at the car. No one—not his wife, or ex-wife, or the brothers down below in the mud—knew his brother the way he did—a duplistic incarnation of love encased within the hard vitriol of his own self-defense.
Doans   You get 'em to sleep?
Emanuel   Finally.
Doans   I was worried.
Emanuel   He gets an idea in his head an' he's pretty hard to stop. You want a beer?—*holding it by the neck, like a billy club.*
Doans   No thanks, man. I got my iced tea.
Emanuel   Gabe?
Gabriel   No, thanks.
Emanuel   Man—*and he sits where they sit, legs crossed like scissors out into the hot mud.*
Doans   He won't go anywhere, will he?
Emanuel   I got the keys.
Doans   He won't wander off?
Emanuel   Hope not. He's tired.
Doans   Hector. . . Hector, man. . . *To himself, bouncing a wanderlust leg on the knee that's been fulcrum for witnessing a thousand back alley crimes and feats of true heroism. Nothing is a*

true surprise to him anymore, yet he is hard-wired for unedited, visceral response—something no amount of same-old-same-old can wear down. What'd you have to go an' marry Moondog for? Man, why don't they outlaw marriage for dudes under thirty to prom queens, preacher's daughters, an' any ol' I Dream a Jeanie who opens doors with just a smile?

Emanuel She's not all of it.

Doans Yeah, she ain't the whole enchilada, *but. . .* Come into my parlor, said the fly to the spider. Here—*lifting his shirt to his neck*—take a look at these cantaloupes. . . Yowwwwza! . . . Can I feel those things? You mean, you're really gonna let me put my Average Joe hands on those milky white orbs a perfection? . . . *Really?* . . . Who's wrappin' who, you know what I mean? It ain't always so obvious.

Emanuel Bad women can fuck you up, man. It's a crapshoot.

Doans Yeah, unfortunately that's pretty much what it is unless you got some pre-determined blueprint yo' workin' from. That counts all of us out.

Emanuel You think Uncle Abe ever had a girl?

Doans He did.

Emanuel You mean you think he did, or you're sayin', for a fact, he did?

Doans I'm sayin' for a fact he did. Mom told me.

Emanuel How old was he?

Doans *Shaking his head, flicking his fag*—I'm not too sure. . . *taking a puff. . .* but I think he must a been in high school. Maybe a little older, but not much. A young buck, as I recall. A strapping young lad.

Emanuel What happened?

Doans Man—*he turns, his eyes wincing*—you wanna know what happened? I'll tell you what happened. He broke it off. He broke it off 'cause he didn't want her to be saddled with a cripple for the rest a her life. Can you dig that, man?

Emanuel Knowin' Uncle Abe, I believe it.

Doans Well, hell yeah, you're gonna believe it.

Emanuel Man, that's. . . tragic.

Doans   That's some serious shit, is what it is. That's deep, deep shit.

Emanuel   So for the rest a his life, he worked that farm. No woman. No kids. Aunt Pearl the livin' saint on one side, an' Aunt Minnie the thorn in the side on the other. Jesus. . . *He remembers those early visits to the farm, Uncle Abe, the only other cripple he knew, sitting with his single wooden crutch leaned against his chair, and dad, his two aluminum shafted crutches lying as seeing eye dogs against the wall. There was the old whetting stone, warped, up the drive. The barn, ragged, waning, barely used. Aunt Pearl and her hunched back. Aunt Minnie and her garden. The two well pumps—never to be used for play, but only for true thirst. The outhouse. The creek. The cellar. Rhubarb pie. Frozen apple sauce. The dry sink. The austere acceptance of their days. The time tunnel to living ancestry.* Jesus, Doans. . .

Doans   You ever see his wound?

Emanuel   *He turns late, away in a million mile time warp to belated awe*—No, man.

Doans   Yeah—*another deep drag, wince, and nod.* It was on his leg, just like dad's. Every night Aunt Pearl or Aunt Minnie— they'd dress it. You know, clean it. Wash it. Caress it. Give that ol' wooden heart a little tenderness, even if it did come from a sister.

Emanuel   It doesn't matter, man.

Doans   Naw, it don't matter. . . Yeah, well so anyhow, Dr. Mint caught wind of it an' brought 'em up to Akron. All he needed was some penicillin, man. Well, Dr. Mint arranged for 'em to stay in the hospital for like three or four days. You know why? . . . So he could watch The World Series.

Emanuel   *He grins only, thinks, then breaks into three-dimensional laughter*—That's fuckin' great.

Doans   What was he—like fifty years old? Livin' his whole life with that wound. An' all it took was a little fuckin' penicillin.

Emanuel   You'd think Aunt Minnie would a said somethin'. She was out in the world for a time. Man, she knew about penicillin.

Doans   I don't know. Maybe he didn't have insurance. Like, what's a little more misery to somebody like him? He probably liked it until he got old enough to not wanna deal with it anymore.

Emanuel   Mom ever tell you about Aunt Pearl?

Doans   What about her?

Emanuel   She almost went crazy, man.

Doans   Crazy? Naw—I didn't hear that one.

Emanuel   You know she went to the convent.

Doans   Sure.

Emanuel   Well, you know, I always knew that as a kid, an' knowin' what a sweet woman Aunt Pearl was, I wondered why she left the convent.

Doans   I always thought she came back to take care a Uncle Abe.

Emanuel   That's what I thought. But mom says she had a nervous breakdown at the convent. She felt like she was lettin' God down.

Doans   Lettin' God down? *Her?*

Emanuel   Somethin' about how she wasn't good enough. She wanted to be perfect, or at least be the perfect servant. She was real hard on herself. An' when she wasn't perfect—somethin' snapped. She was inconsolable. They watched her, an' I think she was even suicidal. After a while, when she didn't snap out of it, the nuns sent her home. As mom tells it, she was just a mess for a while. I don't know how long. An' I don't know how she snapped out of it. . . Ain't that somethin' else, man? Aunt Pearl, the nicest, sweetest lady in the world, an' she nearly went bonkers.

Doans   There's probably somethin' to it we don't know about—nobody alive knows about—an' all we got now is some textbook synopsis like some ancient Egyptian sarcophagus frieze relayin' the big picture of effect without the pearl string a little pictures tellin' the cause. Maybe she wasn't pure. . . *The Groucho eyes toss the bucket of gators, then run and hide.*

Emanuel   Aunt Pearl?

Doans   Fuck yeah, Aunt Pearl. You ever seen pictures a her when she was young?

Emanuel   No.

Doans   Yeah—she was a classic beauty, man, a real A-1 primo

knockout. All I know is, if she got our libido genes, there would a
been some big ass battles ragin' in that little bod'.
Emanuel   Pure speculation, man—*the young one grins.*
Doans   I know. I know. But somethin', as in some specific
inner Battle a Hastings, drove her to despair cliff, man. She was
real. There must a been a real cause.
Emanuel   It could a been nothin' more than normal urges, you
know? I mean, maybe she didn't act on 'em at all, but just the fact
that maybe she was thinkin' about—hell, I don't know what—I
could see that drivin' her to the edge.
Doans   Sure. Those were the prison bars a the times, man.
Guilt was like your sidekick—you an' it in a three-legged race to
eternal purgatory.
Emanuel   *The thought of his great aunt in innocence, when the
word meant a specific kind of innocence, beautiful, ripped apart
by the Goliath—hormones—on one side and the Cyclops—
propriety—on the other. . . the thought shuffles all his inner
papers.* Doans?
Doans   Yeah, man?
Emanuel   Do you think hers was a wasted life?
Doans   Wasted life? . . . Naw, man. Why you say that?
Emanuel   I don't know. No husband. No kids. No adventure. . .
Whenever we'd go down an' see 'em, I always got the feelin' she
was fightin' somethin', you know, that her smile wasn't happiness
really, but maybe an apology or a submission.
Doans   To what, man?
Emanuel   To life. To work, pain—her humped back maybe.
Loneliness, an' the drudgery in the wait for death.
Doans   So?
Emanuel   So anyway. . . *speaking softly, dropping his gaze.*
Doans   No, man—real astute. I knows. . . I knows. . . But what
I mean is, like so how's she different than you?
Emanuel   I don't know. . .
Doans   I mean, where're you on the smiley-happy meter?
Emanuel   The battery's dead—*he jokes.*
Doans   Maybe you're tryin' to go up, an' she never wanted to

go up—you know? . . . Things moved real slow for those three.
They had on a different set a glasses, man. An' I don't know if you
can necessarily see their life movie show through your own pair. I
always got the feelin' they were pretty content. . . But you think
they should a had more highs an' lows?

Emanuel I really don't know what I think, Doans. It's not really
a thought, but a feelin' I always had.

Doans Feelin's are legit, man. Real legit.

Emanuel *For the first time in his life, the pulse he always took as
a concern for others rears up not as a lion, but as a snake, coiling
around his self-image. It occurs to him that his pity for her, for his
brother, his father, and a thousand others, might be nothing more
than a cloaked envy.* Sure, man.

Doans I thought I had the comet by the tail when I was young.

Emanuel Yeah?—*a bewildered, at-peace, sleepy-eyed glance.*

Doans An' I think I did. I know I did. An' I thought not that
folks like Aunt Pearl an' Uncle Abe were on the outside lookin' in
necessarily, but I thought, *hmmmmm.* . . me an' my friends—this
youth movement—youth revolution, or whatever it was—it was
like—*he grasps the air in an attempt to place his hands around
something profound, much bigger than this world*—I guess closer
to the bone. Had karma wrapped around this plug-an'-chug work
world like a piggy-in-a-blanket. Like, they were all just ignorant,
man. Thank-you so much for your toil an' trouble—clearin' the
land, ridin' that plow from dawn till dusk, beatin' back the
Nazis—but we hippie folks'll take it from here. *Yeah!* That's what
I thought, man.

Emanuel You lived in a beautiful time, man. They're gonna
write about it for centuries.

Doans It *was* a beautiful time. . . but we were just dreamin',
man. Mad scientists on dope.

Emanuel What do you think they thought about it all?

Doans They probably thought we were a bunch a pretentious
kids with too much time on our hands.

Emanuel Fuck, man—*he kicks a foot toward his brother, a smile
and laugh*—they were right.

Doans   Well, hell yeah they were right. But then that's the way it's always done, man. Those big new eggs gotta have fertile ground, an' time to ripen.

Emanuel   You think they envied it?

Doans   Sure. But I'm sure they were too scared to think too much about it. An' too old to latch on without lookin' desperate. Man, like all those guys were voyeurs anyway. You can shut off your mind, an' you can probably shut off your mojo; but then some bus load a long-haired freaky flower children break down in your drive an' your black an' white world goes Roy G. Biv whether you're ready for it or not. *Of the farm he thinks, of warped wooden barn boards, big rusted tools, the old oil pump that moved as if in need of winding, whirling dirt, and the rationing of effort and resources. Cinnamon buns, asymmetrical apples plucked from the tree, jumping from the hay loft into massive golden piles, shooting rats under the corn bin with dad's .22, grass so tall it tickled your face while sitting within its amber waves, listening and only listening—the child seen and not heard—as the adults sat in shade stretching legs and sipping iced tea. . . His eyes wander out over the river and he becomes not sentimental, but appreciative.* They watched men land on the moon—*he whispers to the water more than to his brother.* From horse an' buggy to Neil Armstrong on the *moon*. . . an' we think *they* were envious?

Emanuel   I used to sit in the parlor. Remember the glass case? It had a model car in it. No—two. Some books, some arrowheads in a frame. Some other stuff, I can't even remember now. But man, I'd sit there not sayin' a peep wishin' I could have one a those model cars. Every time I went, I'd think Uncle Abe had to see it in my eyes, the hunger for it. It was so powerful—I just knew he was gonna open that case, reach inside, an' hand one to me. I thought if that happened, I don't know, it would a been like the end a the world.

Doans   Let me guess; he never gave you the car.

Emanuel   I don't think Uncle Abe ever gave me a damn thing!

Doans   He gave me a lickin' or two.

Emanuel At least it's somethin'.

Doans The older you get, the more you get it.

Emanuel *He stares, smirking, at his brother-in-law.* Gabe, you're not sayin' anything.

Gabriel I'm just listening. I'm saying all I want to say by having my third beer.

Doans Chime in whenever the planets align, man.

Gabriel I will.

Emanuel I get it, man—*back to Doans.*

Doans Good, good—that makes one of us.

Emanuel Can you imagine. . . what'd they get—like a whole section, man?

Doans I think so. What's a section, about 400 acres, Gabe?

Gabriel I thought it was more like 660.

Doans 660? Yeah?

Gabriel I think it's a square mile, however many acres that is.

Doans Wow. That's a big chunk a the Ponderosa.

Emanuel *Not listening, his mind staggers, then flops forward.* Covered from the Atlantic to the Mississippi with trees, man. You could stamp a whole mess a Englands just east a the Mississippi. An' all trees. . . Here, young man, it's yours. All yours. You just gotta hack all them trees down an' start a farmin'. . .*fuck*. . . who the fuck did all that?

Doans I don't know. . . The Jolly Green Giant an' all his kin, I guess.

Emanuel You ever take out a tree root, man?

Doans A couple, think.

Emanuel I've taken out a few an' I'll tell you what—it was hard fuckin' work!

Doans They had horses. They probably burned out the stumps.

Emanuel Still. Man, they fuckin' wiggled their way outta The Grim Reaper's ball an' chain each mornin'—they probably had rawhide for breakfast an' buffalo balls for lunch.

Doans The birth a the American work ethic, that's what you just laid out, man.

Emanuel   I mean *fuck*. . . Uncle Abe, Aunt Peal, an' Aunt
Minnie—they were like only two generations away! A sniff an' a
scratch from real-live buffalo roamin' while the deer an' the
antelope played. Heard stories about Indians—first-hand—the way
we heard stories about World War II from dad. The Civil War was
somethin' a lot a dudes—dudes still scrapin' the land—knew
firsthand. You didn't need no history book to learn about it; you
fuckin' listened to grandpa talk about it around a fire! . . . *fuck*. . .
Doans   I knows, I *knows*. . . like, two hundred years ago was
prior War a 1812. This great big state a concrete an' rust was just
the itch in a bunch a pioneers' crotches. . . an lookie how far
we've come, man. Look at all the wonderful secrets Pandora's
Box had waitin' for us all those years.
A sudden whiff of river air; a sudden shift in collective thoughts.
The young one, as he loses the sharpness of complete sobriety,
frets over the sun and how, unbelievably, it kept spitting out heat
and light, and what we would do if it ever stopped. He is not a
neurotic, just a perpetual thinker.
Doans   Man, I don't know how to get the fur outta my ears—
at first only a dainty feel, then a crooked pinkie, too close to resist,
went digging. I need a miniature razor. Do they make ear razors?
Somebody oughtta invent one.
Emanuel   I only have nose hair.
Doans   Yeah, I remember when I only had nose hair too.
Emanuel   Is that what finally makes chicks quit lookin' at you?
Doans   You got chicks still lookin' at you?
Emanuel   Only a few times a year.
Doans   Wow. Lucky you.
Emanuel   Mostly at night at stoplights. I think it's fear.
Doans   Naw, man. Chicks don't look at me anymore. . .
Emanuel   It's weird, man. I'm almost forty, but I don't feel like
it. I don't look at myself like I'm forty—you know? I mean, what
is forty?
Gabriel   Younger than fifty.
Doans   Yeah, that's right, man.
Emanuel   Yeah, but older than twenty, thirty, an' thirty-five.

Gabriel   You're not having a mid-life crisis, are you, Manny?

Doans   Naw—*laughing*—he's just in one long On The Road crisis with like a hundred Blondie's standin' in the dirt with boxin' gloves on. Manny's too far ahead to be havin' a mid-life crisis. No Corvette or college bimbo in sight.

Emanuel   I still come home an' wanna fuck my wife.

Doans   Do it, man.

Emanuel   Well—*in a very good, soft-spoken Ronald Reagan parody*—it's kinda hard to pull my dick outta this cocoon she's got me in.

Doans   Yeah, that's a toughy.

Emanuel   I mean I wanna fuck her, really fuck her like I used to. On the banister. Across the table. In the back a the pickup. In the alley behind the movie theater. . . I mean, how the hell do you like that shit one day, an' then *wham!*—suddenly you think that's all dirty?

Doans   Only famous rock stars can get away with livin' their whole lives the way they actually feel. Well, an' we art—*eests*.

Emanuel   But how do you *do* that?

Doans   Man, like chicks got that denial knob fine-tuned like you wouldn't believe.

Emanuel   But why deny it?—*blank-faced, at a loss*. What's the point?

Doans   Why? . . . Fuck, man, I ain't a chick, how the fuck would I know. . . Why? . . . Well, hmm. . . let's think about it. . . It's probably got somethin' to do with those crazy hormones. I mean, chicks are digital machines, whereas we're like analog. They're on or they're off. When they're on—they're fuckin' on. They'll take on F-Troop. When they're off, you might as well be wavin' that Johnson in front a yo' pet hamster.

Emanuel   You mean like somehow all a her estrogen got flushed outta her system?

Doans   Maybe.

Emanuel   Well, somethin' got flushed outta her system.

Gabriel   Yeah, *you*.

Emanuel   It's not just the responsibilities I have now. I got no

problems with that. But, there's these certain expectations people
have with somebody who's *forty*, an' I'll tell you what; I just can't
swallow it.
Doans   Don't. Don't, man. Spit it out—*he makes the proper
barf demonstration with a finger to the throat*—like a White Rock
carp.
Emanuel   But if you don't, you're fightin' against it all the time.
Doans   Naw, man. You don't need to fight nothin'. You just
gotta let go—go your own way. You ain't like them anyhow.
Emanuel   I know I'm not. . . . *His words had more resignation
than defiance in them; he stares at his own head shadow in the
speckled egg mud.*
Doans   Then what's the problem?
Emanuel   I guess I'm just lonely.
Doans   You care too much about what other people think.
Emanuel   No, man. It's that everybody else has moved on.
They've evaporated into thin air.
Doans   That's life.
Emanuel   I know it, brother. . . I mean. . . I still get surprised,
every day, an' I still get mad, an' frustrated, an' depressed. It
seems like everybody else, they don't. It's like they've formed
their opinions, they've constructed this shell around their beliefs,
an' nothin's gonna break through. They refuse to *think*, they won't
lower the drawbridge. An' you know what their views a life are
made of? . . . Money an' security.
Doans   Money an' security, money an' security, doo-dah, doo-
dah. . .
Emanuel   I can't talk to anybody anymore. How can you have
any sorta intelligent dialogue with somebody whose sole objective
is to stuff their 401K full a cash? That's life they're forfeitin'
today, for the security a jerkin' off in money when they're *old*.
Doans   *Singing*—The times they are a changin'. . . Man,
somebody throw'd this locomotive in reverse.
Emanuel   You don't know what office talk is like, man. It's a
form a torture.
Doans   You gotta play that game if you wanna take home first

prize.

Emanuel   Turning his leapfrog crouch toward the elder; he is eager to divulge what seems to him gossip worth passing on. Listen to this, man. This guy I worked with was called into the director's office an' really chastised; you know why? . . . For *readin'*.

Doans   Readin'?

Emanuel   Yeah, readin'. Not while he was workin'. On lunch break. He'd sit on one a the small tables in the mezzanine an' read. Ms. Wants-A-Dick told 'em his readin' looked bad. She said it made 'em look like he wasn't serious about his job. *His face puckers.* Can you believe that?

Doans   A course I can believe that. That's Pinocchio *demandin'* to be a boy.

Emanuel   Pulled into the director's office an' told not to *read*. How do you ignore somethin' like that?

Doans   With a smile, an' since the director's a chick, a wink.

Emanuel   All I want is to be able to sit down at lunch with a group a guys an' say hey, the fox is in the hen house. . . *He's* goin' after corporate fraud? . . . An ex-coke head's in the White House, an' *he's* runnin' The War on Drugs? . . . So, Tom, what do you think about *that* one?

Doans   Do it, man. Stir up the pot.

Emanuel   I have. The pot don't stir. I end up with this swastika knifed on my forehead.

Doans   Man, like you *are* the enemy!

Emanuel   The last time I had any sorta political discussion at lunch was two years ago. It was about Clinton. I tried to make it very clear that I wasn't defendin' his dick or his ethics, just that what he does in the halls a the White House with some chick is pretty damn irrelevant on the global scale.

Doans   He lied, man. He lied under oath.

Emanuel   Yes. I know. I know the argument. If they'd asked every senator in congress if they've dipped their wick in anything but their wife's crankcase, how many a them would a lied too?

Doans   Who knows? But, man, they weren't asked the

question. He was.

Emanuel   Look, man. If you're black, gay, Hispanic, female, a redwood tree, or a Catholic in Northern Ireland, Clinton was the best thing to come along in the white romper room in a long, long time. So lily-white America wants an *honest* president, a man with integrity. Okay. What does that mean? You mean somebody who plays exactly by the rules as prescribed by the potato head rulin' class? So, by definition, you can fuck people over as long as you do it within the laws?

Doans   Man, you can't allow the pres-o-dent of these United States to lie under oath. You just can't.

Emanuel   I ain't sayin' it's not a real touchy thing, man. Like it's cool to be lyin' under oath. All I'm sayin' is if we're gonna disqualify our elected officials on the basis a philanderin', there ain't gonna be nobody left except maybe some farmers an' eunuchs. The Republicans wanted 'em out—that's the bottom line. How they went about doin' it punched a bigger hole in this country than Clinton lyin' about where he put his Willy. . . *Trying to tease, to avoid the spark that lights the fuse that travels twenty feet to ignite the dynamite.* You like Bush, man?

Doans   Naw, man. I think the guy's scum.

Emanuel   He's filled every single staff position with corporate moles. He couldn't a told you what hemisphere Afghanistan was in three years ago with a heap a Cliff Notes in his lap. An' now he's sellin' out America to anybody that throws enough cash his way. All I'm sayin', man, is I'll take a guy who's got the constant pussy hornies over a guy who's got the petrol hornies—any day. *Oil*, man. The guy's got *oil* in his veins. Clinton's just white-trash. A guy from nowhere who rose to become leader a the free world. That scares the shit outta those Republicans!

Doans   He's a Bible totin' Yosemite Sam, if I ever done seen one. *Yippie-yi-yayyyy!*

Emanuel   This guy might set us back two hundred years. He might get us all wiped off the face a the planet.

Doans   I hear you, man. But when Clinton said—I don't inhale. . . man, my whole generation went like—W*hat?* Did he just say what I think he said?. . . It was all over.

Emanuel The guy's got balls, you gotta give 'em that.

Doans Yeah, well, so do donkeys an' rats, man. Yeah, he's got balls.

Gabriel The guy's a shmuck. He got what he deserved.

Emanuel He did. But most people don't. Anybody who looks to Washington for moral guidance needs to have their head examined. Simple, honest people don't go into politics, man. They go to their kids' soccer games.

Doans What do you think about Bush, Gabe?

Gabriel Bush? He's a shmuck too. They're all shmucks.

Emanuel He's ambitious, he's impressionable, an' he's not very bright. That's one lethal cocktail for mother earth.

Doans Carter—he was bright, but had too much Alan Alda altar boy in his jockeys. He never knew how to keep the neighborhood bullies off his back. An' like it or not, the halls a congress are full a nothin' *but.*

Emanuel I'll give Bush that—he does project confidence. You can't deny it. Folks like a man who promises to kill criminals—not with a somber puss, but with Alfred E. Newman's shit-eatin' grin.

Doans Yeah, Carter. . . hmm. . . well, he never understood the pacin' it takes to be pres-o-dent. He didn't know when to give the thumb's up or thumb's down. You can't sit on Tom Sawyer's fence all day when you're the prez.

Emanuel No, an' you gotta *be* Tom Sawyer an' get somebody to do your shit for you.

Gabriel He did get Sadat and Begin together.

Doans Yes, he did. Guess he should a been a diplomat.

Emanuel He sorta is, you know.

Doans Oh yeah, I forgot. Hey—how about ol' Billy peein' on the sidewalks? He knew how to douse a flame.

Emanuel Jimmy only lusted in his heart. I guess that makes 'em an okay Joe.

Doans Amen, an' God bless 'em.

Emanuel How about JFK, man?

Doans Mom's favorite philanderer.

Emanuel   Is that why she hated 'em so much?

Doans   You know, I've never been able to figure that one out.

Emanuel   He's *Catholic*.

Doans   I know! You'd think she'd pardon 'em for that.

Emanuel   You think it was Marilyn jumpin' on the trampoline?

Doans   It was the way he flaunted it, man. Like, I'm the prez an' I can have orgies in the White House if I wanna. Mom don't cut you no slack on infidelity, man. Not after what she's been through an' how she stuck with dad all these years.

Emanuel   I think it was the whole clan. It started with ol' Joe the rum runner. Maybe his Nazi sympathizin' had a little to do with it.

Doans   Man, but she drinks.

Emanuel   Yeah, but she's against crime. Especially when you use your privilege to go above the law. She don't go for pretty boy, fraternity types.

Doans   Thank God dad came from a broken home.

Emanuel   Kennedy was just Clinton before America cared about cigars an' dress stains.

Gabriel   It was before a White House intern would have made a peep about having an affair with the president.

Emanuel   True, Gabe. Good point.

Doans   The perfect man for the times. He did have charm. Elegantly hip. An' he had a first lady you could have some serious fantasies about.

Emanuel   But not a great president.

Doans   A decent one. Kennedy, he was all right, man. Your man Johnny had some decent-sized balls. He took the job more seriously than Clinton. That glossed over Marilyn an' the Beach Blanket Bingo.

Emanuel   Yeah?—*cocking his head, a bit surprised.* He give you a warm an' fuzzy, man?

Doans   He did a lot a good—*in a snap, the rage and repulsion of that moment years ago.* Fuck!—then they shot 'em! They fuckin' shot this—I don't care if he came outta some white bread wrapper or not, man—they shot like this brilliant white light just as we were comin' outta the stiff collar a the 50's. They shot 'em

*dead. . . Leaning forward he wipes his face, then clutches at his
sagging jowls.*
Gabriel   Then Martin Luther King—*bang!* Then Bobby—
bang!-bang!
Emanuel   They were good men—*the younger says solemnly.*
Doans   They were fuckin' great men. They understood where
the choo-choo train was goin', an' they shoveled more coal into
the fire.
Emanuel   Like Lincoln.
Doans   Yeah, man. Exactly. Saints sprung from circumstance,
but saints just the same. Shot dead. Fightin' Mr. Status Quo. The
static conservatism. Men with hearts still alive!
Emanuel   You think JFK would a balked, man?
Doans   Balked about what?
Emanuel   If Marilyn would a sent one a her dresses in for some
DNA tests.
Doans   Sure.
Emanuel   *Trying very hard to get his hands delicately around the
perceived double-standard without challenging Mr. Hamilton to a
duel, he asks*—Well, how come Clinton got buried then?
Doans   How come Clinton got buried?
Emanuel   How come he got buried an' Kennedy didn't?
Doans   You wanna know why?
Emanuel   Yeah. I would. I'm fuckin' baffled.
Doans   'Cause, man, Kennedy was fuckin' Sean Connery an'
Clinton's Roger Moore, *maybe*, on a *good* day.
Emanuel   You're fuckin' right, man. Okay. Yeah—I get it.
Doans   Yeah? You dig what I'm sayin'? Forget DNA, man.
Forget this era versus that era. Forget media scrutiny today versus
maybe the media wink-wink a those days. Kennedy could a been
the one backed up to the wall with Monica down on her knees an'
he'd a come out just some naughty boy. The Republicans wouldn't
a gone on no witch hunt 'cause it would a been political suicide.
The people loved Johnny Boy. He was every housewife's wet
dream, an' too cool for the husbands to sneer at. The guy was
Elvis. Elvis in the fuckin' White House. . . an' like dad told us

about a million times—life ain't fair. He did a whole lot more than poke a see-gar up some oyster an' guess what? . . . The world yawned.

Emanuel An' he didn't even have to lie. . .

Doans That's right. An' he didn't even have to lie. Except maybe to his wife, I guess.

Going Home Ain't Home

Darkness has fallen. Spirits ricochet back and forth against the seamless, timeless walls of thought-imagery. Doans, uncomfortable with barren lap, has fetched a guitar from the shack. It's a handmade model. His father built this one, along with two others, from the specifications he drew up. He has it unplugged and uses a pick to slowly strum rockabilly chords and hum-sing in his layman's, polio-affected voice. . . The water tinkles in delicate femininity. The air, stale, begins to fall away. Emanuel lights a fire, to which Gabriel now gives his full attention—up, down, pacing, challenging it as though it were a cornered, but not yet captured, rat.

Doans Don't let it get away—*he raises his eyebrows to Groucho. Gabriel hears, but flinches not.*

Emanuel Better than Hector could a done himself.

Doans Yeah, an' he's about the best dang pyro this side a somethin' or other.

Gabriel Nobody can top Hector.

Doans Yeah, probably right there, man. The kid's got that, I don't know. . . desire to see things disappear. Manny—*twisting his head*—was he always a fire starter?

Emanuel *He watches Gabriel and remembers when he married Abby. Abby had just been divorced after ten years of clawing a bitterness mural with her first husband. He remembers the wedding at their house and Hermie, the flower boy, Abby's son, standing at the top of the stairs, refusing to come down. The image of that little boy, told to put on a happy face as this new man stepped in, frightened out of his mind. . .* He burnt down Hane's field. . .

Doans   Oh, do pray tell.

Emanuel   Yeah, he an' Jessie an' the other hoodlums a the neighborhood burnt it down. *The dialogue breaks his gaze and his going-nowhere, everywhere-at-once thoughts.*

Doans   On purpose?

Emanuel   Fuck if I know. I don't think so. I think it was just some firecrackers that got outta hand.

Doans   Innocent boyhood melodrama. . . yeah, well. . . *The low rockabilly gets stuck on some forgotten lyrics and side-steps into even lower bluesy rough drafts of his own making.*

Emanuel   Hane's field, man. . . Hane's woods. That was our Sherwood. A million miles from menopausal primal screams an' a billion other insecurities. *Shaking his head—*Now it's condos—*and takes a swig.*

Doans   Oh, *maaaaan. . .*

Emanuel   The whole fuckin' town. It's wrapped in a doughnut a cowardice, kickbacks, an' crass.

Doans   Cozy.

Emanuel   When me an' Hector go up for a visit we sit in the sports bar where we used to catch frogs.

Doans   Across the highway?

Emanuel   Yeah. That all used to be fields, man. All of it. The only thing across the highway was Gillam's Market. We'd ride our bikes over an' get—shit—like gum an' comic books an' maybe an ice cream cone. Barely a car on the road. That whole north part a town's a workin' example a suburban sprawl at its finest.

Doans   You ever bump into anybody up there?

Emanuel   Not too often. I mean, I specifically look around the bar for people about my age, but I never see anybody. I go to the store to get some bread an' milk for mom an' dad an' just stare at faces. . . Nothin'. . . Nobody. Hey—it's Invasion a the Body Snatchers, an' it's in my home town.

Gabriel You're looking at people too young.

Emanuel Yeah, Gabe?

Gabriel Take if from me; you're looking about ten years too young. Look for guys you think look old. You're looking right past them. *He doesn't crack an expression, but continues fiddling with the fire.*

Emanuel I bumped into this guy about a year ago waitin' in line for a pizza. He acted like he didn't know me.

Doans Did he?

Emanuel Oh, yeah. I think. . . I think he was embarrassed.

Doans *The blues chord hits a sours snag, and Doans recoils— only in the corner of his mouth—with apology.* Bummer.

Emanuel I was embarrassed too.

Doans What for, man?

Emanuel He's still pissed about the time I nearly strangled 'em.

Doans I imagine you had a good reason.

Emanuel He was at the wheel stone drunk, drivin' like a banshee runnin' stop signs, goin' about 60. I told 'em to slow down or I was gonna rip his heart out.

Doans You gotta love our tact.

Emanuel It mighta saved my life.

Doans You'll never know.

Emanuel Yeah, so dad—you know what he says to me an' Hector just before we head out last time we were up? . . . He offers to fuckin' pick us up in his van.

Doans From the bar?

Emanuel Yeah, from the bar.

Doans Go, dad. *Yay—yeah!*

Emanuel Like, where was he in high school—you know?

Doans Waitin' at the bottom a the steps for you to carry 'em up, probably.

Emanuel He was dead serious, man. He offers to pick us up in his *van.*

Doans How sweet.

Emanuel It was sweet.

Doans Aw, man, you should a taken 'em up on it.

*Emanuel   The thought strikes him. He pictures it. 2:30 in the
morning standing out in the cold as the bar empties. His dad
creeping along the curb in the green van. Not one single wrinkle
of admonishment on his old brown brow.* Fuck! We should a!
Doans   Should a, would a, could a. If, dog, rabbit. There's
always next time.
Emanuel   Maybe we will. . . *The picture of the green van stays
put. Inside, the silhouette of his dad, small, frail, desperate to
make amends. He weeps inside. Every day, at lunch, driving, or in
bed lying awake, he sees his dad and weeps. The pain has become
a pillow on which he can feel at home, if not soothed.*

Tribute Paid As Servitude

They sit, three points to the triangle, about the fire. *Gabriel,
satisfied, stares into the feather flames that warm his cheek with
its brother, alcohol. The obsessive fretting about the harmonicas
has mellowed into wry humor. This humor has no verbal
expression, not even internal wit for his octagon-psyche to
appreciate. It flows as heat-comfort through his body and mind.*
Doans   I'm worried now, man. Jules should a been here by
now. Aaah. . . maybe he stopped somewhere. Some barfly
probably barfed on his smock after singin' Moon River. He's
probably in some all night laundry joint. Yeah, maybe that's what
it is.
Emanuel   He got a cell phone?
Doans   I think so, but there ain't no phone in the cabin.
Emanuel   Wanna go to a phone booth?
Doans   Naw, he's all right.
Emanuel   You sure?
Doans   Naw, man, he's all right. He's late all the time.
Emanuel   Maybe he's comin' in the mornin'.
Doans   Yeah, but Jules knew we were fishin'. He wouldn't

wanna miss fishin' on the Ohio. Don't tell 'em it ain't the Ohio, man. Jules always wanted to fish on the Ohio. This river's big enough to fool anybody.

Emanuel When I was a kid, I wanted to float from the Tuscarawas all the way down to the Ohio.

Doans Yeah?—*he leans forward rubbing his hands together.* Cool. What kind a boat would you take?

Emanuel I thought maybe a canoe. But maybe a small fishin' boat like dad's old fishin' boat would be better. All you'd need's a ten-horse engine. You could camp out along the banks, or on islands where nobody lived.

Doans What would you eat?

Emanuel Aw—you'd eat good, man, real good—*joining his brother in hand-rubbing, his mind salivating.* Bacon an' eggs for breakfast. Ham sandwiches in the afternoons. Maybe some rice an' beans or roast chicken for dinner. You'd have to watch out for dogs an' crazy river people. They're all along the river, you know.

Doans Maybe you'd have to take a gun.

Emanuel Maybe. But I never handled a gun too much. I'd be better off with some pepper spray for the dogs, an' a machete for the crazies. I'd hide a knife underneath one a the seats in case I got tied up, or somebody pulled a gun on *me*, or they took away my machete.

Doans Sounds like you thought this thing through.

Emanuel I have. You'd have to be ready for anything.

Doans *Without chains—ever—his imagination opens like the Red Sea itself.* Mermaids. Sirens, maybe.

Emanuel You never know. Seriously. You got some wild shit happenin' back in the woods. You got those wild dogs. You got devil worshippers an' KKK gatherin's. You got inbreedin' out the wazoo an' guys in camouflage smellin' you a mile away an' shootin' at you for sport. You got stories a Bigfoot that I don't know if they're true or if they're just stories. You got the occasional bear passin' through. You got chicks havin' lesbian skinny dip parties. It all happens.

Doans Lesbian skinny dippers? Really, man?

Emanuel I've heard—*tossing his hands, shrugging his shoulders, rolling his torso at the prospect.* I don't know. You might be lyin' in your canoe fast asleep when a gang of 'em suddenly comes splashin' into the water. White bodies flashin' in the moonlight, gigglin' an' ticklin' each other. A dozen pair a boobs starin' straight into the night.

Doans Wild, man. *Wild.*

Emanuel Maybe you'd just peek over the edge a the canoe, you know, tryin' to take it all in. . . but then they see you!

Doans Fuck, man. . . *No!* . . .

Emanuel They might drag you into the woods. They got their fire goin'. They'd be standin' there, chests heavin' up an' down—like a band a real-live Amazons, lookin' you over like Sunday's roast, decidin' what to do with you.

Doans Amazons don't like dudes, man. They'll cut off your dick an' feed it to the carp!

Emanuel Yeah, but maybe these ones are curious. You know, curious about what it's like to do it with a guy.

Doans Yeah, man. . . lucky you. . .

Emanuel No shit. They're all sweatin' an' pantin'. Their fingers are on you like a thousand octopuses. They ain't gonna kill you, man, or chop your balls off; they're gonna have their way with you! A dozen Amazon virgins!

Doans *Wow!* Where do I sign up?

Emanuel *He stands, wobbles, staggers to the cooler, takes a bottle between middle and forefinger, opens it on the side of the cooler, and strolls back to his tree stump like some fat cat.* You believe shit like that could happen?

Doans Sure, man, all the time. Just not to li'l ol' me.

Emanuel Problem is, I got Mazzy, you know.

Doans That's right, man. You got Mazzy to consider.

Emanuel I wouldn't wanna hurt her, man.

Doans Better tell the lesbian virgins maybe another time.

Emanuel It's not like I need anybody else. She's all I need, man.

Doans She's a sweetie.

Emanuel Unless they tied me up to where I didn't have a choice.

You know, threatened to cut my dick off if I didn't cooperate.
Doans   Then you'd have to suck it up, man. For Mazzy's sake.
So your wonder bar don't end up on the cuttin' room floor.
Emanuel   I'd be thinkin' about *her* the whole time.
Doans   Sure, man. How else could you keep it up?
Emanuel   *The thought of such a blissfull bounty of bouncing
breasts saddens him, strange enough, and he jumps to the next lily
pad.* Doans?
Doans   Yeah, man.
Emanuel   Tell me about the seminary.
Doans   What do you wanna know?
Emanuel   How long were you there?
Doans   Just went one year, man. My freshman year a high
school.
Emanuel   You hitch a ride with Junior?
Doans   Junior went three years, then came back home for his
final year. I already signed on the dotted line when he backed out.
Emanuel   You like it?
Doans   Man, it was great. Yeah, it was a good time in my life.
I got real fond memories a the seminary.
Emanuel   Yeah? What'd you do there, man?
Doans   Everybody had some responsibility. Like a part-time
job, man. Doin' dishes, peelin' potatoes, scrubbin' the john. For a
while, I cleaned out the stables.
Emanuel   You had stables there, man?
Doans   Oh, *yeah.* I mean, this place was like in the middle a
the Pennsylvania mountains. Like some medieval castle. Nothin'
around it for miles, except one small little town.
Emanuel   Like Narcissus an' Goldman, man.
Doans   Yeah! Just like that! No kiddin', bro'. . . . Yeah, so there
I was, Narcissus the stable boy. The place was full a rats. Man, I
was scared to death a rats. But I didn't have no choice. It was kill
'em or lose face with the other kids. So, I became the rat killer.
We had this ice scraper, man, an' that's how we hacked the rats.
You'd stand there an' wait for 'em to move in the straw, then
whomp!—hack their heads right off! I got real good at it. I loved

killin' them rats. I looked forward to it every day. I kept this log in my head a how many I got outta how many tries. I wore that rat killer badge with pride, man. Rats don't bother me no more. Not after killin' all those rats in the stables. Man, it was like nothin' I ever did in Akron.

Emanuel   Doans, on rat patrol—*he nods.*

Doans   You got it, little brother. *Rat-tat-tat-tat-tat. . .* We had a surprisingly large amount a free time. We had this PX-type store on the premises. They sold cigarettes there like candy. Wild, ain't it? True. Everybody smoked, man. The priests, the students. Everybody. I think they liked us havin' somethin' to do with our hands, if you know what I mean. But they were cool. The priests, all in all, were groovy. That's where I learned to play the guitar, right there at the seminary. This young Jimmy Stewart-lookin' priest gave lessons. I signed myself up. Learned to play gee-tar at the *seminary*. We played a lot a Bob Dylan an' Joan Baez an' Kingston Trio. All the folkies. . . There were books bein' passed back an' forth at night. Catcher in the Rye. The biggest, baddest, wildest book goin' round. Man, I read that book an' thought *wow!*—what's this? *Whoa-hoe. . .* This Holden Caulfield guy's not your average Leave It To Beaver. Now, here was somebody I thought I knew—*him*, the redheaded stepchild with the drippy nose sleepin' in the bunk next to me. Like, I could rel-*late* to his teenage angst. His wit. His deadpan mind. . . It was beautiful back in those mountains. Just beautiful, man. . .

Emanuel   Why'd you leave after just a year?

Doans   Look—I mean, I was fifteen years old. You know who got sent to the seminary? Kids who didn't get sent to military school. Kids with behavioral problems. Kids whose parents didn't want 'em around. Nobody went to the seminary 'cause they *wanted* to.

Emanuel   Sounded to me like you did.

Doans   Well, sure. Follow the big brother. It paints you into all kinds a psyche-scarrin' Night Galleries. An' I wanted to escape the zoo at home too, man. No offense.

Emanuel   None taken. I'm used to it.

Doans   I never really wanted to become a priest—are you kiddin'? I liked *girls*, man. I liked 'em before I shipped out. When I came back home, things were *movin'*. The country was in the middle a this great big ol' belly flop. I think Sgt. Pepper's came out that year, maybe the year after. It was like there was this thing called America, this tight-fisted, tight-wad hemorrhoid-cluster. . . an' it was openin' up into this gorgeous sweet-smellin' rose is a rose is a *rose*, man. For the moms an' dads an' Juniors—Patton wanna-be's a the world—it was like, Hey—who pulled the plug? I thought we had this thing under con-*trrrrrooool*. I think my sophomore year I started takin' art lessons.

Emanuel   When did Junior make the switch from the seminary over to the Army?

Doans   Man, Junior was military from the word *go*. From the womb. From the first time he heard The Battle a New Orleans an' The Sinkin' a the Bismarck. We had folkie-hippie records; Junior had battle marches. The seminary, you know, it taught you how to study, which I don't think Junior had down too good before. It gave you a taste a military routine an' discipline. I think he joined ROTC his senior year.

Emanuel   He was all gung-ho for Vietnam.

Doans   Sure. Let's go sink the Wong Dong Bismarck. Let's wipe them Gooks from the face a U.S. Earth. Push back that Red tide. It's our duty, man. Our chance as the sons a Normandy. Our opportunity. *Our* war.

Emanuel   But he only went to Germany.

Doans   Junior never made it into those rice paddies, man. Only Adam.

Emanuel   Adam volunteered.

Doans   'Cause I think he knew his number was up. But he was like a lot a guys. Itchin' to go. Testosterone thumpin'. No fuckin' clue what was waitin' for 'em on the other end a that high school diploma. Mom an' dad, they wanted 'em to go real bad.

Emanuel   That's wild. . . Unbelievable.

Doans   Yeah, well, sure—insanity-in-a-jar. But you gotta remember, there wasn't nothin' like Vietnam before, man. Korea wasn't no Vietnam. It wasn't no WWII, but it wasn't no Vietnam either. There was nothin' for anybody to say hold on a minute, Jack; remember that great big stinky fiasco over *here*? Remember them body bags a rollin' outta those airplanes like eggs from a queen termite? All that fightin' for what—dead sons an' world disgrace? *Noooooooooooo...* I think this sounds mighty fam-il-eee-yer!

Emanuel   Sure, but it wasn't like people were totally ignorant, man. By the time Adam went in, protestors were in full force.

Doans   They were. But Adam ain't like you an' me. He wanted to please the ol' man. He's spent his whole life on that sticky road. He thought the protestors were punks. In his mind, he was doin' the right thing. Ain't that what any red-blooded American eighteen-year-old boy does? Go fight in some war. Kill some enemy folk. Come back to a hero's ticker tape parade an' all the free pussy you want. Nobody ever thinks details, man. Agent orange, burnin' villages, booby traps, body parts. Nobody ever thinks they're gonna get *killed.*

Emanuel   Or have to kill somebody else.

Doans   You went to Vietnam, you were in the jungle shootin' people. This wasn't no World War II where lots a dudes never saw action. There wasn't no filler, man. It was real lean in terms a utilizin' young, innocent male flesh. They needed your ass up front.

Emanuel   You wouldn't a gone.

Doans   You kiddin' me, man? Hell no, I wouldn't a gone. You mean if this eye was all right? You outta your cotton pickin' mind? Like, I be singing *Oh, Caaaaa—na—daaaaa...*

Emanuel   Dad would a been real pissed.

Doans   Dad ain't crazy; he's just a product a his times too. I thought he was outta his mind back then, but I was comin' from a whole different world. He thought I'd lost it! As hippies go, I was one a the more conservative dudes. Let me restate that: I was into the freedom scene, the rebellion against the establishment, the re-creation a this here democratic experiment on the grandiose scale. But my roots were still in Catholicism, my art, an' the discipline that both required. Dad, for all his squareness, saw through the hair, man. He thought I oughtta get a real job, naturally. You know him. Do your art on the side. Everybody needs to have a hobby, son, but you gots to make a *livin'*. But he knew I wasn't in it just for the wild ride. I mean, I *was* in it for the wild ride, don't get me wrong. But too many a my comrades-in-craze lost sight a where they were goin'. I was too scared, man! Like, I didn't want this Tasmanian Devil to gobble up my precious brain cells. . . I think dad's real—well, sorry ain't exactly the right word—maybe less sure, I suppose, about how he maybe rubber stamped Adam's 747 to Vietnam. Hey—Adam might a gone anyway. Probably not, if dad wouldn't a given 'em the ol' thumbs up, an' I think he knows it.

Emanuel   He remembers the time just before his brother left for Vietnam. His father with the electric shears, giving him an Army haircut. Adam used to pull his hair down in front and put it in his mouth—to the amusement of his younger brothers. Now he sat perfectly still, beneath the pale yellow of the kitchen light, as it was shorn off. There was no humiliation or sorrow in this practical matter on Adam's part. But Emanuel felt something valuable from his brother floating away, and he automatically felt guilty. I was only six when he went over. It was just a word to me. A place. Somethin' that was in the air. . . I've never heard 'em talk about it.

Doans   From the time of their youth, Doans and Adam were the Romulus and Remus, after the given royal status of the firstborn, Junior. The next runts, the up-and-coming work hands. They waged war against one another in a love-hate saga of extremes, the lasting effects of which upchucked years later as resentment and jealousy in both men. But during Adam's tour in Vietnam, they were tight. Man, we used to send these tapes back an' forth. He was real vague about the details, an' I didn't ask. Most of 'em were when he was back at base an' he was on reefer lookin' up at the stars a war, an' I'd get 'em back an' light a joint an' look out my window at the stars a peace. A lot a tangent monologues about Dylan—Desolation Row, in particular. He

wanted to dissect it. Mash it up into corn meal an' make some kind
a at-peace bread with it. I sent 'em Pat Garett an' Billy the Kid,
an' you know, as soon as he got home he got hitched an' they
went out to New Mexico. He just wanted to hide in the mountains,
I guess. By hide, I don't mean like the Grizzly Man, I just mean he
wanted to take his pickup up there in those mountains at night and
lie in the bed an' look up at the same stars he used to watch in
'Nam, only instead a the smell a guns an' blood he had the smell a
his woman with 'em. . . Yeah, we sent those tapes back an' forth
every week. There was music talk—he wanted to hear about the
family—an' all kinds a fantasies an' a lot a incoherency, if I recall.
Like, maybe I was a pinkie in his effort to stay clung to the wall a
life. . . Fuck—I was in college an' anti-war an' just about as
ignorant as you an'. . . you were only—what'd you say? Eight?

Emanuel   Six.

Doans   Yeah, six. I was in another corner a the galaxy, an' I
knew it.

Emanuel   This fuckin' world. . . The dice came up with
Vietnam—not for me, or for you, or for any of us. . . only for
Adam. You don't get up after takin' a hit like that, do you,
Doansy?

Doans   *He takes a last hit from his cigarette, all the way until
it goes out, then flicks it into the fire.* From the guys I've seen, an'
there's been a lot of 'em. . . naaah. . . they generally don't bounce
back. I mean, not really.

Emanuel   You ever feel guilty, like you got let off the hook?

Doans   You mean 'cause a this eye?

Emanuel   'Cause you didn't lose your legs like dad, an' you
didn't lose your heart like Adam.

Doans   Sure. How else are we gonna feel about it?

Emanuel   Dad, askin' if he was AWOL. . . *Kicking at the dirt, a
practiced diversion to bat away the pain.*

Doans   You mean when he came home on leave? Yeah. . . Hi,
dad. I'm your son—remember me?—the ghost a Christmas
present come to wish you Happy Holidays, straight from the
defoliated jungles a hell. . . Am I what?. . . Am I *AWOL?* . . .

Emanuel   That's pretty fucked up.

Doans   That's dad, man. What do you expect?

Emanuel   Half a Adam's fuckin' platoon dead. . . what do I expect? I expect 'em to jump outta his wheel chair an' rush over to feel his own flesh an' blood, to see if he's really there, really alive! I expect 'em to weep like a baby. . . Fuck—Adam probably smiled the whole ride home thinkin' about how he was gonna surprise the ol' man, an' first thing he gets when he opens the shop door is— *are you AWOL?*

Doans   He probably wasn't too surprised.

Emanuel   Aw, man—are you kiddin' me? I bet it killed 'em.

Doans   Well, yeah, sure it killed 'em. I just don't see how you can be surprised by what he said, that's all.

Emanuel   'Cause, man, that little kid—I don't care how old you are or how many times you had the vice dropped on your toe—that little kid inside is always lookin' for a smile, an' maybe a few nice words.

Doans   Yeah? . . . Yeah. . .

Emanuel   It doesn't hurt less; I think it hurts more as you get older. You figure—can't he drop the Papa bullshit? We're both grown men now—can't he just let it go? But then he doesn't, an' that really gets you thinkin'. Like, why, if he loved me at all, would he keep goin'?

Doans   I know. He's hardcore John Wayne, man. Don't let a little mellowin' fool you. He's still the alpha male an' you is still the *whiiiiiite* nigger.

Terrorism Is Peace

It's amazing what an hour with your head *coiled around a steering wheel can do for you. Hector, re-emerged from what for any of the other three would have been all night slumber, is fresh as a day's early morning breeze.*

Emanuel   We better get this fire goin' again before it peters out.

Gabriel   You wanna help me get some wood? I found a big pile over by that tree.

Emanuel   Okay, Gabe, lead the way—*and off they go, the worker bees, while the king and queen hold court.*

Hector   Wanna beer, Doans?

Doans   Naw, man, I'm cool. *He watches load after load, in wrought-iron arms, carried and dumped beside the fire*—Gabe, Manny—you guys are doin' all the he-man work. Need some help carryin' those pieces a fallen timber?

Emanuel   Relax, man. Only one more load, I think.

Doans   *The other eye is on the rough-sketched Hector, pyro at age three, tinkering and blowing on the remnants of Gabriel's fine efforts.* . . Hector, way to go! You resurrected the fire! I want you on my team if I'm ever stranded in Peru with only a toothbrush an' a putty knife. *Yowzzza.*

Emanuel   There you go, man. *The last of the wood having been dumped, he brushes his hands together.* Wood enough for a rescue fire.

Doans   Thanks, brother. Thanks, Gabe. The lumberjacks of Eden.

Gabriel   That should be enough to get us through tonight.

Doans   Tonight? You got enough wood there to keep the fuckin' Lighthouse at Alexandria roarin' for days! No sneak attacks tonight, man.

Gabriel   *Still standing, thumbs in his front pockets*—So, Hector, how are your folks doing? *He directs his question at the big man; it's his way of blowing on the flames of dialogue, which he likes to rouse and then sit back and watch.*

Hector   Pretty good, man.

Gabriel   I haven't been up for a while. Your dad take his gliders out lately?

Hector   He's not doin' the gliders anymore. Now he's into these penny planes.

Gabriel   Oh yeah—I heard he was going to do some of those.

Doans   What the hell are penny planes, man?

Hector   They only weigh a penny, man.

Gabriel   That's amazing.

Hector   Yeah, man. He flies 'em in auditoriums. They stay up for about a minute or two, but they'll go all the way up to the rafters, around an' round in a great big circle—*his finger demonstrates against the ferocious flapping of orange flame.*

Emanuel   Man, they look like big—*his hands, hulkish crushers of air*—big, ancient mosquito-dinosaurs!

Gabriel   No kidding.

Doans   *Wild!*

Emanuel   They're cool, man! *The boy was lying. He had never been with the old man to fly his gliders, or his penny planes. He had felt used by his father from early on. Where the others played the game—or like Doans, fought it—he merely stepped away, quietly, understanding his utilitarian standing. Even as his father aged, mellowed, reached out, those ties that bind had been burned off so that the boy struggled each minute of each day with a heart that wanted to open, but automatically retracted in defense.*

Hector   Gabe, you ever do any flyin' over in Youngstown?

Gabriel   You mean my machine?

Hector   Yeah. Ever stop in to see your man, Traficant?

Gabriel   No, man. . . *Laughing impishly, wishfully at what Hector's wit implied with such casual deadpan.* I heard he was on his way to the toupee shop before heading for the clink. That guy's a riot, isn't he?

Hector   Just your average elected official.

Gabriel   Yeah, I guess so. I don't know. To tell you the truth, I haven't been keeping up on the whole mess.

Hector   So people floated some cash his way for jobs?—*the pain in his face.* Nobody else seems to care about dead towns. Towns that were sold down the river to Hong Kong or Mexico or Tex-ass. . . Come an' take *this.* . . *He turns to the fire and lets one rip.*

Gabriel   Yeah. The guy's no different than any other regular working class stiff who bought his way to the top.

Hector   He's doin' 70 in a 55 zone, but everybody else is still passin' 'em doin' like 90. . . An' they stop *him*?

Gabriel   Nobody else flipped off the cop sitting in the doughnut shop. That'll make Barney get out his bullet real fast.

Hector   We're supposed to get all whacked out about some dude in Youngstown takin' small-time bribes? I'm supposed to break out my Caesar-dicin' knife over *that*?

Gabriel   Of course you are. I saw you fall off that turnip truck not two hours ago.

Hector   *He turns, stepping closer, as though cornering a prospective client at a convention*—So what do you call a no-bid contract, man? Huh? How about a ten billion dollar no-bid contract handed out to a company I used to be CEO of?

Gabriel   Which contract is that? *He knows Hector means him no harm, but his close proximity elicits an automatic reaction and his hands migrate toward his crotch and then clasp together.*

Hector   Hypothetical—*he smirks*. By anybody. Anywhere. Maybe a hundred billion dollar contract—what the fuck—I mean why think small, right?

Gabriel   Sure. Think big. The bigger the better—that's what this hooker used to tell me.

Hector   Here's the deal, man. We got this shit—these zombies—all over the fuckin' country, gropin' into every jockstrap an' skirt. . .

Gabriel   Not some new kind of VD?

Hector   It's called our government, man.

Gabriel   Oh yeah. That was my second choice—*he grins wide, to keep it light.*

Hector   The *government*. . . what is it? . . . Mm? . . . They take your money. They finance their own investments. They start wars that nobody but rednecks an' Christian fundamentalists want—*shooting his middle finger into the air to make his point*—granted, the intersection of those two groups accounts for nearly half our population. They build roads an' used to—a long time ago—fund these places called public schools—can you say hello again, separate but equal? They sell off our jobs like they were junk bonds, an' then have the gall to tell us we're better off because of it. . . *The pain in his face turns to ghastly agony as he squats like an ape.* Hold those bed rails an' squeal like a *pig.* . . fuck. . . *me.* . .

Doans   *Wincing*—Oooooh, man. . . easy on them metaphors.

Emanuel   *From the side of his mouth*—He uses that one a lot. Wonder what that means. . .

Hector   *He stands, animation vanished.* So then you got this other thing called organized crime. Let's say you gotta pay Mr. Rigatoni x-amount a dollars a year so you can sell your tomatoes on the corner. But at least Mr. Rigatoni, 'cause he has a personal stake in your success in sellin' those tomatoes, gives you some protection when the fucker down the street wants to set up his own tomato shop an' possibly run you outta business. Now, let me ask you; who's gonna provide you with more tangible services for the money you gotta shell out?

Gabriel   The Dago, man, but of course.

Doans   The country's too big, man. Nobody ever thought it was gonna get this big.

Emanuel   Tribes. We were meant to live in tribes.

Doans   You may be right, bro'. Yeah.

Hector   I mean, Machiavelli would be *proud* a Congress. . . wouldn't he?

Doans   Like, he was just doin' satire, man. Nobody oughtta take the dude seriously.

Hector   I know, man. But they *do* take 'em seriously, Doans; an' our whole corrupt system would get an A+ for emulation.

Doans   Look—it's outta control—the social contract ain't no more. It's been stretched an' stretched—government sailin' off to yonder green pastures far, far from the common man. They're outta touch, man, an' the proletariat feel as though everything's gonna work out fine, like the Olympus-chicanery still has a pulse on what's happenin' down in the trenches. But it don't. It don't, as a body whole, have but that one hand in its pants.

Hector   Now the thing is terrorism. Everything ties back to terrorism. Anybody doin' anything that doesn't fall in line with government policy has somehow got ties to terrorism. Anybody that says anything against the next war, anybody in the neighborhood sellin' an ounce a pot—he's a potential terrorist cell. And now—'cause the White House in one fell swoop wiped out whole search an' seizures rights—they can now enter your house without any reason, other than you're a suspected terrorist. Give. . . me. . . a. . . *break*. Wake up, people! Read your history books! That's pre-fascism stuff! . . . Think about it; the government can now enter your house, tap your phone, snoop on you as you're surfin' the net, an' they don't need a warrant, they don't have to tell you they're doin' it. . . Shouldn't that bother you?

Doans   No, it don't bother me, man, 'cause I'm a white collar dog workin' at Bung-Holes-R-Us. I got twenty years a savings stashed away in Internet stocks that are now worth about ten cents on the dollar—turn the knob on that treadmill up to high! I'm a farmer sellin' milk at half a what I could be gettin' 'cause the government keeps prices artificially low—then turns around an' pays me for not plantin' on my 1000 acres across the road, while hungry folks in the Congo are lickin' rectal thermometers from garbage bins. I'm a twenty-year-old high school grad choppin' chicken at Chipotle's—I'm up to my armpits in debt 'cause as soon as the Towers were hit, the prez told me to buy, buy, *buy*. It don't bother me 'cause I didn't *see* it, I didn't *hear* it, I know no—*thing*!—ya volt, herr kommandant! *He rubs his hands together conspiratorially.* You fine feathered generals seem to have things under control. Ya'll seem to know what you be talkin' about. I think I'll just close these shutters for a spell an' turn up the volume on this hear Radio Free Europe. . . Jews, gays, Mexicans, Muslims. The same smelly scapegoat 'neath different wool. Walk on by, neo Gestapo, to door number 2, an' I'll lay low, keep quiet, buy your war bonds. . . Naw, man—like it don't bother me 'cause I *believe* in this system we call The United States of America. Like, we own the fourth quarter, no matter what the score is. From McCarthy, to Vietnam, to Watergate, to Iran-Contra, to Cigargate, to Enron—we back our way outta the deepest tar pits ever self-inflicted by man. Now—*his hands go wide*—the only problem with such a faith, is there's this prerequisite that the *people* be watchdog for it all, that the *people* are vigilant, are demandin' a their elected officers. . . Man, that's ancient history! Like, things got too comfy. We don't wanna see what goose is steppin' beyond those shutters. We need a good war to shake things up. The Twin Towers was a good thing! I hope the recession goes on for ten years, man!

Emanuel   *That perks them up. Nobody wants to ask, but somebody's got to.* You don't really mean that.

Doans   Like fuck I don't. I'm talkin' about sacrificin' the arm to save the body—you understand me? I'm sayin', what I'm tryin' in my somewhat modest state a inebriation to tell you is, if somethin' don't wake us up soon, if somethin' don't wake up *him*, Mr. Biggie Size It i-pod fantasy football slug; if he don't wake up like soon, this country is history. You hear what I'm sayin'? You wanna put a smiley face on that one? His-tor-*eeeeee*.

Gabriel   He's right.

Emanuel   But don't say it outside a this circle—*he whispers.* Big Brother is now up an' runnin'.

Hector   *Making his hands into a tunnel*—Terrorism is peace.

Doans   What do you think newscasts are for, man? Fuck yeah—to scare you shitless. A public perpetually under the threat of attack is a public willin' to perpetually fight. A public willin' to bite their tongue, step in line—*obey*.

Hector   Terrorism is peace.

Emanuel   They can read your emails.

Gabriel   Aw, they've been able to do that for years.

Emanuel   Obtain records a what books you read at the friendly neighborhood library.

Gabriel   I knew I shouldn't have gotten that biography on Yassir Arafat.

Emanuel   They can haul you off to places unknown, with charges unspecified, an' tell no one.

Hector   Terrorism is peace.

Emanuel   Satellites can determine the color a your wife's pubic hair, man. They can see through walls. Political correctness evolves into The Ministry a Truth. The re-writin' a historical facts.

Gabriel   They've been doing *that* for years.

Hector   Terrorism is peace.

Emanuel   The erosion a civil liberties behind the mask a patriotism, behind the face a the idiot a the moment, the hand a pharaoh an' pharaoh's legion—corporate Earth. *Jumping on a beached tree limb*—Smash the insidious arm a the cookie cutter machine! Destroy the labs where humanoid cocktails fester in beakers a genetic wizardry without the slightest pause given to what monsters they might unleash!

Gabriel   We need another Washington on horseback with a Lincoln back at the office. Thomas Paine on the street corner sellin' the truth.

Doans   Michael Moore's the closest thing we got, I guess. But he's a little over-the-top, man. Like, I dig his theme song, but his choreography could use less hot pink.

Emanuel   Every canary in every coal mine has to be part Chuckles the Clown. You gotta get attention somehow.

Doans   True. Yeah. I agree. But then how do you take that laughter an' turn it into some serious head-scratchin'? There's a built-in credibility goose egg in your way.

Hector   It's not gonna matter until people put down their joy sticks an' pay attention.

Emanuel   Pink Floyd, man. We're bein' entertained to death.

Doans   Touché, an' what do ya know. Veni, vedi, vici says the puppet master.

Emanuel   Weebles wobble but they don't fall down.

Gabriel   Why don't we do it in the *rooooooow*—ode?

Doans   *Ring, ring, ring goes the bell. . .*

Emanuel   *Zing, zing, zing goes my heart strings, when the lid on Pandora's Box fell. . . open. . .*

Your Mother's Pie

The burning eyes of mid-life sleep deprivation, *dead ends taken,*

*crawling over flints razor sharp back upstream to begin again—
toward whatever appears to have been lost or breached. . . These
men sit around the fire now, having been reborn—each one—
once, twice, a dozen times—beyond the beyond—into the black
holes of witchcraft, statecraft, and Starcraft weekend follies—re-
evaluating, regurgitating, rewinding, and rewarding their own
belly fire efforts with well-deserved rest, peace, and the rare treat
of thought-exchange with fellow hermits. Hector is nearly gone for
the evening, his chin resisting the futile pull of gravity from his
chest. The others, losing the fight to sleep, yet wanting a night of a
thousand hours, trudge on. The river chants to itself, and the lofty
leaves of ancient trees murmur, eavesdropping on their own god.
The fire melts low; only residual, soft-edged flames slither up from
the glow of smoldering furor.*

Emanuel   The walk to school was like magic. It was almost a
mile. There were gobs a kids all over the neighborhood, an' they
all came out like rats at the same time. In the winter we'd stop at
the Nazarene church an' break off icicles from the gutters. Ain't it
funny; now when I see a big icicle hangin' from a corner a my
house, all I can think about is how it means the gutters are full a
leaves an' maybe the soffets are rottin' away. Well, anyway, we'd
break off these really monster icicles an' suck on 'em for a while
or have sword fights or wing 'em as far as we could like javelins
into snow drifts. They always tasted like rust—didn't they?
Sometimes I'd carry one the whole way until we crossed High an'
went down the big hill to school, an' right before I got there I'd
toss it into the creek where I once saw an otter or muskrat or
somethin'. There was this field we'd have to walk through an'
when school first started, in August an' September—Jesus, it was
full a grasshoppers. You know—those big, fat, brown ones that
hunt mice for dinner. I don't know why, but I was afraid a those
things. We'd catch 'em sometimes, but it'd kill me every time.
We'd walk through that field—the sidewalk cut right through it—
an' grasshoppers'd be flyin' in zigzags all around. It was kind a
neat, but creepy. We were little an' had no choice. Seemed like
every day there were things you had to deal with like that—things

that really unnerved you—but they'd come an' go like that an' really weren't any big deal. . . On the last day a school in June we'd race up the hill to see who could be the first one up. I won in fifth an' sixth grade. When I got to the top a the hill that last year, there sat the crossin' guard, Mr. Whipple. Mr. Whipple was a nice old man, like two hundred years old. He actually lived just a few houses down from us, but we never talked to 'em much. He had a wooden leg. Well, I think 'cause I got up there first without makin' any noise, you know, the way kids'd usually come up on normal days, he didn't hear me. He was sittin' in his car with his door open suckin' on his pipe. He always had that pipe in his hand, even when takin' us across the street. I could see his face. I was hopin' he'd hear me. I didn't try to make noise on purpose, 'cause then he'd know how I pitied 'em. But I wanted to make enough noise so he'd see me an' come out of it. I mean, he was just starin' into the ground sittin' sideways in his car. His pant leg was up enough so I could see his sock around his wooden leg. It was thin, like a puppet ankle. But the black sock covered it an' I was real glad it did. I guess he looked too much like dad when you'd catch 'em with his guard down. It was the exact same look, an' I felt the exact same thing watchin' 'em—like, is that where we all end up when we get older? I know both of 'em were cripples, but they were just obvious cripples.

Gabriel   So what happened?

Emanuel   When he saw me? Oh, I think I just made sure he saw me first—I was probably swingin' a stick at the ground or somethin'. By the time we made eye contact he was back out of it.

Gabriel   You ever find out how he got the wooden leg?

Emanuel   Nope.

Gabriel   I hate that.

Doans   Man, I had to give my lunch money to the bullies at North every day. Nobody ever took your lunch money?

Emanuel   *He shakes his head.*

Doans   Yeah, it was like this tribute to the Romans, man. I give you my lunch money, an' you don't beat the crap outta me.

Emanuel   We didn't have gangs, man. This was suburbia-country

life. I had Hector four years ahead a me. Nobody was gonna mess
with his little brother. Plus, nobody my age was really gonna mess
with me anyway. I was a tough little fucker. I was gettin' in fights
all the time in grade school. You know—piss ant little fights
where you're grapplin' on the ground one minute an' then
swappin' Bubs Daddy the next.

Doans   The only ice breaker I had ahead a me was Junior, an'
he was as small as me. Plus, he was off at the seminary for three
years durin' which time I took my daily dosage a ass-whuppin's.
How about you, Gabe? What was central Akron like for a buddin'
young James Dean?

Gabriel   Aw, it was all right. Nothing out of the ordinary from
you guys.

Doans   No bullies on the block?

Gabriel   Yeah, sure. But you learned how to run real fast, and in
my case, what kind of fifth grade contraband could keep your nose
straight.

Emanuel   *Not listening, but dreaming back, back to a flourish of
real worth memories*—Fuck, Doans, remember mom's bread!

Doans   Yeah, man.

Gabriel   What bread?

Hector   Oh, God—mom's bread. . . *Without lifting his eyelids,
his voice like a Pete Townsend guitar, he scratches his middle and
then his big hands fall dead there, rising and falling with the tides
of his labored breathing.*

Emanuel   You awake, man?

Hector   Jesus Christ. . . that bread. . .

Gabriel   What the heck are you guys talking about?

Hector   Gabe—*and for this the sleeping giant opens a single
eye—the one farther from his brother-in-law. He realizes his
blunder, closes this eye, and opens the other, barely*—our mom
used to bake bread every couple weeks.

Gabriel   Yeah?

Hector   Gabe. . . you don't understand. This bread was like the
fuckin' best bread you ever had. It took her all day to make, man.
All *day*. She'd mix it up, an' then let it rise—*his hands, like those*

of Moses before him, levitate for the parting miracle. . . She'd put a damp paper towel over the yellow bowl—

Emanuel   The yellow bowl. . .

Doans   The yellow fuckin' bowl, man!—*Flashes of late Saturday night popcorn in the kitchen, Junior standing in his ROTC greens, the girls in their Catholic nightgowns, the AM radio tuned to American blues bounced back across the sea in moptops and Rolling Stones.*

Hector   If it was summer, the dough'd rise up over the bowl like a pregnant tit, spillin' over the sides—*he makes a fist, hits it into his palm.* She'd pound it down—wham!—and it'd deflate like a shot hot air balloon.

Emanuel   Sometimes she'd let you do it.

Hector   Yeah, sometimes, for those who never actually felt a real tit, you'd get the chance to maul a fake one.

Emanuel   I admit it—*raising his Cub Scout hand*—I snuck into the kitchen on more than one occasion an' felt that big mama dough tit.

Doans   Sure, man. The only thing it didn't have was a nipple, an' you could remedy that with a delicate pinch an' lift.

Hector   *Raising a quizzical eye*—Sure, there it was for the gropin', if you didn't have the real thing at your disposal. Myself—*hand to chest*—I never had the need, although I can appreciate the temptation for some. Gabe—*both eyes open now, black in the dimming firelight*—you'd have to knead an' knead the dough. Squeeze all the air out until it shrank back down. She'd form it into a perfect ball again—*hands working, working*—put it in the yellow bowl, dampen the paper towel with hot water an' drape it across the bowl an' wait for it to rise *again*. Three times!—*his arm thrust into the darkness, three fingers aloft.* She did that three times! . . . Rise, pound it down. . . Rise, pound it down. . . rise *again*, an' pound it down. She'd make six loaves at a time, Gabe. The house'd be filled with the smell! You could be down in the basement doin' homework, on the steps on the phone, in the bathroom—it didn't matter where you were—you smelled that hot, yeasty, outta this world smell! An' fuck, man—when the

loaves came outta the oven. . . she'd take a hard stick a butter an'
roll it across the tops. The crust, it'd fuckin' crackle when the cold
butter hit it. . . . An' then you'd have to wait. You couldn't cut it
right away 'cause it was still too soft, man. It'd fall apart. It was
too hot! When you cut it, you turned it on its side, the down side
away from you. It cut easier an' straighter that way. The slices,
Gabe. . . *Gabe*—were these huge pieces with big mushroom heads.
So fuckin' big you had to lop 'em off when you made toast—they
wouldn't fit in the toaster if you didn't. . . It'd be just barely cool
enough to cut—

Emanuel   We'd be hoverin' around by now droolin' like wild
dogs—

Hector   The pieces'd be just steamin'. You'd slather the butter
on. The butter'd melt into these small puddles. . .

Emanuel   We'd eat two loaves right then an' there, man. We'd
keep goin' until our mom pulled us away from the bin.

Gabriel   You guys are giving my mouth a wet dream.

Emanuel   That was just her bread. Her spaghetti was outta sight,
man. Fuck—we lived on North Hill—Italiano Americano—there
were like spaghetti recipes floatin' in the air.

Doans   An' since we were not a the Old Country, so to speak,
we were only one crotch kick ahead a the blacks.

Emanuel   Hector, remember when Ramie tried to pound a nail in
your head?

Hector   I remember when they put his ass down that sewer an'
put the lid over 'em.

Doans   Yeah, that was a choice moment in the neighborhood.

Emanuel   Or when Mike Ferroni stole mom's car.

Hector   Twice—*arm thrust, two fingers.*

Doans   An' then the poe-leece came knock-knock-knockin' on
heaven's door one bright good ol' Saturday mornin' 'cause Mike
stole Junior's draft card an' got busted for I can't remember what;
but those cops were lookin' for Junior, Mr. Squeaky Clean
himself.

Hector   An' here comes dad, crutches a squeakin', madder than
Ralph Cramden on a bologna sandwich Monday—

Doans   But we digress. North Hill will always be remembered as the sponge where all germs fester equally; just some germs a Catholic Italian descent are more equal than others.

Hector   Emidio's pizza, man. . . God damn. . .

Emanuel   Mom's spaghetti.

Doans   Naw, man. Her hash.

Emanuel   Now you're talkin' Wheeling make-somethin'-outta-nothin'-taste-bud-nirvana, man.

Doans   I'm talkin' sweet Jesus come take me home warmed up in a buttered skillet at 1:00 a.m. after warblin' in Adriane Rotolo's ear all night long.

Hector   Her hash!

Doans   *He had been flicking a stick into his hand every few seconds. He sits up, pokes the stick into the mud for support, and leans toward the supine Gabe slumped in his fold-out chair.* You ever have real good hash, Gabe?

Gabriel   Only the canned stuff in the Army, Doansy, and I tasted puke better than that.

Doans   My dad used to get a side a beef an' freeze it. He had steak every Saturday night.

Hector   We had hamburger—*protesting with a hand*—but since there were starvin' kids in China, we were thankful for it.

Emanuel   Hash on mom's homemade toast. . .

Hector   *Christ.* . .

Doans   So, like our mom, she used to do up a roast about once a week. With all those baby wolves to feed a lot a times there wasn't anything left. But when she made a big one, an' baked maybe a whole bag a Idaho potatoes, there was gonna be hash the next night.

Gabriel   Nothin' like the Army stuff, you say?

Doans   Oh, man. . . naw, man. . . She'd get out this old grinder from one a the kitchen drawers. This Iron Age, last forever gizmo from Thomas Edison's 8th grade science project. Steel pieces like they come from Robbie the Robot's innards, with some rust patina from the last time they were washed an' not dried all the way.

Hector   Probably your turn for dishes, Doansy. In some rush to see a chick or a band.

Doans Yeah, well, I don't doubt it—*he lights a cigarette, waving the match in the air three times until it finally goes out. Inhaling, holding the smoke a moment, he exhales like a gushing creek.* Assemblin' that thang was always a mystery to me, man. But I liked to help mom when it was time to turn the crank. . . *He remembers, as if it weren't memory at all.* The potatoes, we'd cut into cubes. We'd cut the meat into chunks too, against the grain. Then in they'd go into the mouth a the grinder with that corkscrew a churnin'. An' then Gabe, out it'd come, brown an' white, in these finger-width tubes into the bowl. When she fried it up, she used milk. The milk made it brown an' crusty on the outside. Put that shit on some a her homemade toast, some salt, some pepper, an' yowza-bow-wowza.

Emanuel Remember when she'd make it with tongue, man?

Doans Tongue? Naw, we didn't have tongue when I was in the house.

Emanuel Yeah man—tongue.

Gabriel For the hash?

Emanuel Well, if there was some left over, which there usually was, then she'd make hash out of it the next night, just like she would with a roast. But the first night it'd be just plain tongue. I don't know how many times I'd come runnin' into the kitchen home from school, drop my books on Mr. Doppler's bench, an' with that gorgeous roast smell in the air lift the lid on the pot. . . an' there sat a tongue.

Doans You eat it, man?

Emanuel It was one a the few things I didn't. Peas, cooked carrots, an' tongue. I'm sorry, mom, God bless you, but I couldn't do it.

Doans Dad must a liked it.

Hector You put enough gravy on anything an' it's not too bad.

Emanuel How about her pies, man.

Doans Oh, fuck yeah.

Emanuel What was your favorite?

Doans Mincemeat.

Hector   Aw, fuck—*making a face.*
Doans   No, man?
Hector   I could never do mincemeat.
Doans   Like—*grinning*—there ain't no meat in it, man.
Emanuel   Elderberry pie, Doansy. You missed out on it.
Doans   Naw—I had some elderberry, I think at Christmas or Thanksgiving one year.
Emanuel   We had elderberry bushes growin' on the opposite side a the fence by the highway, Gabe. Gobs of 'em. Elderberry's real tart, runny, but damn good.
Hector   *Like the king lion himself, contentedly drifting to sleep*—Her apple fuckin' crisp was the best, brothers. . . an' pumpkin pie. . .
Emanuel   Gabe—she'd make grape juice. She put like twenty grapes in a jar. They'd float in those jars all winter long, an' they'd go kinda pale. But when you opened up a can, spooned out the dead grapes, it was real fresh, man. Real good cold straight from the basement.
Hector   Her baklava. She made baklava like nobody. I got this Greek restaurant around the corner an' it ain't even close. . . baklava. . .*fuck.* . .
Emanuel   That was pretty God damn good. She made a whole cookie sheet at a time.
Doans   Mom—*the elder says, lifting his cup of tea*—here's to you. *The others, with beer cans, follow his lead.* How you did it, I got no clue.
Hector   To mom—*the nearly gone champion wheezes. He thinks of his mother in the kitchen, humming to herself.*
Emanuel   Here, here—*the younger says in a smooth, mellow voice. . . Looking over in wry curiosity at his brother, who had dropped his eye lids.* Hector?
Hector   Yeah, little brother.
Emanuel   What do you think dad thinks about?
Hector   When he's alone?
Emanuel   When he's alone, or lookin' up at the stars.
Hector   Probably fishin'. Or mom.

Emanuel   Yeah. . . The thing is, she probably thinks a him too, still, after all these years. He doesn't know what it's like bein' Romeo without a Juliet, does he.

Hector   Fuck yeah, he does. Why do you think he never complains?

Doans, slumped in a folding chair washed up onto the mud from a long ago spring deluge, tea mug still hooked by a finger bearing down ever so lightly on his chest, feet crossed over a tree limb; Gabriel, his last waking thought being high in the sky looking down on the magnificent river fringed with washed-out green, has his big square head back and would soon awaken with a stiff neck; Emanuel, curled on some leaves with his back against the log, thinking of his Mazzy and her golden hair and the way they used to be when they were truly free and roamed the Western states as gods; Hector, fighting battles without names or easily identifiable armies in his soul, snoring now, already taken by the nightmares of his father's tragedy and the acid it sprayed on their family.

~ PART TWO ~

Sunrise

The throat cancer cough of a Harley, *above the stilts and water clacks, rouses those who otherwise would have stayed comatose for hours longer. Two herons, audacious, turn beaks at the water's edge as a black snake rises gracefully from below, its wake dividing them. A robin cleans its beak on the low, languishing branch of the willow. The sun rises white-pink over the river trees, stiff in the morning's mood of pause and reflection.*

Emanuel   *The younger sits up, his equilibrium lagging. The first thing hitting him is the sun like an ice pick in the eye. Then, Hector, already erect, a sight to see. . .* Jesus. . . You all right, man? *He stares openly at his brother's face, which looks like a beaten peach.*

Hector   Fuck. . . what time is it?

Emanuel   I don't know.

Gabriel   It's eight o'clock—*he says, moving about the white ashes of the fire now resurrected.*

Emanuel   Eight? What're we doin' up so early for, man?

Gabriel   The sun.

Emanuel   Oh yeah—*rubbing his eyes with his knuckles*—the sun.

Hector   Did we all sleep outside?

Gabriel   Sort of—*he says, flipping flaring pieces of driftwood. He adjusts the dented old coffee pot sitting on a rack above the fire.*

Emanuel   You mean there were two couches up there that nobody used?—*he shakes his head*. . . Jesus Christ. . .

Hector   Where's Doans?

Gabriel   He was lying in the dirt until about an hour ago, and then he went up to the cabin.

Emanuel   He got one a the couches—*he says, cold epiphany branded into his eyes.*

Gabriel   Looks like it.

Emanuel   *His head shakes again.*

Hector   Is that coffee?—*he eyes the pot on the derelict rack, balanced on stones above the new fire.*

Gabriel   *He nods*—Be careful, it's full.

Emanuel   Gabe, I love you. *The brothers rise and approach the coffee pot simultaneously. The younger defers, naturally, and allows Hector to pour first.*

Hector   . . . and the fire's still goin'. . .

Gabriel   The coals were still warm when I got up. I had to add a few pieces to fire it up again.

Emanuel   Good man. *Hector sits back down with his back to the sun. Emanuel sits on the same log he slept against, face turned directly to that burning ball of life. Again, he stares openly at his brother's face.* Man, you look like somebody on the losin' end of a fight.

Hector   Yeah? *He'd laugh if anybody but his little brother had made the comment.* . . You don't look so hot yourself.

Emanuel   You sleep on a piece a rebar or somethin'?

Hector   Why?

Emanuel   You got this line across your face.

Hector   What kind a line?

Emanuel   I don't know, man. Just a line. A long red line.

Hector   *He passes his hand over his face, but feels nothing.* It doesn't hurt.

Emanuel   You bring anything for breakfast?

Hector   I brought some Amish sausage.

Emanuel   You bring any eggs?

Hector   Amish eggs.

Emanuel   Bread?

Hector   Amish bread. An' potatoes.

Emanuel   Well, don't just sit there, man. I'm hungry as a hog.

Hector   *He says nothing and then, the temptation too great, he begins fiddling with the morning fire. After another cup of coffee, he pulls the goods out of the cooler and begins preparing the breakfast.*

Emanuel   You need any help, Hoss?

Hector   You can cut up the potatoes.

Emanuel   *Without a cutting board, he uses the top of the old cooler. Hector locates several grapefruit-sized rocks and puts them in the burning coals beside the rack with the coffee pot, then tries it out placing the old black frying pan ontop of them.* Some day the Amish are gonna run the world. They're gonna have a monopoly on sustainable life. *His face in homage to dawn sun, he cuts the potatoes into small cubes, his eyes in just-woken Phantom of the Opera downward stare.* Jules get in last night?

Hector   Don't think so.

Emanuel   I wonder what happened?

Hector   Maybe he chickened out.

Emanuel   Chickened outta what?

Hector   *Shrugging*—Beats me. Afraid a our conversations.

Emanuel   Naw, man. Jules is laid back, not afraid.

Hector   You know 'em better than me. I only met the guy once.

Emanuel   Maybe he did get lost.

Hector   Sure.

Emanuel   You never know.

Hector   Sure. Born an' raised in Zanesville.

Emanuel   Maybe he went the wrong way on the Y-bridge.

Hector   Maybe he just got lost in a painting.

Emanuel   I hope he did.

Hector   You gettin' any tomatoes yet?

Emanuel   We're gettin' tons. The heat's killin' 'em though. All the new flowers are shrivelin' up an' dyin'.

Hector   How about squash; you gettin' any squash?

Emanuel   Hell, we've been gettin' squash for about two months.

You mean zucchini? Almost tired of 'em. Now the peppers are comin' on, an' cucumbers an' peas. But I got the peas in late.

Hector   You sell the other house yet?

Emanuel   Sell it? We don't even have it up for sale yet. We gotta finish the upstairs.

Hector   I thought you would a had it sold by now.

Emanuel   She wants everything just so.

Hector   Even though you're sellin' it?

Emanuel   Don't ask me, man. All I know is I worked on that house for three years, an' I ain't workin' on it anymore. I told her she's in charge. Get it done—hire it out—I don't care. She just needs to hop on it, 'cause this two mortgage thing is killin' us.

Hector   So you like livin' on the farm?

Emanuel   I love it, man. It's real peaceful, you know? The evenings are real quiet. All you hear are crickets an' frogs.

Hector   You lookin' for another contract?

Emanuel   Not right now.

Hector   Think you'll go back?

Emanuel   I hope I don't have to.

Hector   Sid's been cool about me bein' off. She makes okay money. At least we're not goin' backwards. I got the child support I gotta hand over to Moondog—right into her vacation an' new car account. That bitch. But our house payment is pretty low. She says she doesn't care what I do.

Emanuel   *He winces*—I tell you what, man; I don't think I can do it anymore.

Hector   I hear you.

Emanuel   I'm dead serious.

Hector   I know.

Emanuel   You wanna open up a bar?

Hector   There's an idea.

Emanuel   Why not?

Hector   Bars are risky propositions.

Emanuel   So's bein' hunched over in a cube all day, man.

Hector   *He makes a face*—Yeah. I'm just sayin'. . .

Emanuel   I'm just talkin' about some corner neighborhood bar—

somethin' to do for the next few years. It's not like we gotta make much money. Just somethin' for a few years till I figure out what I wanna do with the rest a my life.

Hector   Why you think you're gonna figure that out?

Emanuel   Yeah, well, I know. . .

Hector   Sid'll love that. Honey, me an' Manny are gonna open up a *bar*. What do you think about *that*?

Emanuel   Aw, she'd think it was great.

Hector   Actually, she'd be cool with it. What kind a place?

Emanuel   A small, quiet, comfortable place.

Hector   An old man bar.

Emanuel   Maybe not.

Hector   Not a drunkard's bar.

Emanuel   A place where guys like us can come in an' listen to music, maybe get away from their naggy wives for a while.

Hector   What makes you think everybody has a naggy wife?— *he deadpans.*

Emanuel   You know what I mean. Come on. Instead a the basement.

Hector   Yeah, but why would guys wanna hang out in a bar like a basement, when they could just hang out in the real thing?

Emanuel   Not everybody's got a finished cedar basement like you, man.

Hector   Most a the guys I know are at least workin' on it. You think all those naggy wives are gonna let all those basement dudes out?

Emanuel   We'll send 'em chocolates an' flowers an' Brad Pitt posters for the peace offerin', man. Look—it'll be a simple, comfortable place for dudes just like us who maybe wanna listen to some Joni Mitchell, or Roxy Music, or Dylan, or Neil Young. We'll put some a Doansy's paintings on the wall. We'll serve good beer an' hire waitresses in art school. We won't get rich, man, but it'd be somethin' to do for a few years.

Hector   *He allows himself the fantasy. For a moment he digs without looking over his shoulder.* We'd have to find a cheap place.

Emanuel   We'll find a cheap place.

Hector   You gotta find a cheap place not in some ghetto, man, if it's gonna be a corner bar.

Emanuel   I already got a few places in mind.

Hector   *Raising one eyebrow*—You do?

Emanuel   I can show you when we get back.

Hector   You got a name?

Emanuel   Nope. Why—you got any ideas?

Hector   *Thinking for a moment, then shaking his head.*

Emanuel   We'll serve Guinness the proper way. Foam cut off with a knife—no head.

Hector   People like head, man.

Emanuel   Workin' Irish don't.

Hector   Irish pubs're poppin' up all over the place.

Emanuel   It won't be an Irish pub. But I wanna serve the only proper Guinness in town.

Hector   You wanna import one a those pubs from Ireland, man? Are you crazy?

Emanuel   Look—I told you, it's not gonna be an Irish bar.

Hector   Then why're you so hung up on the Guinness, man? You can get Guinness at a sports bar.

Emanuel   Not lined up ten in a row—a fifteen minute pour from start to finish. Not cut off with a knife.

Hector   You're really hung up on that knife thing, aren't you. All right. Fuck—I don't care.

Emanuel   Just think about it.

Hector   I'll think about it.

Emanuel   It'd be somethin' different.

Hector   Long hours. Late nights too.

Emanuel   We could take turns closin', an' hire an assistant manager with torpedo tits who could close sometimes. We'd each have to close maybe two nights each per week. . . Think about it, man.

Hector   Yeah, I'll think it over.

Emanuel   I'm not talkin' about anything fancy.

Hector   *He starts chuckling to himself.*

Emanuel   What?

Hector   Were those crabs you got from that motel?

Emanuel   At the beach? Naw, man, they weren't crabs.

Hector   You sure?—*the pan smokes with hot grease.* I told you not to sleep under the covers.

Emanuel   You had the air conditionin' cranked all the way up. Man, I was *freezin'*.

Hector   *He scoops the cut potato cubes from the cooler top and dumps them in, still chuckling*—I told you not to. I always sleep in my sleepin' bag.

Emanuel   They bite, man!—whatever they were.

Hector   I know. I saw your welts. Fleas, maybe. Maybe real-live bedbugs.

Emanuel   Don't laugh. It's not funny. Mazzy wouldn't let it go. She kept askin' me how I got all those bites.

Hector   What'd you tell her?

Emanuel   I told her they were from crabs.

Hector   You didn't tell her that.

Emanuel   Yeah I did.

Hector   You must like sleepin' on that couch, man.

Emanuel   Like it's gonna make any difference. *He takes three potatoes in his hand, drops them on the cooler, and begins cutting anew.*

Hector   Yeah, I guess. . . Why'd we come back?

Emanuel   The rain, man. Remember the rain?

Hector   *He had meant the question in the broadest of terms.* Man, why'd you leave that cooler in your tent?

Emanuel   I told you. I knew we were gonna get a storm, an' I thought it'd weigh it down.

Hector   With *bait* in it?

Emanuel   How the hell did I know we were gonna get a monsoon?

Hector   We're lucky bears didn't eat us alive in the mountains.

Emanuel   Yeah, well, it wasn't really a thrill to sleep with you. *After he says it he glances up at his brother, looking for signs of hurt.* I gotta get rid a that thing, man. It was stinkin' up the neighborhood.

Hector   Remember my roommate at Kent who got crabs? We had to fumigate the apartment. He had to shave his whole body except his head.

Emanuel   I sorta remember that. I remember the chick who wanted to tear your head off.

Hector   Oh, there were lots a them.

Emanuel   I'm talkin' about the fifteen-year-old who knocked on your door that one night askin' for you. Man, she laid into you that night at the bar.

Hector   She wasn't fifteen. She was seventeen at least.

Emanuel   Why wouldn't you see her?

Hector   'Cause—I didn't know she was still in high school. I didn't need any a *that* kind a trouble.

Emanuel   Well, I'll give you credit for that. But didn't you think she looked kinda young, man? You could a asked her *before*.

Hector   It was dark.

Emanuel   You ever hear from Ricky?

Hector   Not in about ten years.

Emanuel   He still livin' near town?

Hector   As far as I know.

Emanuel   Man, why don't you call 'em up? I would.

Hector   She'd just hang up, man. She's the phone police, an' she'd just hang up on me.

Emanuel   *Shaking his lowered head, laughing, then raising it up again*—She really thinks you were the big bad influence on her little Ricky?

Hector   Fuck yeah.

Emanuel   Why don't you just stop by the house? What's she gonna do—call the cops?

Hector   Probably.

Emanuel   Fuck her. It's none a her business who her husband's friends are.

Hector   Last time I was up to see mom an' dad I drove past his house. I almost stopped.

Emanuel   Do it, man.

Hector   Yeah. . . *With a fork, he rolls the sausage links aligned side-by-side, sweating hot.*

Emanuel   What happened between you two?

Hector   Nothin' really—*he shrugs only his left shoulder.* It was about me an' her. She didn't like me from the word go. She wanted control over her boy an' she finally got it.

Emanuel   Yeah, but Ricky didn't have to listen to her.

Hector   Sure. I know. But Ricky'd been treatin' her pretty bad for years—since Kent. She was always this mousy, frail thing, an' she grew teeth. Got bossy, got bitchy. I think he woke up an' took a look around an' saw who was wearin' the panties an' who had the whip.

Emanuel   How about Buck?

Hector   I saw 'em at our twenty-five-year class reunion. He lives in Florida. He's a foreman in some wood shop. He's the same old Buck.

Emanuel   You gonna go see 'em some time?

Hector   I don't know.

Emanuel   I'll go with you, man.

Hector   Sure, if I ever go, you can come along.

Emanuel   You guys still have the mile relay record? *He asked the question every time they talked about Ricky and Buck.*

Hector   I'm not sure. . . *He knew for certain that they did. At least once a year, until recently when they initiated a closed-door security policy at the high school, he would walk through the halls, gazing into old classrooms, the weight room, the commons, ending up at the masonite board outside the gym that had the school track records painted on it. There his name, along with three others, were not dead yet—mysterious ghosts to the current throng of angst-and-anxiety that inhabited the school.* Probably, since they've been usin' meters for a long time now.

Emanuel   God, the fivers, man. . .

Hector   I still have the record for the fastest time.

Emanuel   You sure, man? I think I do.

Hector   I do.

Emanuel   That's only 'cause they didn't keep those records by the time I was there. We only cared about real records outdoors.

Hector   As far as I can remember, you never had any records.

Emanuel   Oh yeah. Sure, I did.

Hector   I never heard a any.

Emanuel   That's 'cause I never liked to brag.

Hector   You used to talk all the time about winnin' the pine wood derby in Cub Scouts.

Emanuel   I was just tryin' to make dad feel good. Everybody knows the dads make those things.

Hector   Yeah. Sure.

Emanuel   *He raises his hands in surrender*—I'm tellin' you. . .

Hector   *He pokes at the potatoes crusted brown, flecked with salt and pepper, then scrapes those that are stuck to the cast iron pan, turning them over. The fork grows hot and so he uses the bottom of his shirt as a pot holder.* So, you ever gonna forgive Jessie?

Emanuel   Where the hell'd that come from?

Hector   I've just been thinkin'.

Emanuel   Why should I?

Hector   I don't know what it is you gotta forgive 'em for.

Emanuel   Yeah—*sarcasm*—it wasn't like you were there.

Hector   He took the brunt a mom's midlife whack-out. He was the worst possible fit for that time in her life. She was cruel, man. I was there for that too. Maybe you didn't see it, but I did. If you think he was bad to you. . . he had it come his way too.

Emanuel   *He nods toward Gabriel, who is dutifully collecting the empty bottles and cans.*

Hector   He can't hear.

Emanuel   I don't know why I care if he knows. I guess I'm ashamed by association.

Hector   Is that it?

Emanuel   You mean is that why I still got a beef with 'em? No.

Hector   You sure sound like you do.

Emanuel   Yeah, I do. But it's not 'cause a that.

Hector   Then what is it?

Emanuel   *He pauses for a moment, picks up the fork lying in the pan, and fiddles about with the potatoes.* You wouldn't understand.

Hector   Tell me.

Emanuel   You're you. You're not me. If you understood you wouldn't be askin' the question.

Hector   Try me.

Emanuel   *He had tried, in various ways over the years, to explain things not only to him, but to the others. Their failure to absorb, to accept on his terms and not theirs, only burned him deeper. But the morning sun and the warmth it gave roused a new hope.* You think it was that? The big secret nobody talks about? . . . Well. . . if that's what made 'em so cruel, then maybe that is what it was. An' I'm sure it's what fueled his rage. But, it's not that directly. I mean, how could it be? I didn't even know till about ten years ago. An' it's not like I don't feel for 'em—'cause I know he didn't ask for what he got, just like I didn't ask for what I got. You don't understand, man. I love Jessie. I loved all you guys. . . but that love got sucker punched in the gut a thousand times. It became pretty plain nobody wanted me around. The older guys, they were outta the house. They were so much older, they were like another family anyway. But Jessie an' you, you were both there. . . I didn't get the feelin' it was just an older brother not wantin' his younger brother to tag along. I felt, clearly, that he wished I didn't exist. . . *Looking up.* . . . You didn't have that. Nobody else had that.

Hector   Junior was pretty hard on Doansy, from what I hear.

Emanuel   Junior wasn't seven years older than Doans. I never heard a any stories where Doans went flyin' across the room from the back a Junior's hand. Look, man, Junior's got a temper. We all got that gift from dear ol' dad; but what Jessie had, what Jessie *has*, is a will to do damage.

Hector   You can't blame *him*.

Emanuel   No, I can't. But as a man, I can say stop—no more. You think it's about what he did thirty years ago? Man, it's not about that. It's about what he does to me every time I see 'em. I'm still the little fucker he wishes weren't alive. An' you know what? I don't take that shit from him, or anybody anymore.

Hector   We all took it from dad. . .
Emanuel   Yeah, I know we did. But dad, I can forgive.
Hector   'Cause he's in a wheel chair?
Emanuel   'Cause he's apologized. 'Cause he's wept on the phone
with me when I spelled out his collateral damage. 'Cause he cared
more about my pain than his self-image. 'Cause he's *changed.*
Hector   Yeah, I know, man. . . but. . . *Gabriel had disposed of
the garbage up at the shack, and had come back down. He puts his
big square mug over the potatoes and takes a deep breath.*
Gabriel   God, that smells good. Are you gonna make some
eggs?
Hector   You're just in time, Gabe-mon. Have a seat. You want
yours scrambled or sunny-side-up?
Gabriel   Can you do sunny-side-up?
Emanuel   *No.*
Hector   Hell yeah.
Gabriel   Great. I'll take three.

Calling All George Jetsons

*He lies awake on the bed. He is thinking of his father. The pulled
muscle that was their relationship could never be completely
healed, no matter what tactics he used. The pain his father
endured was his pain. He thinks to a conversation he had with his
mother a few months ago when she told him about the gasoline
fire that burned his father's legs. The war had ended. He was
biding his time as the logjam of GI's came pouring back home.
His mother, in the telling, had been bitter. The Army didn't
discharge him for the burns, and so he wasn't eligible for
compensation. She'd wanted to pursue legal action—an unprecedented act—but he wouldn't hear of it. The burns wouldn't heal,
and when he contracted polio in '52 it killed any hope of them
ever healing by cutting the circulation to his legs. He lived with*

the deep scabs for the rest of his life. . . Doans remembers his
mother telling the story. He considers her backseat life, as his
father took blow after blow from the barrel of God's tragedy gun.
He wonders about their dialogues in those early years; most
certainly she had been conditioned to suffer in silence. Her silence
became her children's legacy of sacrifice to a void, posing as
deity, lighting the flare of madness in their souls. . . He rouses,
piles his bedding on the corner of the couch, and goes down to
where the others are slowly coming to life.

Doans   Hey, look who's up. If it ain't Larry, Curly, an' Shmoe.
Hector   Doans. I thought you just went to bed?
Doans   Naw, man. Me?
Hector   Have some coffee. We're havin' breakfast.
Doans   So I smell, so I see—*he closes his eyes and takes a*
deep whiff. If that don't smell like a Moanin' Lisa in a fryin' pan.
Hector   You want some Amish sausage an' Amish eggs?
Doans   Fuck yeah, I want some a that there chuck wagon grub.
Emanuel   How'd you sleep?
Doans   Not too bad until maybe around three o'clock. Then
they started fightin'.
Emanuel   Who started fightin'?
Doans   You mean you didn't hear 'em? The 'coons, man. You
didn't hear 'em? Holy mackerel. It was like two witches fightin'
over a broomstick. . . *Suddenly he notices.* . . Man, what happened
to your face?
Hector   I slept on a stick.
Doans   You slept on somethin'. . . *Christ.* . . You should see
your face, man. Wow. . . So, you guys didn't hear no raccoons? I
sure as hell heard 'em. I thought they'd go at it for a while an' then
walk off somewhere else; but they hung around. I swear—it
sounded like our sisters clawin' over each other to lick the fudge
pan.
Hector   I didn't hear a thing.
Emanuel   Me neither. *They both shrug.*
Gabriel   Nope—*he says shaking his head.*
Doans   How couldn't you hear *that*?—*rubbing his Keith*

Richards face. It was like stereophonic knock-my-socks-off torture chamber music. Man, like I thought I woke up on the set a Blair Witch.

Hector   Have some coffee, man—*and he hands him a hot mug.*

Emanuel   How was the couch?

Doans   The couch was great, but I barely got to sleep an' then I heard somethin' peckin' outside. I looked out the window an' saw this crow, man. Yeah. Peckin' at this hubcap on the side a the road.

Emanuel   Didn't hear that either.

Doans   You didn't hear that? I couldn't believe it. Yeah, man, it was just about dawn. . . I *think.* . . So like I lifted up the window an' told 'em to shut the hell up.

Emanuel   I heard *that.*

Doans   *Still rubbing his face*—Somebody didn't want me to sleep.

Gabriel   Doans, here's your pocketknife. . . Your hand all right?

Doans   I think it'll be okay. *He holds out both hands and his eyes look back and forth—unsure which hand it is—until he spots the gash near his left thumb.*

Emanuel   What the hell happened to your hand, man?

Gabriel   Me and your brother, we had this great idea last night.

Emanuel   Christ—how late were you guys up?

Gabriel   This was after we all went to sleep the first time. Hector—you thought we were out of our minds, which we were. We were going to send smoke signals to Mars. Only problem was, neither of us knows any Morse Code. SOS—dash, dit, dash? Or is it dit, dash, dit? We didn't know which one it was, so we did 'em both to cover ourselves. Then we got this bright idea. You know how you get these bright ideas at two o'clock in the morning? We got one. We decided to carve something in the mud.

Emanuel   In English?

Gabriel   In English. We figured any George Jetson that's gonna pick this thing up on his Sears telescope is gonna be light years ahead of us in the intelligence department, and he'll be able to catch onto English real quick. We had the hardest time trying to

come up with what to say. It had to be short, you know, because
we didn't have too much mud to work with.

Emanuel *Eating a plate of potatoes*—So what'd you say?

Gabriel It's still there. Right there it is—*pointing to the spot,
then walking on over.* We kind of smeared it later on when we got
that big carp on.

Emanuel So what'd you say?

Gabriel You have to give credit to your big brother there. He's
the one who thought it up. . . He says, how about *Chicks like
Dicks?*. . . *Chicks like Dicks*—not too shabby, eh? Me and Doansy
start chewing on that for a while, seeing if we can improve it any.
Then Doansy comes up with this. He says hey, man—*Chicks like
Dicks*—yeah, true, touché; but it's sort of too short. Maybe they'll
think we smudged the C and think it says *Dicks like Dicks*. Or
Chicks like Chicks. . . Doansy says I got it!—I got it! How about
Big Dicks Get Nice Chicks. As soon as he said it, that was it.
That's what we wrote. It's now circling the galaxy like a turd from
the S. S. Minnow.

Hector I still like *Chicks like Dicks* better. What more is there
to say?

Gabriel It's pretty good, Hector. You get 85% of the credit. We
only tweaked it a little.

Emanuel So, do you mean chicks like dicks—like assholes? Or
chicks like dicks—like the real McCoy—the meat?

Doans Chicks don't dig assholes, man, if you mean literally
assholes. . . Or you mean assholes—like pricks?

Emanuel You're confusin' the hell outta me, man.

Doans How about fucked up dudes, man? How 'bout that?

Emanuel Okay. Now, that I can understand.

Doans I think the beauty a the statement is that you can take it
either way; the meanin' is valid from either eye. Chicks like
fucked up dudes with long erec-shee-own-ayyys.

Gabriel All George Jetson needs to know looking out from his
hobbit hole in the sky.

*They eat breakfast. Scrambled eggs on sagging paper plates,
black-brown links of sausage, torn-off hunks of plain white bread.*

Nobody sits, except Hector, who is cook to these wagon train scouts.

Doans   Gabe, you gonna take your machine up today?

Gabriel   I was thinking about it.

Doans   Wow. Great, man. Do it.

Gabriel   I'll have to see what the weather's like. Anybody hear what kind of wind we're supposed to have?—*he turns his body left and right, but nobody says anything until Hector takes note and shovels some eggs into his mouth and makes something up.*

Hector   Repeat a yesterday. Hot as shit, an' no wind.

Gabriel   Hot's okay. No wind is what I like to hear.

Doans   Groovy, man. Today Gabe's gonna fly.

Emanuel   How you get up in the air, Gabe?

Doans   He runs as fast as he can—like a turkey on Thanksgivin'—an' if he's lucky he's up, up, up an' away.

Emanuel   You always get up on the first try?

Doans   Naah, man, sometimes he's runnin' back an' forth for like a half hour.

Emanuel   Jesus, Gabe.

Gabriel   It's pretty damn heavy.

Emanuel   You're a fuckin' animal.

Doans   Yeah, he is.

Hector   Doans, you talk to the dude about the mural?

Doans   The Texas guy or the Oklahoma guy?

Hector   I thought the Oklahoma guy was the one who was interested.

Doans   Yeah, he is, man.

Hector   What's he gonna do?

Doans   I don't know what he's gonna do. I'm hopin' he'll see the light an' give me the green light.

Hector   But it's a mural about Texas. . .

Doans   Well, yeah, it *can* be. Texan musicians. But there were a lot a Oklahoma musicians who could be in it too. I can swap a few faces no problem.

Hector   He gotta find a site—is that it?

Doans   *Nodding*—He's gotta first say yeah, he'll sponsor it. He don't have to put up a dime. He says he'll sponsor it, that he's got a site, an' then I go get the cash. Cash ain't directly the hard part. If somebody like him says he's got a site an' he'll sponsor it, gettin' money ain't no big deal. Well, it ain't no *real* big deal. It's still a big deal. But first the dude's gotta say yeah, I'll do it.

Emanuel   Then what's he got holdin' 'em back, man?

Doans   What's holdin' 'em back? His reputation. An' the fact that he'll be the cog in the whole wheel. I mean, I'm sure he'd have his secretary or some other flunky do the day-to-day communication; but it's still a commitment on his part. He's like the busiest dude you ever seen.

Emanuel   An' he's the real deal.

Doans   Dude, he's the biggest name outside a Nashville. He's like seventy-five years old. He knows what this kinda mural means history-wise to country music. You drop his name an' shit happens.

Emanuel   An' so you're just waitin' for a phone call, man?

Doans   Me?—*laughing.* He ain't gonna call me back. Naw, I'm givin' 'em a week to think about it. He said call 'em back in a week an' I'm gonna wait like 10 days. I sent 'em the plans. His gears are workin' on it right now.

Hector   Good luck, man.

Doans   Luck is what I could use right now—*his eyebrows jump enthusiastically.*

Hector   Big money?

Doans   Let's put it this way: If I get the green light, I'll be workin' on this thing for two, maybe three years.

Gabriel   That's a lot of cash.

Doans   You ain't a kiddin'.

Hector   Doans, you ever think a doin' some jewelry work?

Doans   Jewelry?

Hector   Me an' Manny were talkin'—

Emanuel   Hey—*putting out his hands*—don't drop my name in your hat.

Hector   What do you mean? We were talkin' about it on the way down.

Emanuel   *You. . . You* were talkin' about it. Leave my name out, man. *He is serious, with serious eyes.*
Hector   All right, whatever—*the condescension, out of habit, rolls in like the tide. . . Then back to Doans and he is all humble pie sincerity.* I was thinkin', you could open up a little shop. Pump out jewelry, you know, somethin' distinctive—somethin' everybody knows is your work by sight. It'd still be a creative process. The overhead'd be low; silver doesn't cost that much these days. *Under his breath*—Not since dad lost a bundle in the 70's. You an' Chelsea could do that for your livin' money, an' then do your paintin' in between. . . All I'm sayin', man, is it'd be nice to have somethin' regular comin' in instead a hopin' for one a these big projects to come through. You know? I'm not tryin' to tell you what to do. Manny says—
Emanuel   Don't—
Hector   Well fuck, man, you did. You said you were in Ireland an' this chick had this tiny jewelry shop, an' she was rollin' in the customers. You said it was some small touristy town no bigger than Doansy's, an' she was doin' real good. . . Didn't you?
Emanuel   I was just talkin' out loud. . .
Doans   It's all right, man. We're all just talkin' out loud.
Hector   I still got dad's lapidary tools. Fuck—you guys're artists. It'd be cake. You just need some kind a brand, some distinctive look, somethin' yours you can place in all the little gift shops for a hundred miles.
Nobody says a word. They scoop and chew and swallow dry swallows. With over-exaggerated pain Gabriel gets up and holds out his plate for more. Hector, over-zealous, gives him more with the tea spoon.
Gabriel   Man. If this isn't the best breakfast I've had since my mom used to cook me omelets every morning before school.
Everybody, too-fast, laughs like hyenas at the carrion trough.

Dali's Workshop

Hector, paper toweling the cast iron skillet; the others, at the end of a coffee round table—the whole wide river there for the taking.

Gabriel   Anybody wanna take a stroll?—*his fingers, but for thumbs, are in the front pockets of his dark blue jeans.*

Emanuel   I think I'll pass, Gabe. I'm gonna sit here an' try an' get some sun, an' appreciate the silence a this beautiful river.

Hector   No thanks, man.

Doans   You goin' down by the dam? Yeah—let's walk down by the dam—*standing up, padding his chest pockets for cigarettes, squeezing the lump in his jeans pocket for his lighter.* You two harpies hold down this here fort an' don't let no witch-raccoons steal our cache a goodwill an' fraternity in this New Age ziggurat.

Hector   Chow, man. Be good.

Doans   Yes, dear. . . Yes, *dearie*. . . *Mom*. . .

Hector   An' don't drag home no stray cats into this here house neither—*waving the skillet.* I slave all day on my hands an' knees scrubbin' this floor; I don't need you muddyin' it up right after I clean it. You hear me?

Doans   Okay, ma. I promise.

Hector   Be off with you! *Shoooo!*

Emanuel   You sure you don't wanna go with 'em?—*he says to his brother. Part of him wants to be alone, though being with him is just about as good.*

Hector   *Already the skillet is back on the rack and he's at the fishing rods. Two are still leaned into their sticks; the others are lying in the mud.* I wanna fish. Let's toss these lines out an' see what we can catch.

Emanuel   Might as well put all of 'em out. *He squats in the mud and lifts a pole up. It sticks, then springs back and wobbles, and then Hector tosses him a dirty rag and he starts wiping down the shaft and even more importantly, the line.* You bring any lures? I thought we could do some surface fishin'.

Hector   All I brought was bluegill an' catfish gear.

Emanuel   Eddie's got some tackle up there. What do you think?

Hector   Go for it, little brother. Me, I'm gonna go for the cats. I've been thinkin' about haulin' in a great big bullhead for about a month.

Emanuel   They got bullheads this far north?

Hector   I don't know, man. Why not? I mean, say this bullhead's livin' somewhere down in the Mississippi swamps, in some tributary a the Mississippi River, an' he gets this itch to head upstream. What's stoppin' 'em from workin' his ass all the way up to the Ohio, maybe even all the way up to Marietta, to this very spot? There's gotta be antsy catfish, just like there's antsy people. Now, if it was the middle a winter, I'd say your odds are pretty fuckin' slim. What kind a outta-his-mind catfish from Mississippi is gonna head north just so he can freeze his ass off? I figure maybe they wanna come north for the summer an' beat that southern shake-an'-bake heat; though I'll say, it hasn't exactly been like the North Pole around here this summer, that's for God damn sure. *The first line still has a dough ball on it. He pinches it off, tosses it in the grass, and wipes his fingers on his jeans. He forms a fresh dough ball, making it round without any cracks, pushes it onto the hook, closes the dough around the crevice, then tosses out the line. He cranks the line tight, sets it into the Y-stick, then tightens it a final time until there's a slight bend in the rod. He moves onto the next pole.*

Emanuel   *Already without a breeze, the air sticks in pockets along the shore and he begins to bead sweat. He watches a woodpecker hop around the bullet-holed, skeletal trunk of a dead cottonwood.* I'm gonna see if this river's got any bluegill big enough for a White Rock hook. I got plenty if you want any, man—*he offers, raising and then wiggling the cup of maggots.*

Hector   Maybe I'll try that after I lose all my dough balls.

Emanuel   I got Mazz one time.

Hector   Hooked her?

Emanuel   Yup.

Hector   Where at?

Emanuel   In the head. I thought I just got her hair. She's got a lotta hair an' as soon as I felt my line stick I thought to myself—

aw shit, I hope to God it's only in her hair.

Hector No dice, eh?

Emanuel Naw, man. Got her with two barbs. . . *Turning away shaking his head*. . . We had to go to the hospital, which was about an hour away.

Hector Jesus. Where the hell were you?

Emanuel In the boonies a Georgia. Her brother has this cabin on some lake down there. Yeah, so like none a the doctors wanted to deal with it till finally this Indian guy comes in an' takes out a pair a regular pliers. These things, they were rusty as shit. Just regular pliers. He didn't even wash his hands—I watched 'em. Hell—I could a done that.

Hector Next time save yourself the co-pay an' break out the needle nose.

Emanuel Yeah, no shit.

Hector Bet the brother-in-law had a laugh.

Emanuel All weekend long. All of 'em.

Hector You the Beavis a their Christmas parties?

Emanuel The Beavis, Butthead, an' Big Bad Wolf—all rolled into one.

Hector You're not blood, man.

Emanuel I know.

Hector We all know—*nodding*—*tossing another line out. It lands with a loud plunk where the sunlight whites out the water surface.*

Emanuel You want any help gettin' those out?

Hector Naw—I only got two more. I wanna see you haul in a big, fat bluegill. Remember how dad liked bluegill?

Emanuel He loved to fish, man. An' he loved to eat bluegill. *He visualizes, as clear as day, that oft repeated summertime gathering. Their father, after fishing all morning before others arrived, now in charge, seated in a kitchen chair at the plateau of the sloping driveway that dropped down to the hustling traffic of Prospect Avenue. Their mother or one of the girls at his side, taking fish by the tails from the heaping plateful, rolling them in flour, piling them on another plate. He, still virile, easily reaching*

*above the fryer forking the curling fish, scooping them out, piling
them on a third plate. . . Behind them in the backyard, a sea of
running kids. The swimming pool—a volcano of squeals and
erupting waves. Boys in the garage, sitting on the twin Honda 50's
like they were mechanical magic carpets. Aunts with cigarettes
and jangly drinks and sudden, jubilant laughter. Uncles with cans
of cold, cheap beer in short-sleeved dress shirts unbuttoned,
bellies like lamb shanks in butcher shop windows. The sun
spraying down on them all like God's firey semen. . .* What'd they
talk about, man?

Hector   Those guys probably talked about the same shit we talk
about. Instead a us worryin' about them, they worried about the
farm. Instead a wonderin' about the ozone, they wondered when
Kruzchev was gonna send the nukes over.

Emanuel   Yeah, I guess so.

Hector   Maybe the man on the moon. They probably talked a
lot about shit like that—in between the whisky sours an' slurps a
beer.

Emanuel   Do you remember those drills, man? The nuke drills
where everybody got under their desks an' prayed to their favorite
God?

Hector   Naw—I think they discontinued that program when
they figured what the hell—they'd be better off tellin' kids to
fornicate an' smoke an' booze it up with your fellow classmates; I
mean, what the hell's hidin' under a desk gonna do when the
nukes're rainin' down?

Emanuel   I think Vietnam put a nail in that charade—for a while
anyway.

Hector   Only for a while. A new generation a kids come up
without any memory a that shit an' bingo—the next war's blood
an' guts is in the chamber.

Emanuel   We were lucky, man. We landed in between Vietnam
an' this new surrealism.

Hector   Yeah, we were.

Emanuel   We had our own surrealism, though.

Hector   Doin' wheelies in dad's wheel chair?

Emanuel   All the shit comin' at us everywhere, man. You remember when Planet a the Apes first came out?
Hector   Sure. My hair was just fallin' over my eyes.
Emanuel   Jesus. . . I remember bein' out in the lobby a The Strand. That big, dirty lobby with like yellow tile an' beat up walls—the seats in that place, man, were like Petri dishes for germs. I was out in the lobby waitin' for my buttered popcorn, probably with a hardon from all those naked tits in Logan's Run, or maybe peein' my pants from Willard—
Hector   Or ready to go monk from Jesus Christ Superstar.
Emanuel   Yeah, somethin'; whatever ten-year-old, mind-bustin' shit mom an' dad were lettin' 'em feed us. . . I'm standin' there an' I see the poster for Planet a the Apes. You talk about some freaky shit. . . I got up real close an' stared at those apes, man. I stood there an' asked myself where the fuck is this mystery train *headed!* . . .
Hector   It's on a bee-line straight to Eye-rack!
Emanuel   I think back an'. . . *damn*. . . the shit comin' at us.
Hector   It was a crazy time for young minds.
Emanuel   I mean, you're off to school in the mornin', hit Cub Scouts once a week, watch some streaker—maybe Jessie—weave in an' outta traffic, get down an' dirty with the Black Panthers— which just so happens to be the name a your Pee Wee Football team, go to sleep listenin' to peace an' love, an' then Gollum creepin' Close to the Edge—so fuckin' real in your mind you're *there*, man, you're *there*. . . Body bags, an' Patty Hearst, Tommy, an' Alice poppin' pills down the street. If you were like me, a kid with wild thoughts already bouncin' like ping pong balls in his head, maybe a dreamer but bein' hit over the head with discipline an' guilt from ol' man Ironsides at home. . . good luck, Dali, 'cause you couldn't a painted a crazier wonder world for my brain if you wanted!

Let The Buffalo Roam

Years ago, you, oh great Muskingum with your silent eyes and billion feet—traveler and sojourner—wonderer and morning warbler—your waters, gathered from the chance soak-and-squeeze of the invisible sponge, flowed where the ruts of chance scored victory, overflowing when the deluge of spring turned into rank, immovable guests. And then came The Second Man, divorced from mystery, averse to riding your whetted whims—he came with God on his side and Manifest Destiny in his loins—your eyebrows were plucked!—your tummy tucked!—segmented, you were, from seamless snake to discrete centipede! The dams of a regimented life changed you forever—from capricious spirit to pastoral ghost. . . And here they now sit, generations later, visitors to your incarceration, the blissfully ignorant, appreciative accepters of your manicured profile.

Gabriel   The meteor shower should be visible tonight.

Doans   Where at, Gabe?—*they dangle feet over the wall of concrete, watching the happy fall of water over the speed bump dam.*

Gabriel   I think the northwest. But we should be able to see 'em all over the sky.

Doans   Is this like shootin' stars? Is that what kind a display we're talkin' about?

Gabriel   Well, they're meteors, so they're not really shooting stars. What most people think are shooting stars are really meteors.

Doans   Wow, yeah—all right! What time, Gabe?

Gabriel   Right after sundown. But I think you can see 'em most of the night.

Doans   *Turning to his right, hand fumbling in his shirt pocket*—Hey, man, you wanna try some a this weed?

Gabriel   Sure.

Doans   *He has a joint already rolled. He takes the joint, gives it to his brother-in-law and says*—Take this, my man, an' *smoke it. This is my mind, which will be given unto you.*

Gabriel   Thanks. *He takes the peace offering, allows Doans to light it, and takes several hits.*

Doans   So here we are!—*scanning the flowing water and gray-green morning trees*—Two turtle doves down the lane a what's-up-ahead out from their female cocoons, awakened to the thump-thump-thump a life!

Gabriel   Away from the governor of muscle!

Doans   Gabe, my boy. . . Why, you're *alive!*

Gabriel   *He shouts*—I said, let the buffalo roam! Open the dams and let the waters gush! The coyotes must eat too!

Doans   Amen, brother! Like, Gabe, we've been prayin' for your poor hen-pecked soul to pull them pillars down. *Pull,* Sampson, *pull.* . . Like, why do you put up with it, man?

Gabriel   Why? . . . I don't know. . .

Doans   No, man—we all put up with it to some degree.

Gabriel   To some degree.

Doans   Yeah—*in his we're commiserating with you, not laughing at you, caramel voice*—to some degree we all get the third degree. Just not to the constant four-hundred fifty-one degrees you get. Naw—Abby's pretty cool. At least you can talk to her—you know? Yeah, she's great. . . a man in a woman's straight jacket, that's her problem.

Gabriel   You think?

Doans   Yeah, I fuckin' think. Man, I ain't sayin' she's a dyke. I'm sayin' her brain ain't a female brain. It's got command-an'-control written all over it.

Gabriel   From what I hear, she an' Manny used to get into some pretty hairy fights.

Doans   Yeah, I think they did.

Gabriel   Her problem is, she won't listen to reason until she's already hyped-up. She gets an idea in her head and then *wham*—she's on you like a pit bull. She thinks way too much, analyzes everything. . . And look—I'm not your dad!

Doans   I know!—I know, brother! Fuck—*we* ain't even our dad. You gotta take the bull by the nuts, Gabe. You let your woman wear a strap-on. First mistake. Never let a woman have a dick.

Gabriel   I don't want any trouble. I just wanna do my job, come home, and not be nagged at.

Doans   Okay, like what's she been doin' lately to ruffle your feathers, man?

Gabriel   Well, like the other day, I was down in the basement.

Doans   What were you doin' down there, man?

Gabriel   What do you think I was doin' down there?

Doans   *Sarcastically*—Okay, I *know* what you were doin' down there. Aside from the obvious—what specifically were you doin' down there?

Gabriel   I was cutting pieces for your guitar on the band saw.

Doans   Yeah, man?—*an appreciative smile.* Cool. . .

Gabriel   All of a sudden, I hear this scream from the top of the stairs. I come running up—I thought something really bad happened.

Doans   Somethin' really bad *is* about to happen, I think.

Gabriel   She'd asked me to put up this bracket on her gazebo for a new bird feeder. I forgot. I always seem to forget. She laid into me about how thoughtless I am, and why can't I be more considerate. She was actually crying. It happens all the time.

Doans   Sure, man. I'm sure it does.

Gabriel   Usually, I just ignore it. I mean, I listen to her. I try and understand her. But I don't know what there is to understand.

Doans   You're damn right there ain't nothin' to understand— 'cause it ain't about *you*, man. You got nothin' whatsoever to do with it. That is, unless you're gonna blame that wall for bein' in the way a that fist. . . You need to show her who's boss in the sack, man. You ever toss her 'round in the sack?

Gabriel   Not really.

Doans   Yeah, well, do it some time. Chicks dig it. They might not admit it to you, but they really get off on it. An' not only that, but it carries over into the jeans-an'-T-shirt world. How can a chick take you seriously, man, when you're fawnin' all over her all the time?

Gabriel   I thought that's how you were supposed to be?—*his head and eyes in disjointed confusion rise two steps apart from one another.*

Doans   Gabe, you poor brainwashed boy. Chicks dig bein'
controlled, man. They *dig* it. They need it. That's biology—see?
I'm not talkin' politically correct, we-all-be-the-same bullshit. I'm
not talkin' talk show trash. I'm talkin' trial an' error, what works,
what don't. Need-based responses as opposed to fairy tale meat
grinder hogwash. When things are goin' not-so-good, you know,
maybe you an' the missus are goin' in polar directions for a while;
the best thing you can do is give her a really good fuck. They love
it. They love it not 'cause it feels good; well, that's *part* of it. No,
man—they love it 'cause it shows 'em you *care*. The king a the
pride has come back to claim his harem. You're like takin' care a
business. . . You gettin' all this down, Gabe?

Gabriel   I don't think Abby would respond too good to that—

Doans   Gabe! Abby's got the cranks 'cause in her eyes you
ain't playin' your caveman part. She's waitin' for you to knock her
on the head, drag her by the hair back home, an' force her to do
unspeakable acts. She's danglin' the worm—her bitchiness—but
you ain't a bitin'. The more she wiggles, the more you back off.
You're in a three-dimensional Star Trek chess extravaganza—you
ain't a playin' dominoes.

Gabriel   *He thinks about it, gets gun-shy with a response, thinks
some more, and then goes on*—Yeah, I know. But every time I've
stood up to her, she just cuts me off for a month.

Doans   Then bring home a Playboy. Bring home a Playboy an'
put it on the back a the toilet. Let her know she ain't gonna stop
this testosterone train from rollin'.

Gabriel   I don't know, man. . .

Doans   Listen!—*he reaches out and puts his hands to
Gabriel's neck and mimes a strangle.* You're involved in the most
epic power struggle known to mankind! Now, you want harmony
or you want blue balls for the rest a your life? 'Cause right now
the wrong pair a legs is in those pants, an' it's thrown the whole
man-woman, pre-determined seatin' arrangement outta whack.
She's mad at you 'cause she's in the driver's seat, an' no chick
really wants to be in *that* driver's seat. *Ouch!* Hey—you know

what happens to lions that don't kill, Gabe? They don't get no pussy, an' they don't get no food. You can't change the rules a biology, man. Either go with 'em, celebrate 'em, or whine about 'em an' be miserable.

Gabriel   Maybe I'm just not cut out for it.

Doans   For what?

Gabriel   Abby. You know, women in general.

Doans   Well a course you're not, man. Who is? You think I am? You think Batman an' The Boy Wonder are? Naw, man— we're fish floppin' in the sand just like you. But here's the thing; you gotta learn to be a student a the game. Fuck, man—you just learned to fly. Anybody with half a brain can learn shit. You learned to fly, you can learn to read the roadmap to Atlantis.

Gabriel   I think flying might be easier.

Doans   True. But—look—you gotta quit hopin' for things to fall into your comfort zone. Forget it. Get that poison outta your head.

Gabriel   *He turns away, looks to the sky, and wishes he were up there.* It's a hell of a lot of work. . .

Dante's Omission

They stand where the leaves and mud wrangle. For Hector, it's watching the tight lines, reeling in and checking the dough balls, tossing back out far, far beyond Emanuel's bobber. And for Emanuel, it's standing back a little from shore, gazing at everything and anything in the bleached flour day.

Hector   Yeah, that's crazy as fuck. A hunk a ice the size a what?—Rhode Island?

Emanuel   You seen pictures of it?—*twitching, ticking, cranking. His eyes are mesmerized by the thin, white shaft of the bobber.*

Hector   Yeah, I saw some pictures of it..It's crazy.

Emanuel   Rhode Island's a state.

Hector   I know.

Emanuel   A small state, but a God damn state. You get what I'm sayin'?

Hector   It's fucked up as shit.

Emanuel   I'm sayin' that's a big fuckin' iceberg. Not even an iceberg—a *state*. A *state* just broke off a the bottom a the world—hasn't ever happened in our turn on the watch tower before—an' nobody seems to worry too much. Ho-hum. . . One more attachment emailed from a friend. . . I find that pretty surreal, man.

Hector   It is surreal. This whole thing's surreal.

Emanuel   It's not the only chunk to break off. Another one almost as big broke off two months earlier. There goes Antarctica, right before our very eyes. How long we been pumpin' shit into the sky—a hundred years?—an' really most of it in the past fifty years? This is the product a only a few human generations. Think about that.

Hector   *In parody*—Don't you know all those liberal scientists are just tryin' to scare people?

Emanuel   I'll tell you what, man. The next World War—I don't mean this Iraq-Afghanistan terrorist shit goin' on now—but the next true big-time war where everybody sends his first, second, an' third born over with a pea shooter in each hand; it's gonna be one side a the Atlantic against the other. Us, as in the U.S., against the European Community—'cause we're headin' in two totally different directions about too many things.

Hector   Them or China. While we bleed ourselves dry fightin' this next war, they'll be rakin' in the cash.

Emanuel   The lines are bein' drawn. This president's buildin' walls around our shores. A rootin' tootin' Yosemite Sam, just at a time when we need somebody with some guile an' a real grasp a international politics. He's got us goin' full steam ahead for the falls, man. You can't hide your head in the sand forever.

Hector   Tell that to Bush an' his gang.

Emanuel   This ain't a fuckin' DVD, man. It ain't a TV show—it's not Spielberg—it ain't out *there*. It's right here, right beneath our feet. It's arrogant as fuck, that's what it is. Plain arrogance. I wish they'd find the arrogance gene, along with the religion gene, an' zap 'em in everybody.

Hector   Some day they will.

Emanuel   That, an' sterilize anybody with kids who ain't really a parent.

Hector   Amen—*he says, grinning.*

Emanuel   An' make president-elects take a course in what wars are. You know?—really. Ship 'em off to Camp David, set 'em down like the guy in A Clockwork Orange, an' make 'em watch reel after reel a war footage. Have some college professor come in an' connect the dots a dumb-fuck moves—superficially benign, innocent administrative moves today—that get the wheels a catastrophe goin' for the future.

Hector   Hey man, as soon as they're elected they got tenure.

Emanuel   *Under his breath*—I'd like to sit my wife down sometimes an' make her watch some things.

Hector   You two patch things up?—*he remains fixed on the lines, and at the water where they disappeared.*

Emanuel   What's there to patch up?

Hector   I thought Doans said. . . Not really?

Emanuel   Not really.

Hector   We've all been there, brother.

Emanuel   Yeah, I know, so I've heard.

Hector   Couches are a drag. Maybe that's what did my back in—all those nights fallin' in the crack.

Emanuel   I thought it was pole vaultin' in high school—*he says, giving his brother a look.*

Hector   Yeah, I don't know.

Emanuel   *He wipes his face—suddenly*—I don't know how much longer I can go on.

Hector   I wouldn't a brought it up, only Doans said you guys were on the mend.

Emanuel   *His eyes narrow, and his mind digs up memories buried with only a cursory dusting—for each day, without exception, he unearths them, hoping for a return to what they had.* God, she used to be different, Hector. I'm serious. I don't even know her anymore.

Hector   Icebergs breakin' off the South Pole are small potatoes compared to your troubles.

Emanuel   Yeah, everybody's got a sob story.

Hector   You might wanna give that a little nudge—*he points to the bobber.* I saw it go under a couple times.

Emanuel   *He does, prompting only teasing nibbles, and so he cranks it in to check his maggot. Half gone, he digs for another in the styrofoam tub.* You take a lot a movies a Corrie when she was little?

Hector   Reels an' reels.

Emanuel   Yeah, I did when Rahe was real small. I don't take as many as I used to. When the camera was new an' Rahe was new, we were takin' 'em all the time too. I've been watchin' ours, you know, on weekends after they're in bed. You forget a lot a your life, don't you.

Hector   Probably about ninety-percent.

Emanuel   I'll watch somethin' an' see shit that if I didn't have those videos, I'd never even know was part a my existence.

Hector   Like what?

Emanuel   Like things in the house. We've been in three houses already. You forget about the other houses, but as soon as you see 'em on video you're right back where you were, maybe with the same feelin's you had while you were livin' there. . . We made some good porno flicks, man. Like six months after Rahe was born when Mazzy was still nursin' an' her boobs were like bazookas. Jesus Christ, she was gorgeous.

Hector   An' I bet she thought those things were just a pain in the back.

Emanuel   Sure. Of course.

Hector   You can't tell 'em you love their tits too much, 'cause you don't want any flack later when God taketh away an' they deflate down to regular size.

Emanuel   Yeah, you're screwed either way—*he barely hears his brother. He's trying to figure out a puzzle in his head. The puzzle with missing pieces and changing images.* I'll see maybe how I

used to be with Rahe, or the way I was with Mazz. I'll see
expressions on Rahe's face that're still there—you know? They
don't change much. The way she lifts her eyebrows an' the way
her forehead wrinkles up—one side of her mouth pulls like it's
hooked. Then how she goes into a laugh.

Hector   It's cool, man.

Emanuel   It's kinda cool, but it's kinda not cool.

Hector   Which part?

Emanuel   What I mean is, it makes you see how precious they
are, but how fragile too. How fast they can be taken away. It
reminds you how much you forget, what you don't have anymore.
How you can't go back. You see time skippin' along laughin' at
you. . . I was up the other night. I think it was Saturday night. I
just couldn't get to sleep. I went down an' turned on the tube
an'—fuck, I don't know what I even watched. But I just broke
down, man.

Hector   Cryin'?

Emanuel   Yeah.

Hector   So what?

Emanuel   So, I feel like a fool.

Hector   Don't.

Emanuel   Then. . . you too? How come?

Hector   Hell—*twisting his body to stretch his back, wincing*—
hell if I know. Same as you, probably.

Emanuel   It's like I want God to be nice. Like for the first time in
my life, I got somethin'. I'm goin' through the ringer, but I got this
beautiful little girl too. I got this beautiful wife, but she doesn't
even hear me anymore. In the spring the buds come out on the
trees, the grass turns green, it's another sunrise without any sign of
a mushroom cloud over the horizon. . . I want God to have mercy
on me. I'm humbled, man. I'm humbled as shit to be where I am
right now. I just want the world to hold together until at least
Rahe's gone.

Hector   That's not weird, Manny.

Emanuel   It feels weird. There's times when I'm alone. . . it's
like I can feel the bomb killin' millions, an' I can see Rahe's face.

I don't understand it. I don't feel sure about anything like I used to, even when I was fuckin' around at college an' thought I was gonna end up a garbage man. *He raises his eyebrows and looks at his brother.* You think there's gonna be a war?

Hector   Of course there is.

Emanuel   I got nothin' philosophically against wars. Some wars are self-defense. But. . .

Hector   Yeah, *but*. . .

Emanuel   Maybe this *is* it. The next big one.

Hector   Could be, man. We're slidin' in that direction, for sure.

For a while they stand without cranking in their lines; the water flows with swirling eddies big and small—dizzying masquerades in which they find black holes going straight to their youth and to their fears.

The Farm

. . . The acres upon which their Scotch-Irish ancestors landed, cleared, and declared independence from hopelessness. The tract studded solid with maple, oak, hickory, beech, and buckeye. Land of the Indian's criss-crossing sagas of serpent mounds, agricultural largess, warring parties, and retreat into white footnotes and too-late apologies. The house, broad, big, honest in its purpose. A garden behind, a corn crib, outhouse, barn, orchard, two wells, whetting stone, and rolling black dirt. Opportunity never presented itself with so much challenging allure, nor lured so many to their withered-hands burial plots where only, years later, sentimental family jackals would circle the wagons in wide-eyed wonder.

Gabriel   Didn't you and Adam go down there one summer?

Doans   *He makes a bitter face and hides himself in his hands—* Yeah. Me an' Adam an' Junior.

Gabriel   That much fun?

Doans   What do *you* think, man? Like, why would any parent think it'd be anything but torture to spend more than about two hours with your great uncle an' his two old maid sisters?

Gabriel   They didn't. That's *why* they sent your ass down there!

Doans   Well, fuck man, I was too stupid to figure *that* one out.

Gabriel   Was it really that bad?

Doans   Naw, it was all right, man. After they dunk your head in that cold bucket a water, you get the idea an' adjust real quick.

Gabriel   How long were you there?

Doans   Like a week, maybe two. I can't remember exactly. Uncle Abe was like our dad without a sense a humor.

Gabriel   Your dad has a sense a humor?

Doans   That's what I mean. That guy was straight outta American Gothic, came right off the Mayflower. We'd get up in the mornin' when he got up, which was like five o'clock or some insane time, an' start workin' before breakfast, which is what he did. He'd milk the cows first thing while Aunt Pearl or Aunt Minnie got the chow goin'. We'd go right out an' start paintin'. It'd be foggy, the grass still wet, man. Sometimes freezin'. We'd go at it about an hour. When he came in for breakfast we'd put our brushes down, climb down the ladders an' eat without sayin' boo. It was like bein' in a household a mutes, chow time.

Gabriel   Good breakfasts?

Doans   Sure, man. They were some a the best meals I ever had in my life. Bacon an' eggs. Toast an' honey. Milk, which was like cream. Uncle Abe let us have coffee if we wanted it. Dad never let us have coffee until we were seniors in high school. Everything was from the farm. The bacon was just cured. The eggs were fresh that day. The milk was fresh, maybe still warm. Water was taken from the well, ice cold. Very simple stuff. But like nothin' you're gonna taste these days. Aunt Pearl an' Aunt Minnie—especially Aunt Pearl—they were some great cooks, man. . . *The wooden table comes to mind. They ate at the kitchen table, never the dining room table, except Sundays. The small pine table had one leg shorter than the rest. The short end was on Junior's side and he tried at every meal to put his weight on the table so Uncle Abe*

wouldn't notice the defect and be reminded of his own short leg. . .
Uncle Abe'd check on us every once in a while, just like my dad,
man. What is it about old dudes that makes 'em like to stand an'
watch young dudes work? . . . It wasn't so bad. It was a chance to
get away from Prospect Avenue. After dinner we were free to do
what we wanted. We played in the barn, or went down to the
creek. Sometimes we'd go out to the apple orchard. Junior was in
charge, naturally. No monkeyin' around with him in charge. He
loved that sorta thing. He got to order us around an' practice for
when he got to be a real soldier. One night we had chicken. We
were outside, man, just hangin' around, an' Aunt Minnie just
leaned over an' picked up the closest chicken by the neck, laid it
on the choppin' block, an' whack—off goes the head. She shuffled
back inside the house an' told us she wanted it plucked in fifteen
minutes. . . They had regular crops like wheat, corn, whatever. But
then they had the garden, which was Aunt Minnie's garden. Big
garden. Maybe it was 'cause I was a kid, but it seemed like some
labyrinth devised to consume little children an' spit 'em out the
other end half mutated into pupae-moths able neither to crawl or
fly. It was a real neat, orderly garden. Rows a vegetables an' that
was it. Okay, maybe a rose bush in the corner an' sweet peas
clingin' to the. . . was that thing fenced in? I can't remember. . .
Gabriel   I only met her once. Abby and me came down on my
bike one Sunday afternoon. She seemed real mean.
Doans   Mean? Naw, she wasn't mean. She was just an old
maid livin' with her brother an' sister. How'd you expect her to
be? Life passed her by. That ain't meanness. That's just takin' off
your happy face. . . Everybody loved Aunt Pearl, that's for sure.
God bless her. She went off to the convent, like a lot a girls in
those days. The story goes, she had some sorta breakdown. She
got too intense, wanted to do God's will too much. She couldn't
handle her own imperfections. So, they shipped her home.
Gabriel   Jesus—*he says, shaking his head.*
Doans   She laid around for a long time, with what we'd now
diagnosis as bein' majorly clinically depressed. She just couldn't
cope with the reality, man, that she'd failed God. The poor girl.

Mom says she was really beautiful when she was young. Before she got the humped back an' those crippled hands. *Her hands, all burl wood and bone sheathed with pulled skin. He would watch her hands, at the table, the askew angles and bulbous joints, barely moving to their task, reduced to simple grasping. He would look at her hands and they were so far removed from his own youthful omnipotence—he found them quaint and unreal.* Aunt Minnie resented Aunt Pearl. Aunt Pearl was like fuckin' Snow White a the household. Aunt Minnie knew she couldn't win no popularity contest, an' maybe that just made her turn away from people even more. She was educated too, you know, an' Aunt Pearl wasn't. Yeah, she taught mentally retarded kids in Canton. She was a teacher for years. From what I've heard, she was a real good teacher.

Gabriel   Why'd she come back to the farm?

Doans   Why do you think? I mean, you got Aunt Pearl who, let's face it, wasn't exactly real useful with the chores no more, an' Uncle Abe, who had the bum leg an' all. That's what folks did in those days. It wasn't like this big moral dilemma. She went where she was needed, with her family. Only thing was, at home, with them two, all her schoolin' meant like diddly. There she was stuck in that family slot. Man, you go home an' you step right back into those roles. It don't matter how old you are, how much education you got yourself; an' don't think she didn't know it!

Gabriel   What happened to your uncle's leg?

Doans   He hurt it. I don't know how. But he kept it hidden from his folks—they never knew about it.

Gabriel   What do you mean they never knew about it?— *incredulous.*

Doans   I mean they didn't fuckin' know about it. They knew about one leg bein' shorter than the other one. But they didn't know about his sores. He had these runnin' sores on his leg, man, that never got better, just like our dad. The bacteria stayed there all those years. Aunt Pearl an' Aunt Minnie changed the dressings on the wounds I think like every night. ... You know how he got it fixed? My Aunt Sophie's husband—Doctor Mint. He caught wind of it an' got his ass in the hospital. They shot 'em up with penicillin. Doctor Mint arranged it so he could stay in the hospital a couple extra days an' see the whole World Series.

Gabriel When we were there, he sat in the parlor most of the afternoon. He fell asleep in his chair. The Bible opened next to him on the arm.

Doans He was worn out, man. He was the last one to work that farm. The last one. Everybody else went off an' joined the modern world. He stayed back, frozen in the madness a standin' still.

Gabriel Think he ever stepped outside of Ohio?

Doans Probably.

Gabriel *Figuring it out in his head*—He would have been the right age for The War.

Doans Yeah, I don't know when he fucked his leg up, man. The War was in like 1915, 1916, right? Dad was born around. . . I think like 1926. Uncle Abe was the age a like dad's dad; let's say 25 years older. . .

Gabriel He would have been about 16.

Doans Yeah, so he would a missed it.

Gabriel But if he was born a few years before, it would have put him right there.

Doans But we don't know when he fucked his leg up. Man—I think he fucked it up real early, like in high school—*rubbing his chin, staring into his toes long and bony and brown like his sandals.* Yeah—I don't think he would a gone to war. Plus, he was a farmer, man. They were lettin' some farm boys stay home. They even did that in World War II.

Gabriel He saw Lindbergh—*he says with big awe, and big eyes*—and he made it to see the moon walk.

Doans Man, like he was there for the *Wright Brothers*. Like, they was still roundin' up the last Indians right around when he was born. Uncle Abe an' my grandpa—they had a brother. I don't know his name.

Gabriel You know anything about 'em?

Doans Yeah, I know somethin' about 'em. I know he was a

thief.

Gabriel   *Turning out his lip*—Really?

Doans   Yeah, as the story goes, grandpa got 'em a job up in Akron at this grocer's wholesaler. He got 'em a job collectin' money. I think like the money the individual grocers owed the company. Yeah, well, he was dippin' into the till. They caught 'em once. Don't know if my grandpa caught 'em, or if somebody else caught 'em. Anyhow, grandpa gave 'em another chance. The dude did it *again*. So grandpa wrote 'em off. I think he got married. I think he had kids, but nobody mentioned 'em. He fell off the family map. Guess grandpa wouldn't even speak to 'em at Christmas or funerals.

Gabriel   Can't blame 'em. His butt was on the line.

Doans   Hell no, you can't blame 'em. He got two shots at a job most guys would a died for, an' he turned right around an' laughed 'em away. I've seen pictures of 'em. He looked like a real slickster. . . An' then on my mom's side, you had Aunt Lois, the flapper.

Gabriel   The flapper?

Doans   Yeah, the flapper with the rumble seat. My mom said that alone made her a real slut. But mom seemed to like her. She talks about ridin' in that rumble seat every Christmas an' Thanksgiving an' sometimes Easter.

Gabriel   Scandals are okay to ride, but not to be.

Doans   She probably would a fit right in with us. She'd a been the entertainment after all the bottles were smashed.

Gabriel   She was probably too smart.

Doans   Yeah, you're probably right. That's a real hazard for women sometimes—especially in days of yore. Mom never talks too highly a women who don't toe the line; but every time she tells the rumble seat story she gets real giddy.

Gabriel   Your poor dad.

Doans   *He leans back, cocking his head*—My poor dad?

Gabriel   As much as he loved your mom, he had to have known where that kind of stuff came from.

Doans   You mean her wantin' to live some other life?

Gabriel   He's a pretty shrewd dude.

Doans   I do feel sorry for my dad. But he had a life, man.

Gabriel   Your mom had a life.

Doans   She did?

Gabriel   *Shrugging*—you'd know more than me.

Doans   Gabe, man, my dad was a king. A real-live king in modern times. He married his beautiful princess, an' quietly put her in a cage. You dig?

Gabriel   He didn't do anything the average guy didn't do.

Doans   Well, yeah, he sorta did, man. He had us, *an'* he was in a wheel chair. Hey—all I'm sayin' is my mom got left off a every bus leavin' the station to a place called Happiness. . . They had this deal, man.

Gabriel   Deal?

Doans   Sure.

Gabriel   What deal?

Doans   The deal. . . Ready? . : . Okay. . . The deal is this: I'm in this here chair, see. This chair ain't just a chair—it's a castration machine. It done lopped off my main piece a manhood, see? I can't walk. I can't dance. I can't fetch a clean nipple from the middle drawer fo' that cryin' babe. The deal is, I'll treat you like gold. You're my Juliet, my Grace Kelly, my *It Girl*. It wasn't supposed to be this way. Things were hummin' along real nice before polio. The deal is, I'll be your yes-man, yo' slave on earth, your protector. I'm still king. I'm still in charge. But my kingship is the front man for this mirage land band—how we's gonna fool 'em all into thinkin' I got the biggest, baddest balls this side a General George S. Patton. An' all *you* gotta do is not leave me. You pump out the chill'un, an' I'll supply the discipline. You tell me who's rockin' the boat, an' they'll walk the plank. Allow me this, woman, this usage a your pretty, precious life vessel—don't *leave me*—an' everything else is yours. . . Trouble was, man, like what the fuck else *was* there? What's left when you got kids in every corner, an' an old man whose main mood is bein' two heartbeats away from stranglin' the dog? . . . Now, did the dude renege? Was it intentional? . . .

Gabriel　How do you mean?

Doans　I mean, did he make the deal knowin' how each cryin' mouth to feed would push her farther into that birdcage? Knowin' she wasn't a deal-breaker—did he use her gold heart to his advantage? I don't think it *was* intentional. The same way the deal wasn't no deal with words or paper—it was a deal a what wasn't said—a deal a wiped tears. I think my dad probably didn't think that far ahead. Sure, the kids were his codpiece, but I don't think he meant for us to take away her happiness. We *did*. But that was just some tragic icing on this here triple-decker tragedy cake.

Mercy Killing

They sit now, the four of them beneath the heavy collard greens canopy of the sycamore. Though Hector has all those lines in the water, his eyes are on the bobber. It vibrates against the incoming ripples of the steady river flowing, and the stouter ripples of the occasional boat. He is paired with Doans, their feet playing at the edge of the water. A distance away, Emanuel and Gabriel sit on a log like two old timer's on a bench.

Emanuel　Want another beer?—*tossing back his head.*

Gabriel　Thanks—don't mind if I do—*he says, as though waiting to be asked. He goes to the cooler on springy bow legs, and doesn't bend over but goes down in a squat to look inside.*

Emanuel　Nobody tellin' you not to.

Gabriel　Not for another whole day. *He pulls out a bottle, reading the label keenly.* You guys really get serious about beer. Jesus Christ. Made in Kalamazoo, whoop-dee-doo. . .

Emanuel　Gotta make each one count, since I'm only allowed a six-pack a week.

Gabriel　Says who?—*he cracks the beer and goes back and sits down.*

Emanuel　Says my age.

Gabriel   Yeah, I know what you mean. You thinking about 'em now?

Emanuel   Who?

Gabriel   The family. You look like you're thinking about something.

Emanuel   Yeah, well, I guess I am. I'll tell you what. You never know what havin' a kid's like till you have one. Nobody can explain it to you. I didn't think I was gonna have any kids. It was just somethin' I never thought about doin'. Then Rahe comes along an' boom—wow. Just wow.

Gabriel   That's beautiful, man.

Emanuel   They'll keep you goin' when you're on empty.

Gabriel   Yup—*then pointing suddenly to the bobber bobbing*—Hey, is that a bite?

Emanuel   I think it's nothin'.

Gabriel   Yeah, okay. Just checking.

Emanuel   Might be a little one. I'll check it in a minute.

Gabriel   I heard you had a big-ass garden.

Emanuel   I'm off work, you know.

Gabriel   I heard that too. Man—what I'd give for a summer off. You doing all right?

Emanuel   Aw, we're doin' fine. I don't *wanna* work.

Gabriel   I hear you, all the way to my Friday four o'clock migraine.

Emanuel   You get 'em too?

Gabriel   Aw, do I get headaches. . . *He acts crazy with his lit-up face all red and veiny.*

Emanuel   Mine's like an ice pick right here above my right eye. It's always in the same place. Like it's got a root to it. Like some big fuckin' dandelion root that grows back once a month.

Gabriel   Mine comes on every Friday, like clockwork, right before I head home.

Emanuel   You an' my dad. He always got 'em on Fridays too. Yeah, well, take the summer off, man, an' guess what?

Gabriel   What?

Emanuel   No more headaches.

Gabriel   Don't tell me that—I just might join you.

Emanuel   *He eyes a praying mantis perched on some fluffed brown leaves, and brings it up on the back of his hand to look at it. It's a small one, more green than brown, and it seems unafraid and doesn't move. He lifts his hand to show Gabriel, who only makes a wincing face. He waves his hand several times, but the thing won't take off. He remembers how the females eat the heads off the males after mating; in his youth, when he heard it, he only had a vague idea what mating was, and it was only the gruesome prospect of being eaten alive that offended him. The idea had a whole different layer of meaning and irony and bitterness to it now. . . . He lets the mantis go back where he found it, on the same morning-hair fluff of leaves.* Yeah, so I bring Rahe out, you know. I put her on this blanket underneath the tree while I work in the garden.

Gabriel   Doesn't she crawl away?

Emanuel   Sometimes. I'm always over there settin' her back on. It's a big blanket, an' there's only grass around. But we got a lot a ticks out there. The cats are always bringin' 'em in the house.

Gabriel   *He shakes his head and rubs his arms in a shiver—*I hate those things.

Emanuel   I bring toys out for her. I just get waterin' again, or maybe pushin' the beans through the strings, or trimmin' the grass, an' she crawls off an' I have to set her back on again—but it's no different than yankin' a weed or turnin' on the hose or anything else that you don't think about doin'. . . . I'm out there, just about naked, the sun blarin' down on me; I spend half the time waterin'. It's been real dry this year. The groundhogs are bad.

Gabriel   Yeah? What do you do to get rid of 'em?

Emanuel   They don't like goin' in live traps. It's funny but raccoons, who you'd think were real smart, will walk right in. But groundhogs, who live in holes, they're real wary. But lately I've been catchin' a few. The other day I came home an' nobody else was around. I wanted to head right into the house, but I saw the old neighbor on his John Deere lawn mower comin' over. I just wasn't in the mood for talk. Well, we talked, an' pretty quick he gets to the point. He told me he was over poppin' smoke bombs into the groundhog holes an' noticed I had one in the trap. I thought he meant the one from the other day, but he meant today—there was one in there right now. He's an old pig farmer, this guy. Real tall, can barely walk. He's got like five acres between his house an' mine an' he spends half his time mowin'. Anyhow, so he sorta grins an' asks me what I do with 'em once I catch 'em. I told 'em I'd kill 'em, but I didn't have a gun. I said I take 'em out north a town an' let 'em go. He didn't seem to like that answer too much an' says you really should kill 'em, you know. I said yeah, I know. I told 'em about my dad an' how he used to drown the squirrels he caught.

Gabriel   Your dad—the squirrel killer?

Emanuel   Yeah, man. They used to get into the barn an' gnaw on his tarps. Used to piss 'em off somethin' royal. He'd shoot 'em with his pellet gun too, but usually he'd just catch 'em an' drown 'em in the rain barrel. . . Yeah, so the old pig farmer said he had a spear I could use, if I wanted.

Gabriel   A spear?

Emanuel   Like some rod that he ground down on his grinder. I told 'em I'd think about it. He left an' I stood there thinkin' it over, an' finally I thought hey—I got a big plastic trash can. I can drown the fucker in that.

Gabriel   Good thinking.

Emanuel   So I fill up the trash can an' bring the cage with the groundhog over. The handle was broke, so I lifted it with this pitch fork. That damn thing stunk to high heaven. I dumped the cage in, an' the damn thing was like a foot too long. The groundhog climbed up to the top, clingin' for dear life.

Gabriel   *Snickering*—What'd you do?

Emanuel   I didn't know what to do—*lifting his hands and eyebrows both*. I got the plastic lid an' put it on the cage. I thought about leavin' 'em there overnight, you know, an' try an' forget about it till mornin'. But I knew I'd just be thinkin' about 'em all night. I got the hose an' tried sprayin' 'em down into the water, but he just sat there an' closed his eyes an' took it. A little water in the face don't mean shit when you're facin' drownin'. . . I walked over an' flagged the old pig farmer down an' told 'em I wanted to use his spear. He was real happy about that, puttered over to his house, an' came back with this pretty scrawny rod not much thicker than a piece a wire. I had my doubts right off the bat, but I figured this guy killed a lot a things in his time, so I let 'em have at it. I asked 'em if he wanted me to dump 'em outta the trash can, but he said naw, an' so he starts pokin' the groundhog. I'm like lookin' over my shoulder thinkin' some animal rights nut is gonna jump outta the brush an' nab us. Fuck—the rod just bent. So I told 'em I had a plant hanger right around the corner by the daffodils an' he said great, he could grind a real sharp point on it. He left an' came back, this time with a .22 across his lap. He got up an' fuck if he didn't swing that thing across me—I'm like, hey, man, watch it with the gun, ol' timer. He gave me the rod, meanin' this time I was gonna do the dirty work. . . Gabe—*he winces without humor in either look or tone*—it took ten minutes to kill that thing. I went right through 'em three times—all the way through the trash can too—before he hunched over an' his nose went down into the water an' we knew he was dead.

Gabriel   Least you got 'em.

Emanuel   Yeah—*he pauses, makes a frown, thinking, then rubs his moist temple with his fingers.* I never killed anything before, except some bugs an' maybe fish. An' sure as hell not by drivin' a spear into it. I can't say I felt a thrill, but after the old guy left I sat there an' I felt somethin'. I felt like I did somethin' for my family—my kids—that women can't do. I mean, those groundhogs got sharp claws an' sharp teeth, an' their holes're right there next to where Rahe was crawlin'. There's no question about what had to be done. This ain't no fairy tale, man. It's about protectin' my kids. Those things carry rabies an' fleas an' ticks an' who the hell knows what else. They dig holes big enough to break a leg in. I had to kill that thing. . . I felt like a Neanderthal, or just a plain old guy on the frontier doin' what he has to do. I felt like I really did somethin', man, you know? I felt like my woman, in the old days, would a baked me a pie for it.

Gabriel   Those were the days.
Emanuel   'Course there's no way I told Mazz about it. I wanted to leave one good deed untarnished, without havin' her turn it into some crime.
Gabriel   Real smart. Yeah, better to keep it to yourself. It's habit, anyway, the way they flip those things on their head.

Fear The Jazz Musician

Doans   **Man, I remember you were always** gettin' into fights. Mom an' dad thought you were gonna end up in prison.
Hector   People were always pickin' fights with me, man.
Doans   What—like you walk around with a sign on your back—come fuck with me, 'cause I fucked your mama? You have your number on the bathroom wall: Lookin' for an ass-whoopin', give me a call?
Hector   I might as well have. Man, I was husky. Maybe a little mouthy. Dudes for some reason liked to egg me on. I guess they thought I wouldn't call 'em on their shit. A lot of 'em were one or two years older. They didn't think I could kick their ass. They'd get mouthy. I never picked a fight with any of 'em. They always started it, but I always finished it.
Doans   Man, like I was too small to fight. I learned early on I wasn't gonna be fightin' my way outta trouble. No, sir. Right here, man—*thumb to his temple, right between the eyes.* This is all I ever had. My wits. The only thing that was gonna keep my lunch money in my pocket an' my coat on my back. I got tossed around a few times, but never actually got beat up. I steered clear a that kind a trouble. Worst I ever did was sneak outta the house after hours. All my horseplay was with chicks.
Hector   Didn't they have to come back early from somebody's house one time 'cause you weren't in by curfew?
Doans   Oh, man, that time. Yeah—'cause Junior squealed on

me.

Hector   That's a real shock.

Doans   Yeah—I was over at this chick's house. Mom an' dad were like at the Baker's playin' euchre or pinochle. I was out past curfew—that was the big deal. Curfew was somethin' like 11:00 o'clock, or some insane time like that. That's when dad made the fateful call.

Hector   He talk to Junior?

Doans   Who do you think? As Junior tells it, he didn't blab it out right away. Dad asked 'em if everything was okay an' Junior— who could a said everything's just fine, pops—gives 'em the old silent treatment. A course dad, who knew how to read them tea leaves on gaps a silence like nobody else, knew somethin' was up. That's when Junior spilled his guts. Man, like he could a covered for me. He could a said aw everything's fine, daddy-o, you an' ma have a real good time. Drink your martinis. Eat your chicken wings. Don't worry about nothin'. But no. That ain't Junior's style. He lives for moments like that. Everything's by the book, whether it ruins your parent's once a month night out or not. Man, like I was right smack dab in the middle a some Salvador Dali teenage love-puzzle; you think I had my eye on the second hand? They left in like ten minutes. . . Then there was the time I snuck outta the house an' went over to this other chick's house.

Hector   Uh-oh.

Doans   Man, like I'm over there at some ridiculous hour a the night—maybe three or somethin'; an in walks the old man.

Hector   Whose old man?

Doans   Her old man.

Hector   *Shit.* Where were you?

Doans   Standin' with my drawers dropped an' my hand only halfway outta the cookie jar, if you know what I mean.

Hector   At least you weren't in bed.

Doans   Naw, man, I jumped out like the minute I heard Papa Bear come rollin' down the steps. I had my skivvies only half-way on; the room smelled like a whorehouse. I thought he was gonna shoot me. I did, man. He had guns—she told me. He was some kind a redneck.

Hector   What'd you do?

Doans   I tried to get past 'em, but there wasn't no way. He called dad. When dad came an' got me, man—*like it happened yesterday, those lion claws to the heart still hurt*—I knew he wasn't gonna trust me no more. I was like way over on the other side—*his hand wanders out and does somersaults.* There's no second chances way over yonder, man. He didn't say too much on the way home. He looked like I just murdered somebody. That was one long drive home, let me tell you, even though it was only like ten minutes.

Hector   I know that look, man. You remember when mom found the pot in Jessie's dresser?

Doans   Just through legend an' hearsay.

Hector   You wanna talk about lettin' the air outta somebody's tire.

Doans   Mom found like what—a couple joints in his dresser? Was she snoopin' around?

Hector   Supposedly, the way she told it, she was puttin' his laundry away, which hey—let's face it—she probably was. An' even if she was snoopin', you could hardly blame her. That was some heavy shit. Findin' *pot* in your son's dresser in—I think it was 1973. They weren't prepared for that, man.

Doans   Noooooooo. . . not the steak knife through the heart!— *he dramatizes.*

Hector   Dad sat me down an' asked me if I knew, an' I told 'em yeah, I knew. Then he asked me how long he'd been doin' it an' I said maybe a few weeks, which from what I saw of it was true. Finally, he asked me if I was doin' it.

Doans   Were you, man?

Hector   Fuck no. I was only a freshman. I smoked pot in high school maybe three or four times—all later on in my senior year. I didn't do that shit.

Doans   That probably killed 'em!

Hector   I really felt sorry for 'em. Nothin' could prepare somebody like dad for our generation an' somebody like Jessie. It was like stickin' your middle finger in his face.

Doans   Yeah—*he thinks back, remembering his own icebreaking moments with a combination of squeamishness and bravado—*pot, man. A real sweat spray from the Devil's brow.

Hector   Well fuck—Uncle Abe had his glass a wine every night. What's the difference?

Doans   What's the difference? There is no difference, man. Well, okay, there is a difference. You wanna know what the difference is? . . . For Uncle Abe, that glass a wine was like this itty-bitty pinkie a mellow relaxation at the end a bustin' his balls from sunrise to sunset. He figured he earned it. He earned it an' he needed it. Jessie puffin' joints down in the basement after school—that's somethin' else. That's indulgence, man. That's pure pleasure bath without no need for a bath at all.

Hector   So? Who said that was a crime?

Doans   Hey, man, I'm just tellin' you.

Hector   So it's a matter a degrees.

Doans   A course it's a matter a degrees. Man, like Uncle Able wasn't no complete prude—you dig? Mostly, he was. But underneath he was pretty much like you an' me. But those dudes still subscribed to the all things in moderation manual to health an' prosperity.

Hector   What if Uncle Abe had *two* glasses a wine after dinner, man; is that moderation?

Doans   I think it's like, if it looks like indulgence an' smells like indulgence, then it's probably indulgence.

Hector   Then it's all subjective.

Doans   Man—*chuckling with charmed amusement*—like, I don't know.

Hector   *Oh, how he wants to pursue. But still sober, his wits tell him to drop it. The image of Uncle Abe pinching a small glass of wine between his fat, weatherd fingers, sitting back in the rocking chair, his wooden crutches lying beside him on the floor, sunshine bringing out the brilliant wood grain on all the furniture and molding and floor—it stirs in him a longing for things he never had and would never fully understand.*

Doans   Sissy took a lot a heat—*he says, nodding his head.* An'
Abby.
Hector   I know Abby did—the first one to live with a guy,
unmarried—but I thought Sissy was pretty clean-cut.
Doans   She put on a better show for mom an' dad. Abby just
hung it out there—here it is—take it or leave it. But you gotta
remember—Abby's breakaway happened in the 70's. Sissy was
doin' her thing like ten years earlier. She was the real icebreaker.
Hector   But she didn't do anything.
Doans   She did lots, man. She kept it away from the folks—
she's the oldest. She had to keep this image, you know? But they
could see the shape a things by what she didn't do, or by implica-
tion. She *was* Mary Tyler Moore, man, an' that's cool to watch on
TV, but when it's your eldest daughter, an' you ain't a seen
nothin' like this come down the pike before. . . well, it rattles some
a them bones. She made way for pot-smokin', streakin', nude
chicks in the hall, middle fingers at the prez, an' hey—whatever
else I might a forgot to mention. Straight-A Sissy, just by livin' on
her own, goin' to happy hour with the gang down at the tire
factory, gettin' married an'—what's this?—a year later *divorcin'*
that creep. Shit that we might take a snooze over really got the old
folks scratchin' their heads. . . Little did they know what was
comin' around the bend.
Hector   The worst was Abby. . . God damn it. . . I can still
remember her wedding day.
Doans   Yeah? I don't think I made it.
Hector   You remember. They got married at a non-Catholic
church.
Doans   *He looks up to the sky, turning his head as if following
something.* Oh yeah. I remember hearin' about it.
Hector   Why'd they have to be that way?—*real pain—he
wheezes through his teeth.*
Doans   They couldn't help it, I guess.
Hector   They couldn't help it? Fuck, it was her *wedding* day. . .
Doans   You can't cherry pick frowns when it comes to sin,
man.

Hector   But it was *her* wedding day. Not theirs. *His hands, side-by-side, go up*—They had theirs over here—*hands move*—and now it's Abby's turn—she has her wedding over there—*they shift over to the other side.* Why would you wanna ruin somebody's wedding day? Your daughter's fuckin' wedding day?

Doans   I think, man, you sorta just said it. It wasn't their *son's* wedding day. It was their daughter's wedding day.

Hector   An' that's why they weren't freaked out about you gettin' married in the park?

Doans   Oh, man—I was a lost cause. You serious? You're comparin' Abby tyin' the knot the first time in a Protestant church to me an' Yoko passin' love beads in Goodyear Park? Like, it ain't even fair. No comparison. *He laughs heartily.* I was a hippie—or did you forget?

Hector   No, I didn't forget.

Doans   I was a dude—*he begins counting on fingers, starting with the thumb.* I was a hippie, they already knew I smoked pot an' lived with chicks. . . I was an *artist.* That ranks right up there with jazz musicians, from what they heard down at the Brown Derby. An' I'd been causin' dad grief from the first peep in the back a the station wagon. Like, they expected me to do whatever it was I was doin'.

Hector   It was mostly mom. Dad was upset 'cause mom was.

Doans   Sure, man.

Hector   He could a said somethin'.

Doans   Like what?

Hector   Like, back off, woman. This is our daughter. Let her do what *she* wants to do.

Doans   Man, they didn't think that way. Don't you know who your mom an' dad are? Don't you got eyes? Haven't you been listenin'? It's not even in the realm a possibility that they would a said somethin' like that to her. You think the church would a said, like, it's okay, Abby, do your own thing?

Hector   No.

Doans   Well man, like they were just *voices* a the church. Father Whoever might as well a been standin' right there. An' brother, to them, the Almighty Himself might as well a been in on the discussion—He *was*. As real as that river at yo' feet. . . no ifs, ands, or buts about it. . .

A Thousand Ways To Carry The Weight

Emanuel **I probably carried 'em up** a thousand times.
Gabriel Yeah?
Emanuel He wasn't that heavy. Maybe a hundred an' fifty pounds. He would a only weighed, probably, a hundred thirty-five, but he had this gut, you know, from sittin'. Look at anybody with polio, or anybody in a wheel chair, an' they got this gut from sittin' all the time. How the hell you gonna work off a gut just sittin' all day—you know? Aaah—I don't think it bothered 'em too much.
Gabriel A thousand times on your back, and you never dropped 'em?
Emanuel I almost did.
Gabriel Almost? Really?
Emanuel A few times.
Gabriel What'd you do?
Emanuel You mean what'd I do when I almost dropped 'em?
Gabriel Did you shout for help?
Emanuel The worst time was one night when I was drunk.
Gabriel You carried him up when you were drunk?
Emanuel Well, who else was gonna do it?
Gabriel How about Levon?
Emanuel He carried 'em up sometimes. But Levon was usually in bed by the time I came home; my mom an' dad always stayed up for Johnny Carson, an' then sometimes he'd just wait for me. I was drunk every Friday an' Saturday for the last half a high school.
Gabriel What held you back for the first half?

Emanuel   A girl. An' then the last year Levon was gone, an' I
was the only one. . . Some nights he'd go up by himself. But he
was windin' down as far as the stairs went. Mostly, I took 'em up.
Gabriel   Did he know you were drunk?
Emanuel   You know, I've thought about that a lot. I can't
imagine he'd a let me take 'em up if he knew I was drunk. But
how the fuck couldn't he a smelled it on me? . . . Here's what I
think. I think he might a smelled it on me, but maybe he thought I
had only a beer or two. 'Cause he always told us—even though he
was hardcore anti-alcohol himself—he wasn't totally unreason-
able—to just have one beer when we were out at some party. He
always lumped me into the squeaky clean category with Levon.
For those first two years I was. I had a girl. I didn't do any
partyin'. When we broke up, I went hog wild. There was nothin'
holdin' me back. . . So no, I don't think he knew how I could
barely stand up sometimes. I'm tellin' you, Gabe, it's hard enough
climbin' stairs when you got a railin' to grab; but from the top a
the stairs to his bedroom—it was murder.
Gabriel   Is that where you nearly dumped 'em?
Emanuel   *He slowly shakes his head*—Halfway up the stairs one
night, I just lost my balance. We almost went tumblin' backward,
which would a killed 'em, Gabe, seriously.
Gabriel   No kidding. . . What did you do?
Emanuel   I leaned forward—fast—to get the weight on my legs. I
knew if I had 'em on my legs, I'd have a chance. But I was all the
way down. His whole weight was on me.
Gabriel   You should have yelled for Levon.
Emanuel   He was off at college. This was my senior year. *His*
eyes pop out—I was really drunk. I didn't know if I could do it. He
didn't say a peep—he just held on, stranglin' my neck.
Gabriel   But you made it!—*his own eyes big.*
Emanuel   I did. I just got up, somehow, an' climbed those stairs.
At the top, I let 'em down real easy, as easy as I could. He rested,
an' then I fetched his crutches. He had this terror in his eyes, an'
the worst kind a disappointment in me. I think that night he knew.
He didn't say a word about it, but I think he knew.

Gabriel   It kills you, those looks they give you.

Emanuel   I was already fadin', but I sorta gave up after that night. I just wanted.to get the hell outta school an' do somethin'.

Gabriel   Yeah—then the real fun starts: *work*.

Emanuel   ·I bypassed work in favor of an extended childhood.

Gabriel   College?

Emanuel   But a course.

Gabriel   Me—I hit the Army.

Emanuel   Be all you can be, man.

Gabriel   I figured if I joined the Army, they'd feed me and give me a place to sleep at least.

Emanuel   Brilliant.

Gabriel   Wasn't it?

Emanuel   Then what?

Gabriel   After the Army? Then I worked my butt off till I was almost thirty.

Emanuel   Then what?

Gabriel   Then I got lucky. Your sister and I got married.

Emanuel   Then what?

Gabriel   *Laughing*—And then I became night manager of the warehouse of crap in my garage.

Emanuel   You too?

Gabriel   I have boxes and boxes—half of which have never been opened. One whole side of my garage filled with crap. Abby—she comes home with this stuff and I'm like, where do you think we're gonna put those things?

Emanuel   Let me guess—everything was on sale.

Gabriel   Bingo. It's like being on sale puts them under a spell or something. Like they turn into zombies and have to buy this shit— even though a regular sale isn't really a sale at all because they start off these days with a sucker price no human being in his right mind is gonna buy it for, and so like 40% off doesn't mean diddly when you get right down to it. Abby's real smart, but when it comes to shopping she turns into this real dumb little kid in a candy store who can't say no.

Emanuel   They're well trained.

Gabriel   Yeah, I guess so.

Emanuel   I used to think it was generational, which part of it is.
But Sissy's that way too, an' she's on the other side a fifty.

Gabriel   Sissy?—*he pushes up the right side of his face, then
shakes his head looking into the water.*

Emanuel   She's the oldest. You'd think she'd know. But man,
she's always buyin' shit for people. It's real nice of her. She's
always bought stuff for the nieces an' nephews an' my mom an'
dad. But she's always on the edge money-wise. I don't think she
has anything saved for retirement, except maybe what she's gonna
get from workin' in the factory all those years.

Gabriel   An' they'll probably zap that two weeks before she
retires.

Emanuel   Who knows? You can't count on that anymore. It's
scary. She's pushin' sixty. We're not talkin' about somebody even
like me who's got twenty-five more years to save. Retirement's in
her sights. I look at my mom an' dad an' how much they saved all
those years, you know, bein' frugal as shit, an' it ain't like they're
livin' it up or anything. I don't know what Sissy's gonna do, Gabe.

Gabriel   Maybe she can buddy up with one of you guys.

Emanuel   She'll probably have to.

Gabriel   Or maybe she won't retire and she'll keep whirling on
that hamster wheel till she keels over from the stress and strain.

Emanuel   Yeah—who knows? . . . Fuck—my wife—half the shit
she buys is for Rahe. Toys? You wanna see toys? We got a wall a
toys. I'm not kiddin'. We got a whole wall with shelves an' it's
full a toys. Half the shit she doesn't even remember she has, an'
the other half she can't reach. An' another half she doesn't wanna
play with anymore. An' that leaves like only ten-percent that she
messes with on any sorta regular basis. An' then like eighty-
percent a the shit has about a million pieces to 'em. How the
hell're you supposed to keep all the pieces together?—an' if you
don't, then what's the point a havin' 'em? Plus, everything needs
batteries 'cause the toy pimps are in cahoots with the battery
pimps, an' so like everything needs batteries 'cause you sure
couldn't expect a kid to just move a doll around on her own an'

pretend it flies or poops or sings or whatever. Christmas morning's a fuckin' nightmare. Who the fuck came up with tyin' everything down with those twisties, man? I'd like to kill 'em.

Gabriel   Probably the twistie pimp wining and dining the Chinese plastics pimp.

Emanuel   I remember my grandma tellin' me once how they didn't have money for her to have a doll. I don't think she was the only kid on the block in her shoes. She told me they used to cut figures outta leaves an' use 'em. They'd dry up an' curl up, an' by the end a the day they'd just blow away. The next day, if they wanted to play some more, they'd have to cut more leaves. . . Gabe—*he looks over an' shakes his head*—they fuckin' get a toy every time they walk through a set a golden arches. There's no value in shit anymore—you know? Nothin's special outside a the moment they get it. Pressed, colored oil—you said it, man. Plastic—not love—that's what makes the world go round.

Pound For Pound

They are up, standing with toes penetrating the old mud shores made new again by the annual floods. The sun whips them fiercely. The clouds, few that there are overhead, are reminders of scale to their colossal words inside their invisible fish tank.

Hector   We're livin' in a different world now. Don't you think people's attitudes are fundamentally different?

Doans   No. I think people are fundamentally the same as they've always been.

Hector   Explain Waco, then.

Doans   What do you mean, explain Waco? Like, what do you want me to say about it?

Hector   Explain how somethin' like that happens today, when it didn't happen twenty or thirty years ago.

Doans   It did happen twenty or thirty years ago. They's called criminals.

Hector   Not on that scale. Not with the total disregard for innocent lives.

Doans   Man, people've always had disregard for human life. Look no farther than the slave trade, or the Indian round-up.

Hector   Post Manifest Destiny.

Doans   Post Manifest Destiny? Okay. How about the KKK, the tobacco industry, McCarthyism, Vietnam., J. Edgar Hoover, Nike sweat shops, the Moral Majority, to say nothin' about those millions dyin' a AIDS every year in Africa that we could prevent overnight if anybody in Washington really cared. I'm just gettin' started.

Hector   The average, dude, Doans. I'm just sayin' the average dude today, the *average* dude, cares less about his next-door-neighbor than he did twenty or thirty years ago.

Doans   Mmm. . . well, okay, I just might buy that.

Hector   I don't have the answer. But my question is, what's different? What's fundamentally different about the way things are today that permits—possibly encourages—things like Waco, the Unabomber, Columbine, the Anthrax shit, an' 9/11 itself?

Doans   Don't get lumpy, man. All those things don't lump together.

Hector   No, man, they pretty much do. They're events. Recent events that wouldn't have occurred twenty or thirty years ago.

Doans   Well, for one, the Unabomber's right, man.

Hector   The Unabomber's right?—*the sun and the beer and the continual dialogue has loosened the tie around his better judgment; he mocks his brother with a you're-fucked-up face.*

Doans   That's right. You ever read his manifesto?

Hector   No, I haven't.

Doans   Don't get smug, man. We're just havin' a conversation. You're askin' some serious questions here. You're makin' some bold statements. I'm tryin' to give you my own humble opinion, you dig?—*he tosses out a smile, genuine, as an olive branch of diffusion.*

Hector   I'm fine, man.

Doans   You're fine? Well, good. I'm fine too. We're all fine.

Hector   So tell me; what does the Unabomber's manifesto have to say?—*taking a drag from his cigarette, hard and quick.*

Doans   It says that technology has gotten outta hand. That we're standin' in the fork in the road. This way leads to our subjugation at the hands a machines an' the privileged elite—an' that way, if we hurry, might lead us at least to survival as a species. It says that the so-called liberals who espouse to be against many a the so-called evils a society, are actually contribu-tors to the problem. They're hypocrites. This hypocrisy, when applied to the cataclysmic self-destruction industrial nations inflict upon their land an' their people, is pure evil. It must be stopped. Forget your so-called war on drugs. Forget your so-called war on terrorism. This is the war: the war to save the biosphere. The war to return human beings to some sensible means a dignity, an' avoid mass self-annihilation.

Hector   So he sends bombs to college professors.

Doans   How far you think he would a gotten with a letter to the editor, man? Yeah, so he sends some bombs. He drops some tea into the bay. He massacres ol' Golden Hair himself.

Hector   He's nuts. The guy, though I might agree with some a his ideas, is plain nuts.

Doans   Well, sure he's whacko. But any more whacko than the conservative right who puts blind, zealot's faith in the fairy tale a everything workin' out just fine all on its own? Look—in the face a not bein' listened to, desperate people do desperate things. They'll steal. They'll kill. You decide who's the Robin Hood an' who's the terrorist. What side a the fence you sittin' on, man? You in the grass, or in the dirt? You with the folks writin' them op-eds, or you with the folks bein' thrown into the klink for disorderly conduct? You with mother earth, or you with Wall Street?

Hector   Even so, an' I'm not disagreein' with what you're sayin', it doesn't justify the actions. . . You said yourself that 9/11 was no more than some radical Muslims takin' a shit on New York. How's that different than what the Unabomber did?

Doans   How's it different?—*with umbrage.*

Hector   Yeah, I'd like to know.

Doans   How's it different?—*nearly shouting.*

Hector   Why is it okay for the Unabomber to make his point with bombs, when he himself hasn't actually been attacked, but it's not okay for Muslims to use bombs against a country who killed 100,000 people in a war ten years ago for oil, a country who unconditionally supports Israel, no matter what *they* do? . . . Come on, Doans. Explain *that* one to me.

Doans   *On his toes, his body tensed and ready to spring forward*—You serious, man?

Hector   I just wanna know.

Doans   *But instead, he holds his anger, rocking side-to-side on his feet*—Why you so pro-Muslim all of a sudden, man?

Hector   I'm not pro-Muslim.

Doans   Like, you do know that the Muslim world wants to see Israel wiped off the face a planet Earth?

Hector   Can you blame 'em, Doans?

Doans   I sure as shit can.

Hector   I know they lost six million people in the death camps—

Doans   So you do admit *that*.

Hector   Sure. Why wouldn't I?

Doans   Why wouldn't you? 'Cause a lot a you don't.

Hector   A lot a who?

Doans   Forget it, man, it ain't worth it.

Hector   I'll say it again—I know they lost six million people in the death camps. That really sucks. I can't fathom that. Nobody can understand that. . . *He bumps his brother's arm, intentionally, gently, perhaps not a good thing to do.* . . But don't you think to compensate for that horror, by movin' one group a people out— outta *their* Holy Land too—an' movin' another group in. . . Don't you think that maybe, *maybe* wasn't such a good idea?

Doans   Where were they gonna go, man? Like, for hundreds a years they've been dispersed all over the world without a country. Why don't you look at it this way: Don't you think they deserve their own place, just like everybody else?

Hector So we play God?

Doans Somebody's got to.

Hector Why?

Doans Man—*laughing*—for an ex-history major, you act like you ain't read any sometimes. Somebody's always in charge. Don't ask *why*, it just is. An' it's up to the current empire in charge a this here dung heap to make some pretty harsh decisions that don't have no moral grounds—individually speakin'—to stand on. But they maybe got practical grounds.

Hector Or self-servin' grounds.

Doans Always—heck yeah.

Hector I think we gave 'em their land back outta guilt.

Doans Sure.

Hector Well. . .

Doans Well, so what? Look, man—this country—whether you wanna claim it or deny it—has a big Jewish component. It has a lot a Jewish people—you dig? Jewish folks are like woven into the fabric a this society as much as anybody. It ain't *they*; it's *us*. So yeah, *we* support Israel. 'Cause without our help, it goes bye-bye like tomorrow.

Hector But because of it, 9/11 happens.

Doans Those were terrorists, man. You dig what a terrorist is? You don't know what a terrorist does?

Hector I think I got an idea.

Doans Yeah, well good.

Hector That's what I'm sayin', Doans—*imploring with his hands.* Some things are too big to get involved in. We gotta know when to keep our hands outta the—*ouch!*—mousetrap.

Doans If you haven't noticed, the Muslim world ain't like the rest of us.

Hector They're not?—*thinking he had a rope that bound them, it suddenly slips through his fingers.*

Doans *He eyes his brother uncertainly, and grins cautiously. He snickers, looking away, then swings his head back. They stare at each other.*

Hector All right, Doans.

Doans   Uh-oh—*winking to the other two, who are oblivious*—
here it comes.
Hector   I'm all right. There's no argument. We're just havin' a
good discussion between brothers, that's all.
Doans   I dig, man. It's cool.
Hector   Okay. Let's take a look at Northern Ireland.
Doans   Sure, man. Let's do.
Hector   You know the deal there, right?
Doans   I have a rough idea where to put my hands around that
tickin' time bomb.
Hector   Well, we all know how that's been about the biggest
war zone in the so-called Western World for a long time.
Doans   It ain't been no Disneyland, that's fo' sure.
Hector   I mean, there's been nothin' but bombs, barbed wire,
an' a lot a cryin' mothers for a fuckin' long time.
Doans   An' Irish wakes. Don't forget the wakes, man.
Hector   I didn't wanna state the too obvious.
Doans   Groovy. I'm with you.
Hector   Ten years ago if you would a told me there'd be a real
chance for peace, I'd a said no way. Huh-uh—it's not gonna
happen. . . But look at what's happenin'. They're almost there.
The two sides, for the most part, have laid down their arms.
Doans   It ain't over till the good Mr. Adams an' the good Mr.
Paisley get naked an' sing Give Peace a Chance, man. In *bed*.
Hector   Sure. They're not there yet. But almost.
Doans   Close only counts in horseshoes an' hand grenades—
not in peace processes.
Hector   Doans—the point is, here we got an example of a no-
hope situation where now there's hope. The thing could blow up
tomorrow, sure, an' there's a lot a fuckers on both sides that want
it to blow up. But what I'm sayin' is—
Doans   Just what *are* you sayin', Jimmy?—
Hector   I'm sayin', okay, what did they do in Northern Ireland
that maybe we ain't doin' in the Middle East?
Doans   Uh. . . like maybe prayin' to the same God helps.
Hector   True. But it basically gets down to this—*he lays it*

out—world peace—in the palm of his hand. The people bein' shit
on—
Doans   Commonly known as terrorists.
Hector   They are. I agree. You murder innocent people in cold
blood, you're a fuckin' terrorist.
Doans   Whew!—*wiping his brow*—glad we agree on *that.*
Hector   The people—the oppressed people—who yes, are
tryin' to get their point across by violent means—guess what? The
fact that they *are* bein' oppressed is acknowledged. . . *His hands
open. . .* That's all it takes. Quit the stone-wallin'. Quit the denial.
Take a look in the mirror an' say yeah, we're takin' a great big ol'
dump on these poor folks over here. Maybe they don't like it.
Maybe—just *maybe*—that's why they're shootin' our children.
Maybe if we didn't do *that*, they wouldn't do *this.*
Doans   Bravo, man—*clapping in slow, loud claps.* You got a
real knack for squeezin' honey outta even the most stirred up
beehive. But like, they been goin' at it for hundreds an' hundreds a
years. Northern Ireland—man, that's just like a fight between
brothers. It's real messy. It's real ugly. But there's love underneath
all that camouflage. Look—*hammering cold reality in* his *hand*—
you can't give in to terrorists, man. It's like International Protocol
101. You do that, an' you legitimize the violence—you dig? You
do realize that. . .
Hector   I know that if I'm layin' in the gutter an' somebody
takes a piss on me, I'm gonna probably kick 'em. I'll stop kickin',
when you stop pissin'. But you're tellin' me you'll stop pissin'
only if I stop kickin' *first*? Well, sure. I mean, I'm down here an'
you're up there. A course that's what you're gonna say. 'Cause
fuck—you don't really wanna stop pissin' anyway. Doans—*he
lays it on with loud sarcasm now*—how come we never hear about
the refugee camps where all the displaced Palestenians've lived
for two generations?
Doans   *Scratching his head, looking for the common road in
the chaos of the conversation*—I think you got the wrong axe to
grind.
Hector   Here's where our isolationism hurts us. Here's where

the ultra-sensitivity to Israel bites us in the ass. Hop on the BBC or The Irish Times some time, man. You get a whole different take on the Middle East.

Doans   I'm sure you do.

Hector   Yeah. Well, on-the one hand they aren't callin' for war just 'cause Saddam Hussein shaved an r.c.h. off the sanctions yard stick. An' on the other hand—

Doans   The infamous other hand—

Hector   They're not afraid to call it like they see it, an' ask out loud why the fuck it's a given that Jews were allowed to shove Muslims off their land.

Doans   *Laughing like a seagull*—Man, this land is my land, this land is your land; this here land was done got by shovin' people off *their* land.

Hector   That's your answer—*he winces and sneers.*

Doans   No, that's the mirror, man. Take a good look.

Hector ·   It's unprecedented—*thick with disgust.* Where one group a people swoop in an' reclaim the land they used to have like eons ago. You wanna give New York back to the Dutch, man?

Doans   Hey, if they think they can take it, come an' get it.

Hector   Let's give Texas back to Mexico. No more illegal aliens—they'll already be citizens.

Doans   The Catholic church'd love it.

Hector   You can't *do* that. . .

Doans   Do what?

Hector   Go back to scrolls an' promises from God to justify what under any other banner's unjustifiable.

Doans   Why not?

Hector   *He just looks, then stares, real venom in his eyes.* . . Okay. . . Okay. . .

Doans   Like, you're shovin' what oughtta-be down my non-parched gullet. I'm just tellin' you the way things *are.* You dig? World paradigms don't shift on should-be's, man. They move on what-are's. An' listen anyway; if you wanna bring up the point a· unprecedentedness—let me hear you rattle off one other group a people that's been homeless for as long as the Jews.

Hector It happened to other people too, Doans. They just decided to assimilate into whatever culture they called home. When was the last time you saw a Saxon walkin' down Broad Street? How about a Viking? You know what I'm sayin'?

Doans *He takes two abrupt, hard steps back*—Are you sayin' the Jews should a stopped bein' *Jews*, man?

Hector I'm sayin'—really what *you've* been sayin'—

Doans Me?—*he jumps, jester-style.*

Hector Yeah, you. You've been tellin' me to look at what is, not what oughtta be. Well, okay. The reality is, civilizations rise an' fall, man. They take on hats an' coats from other people. They morph, or maybe fall apart altogether.

Doans An' the Jews haven't, man.

Hector Right!

Doans So?

Hector So, maybe they should.

Doans *He takes two more steps back; his eyes bug out—* You're fuckin' outta your God damn mind!

Hector What's more important—peace, or a handful a rituals?

Doans A handful a. . . a handful a *rituals?* . . .

Hector Is it more important to honor—so-call honor—the dead, or the livin'?

Doans *For a moment he can't stand still and jumps about not knowing what to do with himself. He settles then, and the only thing that remains from his wretched fit of anxiety is his foot manically kicking into the mud.* You want 'em to do what, man? Become what exactly?

Hector Fuck, I don't know. I don't *care*. . . Maybe become democratic—that would be nice.

Doans All Jews, or just Israelis in your master plan?

Hector Israel. I'm talkin' about Israel.

Doans They're not democratic?

Hector Can a Muslim become Prime Minister? Israel was *created* to be a Jewish State. That ain't no democracy, man.

Doans An' just what the fuck do you call the whole mess a countries surroundin' her? How about all a them Muslim States, brother? I do believe Israel is outnumbered like a whole shitload to one.

Hector   Yeah—I know. But we call *them* on it, don't we? We wanna ram democracy down *their* throats. We wanna force *them* into a pluralism they've never known before. Two reasons—*he thrusts two big fingers in the air.* One, the Islamic countries got oil, an' we got an' oil president from Texas. Figure *that* one out. Two—you said it yourself—historically we have a big Jewish population an' hardly any Muslim population to speak of. Put those two things together, along with a little Christian fundamentalism poured into the head a Alfred E. Newman the Crusader, an' wallah, Doansy, your manageable mess just got unmanageable.

Doans   I don't know, man—*he rubs his chin, pointed, rough with black and white whiskers*—I don't think I like where that finger's pointin'.

Hector   Doans—*in a mellow voice now beneath the harsh sun*—I got nothin' against Israelis. ·

Doans   I pretty much believe you, man.

Hector   But to be honest, I ain't got any special hardon for 'em either. I'm just sayin, we can't police the world.

Doans   Well, sorta, we do.

Hector   It'll ruin us. Let me rephrase that: It'll ruin us *faster*.

Doans   Man, like there's certain pockets a civilization we gotta keep afloat. You can be politically correct, man, an' say they's all the same, but they ain't. *This time he's the one—he pulls on his brother's shirt, coaxing him to come closer, lowering his gravelly voice.* You're talkin' about a rope goin' way, way back to ground zero.

Hector   I guess that's why we don't care too much about all those blacks in Africa you mentioned.

Doans   *He let's go*—Here we go again. . . *His eyes roll.*

Hector   Look, man, here's the thing. I'm just tired a followin' the same rut that takes me to nowhere but misery—you know? What the fuck do I care if the Israelis wipe the Palestinians off the map, or if the Palestinians wipe the Israelis off the map? I ain't Jewish, an' I ain't Muslim. But if—*if*—you're gonna insist that I invest my tax money an' my anxiety every night when I sit down for a plate a pasta with my daughter, then let's at least be capitalistic about the whole thing, right? I want the most return for my nightly angst. An' pound for pound you can save a shitload more people in Africa than you can in the Middle East.

Doans   It don't work that way.

Hector   Why not?

Doans   'Cause, man, in the bluntest a terms, a pound a African civilization ain't worth a pound a Jewish civilization.

Hector   We got a fuckload more blacks in this country than we do Jews.

Doans   Yeah, an' we got a lot more rednecks than either of 'em. So what?

Hector   So people are people.

Doans   *He chews on that for a while and then, raising his head from the mud to look his brother in the eye:* No they're not.

Hector   They're not?

Doans   You know they're not.

Hector   Funny, but I thought they were.

Doans   That's your guilt talkin'.

Hector   No, I think it's true.

Doans   I'm not sayin' *you* don't believe that, man. But it ain't the way this country sees it.

Hector   I think it is. I think that's why so many people are clamberin' over each other to get here.

Doans   Look—I ain't arguin' the opportunity angle, man. I'm makin' a distinction between opportunity an' points a influence. Points a influence don't come from numbers—they come from a weighted scale. An' that scale is weighted in part by—to a *large* degree by—the power—mostly political, an' surely economic— said culture does possess. . . . Listen, brother—the fact a the matter is Jews got a lot more power where it counts than blacks, Mexicans, or whoever. Plus, I mean, the blacks in this country care no more about the blacks in Africa than you an' me.

Hector   Maybe they will.

Doans   What do you mean, maybe they will?

Hector   Maybe they'll go back an' find out what they're all about. An' when they do, are we bound to their newfound family ties?

Doans   Hm. . . You got me there, brother.

Hector   Is more a my tax money gonna go out the door for somebody in Africa now, on top a Israel, on top a wherever?

Doans   Probably.

Hector   Is the Jew in Brooklyn gonna take up a gun for some black dude in Harlem's 5th generation second cousin in Africa?

Doans   I don't know, man. Like, I think he already has his arms full.

Hector   Well, fair is fair, man. That's all I'm sayin'. Fair is fair.

Doans   Look, man, The Bible didn't come from Africa, it came from present-day Israel. You think this is all new? You think it's really about Jews, man?

Hector   You just made a pretty passionate argument that it was.

Doans   Naw, man. Boil it down, take away the fat, an' what do you got, but we're just the modern protectors a The Holy Land. The Moors conquered half a the Mediterranean. You don't negotiate with somethin' like that. There ain't no politically correct way around it. Just like there ain't no happy pill around the fact that The Muslims want Israel—i.e. The Holy Land—dead or alive. An' you're gonna give that the same headlines as some God damn bushmen dyin' in Africa?

Hector   Yeah—*he says plainly and without hesitation.*

Doans   Then, like, I don't know what to say to you, man. I just don't know what to say. Jesus was a Jew, man—you dig? Jesus— the footer for all a Western Civilization, which like it or not you're part of—was a *Jew.*

Euchre In The Afternoon

***When they were children,** these men trotted faithfully at the heels*

*of their fathers' you-judge-a-man-by-the-shine-of-his-shoes. There
were re-enactments of war battles—Cowboys and Indians, Davey
Crockett and the Mexicans, Patton and the Germans—beneath
July maple shade, on lawns mowed with the soothing whir of
engine-less rotary blades—a last bastion of the free dandelion. All
day baseball games on dirt fields filled with bigger boys bullying
their way into games in progress, backs of necks stinging red
while leaning over between innings gulping water at the drinking
fountain, miraculous catches smacking the palm and saving a
cheek from sure destruction. BB-gun fights, you-show-me-yours
and I'll-show-you-mine, summertime profanity that must be
shaken before school begins again. Chores that tie you to your
home when the gang is roaming unfettered into the blissful dream
of adventure. Skinned knees, flying down concrete hills on bicycle
wings, roaming through the grease-heat of the local fair, running
to get a kiss from exotic lips, boasting in plywood tree houses, and
that first taste of stolen, warm beer from your father's garage. . .
They know themselves not as burl wood, shaped by influence and
reaction—yet that is precisely what they are. Where grass roots
met pop culture, the fireworks lit the night and the spray rained
down on them all. Still, the strings to relics, rituals, and fears
move them toward middle ground, the conservative's wildcard.
None recognize their life's wake as their own. All have contem-
plated this truth and reconciled it, reinvented their expectations,
lowered them, and found that happy mask on the garden floor you
either wear to midnight balls the rest of your life, or stomp to
pieces in bitterness and defeat.*

*The game of the day is euchre. The sun is beyond the noon hour,
barely. Shirts are off. Second, third, fourth beers have been
uncapped. The table—a warped, dirty sheet of plywood—gift from
the river—has been set on cornerstones of ingenuity: a cement
block, a tamping bar, the cooler, and the arms of a plastic chair.
Hector and Emanuel are partners, as are Doans and Gabriel.
They had been otherwise, and will be otherwise, in this musical
chairs of temporary alliance—ruse for the self-promotion of ego*

and intellectual satisfaction..

Gabriel   So Doans, how'd the teaching go? Are you all through for the summer?

Doans   Oh, man. What a nightmare that was. Like, I've been done for almost two months. .

Gabriel   You don't think it's something you'd be interested in doing on a full-time basis?

Doans   Are you kiddin' me? What? *Nooooo. . .*

Gabriel   *He looks around the table for some sort of clue*—I say something?

Doans   It was horrible, man. You got no idea. What a futile attempt at knowledge exchange *that* was.

Gabriel   The kids not listen to you?

Doans   They listened to me, man. You should a seen my evaluations. They ripped me apart—every single one.

Hector   That's a heart—*big brother notes to his little brother, Gabriel having trumped his ace of spades with the jack of diamonds.*

Emanuel   Thanks, man. I don't think I could a figured that one out. *Having to follow suit, he lays the ten of spades.*

Gabriel   That's not necessarily a bad thing.

Doans   No, it's great. I mean, how would I a felt if they would a liked me? No, man. . . They don't wanna learn. They got no inquisitive instinct, no sense a where art's been or where it's headed. It's just baby-sittin', man. I hate baby-sittin'. I got no patience for it. *He plays off-suit and allows Gabriel to gather the trick.*

Hector   They called 'em—what'd they call you, Doans—an art nazi?

Doans   Yeah. An art nazi. They said I was too hard on 'em. They said I was mean. They're clueless, man. Even the ones with talent were more interested in the brand a their shoes than *improvin'* themselves. I told 'em, hey—you guys are in an institution a higher education in the greatest place on planet Earth. You should feel honored. You should have some sense a responsibility. You should take advantage a your privileged standin'. They looked at me like I was crazy.

Emanuel   Art nazi. That's fuckin' hilarious, man.

Doans   Yeah, I guess so. Like, they're all wantin' to show me butt cleavage an' titty tans. Who do they think I am? I'm the teacher, man! They been watchin' too many flicks. One chick went on spring break, an' the next week after class she lifts her shirt to show me her tan lines! Man, I don't need to be lookin' at that shit. Get your tits outta here, man! What *is* this? We're not buddies. This ain't no Room 222 Gone Wild. I'm here to jump-start your wee little catatonic brains. *Gabriel, with the nine of hearts over Hector's queen of clubs, saves the hand.*

Hector   Fuck. Why didn't you trump 'em when you had the chance?

Emanuel   *No answer. A toss of the hands, a non-apologetic smile.*

Gabriel   So that's the end of prof life for you, Doans?

Doans   The end, finito. Ain't goin' back no more. Ain't no point. Ain't no reason. You know how hard it is to get those Gomers to do *anything*? Like, they don't get The Game, you know? Here's The Game: I'm the painter. I'm the teacher. I got this knowledge, this experience, this insight. You don't. I'm here to pour as much as I can from this cistern into your empty well. I talk, you listen. I show, you pay attention. Man, like they're all the time tryin' to tell *me* what's what. Me, me, me. See—that's what they've been used to. Look at *me*. Let me tell you what *I* think about art history. Let me show you how *I'd* paint that cube. Man, they don't grasp The Game. The concept. The purpose. Egocentric, vanilla rice cakes is what they are. It's fuckin' sad is what it is. Like, I got no hope for this here generation, man. What're they about? What's their stance? Where's their flag? . . . Money? . . . Computers? Gadgets, essentially. Like, you're knockin' on their heads an' there's nobody home. Out to lunch. Their brains don't got no capacity for chewin'. They ain't been trained for that. It's like they're still in diapers, man. It's an eye-opener, that's fo' sure.

Emanuel   So what do you have going on now?

Doans   You mean cha-ching-wise, or personal-gratification-wise?

Emanuel   Cha-ching-wise. You doing another mural?

Doans   No more murals, man. Not for a while. Not unless I do the history a rock-n-roll down in Texas. I'm workin' on this sculpture for this cemetery. It's this arc that goes up about twenty feet. An' on the arc are gonna be doves—*he scratches behind both ears at once, having mis-played, causing them to be euchred.*

Emanuel   Doves, man? Killer. What kind a doves? White doves?

Doans   White doves.

Emanuel   What's the material?

Doans   The arc's gonna be stainless steel. The doves're gonna be aluminum, I hope; if I can get somebody to pour it for me. It's gonna sit in this fountain, man.

Emanuel   A fountain. Can't wait to see it. How long's it gonna take?

Doans   I hope to get it installed before winter, man, but it ain't lookin' too good. That's my plan. Right now I'm tryin' to get the prototype dove finished to show the man.

Gabriel   I shot him a dove.

Emanuel   *You* shot 'em a dove, Gabe? . . . Oh yeah?

Gabriel   He needed a real bird to use as a model, so I shot him one.

Doans   Yeah, Gabe got me a real good one too. Shot 'em in the head, just like Davey Crockett would a done.

Gabriel   He keeps it in the freezer.

Emanuel   You mean so it won't go sour?

Doans   Yeah, man. I can have it out for like four hours before it starts stinkin' up the place. Then I pop 'em back in.

Emanuel   A cemetery, eh? I didn't know cemeteries were so well endowed in the cash department.

Doans   It's a private joint, man. The dude inherited it from his mom an' dad. He owns it with his two sisters—a couple a real-live Canterbury hags.

Hector   Hey—maybe it could turn into a full-time gig. You could start with Paul, an' work your way through all the apostles.

Doans   Yeah, man. He'd dig it. He's pretty relaxed about the whole thing. I mean, he's got a steady thing goin'. It ain't like people are gonna stop dyin'.

Hector   Not yet, man.

Doans   Doans and Gabriel lose another hand, and then the game. Doans stays put, while Gabriel and Hector trade places. It's now Doans, Gabriel, Hector, then Emanuel going clockwise around the table. They sit back down and Hector shuffles, then deals.

Hector   Gabe, so what do you think about all the shit goin' down in the church? You guys still go, don't you? *That they did, for the simple reason that Abby could not let go of the last ritualistic thread leading back to childhood.*

Gabriel   Yeah, we still go. I don't know. I think they need to re-examine the whole thing.

Hector   What's the buzz from the pews?

Gabriel   I think people are pretty nervous right now. It's like your mortgage company's just been caught laundering your money and is about to go belly-up any minute. But, pretty much, people are patient.

Hector   Are they?

Gabriel   I think they are. Just the fact that you're attending church at all these days says something.

Doans   Good for you, man—*laying the jack of spades, the left bower, he takes the hand.* One point for the good guys.

Hector   Way to go, man.

Gabriel   People are tolerant. Having said that, people are freaked. They're freaked because the church is hanging by a thread to begin with. They're freaked because ol' Father Ball-buster may be smiling for the same reason those pervs on South Main Street are smiling. Nobody wants to believe it. Nobody wants to go through the agony of yanking out the rotten teeth. Not the Pope. Not the clergy. Not the congregation. I tell you what, though. It makes for some pretty weird shit.

Hector   Weird shit like what?

Gabriel   *Between hands Emanuel is shuffling, so he leans into the table to speak.* For instance: There's this priest in our diocese—I won't name names—who's been pinned with some molestation charges. They go way back like fifteen, twenty years. A couple of teenage boys, one or two extra—ahem—sacraments you're not gonna find in the prayer book; you know, standard stuff these days. So anyhow, I get this letter, see. I get this letter, and guess what the letter says?

Doans   You never got your first divorce to that Cuban transvestite annulled?

Gabriel   *He leans back and playfully slaps Doans with the back of his hand.* No, it's asking for more money.

Hector   Gee, *that's* a surprise—*he slaps down a card.*

Gabriel   Yeah, they want you to dump in a little more than your normal contribution in the ol' Easter Basket come Sunday. . . . Now, I'm no genius, but you've got to be real stupid not to figure out where that money's going. It's going to help out ol' maybe-yes-maybe-no fudge fucker off the proverbial roasting spit.

Doans   Man, you figured *that* out! You *are* a genius!

Gabriel   Yeah, so, you know, I have a real issue with that. Because if this dude really has been packing more than rosaries and holy water in that robe of his, the last thing I wanna be doing is pumping money into his defense. The guy should be strung up by his ears, let everybody in the congregation beat 'em silly with a ruler.

Doans   So, what're you gonna do?

Gabriel   I don't know—*he shrugs.* The letter's still sitting in my office. Some days I think there's no way I'm gonna write 'em a check; maybe it's time to back out of the church altogether. The only reason I go is for Abby anyway. Then there are other days when I feel like, okay, I close my eyes to everything else—why get ants in my pants now? They've been buggering little boys for like two-thousand years. I think, maybe I'll just cover my nuts, stick out my tongue, and say Aaaaaaah-men. . . I don't know if the church is gonna make it. It doesn't seem to understand that it provides a service, and when your service doesn't jive with the needs of your customers anymore, you're gonna be having a red tag sale pretty God damn soon.

Hector   Like the government. There's gonna be a revolution, man. In our lifetime.

Doans   Naw. There ain't gonna be no revolution.

Hector   You don't think?

Doans   People are satisfied.

Hector   I'm not.

Doans   How many do you number, man? People don't move until it hits 'em square in the pocketbook, or deep in the gut, an' neither a them two things has happened yet, or is about to happen anytime soon—*he takes the deck from Hector, his shuffler, and deals out the cards alternately in two's and three's.*

Hector   What're you talkin' about? We're in a recession, man.

Doans   Yeah, like so where is the revolution? . . . Don't you get it? *Emanuel calls spades, on a right and a prayer.*

Hector   Get what?

Doans   The revolution's over. It came an' went. It was called The 60's.

Hector   I don't mean a fringe revolution. I mean the topplin' a the government.

Doans   What do you think it was all about, man? What do you think we, if I can be ever so humble as to include myself in that honorable uphill battle, tried to do? We lost. All we ended up doin' was showin' 'em our cards. They know what to expect now. You think this generation a zombies is accidental? Think again, man. The power structure knows it has to embrace youth, coddle 'em, keep 'em caged up, bring 'em into the fold. Not kick 'em outta the way, speak only when spoken to, like we had it. It can't be no more them an' us—too dangerous—an' more importantly, fiscally suicidal. Why do you think things are so youth-oriented? It ain't so youth-oriented anywhere else, man. Why so? It's 'cause nobody else had a bona fide youth war the way we did. We did— so those in power restructured. Re-thunk. An' it's worked like a charm. How much noise do you see the youth a today makin'. . . about *anything*? This is like the 50's on steroids, man. Kids today *wanna* be part of it. There's no more skepticism. Even with all this corporate treason—they don't give a fuck. The average kid today just don't give one fingernail's fuck. An' if he does, it's 'cause he's concerned about his 401K at the age a 21. You see anybody marchin' in the streets about this war Deja Vu we're gonna be fightin' soon? You see anybody in the gears a intelligentsia— Columbia, Yale, Cal-Berkley, MIT—stirrin' up a hill a ants? No, no, no. There ain't no real fuel for the fire. Blow on your own personal spark, man. Good luck.

Hector I thought you were for a war.

Doans What does that have to do with anything?

Hector I don't know. You sound disappointed that nobody's burnin' bras about it.

Doans Man, like when're you gonna get that line straight?

Hector What line?

Doans The line between endorsement an' observation.

Hector *Pausing to chew it up, he then plays the winning card for the hand—a ten of clubs—and collects the cards for Doans.* So what was the fuel to the fire back in the 60's, then?

Doans What was the fuel back then? How much time you got, man? The fuel was a nation split between crusty old men, an' his sons an' daughters listenin' to Elvis Presley—the first white pop god to use black rhythm an' blues as the springboard to fortune an' fame: It was the beats—specifically Jack Kerouac, Allen Ginsburg, Pynchon, Lawrence Ferlinghetti, Burroughs an' others—who were pioneers—or at least carried the baton—in American literature, American thought, who took sledgehammers to the concept of acceptable American ideals, who glorified the American outcast; they themselves fueled by the jazz undercurrents still simmerin' beneath white, white, white American mainstream—sometimes consciously an' sometimes unconsciously meldin' this hip black beat with their own poetic reverberations. From here, the folkies, led by Alan Lomax an' his chronicle a rural American music, Pete Seeger who along with the greatest of 'em all, Woody Guthrie—a real live card-carryin' commie an' a fantastic lyricist—they slowly, quietly formed the nucleus of a protest movement via pop music—timed perfectly with the change an' upheaval that was headin' down the tracks straight toward the 60's—influencin', pushin' rock-n-roll's voice a conscience—Joan Baez, Peter, Paul an' Mary, Bob Dylan most of all— toward the spark a revolt, introspection, social awareness, an' the throwin' down a the generation gauntlet. You had Vietnam, like an octopus, grippin' the country so that you now had boys bein' shipped off after their last football game to the jungles a hell, who never came back. The media, via television, brought war for the first time in human history to every single American family, scarin' them shitless, horrifyin' 'em, showin' 'em uncensored blood an' guts—our first true, unequivocally morally detestable war. You had the pill. That in itself freed women—for better or worse as far as the nuclear family goes—from the until-then assumed role a mother, homemaker, supporter, glue—beginnin' the volcanic demise a traditional male/female roles, which not only affected those women who chose careers over family, an' those men who had to re-adjust their own way a playin' the matin' game, but the socio-economic infrastructure a the workplace, economy, government—'cause now women were *part* of it. Blacks, for the first time, were able to mount sizable forays into white society via protest, violent uprisin's, civil disobedience, an' legislation—scarin' the you-know-what outta your average Archie Bunker, forcin' 'em to listen an' react. Then there were the Timothy Leary's an' the LSD experiments—drugs for the first time used by a large segment a youth. You had a president durin' the crucial formative years—Kennedy—who understood to some degree the change already takin' place in the country, who fueled it with his unique charisma, his guile in at least allowin' Mr. King to do his thing, by simply *standin'* there before the camera lookin' dapper an' hip.

Hector   So what happened?—*taking a long drag from his beer, head tossed back.*

Doans   *He waits until his brother's head is back down and his attention is undivided.* What happened? The revolution died, as they all do, 'cause by their very definition they're a transient occurrence, a period in the space-time continuum. It got ate up, it morphed. It became disco. It changed a few laws an' then everybody went back to sleep. Institutions bent, but they didn't break. They compromised. What came out was a new, inoculated set a rules, same as the old rules, but safeguarded against any new youth-attacks 'cause it'd been tried already. . . The youth of America is now sewed into the hides a the status quo. The danger has *passed.* . .

Emanuel   Eyes wide like a Christmas morning child's—Hand 'em another iced tea. The man deserves one after that speech.

Hector   Yeah, but The Revolution, capital T, capital R, *The* Revolution, doesn't have to come from the youth. In fact, don't you think that's why the 60's only got so far—*because* it was a youth movement?

Doans   Sure. No question about it.

Hector   Well, revolutions—all of 'em except the 60's—are initiated by workin' people. It's not about ideology. It's about food, man. Shelter. Protection. When the basic elements a life aren't bein' met, aren't bein'—fairly or not—distributed.

Doans   Okay.

Hector   That's what I'm talkin' about. *The* Revolution. 1776, The Sequel. Bolshevik Revisited. Guillotines dusted off. Not college kids dancin' in the mud at Woodstock, all we need is love bullshit. The government—by force—will be overthrown. Et tu, Bruté. Spartacus. The Norman Invasion. Castro.

Doans   Castro?

Hector   Yeah, for example. . . Look—I think if it gets to that point, we're all fucked. I'm just sayin' I think it *is* gonna happen. As an outside observer. 'Cause too much is bein' funneled into the pockets a too few. The fact that people aren't that upset about the dot-com bust an' the Easy Bake Oven accountin' scams are reasons to believe it even more. Everybody's happy—like you said, Doansy—or at least content not to move, not to say boo. . .

He turns his head and puts a hand to his ear. Don't you hear that canary squawkin', man?

Doans   There was a Prague Spring, man. Look what happened.

Hector   I never said it was gonna succeed. I have no illusions about that. Our government, in the name a squashin' terrorism, will turn this country into a military state.

Doans   Dude, like what do you think is happenin' right now?

Hector   I know what's happenin' right now. The Republicans—the really smart ones who see five, ten years down the road—are in a race to pull as many civil liberties out from under us as they can so when the time comes, when people do take to the streets, they can be hauled off no questions asked, in the name a anti-terrorism, for the so-called safety a the country, an' shot in some corn field.

Emanuel   They're just tossin' shit at the wall, man, to see what sticks.

Doans   That's a good way a puttin' it.

Emanuel   That's a tried an' true modus operandi for buddin' fascists.

Doans   Communists too.

Emanuel   Well, they're really fascists in disguise.

Hector   Revolutions are usually bad things.

Doans   I don't know, man. We're sittin' on the land a revolution an' things still look pretty good from here.

Hector   So it took Europe a while to catch up, industry-wise an' freedom-wise. I think they're passin' Go while we're sittin' in Jail.

Doans   Naw, revolutions are usually the backbeat a anarchists who gobbled up Grandma an' are waitin' for Little Red Ridin' Hood to come a knockin'.

Hector   How about revolutions in art, Doansy?

Doans   What about revolutions in art?

Hector   Without revolutions in art, where'd we be?

Doans   I don't know, man. . . still in the caves, maybe tattooin' sheep on our arms. . . Yeah, but man, like all change ain't revolution, you know? There's revolution, an' then there's just evolution.

Hector   What's the difference, say, in art?

Doans   What's the difference? Revolution, I think, is by nature destructive. It says—this thing here's no good. It's obsolete, or not useful, or oppressive, or—*his hands, moving in mid-air, fumble for more*—you get the idea. It seeks to eliminate the status quo. It hates the status quo. It's the antithesis a the status quo. Evolution ain't that at all. I think it's the natural next-step along the same line. A tweak to an already good idea, or at least the same idea. It comes about not as a reaction, but as a means to improve. From what I've seen, man, revolutions might look real good in the beginnin', but the food they take for that long trek up the mountain don't last.

Hector	1776—*he looks to Doans, then to all the others, eerily.*
Doans	Yeah?
Hector	You just explained how an' why we're where we are.
Doans	If I did, I didn't hear it.
Hector	The Colonists, man—some of 'em wanted to work

with England, right? They were sorta the first real niggers a this country.

Doans	Well, not exactly.
Hector	Sort of. I mean, they were pumpin' a lot a cash back to

the mother ship, an' not gettin' their due cut a the pie. So instead a just dumpin' the tea an' leavin' it at that, they took to cuttin' the cord completely. Overnight, everything English was out. The laws, the government, the *culture*. . . *Gone*. . . Not like Canada, man. We opened up the ribcage, hacked out the heart, an' performed a transplant. Without that tie to England—which is the tie to Europe an' a sense a world affairs—we can't help but see anything but ourselves. Canada never cut the cord. That's why they're more savvy in the world arena, even though they're isolated just like us.

Gabriel	Are you saying 1776 was a mistake?
Hector	*His eyes flare*—I don't know. Maybe. Canada's pretty

fuckin' nice.

Emanuel	Unless you really do need a heart transplant—*under*

his breath.

Hector	They're like us without the stick up the ass. 'Cause

they only evolved—like Doansy said—an' didn't kick their culture down the alley.

Doans	This is where freedom rings, man. I don't know. . .
Hector	It did. But did all that freedom turn cannibal? I mean,

is our hunger for freedom what's eatin' the world?

Doans　　Our freedom, man, is like the blueprint for success stories all around this here globe.

Hector　　.That's 'cause there's but one government, an' it goes by the name a *cha-ching!*

Emanuel　　I don't know why we even have countries anymore.

Doans　　*After tossing in his last card, a meaningless ten of diamonds, he plays the surprised stooge*—How come?

Emanuel　　'Cause, man, if there was ever taxation without real representation, this is it.

Gabriel　　Come on—*he says sarcastically.* What do you think elections are for?

Emanuel　　Choosin' between piss an' poo ain't my idea a representation, if you catch my drift.

Doans　　So, okay, how's this world without a country gonna go down? An' don't tell me love's the answer.

Emanuel　　Do I look like John Lennon, man?

Doans　　Not even Yoko.

Emanuel　　I think we're headed for a new feudalism, man, with multi-national corporations as the Caesar, Czar, King, CEO, Ayatollah, an' last but not least, President. Since this is a world economy, the pods a fealty aren't gonna be delineated by shorelines or rivers or a Hadrian Wall; they're gonna be—they're *already*—bein' drawn by specific economies, subsets a economies, brand names. Corporate castle walls. Instead a payin' taxes into a black hole, you're gonna give your thirty-percent to The Sheriff a Nottingham. Only his name might be Shankar or Ling or Fabian or Schultz, an' his castle might be on the banks a the Volga or in Thailand, right beside the new KFC, one door up from the Wal-Mart, two steps down from the Murdock Newsstand. I mean, there's always gotta be some sorta general overall kitty everybody tosses a few pennies into. Somebody's gotta do the roads an' shit like that. But what you pay money into now—which essentially goes to feed this neo-feudalism in its embryonic state—which, by the way, is why you get practically nothin' for the cash you put in—is instead gonna go to Your Lordship: your employer an' all a his sub-contractors. Or some warlord in Africa. Or some neo-communist in Asia.

Hector   Or just your plain mafioso in back a the spaghetti house.

Emanuel   Schools, health care, even armies—all that shit's gonna be decentralized. Privatized. Spread out over the whole fuckin' world, connected by electrons, everybody kept in line by low wages, the threat a terrorism, an' a few carrots on a network a strings.

Hector   They'll probably all be Iraqis, man—*tossing his head back for a swig.* Or Mexicans. God, you notice. . . they're *everywhere. . .*

Emanuel   The money trail is headin' East, for sure. Where oil meets drone, you'll find the new Gold Rush.

Hector   *Not yet drunk, still in control, pricked by the normally suppressed truth-as-he-sees-it—*Which is why for thirty years we've been able to get 50 miles a gallon, but instead a givin' incentives to people to buy *smaller* cars—he gives tax breaks to people who buy SSV's!

Gabriel   What the heck's an SSV?

Emanuel   *Out the side of his mouth—*Saddam Support Vehicle.

Doans   Hold on there, Slick.

Hector   Hold what?

Doans   Hold your loose steerin-wheel through the swamps a truth. Your view on the possibility a sendin' troops over is a well-established, uh, diatribe.

Hector   I prefer to call it a stance—*lifting his chin in metro male, Brando coquettishness.*

Doans   Hey, man, call it whatever you like. But are you tellin' me you don't see the dust a the New Crusade round yonder butte?

Hector   I see Commandments a fear, brother. I see knee-jerk kicks in the balls a the so-called enemy.

Doans   You don't see nothin' else, eh?

Hector   *He pauses, and then—*A man without a clue, lead by a gang a opportunists with a unilateral agenda. Is that what you mean?

Doans   Man, like you're always worried about the tick, an' not the beast it's suckin'. World War III has *begun*. The wheels are a rollin'.

Emanuel   *To Gabriel*—God, I hope he's not right. I just got a home equity mortgage so we can send our kid to the Ivy League.

Hector   You sure we didn't start it?

Doans   I know the prez didn't.

Hector   Okay, so he passed the train wreck on his way to the ball park; he sure as fuck isn't doin' anything to stop the bleedin'.

Doans   Man, I think that's exactly what he's doin'.

Hector   With a war?

Doans   Yeah, with a war.

Hector   Where's the tie?

Doans   What tie?

Hector   Iraq to Afghanistan. Saddam to Bin Laden. I don't see the tie, man.

Doans   Like, there wasn't a tie between Germany an' Japan?

Hector   Japan flattened our Navy, man.

Doans   An' Germany blitzed all our Allies.

Hector   *He lifts hands and shoulders*—So?

Doans   It's called ideology, man. First, the fascists. Then, the communists.

Hector   What?—Now, the A-rabs?

Doans   Now, the Final Assault.

Hector   *Only his eyes, with momentary betrayal, move*—On what?

Doans   On Western Civilization. On Judaism an' all a her sundry children. Look, man, the Rhineland's been run through. You think our prez don't see it? I see it. Thank God he sees it. You think he's simple? Naw—he ain't simple, man. He's just got a clear picture a this here storm brewin' over the horizon. He's wide awake in that grand White House. You think this is just another case a cowboy diplomacy? Well. . . if it is, it is. We need the cavalry on Calvary.

Hector   If we wouldn't a stuck Germany's face in mud after World War I, there wouldn't a been a World War II.

Doans   You're blamin' *us* for World War II?

Hector   The Treaty a Versailles—

Doans   I know all about The Treaty a Versailles—

Hector   Well, then.

Doans   Well, you don't blame victims, man. If I wanna stroll down Howard Street with a I Hate Martin Luther King T-shirt on, I got all the right in the world.

Hector   But you'd be pretty stupid, Doans—*narrowing his eyes, sneering at the gross naïveté.*

Doans   Dude—*he leans across the makeshift table, agitated, scratching his head*—it doesn't fuckin' matter. You just got sucker punched in the face, man. Hit with a two-by-four. You're on the ground. Your attacker is standin' over you an' he's got that two-by-four ready for the next blow. . . You're lyin' there in a daze. . . What're you gonna do, man! . . . What's it gonna be? Flee, fight, or cower in guilt submission, man? Maybe you don't know this guy from Adam, an' maybe you do. The only thing for certain— for absolute certain—is that if you don't do somethin' real fuckin' fast, he's gonna whack your head clean off your shoulders. . . Man, those dudes are serious as serious gets. Maybe you don't like the rules our elected officials in Washington play by, but unless you wanna just get silly an' say they're just as bad. . . they're *not* just as bad, man. Like, why the fuck're you pretendin' that they are? They're gross. They're obscene at times. It's an ugly machine over in that drained swampland; but they're not total cuckoos. But the dudes we're fightin'. . . yeah, they *are* totally cuckoo. They're so cuckoo they look right through the flyin' limbs a babies an' see the word a God.

Hector   Sure, they are. But Doans—they're a pretty small percentage.

Doans   *He stands, on the verge of erupting*—You know what I saw on September 11th, man? You know what I fuckin' saw all over the world with these two eyes? . . . I saw the end a Pax Americana. The sackin' a Rome. . . I saw dancin' in the streets like it was God damn Mardi Gras! Not by a small percentage. By the millions! The whole fuckin' Arab World—on their feet—in

the biggest celebration I've ever seen. . . An' you wanna tell me
the situation at hand is some sorta fringe disturbance by a *handful*
a whackos? Get your head outta your ass. Those guys that flew
into the Towers are the Huns a the 21st Century. They got the tacit
blessin' a the whole Middle East. An' guess who they're lookin' to
put on the end a their rope? . . . You, me, an' your *daughter*, that's
who. . .

Of Love And Loyalty

*The game goes on. The one and only glorious sun of every man's
God flaps down like harpies to claw at their necks. It's Doans
paired with Gabriel, Emanuel with Hector again. From the banks
of the great river, Emanuel has found a rolling pin. He grips one
end, swinging it casually in figure eights at his side. It brings back
memories of being with his mother in the kitchen, and a sharp
agony shoots through him as he remembers how the bright
maternal torch she had held high for all those years has dimmed.
This dimming has coincided with the loss he sees everywhere, in
all things, in all places, so that he walks invisibly, sadly, each day
trying to forget the shooting stars of not only his youth, but of his
nation's.*

Emanuel You know, she went crazy one day—*his voice carries
over the table on a gentle wave.* I heard she just put down her
apron, the oven still on, an' walked out of the house. I think she
was makin' biscuits an' gravy. I don't know who told me—isn't
that strange? She walked down Prospect Avenue to Main, turned
north an' headed toward The Falls. She just kept on walkin' an'
like a little kid, vowed she'd never go back. She bought a lunch in
some diner. How many times do you think she ever went into a
diner, alone, sat down, an' had somebody else make her a
hamburger? I can tell you exactly how many times. Never. She
had a cup a tea, an' a piece a pie. The pie wasn't nearly as good as

hers, but she thought it was. She thought it was the best pie in the world. She went to the cemetery an' sat at her mom's grave. She cried. She had a conversation with her dead mother. I'm not makin' this up. I can't remember who told me, but it's true. She talked to her mom about a lot a things, I guess, but like we always talk about dad an' his polio, she wondered aloud about the rheumatic fever, an' why the doctors couldn't a done somethin' for her. Why did she have to die so young?—she kept asking herself . . . She took a cab to her old house in The Falls. She sat lookin' out the cab window an' remembered way back to her happy childhood—can you imagine that?—the best years a her life were durin' The Depression—an' thought about her mom. . . You know what, Doans? You know why they were so in love?

Doans   Why, Manny?—*he says softly.*

Emanuel   'Cause they really did need each other. It was about survival. Emotional survival. Once they latched onto one another, the choice was over. They each had a life preserver an' weren't about to let go for anything.

Doans   No, man. They weren't.

Emanuel   Hell, she went back. Just like a kid, she didn't wanna leave, she just wanted to be seen. She wanted a break. That didn't come for about twenty more years.

Hector   Mom's never been on an airplane. She's never been to New York, Chicago, or California. She's never bought a car, or a house, or probably even a bicycle on her own.

Doans   She never did a lot a things.

Emanuel   What do you think dad did when she came home?

Doans   You mean the day she left? Probably gave us all the belt an' sent us to bed at like 7:30.

Emanuel   And then what?

Doans   An' then the next day he got up, went into the shop, an' lost himself in a Hasselblad.

Emanuel   She's just. . . *looking for words not there*. . . pretty much gone.

Doans   Yeah, God bless her.

Emanuel   Dad's havin' a real hard time of it. His breathin's worse. He gets outta breath wheelin' from their bedroom to the table. I go up, but it's like I'm in a foreign house. I never know what to say anymore. I don't go up as often as I should.

Doans   You go up plenty.

Emanuel   No—*shaking his head, looking down*—I don't. There's always somethin' that comes up.

Doans   You got a daughter, man. They understand.

Emanuel   I got a daughter. I use that as an excuse not to go up more often. I could make it up every weekend, if I wanted.

Doans .   Yeah, but would you really want to?

Emanuel   *Returning the warm, affectionate smile back to his brother*—Not really.

Doans   Well, then?

Hector   Sissy's there. An' Abby. If it weren't for those two, they'd be in a nursin' home. . . I hope I meet Dr. Dickhead some night behind the pizza shop; I'll break his neck.

Doans   Is it really him, man?

Hector   Is what really him?

Doans   I mean, is he responsible for mom's current condition?

Emanuel   Yeah.

Doans   *He had been looking at Hector, waiting for a response, but now lifts his gaze toward Emanuel.* Yeah? Well, you'd know.

Hector   He's negligent, Doans. It's all about paperwork. It takes 'em two weeks to send paperwork over to the hospital. *Two weeks.* Why does it have to take two weeks to get some paperwork over—which, by the way, you can fax in two minutes—so our mom can get the go-ahead for some tests?

Doans   I know. It's obvious the guy doesn't give a shit. We all know that.

Emanuel   She watches Smiley's People, over an' over an' over. Smiley, or Tinker, Tailor. Over an' over an' over. Like she's never seen 'em before. It used to bug me, you know, how every time you go up she's got the TV blarin' away with Smiley on. I couldn't stand to be in the same room if that shit was on. But then about three months ago, I rented 'em. I started with Tinker, Tailor. I don't know why I did it. I just switched one day from hatin' even the thought of 'em, to wantin' to know more about 'em. It was like I wanted some kind a connection with mom an' dad again, an' I thought maybe I could get it through Smiley. . . So I sat there alone in the back room after Mazz an' Rahe were in bed, an' watched. I pictured 'em up in Barnesville; mom on the couch, dad in his chair, watchin' the same thing. The three of us a hundred miles apart, but connected by George Smiley. The next thing I rented was Bridge Over River Kwai. Then Lawrence of Arabia. Even Star Wars, man. I got everything I could find with Alec Guinness in it. Then I got Twelve O'clock High—'cause I think that was dad's favorite. Midway. The Great Escape. The Green Fuckin' Berets. True Grit. Lonesome Dove. Casa Blanca. Things naturally took me back toward dad. Dad's heart was always an open door.

Doans   You can say that again.

Hector   Yup—when he wasn't givin' us a lickin' or takin' back our Christmas gifts, he had a heart a gold.

Emanuel   He'll sit there an' watch Smiley with her every night— *he looks at them each in turn, thunderstruck with awe*—just to be there with her. Even after she falls asleep, so she'll see 'em when she wakes up. Like a raccoon. You ever notice how you don't usually see just one dead raccoon on the side a the road? That's 'cause they won't leave their mate. They hang around waitin' for 'em to get up. They wait an' wait right next to 'em, an' before too long—boom—they're dead too. Dad's like one a those raccoons. He has to be there, right beside her. Isn't that somethin'?

Hector   Yeah, but he has to leave when the smoke's bad, or the TV's maxed out.

Doans   Fuck yeah—who wouldn't?

Emanuel   Off he goes to fuck around down in the basement. He'll work on a plane, or email one a his relatives who's like a hundred an' fifty an' still kickin', or he'll even knock off a Hasselblad now an' then. He still does 'em for his old customers, even though his hand's shakin' like a leaf an' he loses screws left an' right. Some a those guys won't go anywhere else. They gotta bring 'em to him, the guy who kept their cameras hummin' for forty years.

Doans　That's loyalty, man. That's what that is.

Emanuel　We always thought dad would go first. But they're both driftin' away so fast now. It looks like mom's got a year left in her, if that. Dad keeps up hope. She hates goin' to the doctor— he won't tell her till the mornin' of her appointment that she's goin'. Sometimes it pisses her off. God—that's so weird—how much it must hurt 'em to have her mad at 'em. He's gettin' frustrated. He's depressed. He can barely—no, he can't even— fend for himself, an' now he's gotta look after mom, who's in the late stages a dementia, with a bad heart, a bad hip, an' probably black lungs. If she goes, he'll be right behind her. He won't have any more reason to live. He'll just fade off into those steel gray Copley skies of his youth, before the war, and he'll fly his penny planes till the end a time, mom not five feet away sittin' in the grass.

Concerning Saviors

Emanuel　**I did the photography thing** for almost ten years.

Gabriel　Yeah?

Emanuel　It paid my tuition—all those weddings. Probably half a those blushin' couples are divorced by now.

Gabriel　At least.

Emanuel　Me an' Iggy'd stay out till like two a.m., an' then I'd get up an' do an all-day wedding. He'd run a 10K, or sometimes a marathon. He was a fuckin' animal. . . I did a lot a thinkin' in the back a those churches.

Hector　*Wisecracking*—I hope, for your sake, you did a lot a confessin'.

Emanuel　The ceremonies all blur together after a while, an' what's The Big Bang to that couple is just another gig.

Gabriel　So what sort of things did you think about?

Emanuel   I did mostly Jesus thinkin'.
Gabriel   Jesus thinking?
Emanuel   Lots a starin' at The Cross an' thinkin'.
Gabriel   When I'm at church I stare at The Cross and wonder
who the scrawny dude that modeled for the artist was. It got my
brain worked up so much one day—after Mass I went out and
bought a chisel set.
Emanuel   Yeah?
Gabriel   Yeah, but nothing came of it. It's out in the garage with
Abby's UPS stockpile.
Emanuel   I liked doin' Catholic or Lutheran weddings, 'cause
you'd have a good half hour at least to veg in the back without
havin' to take any pictures. You just had to make sure you listened
for the do you take this man to be your whippin' boy blue for the
rest a your days—an' hop on up to the front to snap their blissfully
innocent faces.
Doans   If only they knew—eh, bro'?
Emanuel   Yeah, but shit—a lot of 'em'll be divorced, but some
of 'em'll be like my mom an' dad. Who the hell can tell.
Gabriel   Don't you think it would be real weird to be hacking
away at the body of Jesus, and when you get to his loincloth. . . I
mean, you don't wanna endow 'em with too much or all the ladies
will have fainting attacks every Sunday.
Hector   Don't forget the priests.
Gabriel   Especially priests—hey, and nuns too! But, you know
what I mean? It'd be a real touchy thing, getting Jesus' genitalia
just right.
Emanuel   Most a the ones I've seen go for the velvet curtain
look. All heavy ripples an' not a hint a anything more. Fuck, man,
if Jesus would a been a bona fide Roman citizen, maybe some
wanderer along the Appian Way, they probably would a fitted 'em
with a see-through toga or somethin'. Maybe they would a let 'em
into the fold a Roman gods an' represented 'em buck naked with
washboard abs an' curly pubes. But by the time the Romans
claimed 'em, he was a well-established Jew a dubious gender.
Doans   *Raising an eyebrow*—What do you mean, dubious

gender?

Emanuel   No offense, Doans.

Hector   I think what he means is, Jesus wasn't your typical hero slash savior.

Gabriel   Sort of like Dylan.

Emanuel   No—not Dylan, man.

Gabriel   Why not?

Emanuel   You mean 'cause a the protest songs? Man, he only half-believed 'em himself. I don't think Jesus was insincere.

Hector   Fuck no. If anybody was sincere, it was Christ, for Christ's sake.

Gabriel   How about Lennon?

Doans   Maybe.

Hector   Lennon more than Dylan?

Emanuel   Sure. More charisma. More followers. More peace an' love. An' he actually *believed* it.

Doans   For a while.

Emanuel   Plus, there's the martyr factor.

Doans   Yeah, the martyr factor. That's a biggie.

Emanuel   Plus, he was the more androgynous a the two. That hen-pecked walrus wanted equal rights for *women*, God damn it. What kind a crazy fool'd want a thing like that, except for a Christ figure?

Hector   I don't know. Dylan in his eyeliner days, man.

Doans   Yeah, but that was just show. That was Ziggy Stardust wave-ridin', get off a my back 'cause I'm Mercury with alliteration-sparks flyin' outta my heels an' I can do anything I fuckin' wanna do an' it'll be cool, even if it's shit.

Emanuel   You gotta go with the masses on this one. Dylan, the critic's favorite. Lennon, charm out the wazoo, charisma galore, adored by every teenage chick born in the last fifty years. Time remembers charisma.

Hector   It remembers influence.

Doans   I think the kid's right on this one. It'll remember the dude who put the goose in the step over simple genius.

Hector   I still think Dylan's gonna make it before Lennon.

Gabriel   Lennon's more likable.

Emanuel   Don't matter, Gabe. That shit gets polished up when the redactors get their hands on it.

Gabriel   Yeah, but Dylan had a real wicked streak in him.

Emanuel   *Waving him off*—that stuff won't make it past the canon delegation. They'll trim that stuff out. It doesn't fit the icon—it'll get hacked.

Gabriel   Yeah, but all they have to do is look at old footage. Read old transcripts.

Emanuel   They'll burn 'em.

Gabriel   They can't burn all of 'em.

Emanuel   They'll discredit the ones that do survive. Say they're fakes. Staged. Taken outta context.

Gabriel   That's a lot of material to wipe out.

Emanuel   Gabe, we got an impendin' prelim to World War III starin' us in the face, based on nothin', an' the entire country is balls to the walls gung-ho for it. It's image, man. Image today, it was image yesterday, an' it'll be image years from now. People believe what they wanna believe. . . Say, for example, they found a new gospel. The gospel accordin' to Jesus' brother. I think it says a hell of a lot that you don't hear jack from His brother, sisters, mom, or dad. All the people who knew the dude inside an' out—an nobody turned a mike on or jotted down their thoughts?

Gabriel   I don't know that they did the up close and personal shtick back then.

Emanuel   No, true. But we're not talkin' about just any historical figure. He's it. There's nobody bigger. An' the guys around 'Em—they knew He was it. So like where're the anecdotes from childhood? How about coffee house snippets from the time a His fifteen minutes a fame?—Why no peep from anybody who knew 'Em best?

Doans   'Cause they probably didn't know 'Em best, man. When you're a social misfit, friends are thicker than blood. Take it from me; all a you guys notwithstandin', a course.

Emanuel   See—I think there probably were accounts from His mom an' dad an' brother an' ex-business pals; but He probably had a few Dylan moments peppered in there too. How do you centrifuge out the temper tantrums, womanizin', bad breath from the symbol—the symbol a *God*?

Doans   Could a been as simple as who cares about that shit?

Emanuel   God doesn't have flaws, man. He *can't*.

Doans   You're assumin' that He did.

Emanuel   I'm goin' in, eyes wide open, is all. I'm startin' with the man, an' sayin' let's see how He fits into the God. Look, Doans, you told me once how we all got better bullshit radars than most guys on account a we watched our dad slog through the daily grind in a wheel chair; we saw *real* up close an' personal what matters an' what doesn't. Who's lyin' an' who's not. Actions are the *only* thing that counts—fuck what somebody *tells* you. . . I'm just applyin' the same radar to the biggest question since who killed the last wooly mammoth?

Doans   I hear you, man. Okay, you caught me at a good time. I'm listenin', an' not necessarily thinkin' all a your naysayin' is bogus.

Emanuel   All right. Cool. Let me address what I started to say to Gabe a few minutes ago.

Hector   You discovered that Jesus was a black dude.

Emanuel   Well. . . I wasn't gonna go quite that far. . . but what if? An' not even Ethiopian Africa—what if Jesus was an Egyptian?

Doans   He wasn't.

Emanuel   Humor me.

Doans   Okay, man, but hypotheticals only come in handy when all other beasts are extinct.

Emanuel   Let's say He was Egyptian. His family line possibly progenitor a the Greeks—a mixed bag at worst. Still, fairly dark-skinned. . . *African*. Let's say He *was* an Egyptian, His mom gets knocked up by some camel trader, gives birth, her husband sticks around anyway. The Dude goes into the family business—wood work—an' then grows up to be this mythical figure, adored by the zeitgeist a His generation, the accepted human manifestation a God on earth. . . What're they gonna do with that? . . . I'll tell you

what they're gonna do with that. They're gonna do a little 1984
Ministry a Truth, it never happened—that's what they're gonna
do.

Hector My barber'd shoot himself.

Emanuel Would he?

Hector In a heartbeat.

Doans Naw—he wouldn't buy it, man.

Emanuel That's right, he wouldn't.

Doans Faith is the mother a all jaw-breakers. We all know that.

Emanuel What if he was gay?

Hector *Laughing*—I'd like to see what the Right would do with that.

Emanuel *Barely hearing his brother*—Really—what would Christianity do? I think there's a good chance He was.

Doans Man, like there's no rope you won't skip across—*he says, chuckling.*

Emanuel Talk about irony.

Hector It'd kinda put a whole new wrinkle in the Twelve Apostles—*wink-wink.*

Emanuel The guy didn't get started until he was thirty. *Thirty.*
Not married. No kids. I think He woke up one day with a hell of a
mid-life crisis headache, heard about this dude John the Rock Star
Baptist, checked 'em out an' said fuck, I can do better than that.
Hell yeah—I think I just found out what I wanna be when I grow
up. I wanna be the guy everybody's waitin' for. It sure as hell
can't be *him*. . . That old wildman? Maybe. . . maybe it *is* me?
Why the hell not? An' off He goes into the wild blue yonder.

Doans Man, like you got more juicy theories than Oliver Stone.

Emanuel Just like in The Man Who Would Be King, man. At the
end a the road, ridin' that donkey into the city, He believes it. He's
been on the road two, maybe three years. He's burnt out. He's
been one-uppin' Himself at every turn, an' now there's no way
out. He's suicidal, man. He's got a death wish. He gets himself
crucified. He's Jim Morrison. Jimi Hendrix. Janis Joplin. Keith

Moon. His drug wasn't somethin' He inhaled or shot into His arm; it was the ever-increasin' burden a playin' the Son a God. At first the rush a all rushes. An' then, the drug that stops His heart.

Roll, Cosmic River, Roll

With arms slippery and foreheads wiped as fogged windshields to keep clear what cloudy avenues lay ahead, and disaster in the mind fizzles to the elegance spreading before them in the round—a few tussles with the legend of Billy the Kid, Custer the Barbarian, Jessie James, The James Gang, and finally, the dead horse that won't die, Jesus. . . They rise, stretch, wobble, and inch their collective toes into the laughing animal that is the Muskingum. Its eyes in a single generation's blink have witnessed the calamity of ethnic cleansing, the rise of an empire, the first war, brave souls in soup lines, the second war, battle lines and black list lines, the third war, demonstrations in the streets, the unthinkable war, the murdering of the best and brightest, men shooting to the moon, the fat cat getting fatter; the first oil war, electrons at your fingertips, the second oil war and with it, finally, the attempted shredding of The Bill of Rights by wolves in evangelical clothing. Today Jessie and Billy are accountants at some California energy bazaar— destined for canonization of their own—when dead of course—into the pantheon of bodacious vaudeville thieves and swindlers. Jesus rides on the backs of the lemming billion. Tolerance is being body-snatched by city-states of fascism everywhere. . . And laugh, laugh you do, Cosmic River. Cleanse these scalloped fields of grain as you have for years. Disregard our singular blip and keep to your wooden sameness—there is untold wisdom in it. But who in this hollow age can recognize it?

Gabriel   Anybody wanna go in for a swim?—*already with shirt off.*

Emanuel   Yeah, I'll go in with you, Gabe—*he turns his back to gather the poles, lines limp, the battle lost, and sets them against the leaning, shoreline sycamore.* Come on, Doansy. Time for you to get re-baptized.

Doans I didn't bring no Bermudas.

Emanuel Go in like you came out. There's nobody around here but us chickens.

Doans *He begins unbuttoning his dime store shirt*—Man, I haven't been traumatized like this since my swimmin' days at the Y.

Gabriel It's cold! . . . *He walks forward in his skivvies, his long gorilla arms gripping himself. The others eye him with affectionate reproach, but say not a word. And then*—Jesus Christ, Hector!

Hector What?—*snickering, standing square-on, pants down.*

Gabriel Now I know why all the country club ladies got your number.

Hector What're you talkin' about?

Gabriel What am I talking about? Holy Shitoly—*trotting splashily away.* Don't stand next to me—I don't need the compare and contrast.

Doans Hey, man, keep your eyes where I can see 'em—*turning to avoid Gabriel's visual go-around.*

Gabriel I have nothing to hide—*standing all blunt knife and chipped flatware.*

Doans Yeah, well, maybe you got nothin' I wanna see, neither.

Emanuel This is great!—*playfully splashing.* Come on, Doansy, don't be shy.

Doans Man, like I didn't know this picture contained nudity. Why didn't somebody tell me?

Emanuel It's an integral part a the story, man. Isn't this where fate an' natural selection have a sword fight?

Doans Cold!—Cold!—*Cold!*

Emanuel Doansy, you got nothin' to be ashamed of—*still splashing.*

Doans Man, like what are you, the beach bully?

Emanuel I'm just messin' with you, man. . . This is fuckin' beautiful! The mighty Muskingum River! Come an' get me!—*and he goes stumbling raucously backward and tumbles in. He remains submerged up to his shoulders waving his arms through the water.*

Hector   Now I wish the women were here.

Emanuel   Which women? Our wives? Naw, man.

Hector   Why not?

Doans   Why're you laughin', man? What'd I miss?

Hector   I'm laughin' at him.

Emanuel   You're laughin' at me? What'd I do?—*standing out of the water.*

Hector   Why wouldn't you want our wives here skinny-dippin' with us?

Emanuel   It's not that I wouldn't *want* 'em here. It's just that with just the four of us, I can pretend anything might happen. Some boatload a cheerleaders might come cruisin' up river lookin' for a good fishin' tip. I might get lucky an' have a carp jump outta the water an' give me a blow job. *Anything.* If our wives were here, I'd be stuck with reality which—hey—ain't so bad. . . Not that I'm not curious about what all your wives look like stripped buck naked; except Abby a course, 'cause she's my sister.

Hector   We used to do a lot a skinny-dippin' out in Montana.

Emanuel   That's the weird thing, man. You go skinny-dippin' with your friends an' their wives, an' from then on whenever you see 'em out waterin' the arborvitaes, all you can think of is what they look like in the buff.

Doans   Man, like what is so *funn—ny*?

Hector   Him.

Emanuel   Me again? I got snot on my cheek?—*brushing the side of his face.* What'd I do this time?

Hector   Nothin', man.

Emanuel   Nothin'?—*he smirks.* Okay, good, bro'. I just wanna see you smile.

Hector   So, Doans, remember White Rock an' goin' to the beach?

Doans   Sure, man.

Hector   Remember peekin' at the chicks in the bathhouse?
Doans   How could I forget?
Gabriel   What bathhouse?
Hector   The changin' room at the beach, Gabe. There didn't
used to be a roof over it.
Doans   Until the MacTear's came along.
Hector   You could go up on the hill an' look right down on top
of 'em. You had a perfect view, man. Chicks changin' or takin'
showers—all the time.
Doans   A few old hags tossed in but hey—what the hell? Just
made the sixteen-year-olds look better.
Hector   You do any surfin' on the net, man?—*to Emanuel.*
Emanuel   You mean porn? Isn't that why Al Gore invented it?
Hector   There's a lot a freaky shit out there, ain't there?
Doans   Really?—*perking up*. Like what?
Hector   Whatever you want. Anything you can imagine, you
can see.
Doans   Yowzzza.
Emanuel   Well, maybe not what Doansy can imagine.
Hector   Yeah, man. . . *Anything*.
Gabriel   I used to look at those porn sites—*he says, surprising
them all*. I liked the upskirts.
Doans   Upskirts? Like, what's that?
Gabriel   These guys, they take these little spy cameras and snap
pictures of women beneath their skirts. They don't even know
what hit 'em. You get a lot of thongs and wedgy shots.
Doans   Man, like where're they takin' these pictures? They
gettin' chicks up escalators?
Gabriel   Anywhere and everywhere. At the grocery store. At the
mall. Waitin' in line for Communion. They don't have a clue.
Doans   Wow. Man, that's far out surveillance.
Gabriel   Just don't get caught.
Emanuel   Yeah, don't get caught.
Doans   How're they gonna know who's ass it is, man?
Emanuel   Not after the fact, man. He means don't get caught
takin' the picture.

Doans   Got any good S&M pictures, man?

Emanuel   Are you kiddin' me?—*making a face of disbelief.* What kind do you want? Doans—I'm tellin' you—it's a fuckin' smorgasbord out there—right at your fingertips—free a charge. . . S&M, hanky spanky shots, whips, chains, master/slave, lezzies, preggos, camel toes, cum shots. Man, they got fuckin' pictures a chicks doin' it with dogs an' horses.

Doans   Come on. . .

Emanuel   No shit. A fuckin' horse. You ever seen the size of a horse? I don't know how they do it.

Doans   Man, like I don't need to be seein' no bestiality pictures.

Emanuel   Naw, me neither. But they got 'em if you want 'em.

Doans   How about pictures a chicks gettin' it up the ass, man?

Emanuel   Doans—I'm tryin' to tell you—they got it all. Anal? You want anal? You got it. Loads an' loads—entire websites with nothin' but your next-door-neighbor gettin' plowed up the pooper by the Italian lifeguard. Blowjobs? Thousands a fuckin' sites. Cum flyin' everywhere. . . It's a strange world we live in when you can click on pictures a nothin' but women with cum on their faces for three hours, an' barely make a dent in the mountain a material out there.

Doans   Sounds like Pandora's Box has been vandalized again. Sounds groovy. Where do I sign up?

Emanuel   Yeah, man, it's cool—but I tell you what. After a while, it gets kinda, I don't know, monotonous maybe. You go through this stage where that's all you can think about, it's all you wanna do. You don't care if World War III starts right outside your bedroom window—just gimmee some more pictures. . . Then everything starts lookin' the same. It's like sayin' the same word five thousand times in a row. It's fucked up. One week I looked at nothin' but pictures a chicks in thongs. After a while, man, I realized all I'm lookin' at are like two round humps with a slice down the middle, maybe a little shaved clam peekin' out every once in a while. It's like seein' the same Gilligan's Island episode every night, over an' over. Pretty soon you don't care if you never see it again as long as you live—*he reaches out*—come on, turn that thing off.

Hector   If you spend *that* much time lookin' at it.

Emanuel   Yeah, sure. That's a lot a fuckin' porn. But guys do it. I know lots a guys who do. Guys you wouldn't think. I mean, you don't ever have to leave your house, an' you can be in porn heaven. Lots a closet perverts've come outta the dark from this shit. Guys who maybe were too afraid or had too much to lose to be seen at the local triple X. It's a whole new paradigm.

Doans   A new porn paradigm. I like it.

Gabriel   Isn't it beautiful—*he says with deadpan sarcasm.*

Doans   A course it's beautiful. Nudity's been makin' the world go round since fertility goddesses. Addiction ain't beautiful. But people are addicted to french fries an' Coca-Cola an' shoppin' an', well, I don't see anybody callin' for limits to be put on how many lottery tickets a guy can buy in a year. People'll abuse anything you put in front of 'em. That's just how it is, man.

Emanuel   You gotta wonder though, what women would think if they knew that every single dude with a computer in his house is lookin' at this shit. . .

Doans   Well, a course they're not gonna *believe* that. You could show 'em, have signed affidavits, an' still they wouldn't believe you. That don't jive with their fairy tale picture a life.

Gabriel   Aren't we lucky—*he muses wickedly.* Our wives always give us more credit than we deserve.

Hector   It's not luck if they expect you to be somethin' better than you are. Then you either have to lie, or if you really are honest with 'em an' like Doans said, they don't wanna believe the truth, all you've done is fucked yourself. They think their brother-in-law is the greatest thing around. Because he lies.

Gabriel   That's true. Better they don't even know.

Doans   Chelsea knows. Man, I don't go for chicks that can't handle the truth. I've been down that lonesome highway; I don't ever wanna go back.

Skewed Lines

Doans sits on a stump, carving a dragon's head in the worn, gray wood. Hector has swum out to a sandbar in the middle of the river. Gabriel, in quiet repose, arms folded, watches him, while Emanuel lounges with his arms asleep on the plywood table. Cottonwood puffs drift by like fairies on the move.

Emanuel Doansy—who'd you wanna be when you were growin' up?

Doans Elvis.

Emanuel Yeah, man?

Doans Every kid wanted to be Elvis. Well, some wanted to be Davey Crockett, but that was before your testosterone jet engines kicked in. Elvis was it, man. He was so big. You can't even imagine.

Emanuel Elvis the Pelvis. I bet parents went crazy, man.

Doans They thought he was the devil incarnate. I'm not kiddin'. Man, an' all the dude did was some cheap bump an' grind routine.

Emanuel An' he sang a little too, Doansy.

Doans What I mean is, they got all whacked out about *that*? Some Adonis hormone machine up on stage wavin' his six-shooter in front of a madhouse full a girls, all on the verge a their first public orgasm? *That's* Satan?

Emanuel It would a been kinda worrisome, man; if you had a daughter back then.

Doans Yeah, but like compared to what's goin' on now; that was tame, man.

Emanuel Yeah, but it broke through the barriers. It wasn't tame to 'em back then, man.

Doans Most definitely not. Tame couldn't a been used in the same sentence, in the same paragraph, unless you wanted to say somethin' like—Young Stud Needs To Tame His Erection. Elvis, he was our man. Our hero. He was on the front lines right up there with Kerouac, J. D. Salinger, an' Marilyn Monroe.

Emanuel You think he was bigger than The Beatles?

Doans   No, man. Nobody was bigger than The Beatles. . . I
don't know. . . Yeah, but even Lennon an' McCartney—they
wanted to be Elvis. Everybody wanted to be Elvis. He was like
Picasso, man. Or Michelangelo, or Mozart. People might a come
after 'em, took the rawness an' sprinkled loosy-goosy, mellow
yellow dust on it—but he stormed the gates, man. You can't storm
the same gates twice, it don't matter how good you are. That's
timin', man. Fate. It's got nothin' to do with you.

Emanuel   How about Dylan, man?

Doans   Dylan. He's a different beast altogether. I mean, Elvis
was a phenom. He had that beautiful, melted butter voice. X-rated
winks in a G-rated haircut. He was a romantic. A lover. Dylan;
now you're talkin' poetry, man. You're talkin' genius. Elvis
wasn't no genius, except maybe in his natural presentation. He
wasn't a *conscious* genius. Dylan, he was the poet laureate of our
time.

Emanuel   Goin' electric, man. . . *He raises eyebrows to raise a
point.* . . Dylan sells out to pop-n-roll.

Doans   He didn't sell out to nothin'. Man—like Dylan was
rock-n-roll way before he went folk. Folk was just an escalator to
fame. Folk was what was happenin' where he was at at the time.
He used it, it used him, an' then they both moved on. Dylan
wanted to be Elvis too, man.

Emanuel   Just a song an' dance man.

Doans   Sure. Ain't they all? But so what? What'd Shakespeare
do? He wrote plays all them Elizabethan folks wanted to see.
What'd the Renaissance painters do? They painted religious motifs
'cause guess who had the fat checkbooks? So what? You think
that diminishes their art? You think that somehow tarnishes what
they communicated? How? They either communicated effectively
or they didn't. Man, without Dylan folk music never would a
made it outta the coffee houses. Well, maybe Joanie. Okay. . . But
he carried folk music on his scrawny little back, if only for a few
years. He put the spotlight on 'em. Newport. . . Give me a break.
Newport Shnewport. Nobody ever heard a Newport before Dylan.
They oughtta lick his toes for what he did to *their* movement.

Emanuel   He still puts out good shit, man, even if nobody's listenin' but fuckers like us.

Doans   I'm honored to be alive an' breathin' the same air as that curly-haired Rasputin.

Emanuel   You ain't gonna hear it on the radio, man.

Doans   The radio station's are just the audio cartoons in this here cartoon nation. Art is secondary to the bottom line. Rock-n-roll, as a vital, mainstream form a youth communication, is officially dead. If I want nonsense I flip on Bugs Bunny, which is high art compared to the shit on the radio, man.

Gabriel   Manny, you need a beer?—*as he digs, hunched over, through the cooler.*

Emanuel   Yeah, man.

Gabriel   Doansy? Another iced tea?

Doans   I'm good. Thanks. I'm gonna fire up old man skull in a minute—*leaning back, he slips his bony artist's hand into his jeans pocket and pulls out his pipe. He rubs it, like he was shining a dull spot.*

Emanuel   Where'd you get the pipe, man?

Doans   Cletus got it for me for my birthday last year. You remember Cletus?

Emanuel   Yeah, I remember Cletus. How's he doin'?

Doans   He's doin' all right.

Emanuel   Yeah?

Doans   Yeah. He's on the comeback trail. He's doin' good.

Emanuel   He the dude that lost gobs day tradin'?

Doans   That's Cletus.

Emanuel   Fuck. How much? You have any idea?

Doans   More than I could afford to lose. Way more. I'd say he's out twenty-thousand G's.

Emanuel   No shit.

Doans   Yeah, an' Cletus don't have twenty-thousand G's layin' around to lose, if you know what I mean. It cut 'em real deep.

Emanuel   That's tough, man. Cletus seemed like a real good guy. He plays the guitar, doesn't he?

Doans   When he's sober.

Emanuel   He should a come down for the weekend.

Doans   Yeah, well, he's not a travelin' sorta dude anymore. He gets real nervous when he's away from his pad.

Emanuel   What's he doin' for a livin' these days?

Doans   He's been makin' signs for twenty years.

Emanuel   What kinda signs?

Doans ·   Laser signs. You know, just signs. Signs for whatever. Plus, a little dealin'.

Emanuel   Big-time dealin'? Small-time dealin'?

Doans   Medium-time dealin'. He's an alcoholic, man—*he says plainly*. That's where his cash flow goes. Right back into his habit.

Emanuel   Man, that's too bad.

Doans   He's gotta pick himself up or the cops are gonna do it for 'em. He lost his girlfriend. He got kicked outta his bar for like the tenth time. I think it's the last time. His place is a garbage dump. . . Cletus used to be a really good artist. He was one a the few artists I've respected over the years. We've been pals since Kent.

Emanuel   You gonna light it up?—*Doans, having produced a bag from thin air, sets it beside the skull pipe on his tree stump.*

Doans   If you want. I can wait if you want.

Emanuel   I could use a hit or two, man. Go ahead.

Doans   This is some real good stuff.

Emanuel   Cletus set you up?

Doans   Jessie.

Emanuel   He grow it out in the desert?

Doans   Don't think so, man. Naw—he don't grow it. I don't know where he gets it. He sends it to me in these little packets—*reaching over the plywood table*—Here, man, take a look.

Emanuel   Wow—*flipping the packet between his fingers.* That's pretty slick.

Doans   He must have some kind a sealer.

Emanuel   That's real cool, man. That's real neat. Pretty risky though, isn't it? I mean, through the mail.

Doans   Naw, it ain't risky. Man, there's so much pot floatin' through the U.S. Post Office—if they ever cracked down on it they'd be outta business like tomorrow.

Emanuel He oughtta go into the biz. That's real tight. That's artwork right there, man.

Doans Yeah, well, I think he kinda is. . . *He takes the bag and opens it with Emanuel's fillet knife, fills the pipe, lights it, take a hit, and passes it back over the plywood. The pipe goes around. Time, in its space capsule on a journey toward re-invention, stays tucked under wing, listening, and yes, even learning.*

Emanuel I remember one night when I was about ten. I was real sick. They pulled out the bed from the couch in the family room so I could sleep there for the night. I had the flu. I kept throwin' up. I threw up seven times—I know 'cause I counted. Each time I'd throw up, it would feel good for a while, an' I'd think that was it. But then that feelin' would slowly creep back, an' pretty soon I knew I'd have to do it again. It was real late, maybe three o'clock. I sat up with the pan on my lap watchin' TV. There was a movie on—some epic like the Ten Commandments or Samson an' Delilah. Maybe Demetrius an' the Gladiators. I don't know which one it was. But I remember the simplicity a the set. It was all about the guy an' the girl, an' they were only wearin' togas an' sandals, an' the landscape was that arid, mountainous Cyprus tree landscape where everything looks like it's through a microscope an' there's no escape for them or for you. I felt like I was right there with 'em. I felt this feelin', like eternal love, like even the hopeless things aren't so bad . . . Mom came down an' sat with me from time to time. She'd lay with me an' stroke my head an' hum her little songs. She'd feel my forehead to see if I was hot. . There was a universe—there—on the pull-out couch with blackness all around except the TV screen with that epic movie, an' mom weavin' in an' out of it all. . . When I remember doin' things with mom, it's always just the two of us. Nobody else is ever around. . .

Doans Don't you wish you were back there right now, man?

Emanuel It was like the sun risin', or the seasons when they're about to change.

Doans   *His thoughts pull him away from the river of petrified wood and haze. His soul spills onto the mud—he gathers it up again, and desires to hear the boy tell his story. He floats in the pleasure dome high where worlds intersect to create music rising in the back of his head.* Tell us about the walks in the snow, man: Tell Gabe.

Emanuel   With mom?

Doans   Yeah. Tell 'em. That's some really beautiful imagery, man.

Emanuel   We used to go for these walks at night, Gabe. Just mom an' me. I don't know why nobody else ever came along. Who wouldn't wanna stroll through soft-fallin' snow at night with their mom? . . . I remember one night when the snow was comin' down real soft, when it was cold an' the snow on the ground squeaked against our boots. We walked all around the neighborhood. The snow was pure an' smooth. We were almost always the first ones out. Sometimes we'd talk. Mostly we didn't. But when we did, I knew I could say anything. Mom wasn't like dad. She thought bigger than dad. She dreamed, an' let me dream. We walked up Eastview, where Hane's field was just a gray mystery off in the distance. The streetlights showed the pace a the snow comin' down. The houses seemed pink, an' they almost all had lights on inside an' none a their driveways were shoveled. It was gonna be a serious snow, I knew, 'cause it came from the northwest, not the southwest, an' it didn't flutter down, but came down heavy an' plump. Eastview was the big hill in the neighborhood—the hill you rode down when you wanted the thrill a goin' fast. But now it was its own storybook land; only a few ruts in the street, an' those were bein' covered fast. It was gonna be a long walk—somehow we both knew. We went all the way down to Akron Road, took it for a block, then headed down Woodland. All the old, rich houses are on Woodland. They're set back from the street an' have huge front lawns. Here, the snow reached out toward us. The old black trees were bein' barraged with snow from the top. The big mansions with their chimneys puffin' looked real invitin', but since we didn't know anybody on that part a

Woodland, we kept walkin' all the way until it ran into Durling Park. The park, like everything else, was deserted. We pushed through the unbroken snow and strolled beside the tall chain-link fence a the tennis courts. I'd never, ever seen mom anywhere near this part a town on foot. I spent a lot a time down at the tennis courts in summer, an' sometimes played baseball there too. Havin' mom there alongside me, in what amounted to the outer limits a her existence, felt real good, an' I knew it was a once in a lifetime thing for us. She didn't know about the anxiety a waitin' your turn for a court, watchin' the other kids, some a who you knew an' a lot you only knew by sight an' by reputation. She didn't know about the taste a bubble gum an' sweat down your back against the hot bench, or when it finally came time to play, the thrill a runnin' onto the court with those perfect lines an' the not-so-perfect, saggin' net, or the beautiful frame around the courts—especially on a summer night when the lights were turned on—with the big trees lookin' down on you, blowin' just a little with a breeze. I wanted to tell her, now that we were there, but part a me felt exposed, like she'd seen me walkin' from the bathroom naked. Like most things, I kept it to myself an' we went on without a word. . . We went downtown. It was light downtown, an' here we found a little more activity. Cars pulled in an' outta the gas station. Now the gas station's a parkin' lot. After it was a gas station, it was a doughnut shop, I think, but now it's just a parkin' lot. That night, cars fish-tailed in an' out in happy, slurpy, slushy sounds. Bill's Diner was still there. You remember Bill's Diner, Doans?
Doans   Naw, man.
Emanuel   Yeah, it was a real diner, like the one in Kent. Right alongside the library. You could see the backs a mostly men sittin' at the counter as you went by. The diner closed about the same time the old hotel closed—a few years after we moved to town. The hotel was torn down to put in a Ben Franklin's, which was our prime destination whenever we rode our bikes downtown. They had the biggest candy selection in town, but the ladies that worked the counter were mean as hell an' always slighted you a little. Mom didn't know any a that. Sometimes I wonder what her life

was like in the same town we both lived in, yet really they were different places altogether. The library was open, but we didn't go in. Beaman's Drug Store was open, an' it had the only swept sidewalk we crossed that night. Mr. Brown was the pharmacist. He talked real loud, like maybe he was hard a hearin' or somethin'; a nice old bald guy—friends with dad—like just about everybody in this world. Beaman's has been closed maybe twenty years. It's been a few things; I think it's a coffee shop now. We came back down High, which had big slate sidewalk blocks an' trees so old most of 'em were half dead on one side, just shiverin' in place waitin' for a lightning bolt or somethin'. Aunt Sophie's place was down Baldwin, but we didn't stop. Aunt Sophie used to walk everywhere in town. She'd walk over to our house at least once a week. Now she's in an assisted livin' place that took all her money, but won't ever boot her out, an' mom says she regrets it, but who the hell knows if that's true 'cause mom is twice as bad off as Aunt Sophie an' a lot more senile. We used to spend the night with her—me, Levon, an' Lynn—Saturday nights. She was cool, but had no patience for regular stuff that kids do. She never had any kids. Well, so on we went along High. When cars came by their sound was muffled; they moved real slow an' cautious, except for a carload a teenagers in this beige Impala who were doin' doughnuts up near the circle a Goode. Mom didn't say a word about how they shouldn't be doin' it. I knew she would a been doin' it herself if she was younger, or could somehow hide behind somebody else's i.d. Down Goode hill on the other side a High was Valley View, where I went to grade school. It was about a mile walk from our house to school, an' we walked it unless it was rainin' or too cold. Up by the abandoned field an' the Nazarene church, up Brouse, down Woodland, an' back home. We hardly said anything, but by the time we got home our cheeks were ice cold, an' when we got inside she made us some hot chocolate, which took a long time 'cause you can't heat it up too fast or you'll burn the milk on the bottom a the pan. . .

Doans   He'd had his eyes closed to better picture what he was hearing, but now he opens them—That's nice, Manny. You an' mom had a special thing goin'. She always had a soft spot for you. You're lucky.

Emanuel   Why couldn't dad be like mom?

Doans   I don't know, man. But that'd a been groovy if he was, in the sense you're referrin' to.

Emanuel   Mom gave you the details to life. Dad gave you the hard nose guts an' glory picture. He gave you the blueprint. I can remember workin' in the garden with mom; it wasn't like with dad. She'd always point out somethin' new. Maybe a color on a flower, or some little bug. Maybe how a leaf looked like somethin' else. Dad was about gettin' from point A to point B. The task at hand. Mom took you on detours.

Doans   God, what a sweetheart mom was. Remember the sports jackets she made us for Christmas that year?

Emanuel   Me an' Levon were too little, we didn't get one. But I remember.

Gabriel   She made you guys sports jackets?

Doans   Gabe—listen to this. It's Christmas Eve, right, an' it's time for the big surprise. Every Christmas there'd be some big surprise, you know, some outta-this-world personal Last Supper that somebody spent some ridiculous amount a time on. This year was mom's turn. All the guys—like, we had these identical boxes. You know what that means. We're out in the middle a the livin' room, just waitin' for the gun. So mom says go ahead, open them boys up—*he begins laughing out loud*. . . Gabe. . . Gabe—like, you ain't gonna believe it, 'cause still twenty-some years later I can't believe it. Our mom made us matchin' John Travolta Saturday Night Fever jackets!

Gabriel   No kiddin'.

Doans   Yeah! Yeah!

Gabriel   That's pretty cool.

Doans   Cool?—*his whole body lurches back.* Are you serious, man?

Gabriel   Heck, yeah.

Emanuel   They *were* cool.

Doans   You are serious. . . Gabe! Like—do you even

·remember the style a jacket I'm describin'? *Disco* jackets, man. I
hated disco. We all hated disco. It was like givin' us all new
beanie hats or somethin'. Man, them things were *awful*.

Emanuel   Hey, at least you got one.

Gabriel   I'd have worn mine—*he says plainly.*

Doans   Hey—no—I appreciate the fact that it took her like ten
thousand hours to make those things. Bless her heart. But, man,
we were stunned. We stood there like we'd just been given
bicycles with trainin' wheels.

Gabriel   You ever wear yours?

Doans   Are you out. . . of. . . your. . . *mind*?

Gabriel   You should have worn it, Doans. Your mom spent all
that time on those things? Aw. . . You should have worn it at least
once, maybe had somebody take your picture. I bet she'd have
gotten a real kick out of that.

Doans   None of us wore 'em. Not even for Halloween.

Emanuel   She used to make us school clothes, Gabe. They were
some a the coolest clothes around. I remember this burgundy
sweater-vest. It looked like somethin' Bobby Vinton would a
worn. I had my Thom McCann platform shoes, my big ass belt
buckle, maybe some paisley pants or a paisley shirt, an' dad's ten-
cent haircut. I was all set, man.

Gabriel   Your dad used to cut your hair?

Emanuel   More like sheared us.

Gabriel   That bad?

Doans   Don't you remember what we looked like?

Gabriel   Sort of.

Doans   What? . . . You think we *paid* for those haircuts?—*he
howls, falling backward.*

Gabriel   I don't know, Doansy. To tell you the truth, I didn't
think too much about it.

Doans   Fuck—he'd have us lined up like sheep which, let's
face it, we more or less were. All us boys took like a half hour.
An' if he was pissed, or we got into hot water about somethin',
he'd shave our heads. *Leaning forward*—Gabe, he *shaved* our
heads. . . Instead a leavin' a layer a stubble, he'd shave it down to

the skin. Man, like we was skinheads before skinheads was cool.

Gabriel   That's raw.

Doans   No shit.

Gabriel   Yeah, but lots of kids were getting crew cuts.

Doans   Gabe, this was like mid-sixties. No—even late sixties.
The guy was a lunatic. I remember once I had this discussion with
'em. You know, like come on, man, let's you an' me talk about
what's gonna transpire here. Let's compromise. Let's be real. . .
Fuck. . . There wasn't no discussion. This wasn't like no Indian
pow-wow. He just laughed, then got mad an' two minutes later I
was a skinhead again. . . *With his hands rubbing, his face pushed
out, his insides in a violent whirlpool.* . . You know, sometimes I
think of 'em like he was just this cripple. That's where he got his
anger. That's why he took it out on *us*. You dig what I'm sayin',
man? That's why I can't feel sorry for the guy now. I love 'em.
Don't get me wrong. I got no bad thoughts against ol' pops. Well,
fuck, I guess I do. I ain't ever gonna work it all out in my head. He
was mean, man. He used the belt on me I don't know how many
times. Just usin' me like some dudes use punchin' bags, or dogs.
Now, in his old age, he's a softy. . . You remember when he fell
outta his van a few years back?

Gabriel   Sure, I remember.

Doans   Well, he was in the hospital. We thought maybe this
was it. Me an' Junior an' Adam come walkin' into his hospital
room—an' you know the first thing he says to us? He says I'm
sorry for havin' so many kids. God—what the hell was I thinkin'?
I'm sorrrrrry, he says. . . He knows what he did, man. But it don't
erase what happened. 'Cause what happened is up here, it ain't
goin' away. It's the roadmap to everywhere I been.

Emanuel   To Gabe—God, I cried once. He just buzzed me. This
was way, way past the time when it was okay to have a buzz, man.
I think he was pissed about somethin' an' tired. . . I ran into the
bathroom. I looked at myself an' just teared up. I couldn't help it. I
felt like I just got my pants lowered in front of a room full a girls.
The thing is, it wasn't my appearance; that wasn't it. It was that I
knew he cared so little about how I felt. You know what that kind

a shit does to you? To this day I struggle with that. I still feel like
I'm worth less than everybody else. Hell—a *course* I feel that
way. I *was* worth less than everybody else.

Doans   My dad, the sadist.

Gabriel   Your old man was great, man. I love your dad.

Emanuel   He was one cruel dude, man.

Gabriel   Your dad? Cruel?

Doans   Man, like when did you ever see my dad? Saturday
night hellos before you an' me peeled outta there? That ain't my
dad. That ain't Thursday night after work an' somebody put a dent
in the car, an' somebody else broke the candy dish, an' he's got a
migraine the size of Alaska, an' we're havin' hamburgers—not
steak—for dinner. Toss in maybe Levon an' Manny are fightin',
there's body bags floatin' across the TV screen, an' he's had two
re-do's at the shop. Man, go fetch the dog for a beatin' or he's
gonna take it out on you.

Gabriel   I know what you mean, I guess.

Doans   You don't, but that's okay. I mean, like my dad would
get migraines all the time—especially Friday after work that'd last
through the weekend. It was all that stress lettin' go. So, it was bad
durin' the week, but worse on the weekends.

Emanuel   Gabe, there was no doubt what I was. A fuckin' thorn
in his side. For that, as far as I'm concerned, he can just fuck off.

Gabriel   Hey man—*rearing up his head, showing real
displeasure with the comment*—that's your dad you're talking
about. Show some respect.

Emanuel   Respect?

Doans   Let 'em go, man—*putting his hand out toward
Gabriel.*

Emanuel   Did you say show my dad some respect? What do you
think my whole fuckin' life has been about? Not pissin' 'em off.
Not doin' anything to make 'em worried, bothered, or stressed.
Not makin' 'em go outta his way for *me*, his *son*. It went way
beyond respect, man.

Doans   But, man—*speaking softly*—he was like that with all of
us.

Emanuel   Once an' for all, Doans, with all due respect—bullshit. I've been hearin' that my whole life. I'm here to edify you, man, that I was *the* A-number one, numero uno nigger a the family. There's a peckin' order, in case you haven't noticed. I'm an afterthought—an after*birth*. . . Tell me somethin'—*with attitude now*—how do you know what it's like to be me? Is that some canned answer you got there, 'cause you don't wanna spend the energy thinkin' about it? You afraid a what you might find out; like maybe you'll have some guilt to deal with?

Doans   Man, you can't put no guilt on me.

Emanuel   An' you can't explain to me what *my* childhood—what still my adulthood—is like in this family.

Doans   You always were a complainer—*looking away, then down to his carving.* Yeah, you were different from the rest of us.

Emanuel   From the mouth a privilege. . .

Doans   I ain't condemnin' you, man. But you weren't the only one.

Emanuel   *Near pleading*—You'll never know; I don't *want* you to know. But Doans, you of all people, to not even consider it. . . To tell me I'm full a shit. Why would I go through all this? You think I enjoy it? You think I'm makin' this up, man?

Doans   No, man. I know you ain't makin' it up.

Emanuel   Then don't twist the knife. Allow me the small solace of acknowledgement. That's the only thing I've ever wanted from any a you.

Doans   Man, let it go—*again, tenderly.* You got the right to feel the way you do, but the sooner you let it go, the better off you're gonna be.

Emanuel   *He's* crippled? That's nothin'. He's got his whole youth to fall back on. Me? It's been one long boot camp—the tearin' down without the buildin' back up. I got nothin'. Nothin' but pain an' emptiness. He took a happy wild hunk a clay an just flattened it. It's ruined one marriage. Now it's workin' on number two. . . He still does it—*looking up at his brother, eyes watering, lips quivering.* The anger, the threats. When I see 'em jump on one a the grandkids for doin' nothin' more than bein' *alive*, I wanna reach across the room an' strangle 'em. I wish he *could* walk! So I could stand toe-to-toe with 'em. So I could say look, man, leave that poor little kid alone. He hasn't done anything wrong. You're the one with the problem. An' if you cut 'em down one more time or lay another hand on 'em, you're gonna have me to deal with. You got that? You got that, Mr. Big Man On Campus? Mr. Egomaniac? Mr. I Love Your Mother More Than Anything— More Than You—So Don't You Forget It? . . . But, you know what? . . . That's a question, man—come on, laugh with me. . . *laugh*—it's the only way! . . .

Doans   No, what, man?

Emanuel   I still love 'em. I love 'em for a thousand reasons, only one a which is 'cause he's my dad. You can't not love the guy. I can intellectualize it. I understand the different universes one human bein' can occupy. He is one truly great human bein'. An' he's also the source a this crippled heart. The two can't be reconciled. I know it, but I still keep on tryin'. . .

Three-legged Horse

Hector climbs the great stairs and comes back down minutes later with a paper sack full of corn. The others, when they see what he has, summon cords to childhood and back porch shucking, and memories of sinking teeth into ears steaming, dripping with butter, peppered, chewy, sweet, sweat dripping from the brow. They sit in a circle, setting aside the makeshift table of plywood, and begin shucking the corn and tossing the clean ears into a large pot.

Hector   *To Doans*—Does Eddie have a grill?

Doans   Don't think so, man. But we found this old rack while you were out yonder. *He holds it up*—Think you can use it?

Hector   That'll work.

Doans   Great. Cool. Okay. . . What's the matter, bro'?—

noticing his brother's eyes darting between the pot of corn and the grill.

Hector   We shouldn't shuck the corn if we're gonna grill it.

Doans   Why not?

Hector   'Cause, you keep the husk on—it keeps the moisture in—an' it steams the corn. If you take the husk off, unless you got it up high off the heat, it'll burn.

Doans   *They pause, stupefied, waiting for somebody to take the flag and run with it.* Hm, yeah, well—I guess we could boil it.

Hector   Fuck—it'll be all right. We'll do 'em slow. *Promptly, he begins preparing a new stack of kindle wood onto the fire's ashes.*

Doans   Don't you guys know you ain't suppose to shuck corn when you're fixin' to grill it? What's the matter with ya'll? You guys are fired. Go back to the unemployment office.

Hector   Toss me a beer, will you, Gabe?—*he says, Gabriel standing bent at the knees in a Sumo squat before the opened cooler.*

Gabriel   What kind?

Hector   Rollin' Rock.

Gabriel   You got it. One Rollin' Rock on the way.

Doans   Manny—you gonna throw your lines in? *He sits down on his tree stump and begins working on the dragon.*

Emanuel   I was thinkin' about it. Might as well.

Doans   Yeah, why don't we give it another whirl. It'll give this weenie roast the added dimension a unrealized anticipation.

Gabriel   You got any bait down here, Manny?—*beginning to crank them in and check them out.*

Emanuel   There are some dough balls and maggots and some worms in my tackle box under the porch there, Gabe. See it? Bring the whole box over. . . I was thinkin'—I may just put some worms on just for the hell of it.

Hector   You'd think this river would be loaded with catfish.

Emanuel   You'd think.

Doans   Hmmm. . . Maybe they're congregatin' conjugatin' along those hospitable shores a Marietta, waitin' with mouths wide open for Lucifer to drop some french fries down from a mini-van cruisin' over the bridge a no return. . .

Gabriel   *Still squatted at the cooler, he looks over with an Alfalfa surprise.* You stoned, man?

Doans   Naw, not even close.

Gabriel   You sure sound like it.

Doans   Naw, man, I ain't stoned. *To the younger*—Hey, man, like will you throw a line out for little ol' me?

Emanuel   Sure, man. You want a worm on it? I'm puttin' mostly worms on 'em.

Doans   You think a worm's the way to go?

Emanuel   Who knows? But we ain't done jack with the dough balls an' maggots.

Doans   Good call. Yeah—*watching his brother at work.* Pierce one a them night crawlers on that barb. Make 'em work for a livin'.

Gabriel   How far down you fishing, Manny?

Emanuel   I think it's about ten, maybe thirteen feet. I'll toss some farther out, an' some off to either side. I figure we'll form a shield around this whole cafeteria no self-respectin' catfish is gonna be able to pass up.

Hector   Gabe—you hear me an' Manny are gonna open up a bar?

Gabriel   You guys? Hey, that's all right.

Hector   It's not a done deal yet, but it looks like it's gonna happen.

Gabriel   Where are you gonna put it?

Hector   In C-town. We're lookin' for some old place close to hipville.

Gabriel   Hip, but not with the hip prices. Good idea. What are you gonna call it?

Hector   MacTear's.

Gabriel   Hey, that's great!

Hector   Our dad's gonna love it. . . Uh, dad, me an' Manny, seein' as how we're a couple a unemployed software drones, thought it would be a slap-happy idea to open up a bar. . .

Gabriel   He'll probably get a kick out of it, as long as he can use his AARP card.

Hector   Yeah, he probably will dig it.

Gabriel   What's it gonna be like?

Hector   We don't know yet.

Gabriel   Doans—*with a piece of line in his teeth, the hook only an inch farther, squatting at the shoreline*—you hear Hector and Manny are gonna open up a bar?

Doans   *He has his legs farther open now that he's carving the left wing of the dragon.* A bar? Grooooooovy.

Gabriel   Guess what they're gonna call it?

Doans   I don't know, man. . . Uncle Hector's Beer Guzzlin' Joint?

Gabriel   MacTear's.

Doans   MacTear's?

Gabriel   It's just plain MacTear's, isn't it? It's not like MacTear's Place, or MacTear's Bistro?

Hector   No, man, just MacTear's.

Doans   Wow. You gonna have dancin' girls an' a salt water aquarium?

Gabriel   Say *whaaaat*?

Doans   I had this friend in New Orleans, he had this bar. He had dancin' girls an' a salt water aquarium. Dancin' girls every Thursday night.

Hector   No dancin' girls—*biting a cigarette and blowing out smoke like he was kissing glass.*

Gabriel   If you put it close to the freeway I'll pop in every time I'm passin' through Columbus, which isn't very often, but hey, what the heck.

Hector   Shit yeah, man. We'll set you up. All brother-in-laws get ten percent off bottom shelf liquor.

Gabriel   Ten percent? Aren't you the generous type.

Hector   I'm just fuckin' with you, man. We'll fix you up.

Gabriel   *With his teeth, he holds the line and then pulls the hook against it, tightening the knot.* You an' Manny hit that acid, Doans?

Doans Sure. Manny ain't no rhombus parallelogram, man.
Ain't no straight lines or sharp angles on that boy—*he raises his
head and grins at the boy.*
Gabriel Was that your first time?—*to Emanuel, but the elder
speaks for him.*
Doans Yeah, an' yes. Curiosity is all it was. He's just a
curious beatnik born in the safe zone.
Gabriel So how'd it go?
Doans Man, like it was some old acid. I knew that when I got
it. The guy threw in a dot an' a half with the pot he sold me.
Gabriel Cletus?
Doans Naw, Cletus wouldn't a even given me shit like that. A
friend of a friend of a friend. Me an' Manny an' Chelsea split it
three ways. No trip, man. Manny said it made the floors roll, an'
he saw Grizzly Adams come outta the speaker. But we never
really took off.
Hector I remember when you brought those mushrooms down
to White Rock. Those things can kill you!
Doans Not if you know what you're doin', man. Did you try
any?
Hector Fuck no—*he laughs.*
Doans Yeah, well it's a lot like doin' acid. Seems like you can
get a bad trip more times on acid. But I never had any really bad
trips on any of it. The last time me an' Cletus did acid, man, we
ran down Howard Street buck naked. *Howard Street*, man. It ain't
too smart for a couple a scrawny white dudes to be doin' that at
like four o'clock in the mornin'. We were yellin' an' bangin' on
doors. Suicidal, is what we were.
Hector Why not just like give 'em the fuckin' gun, you know,
be quick about it?
Doans Us? Naw, man. That ain't no fun. We like to dodge a
few bullets first.
Hector Nope, I never tried acid.
Doans All that shit's about the same, man. It fucks you up for
a while so you're higher than a kite, then maybe you feel like shit
the rest a the day. . . You ever do a chick on acid?—*to Gabriel.* I

tried it a couple times. Man, it was too much.

Gabriel Too much what?

Doans Too much everything. The tempo's all wrong. It's like too frantic for me, man.

Hector I did ecstasy once.

Doans You did?

Hector After I got divorced from Moondog. I was datin' this twenty-five-year-old aerobics instructor. She dropped some in my wine cooler.

Doans She date rape you, man?

Hector I don't know if I'd call it rape, but I'll tell you somethin'; there's no way you're gonna turn anything down on that stuff. She could a called in Richard Simmons an' I would a been game.

Doans Yeah? Yeah? Wow.

Hector It was some powerful shit, man. She was into it. She was fun.

Gabriel Don't you hope and pray our wives aren't as demented as we are.

Doans Oh, they are, man. It just ain't in the same bullring.

Gabriel Yeah?

Doans Women are kinky. When they reach like thirty-five, fortyish— watch out! At that age they're old enough to know that an orgasm's an orgasm, an' the word *husband* is just another word for *masturbation surrogate*.

Emanuel They are kinky, man. They're kinky when they're young, in that experimental sex-gymnastics stage; an' they're kinky after they shed that prima donna stick-up-the-ass, da-da guilt. In between can be a real drag.

Gabriel Remember when all you wanted from a girl was to hold her on the front porch swing and kiss her all night?

Doans I remember those days.

Gabriel Me an' Abby used to sit on your front porch on Prospect Avenue an'—gosh—just watch the cars and make out for hours.

Doans Nothin' like the sweetness a youth, man. I'll take it in a heartbeat.

Gabriel   What I'd give to be there now. . . *He falls into a dreamy trance, and nobody snickers or makes a joke out of it.*

Hector   I had a girlfriend in high school, an' all I did was make fun of her.

Doans   You too, bro'?

Hector   *He nods quietly.*

Doans   Well, that was dad's belt talkin'.

Hector   She was all right. She was real cute. She hung around till she couldn't ignore the insults.

Doans   As I recall, you had a few cute girls in school, man.

Hector   I did—*he says without the usual boasting.* I knew a lot a really cool girls. I had my pick.

Doans   An' you picked 'em apart.

Hector   Only one. I had a real good thing with the others.

Doans   Yeah—*rubbing his face*—I dated this girl at Kent. A classic hippie chick, man. Beautiful, Spanish sorta Joan Baez type, but better lookin'. I spent all summer skinny-dippin' with her an' some friends at the quarry. We'd lie in the grass an' smoke dope an' talk art. She was real cool 'cause she wasn't too political. A lot a those chicks had some fierce viewpoints, which made for some real edgy dialogue lyin' beneath a blue sky. She was mellow an' easy. She had legs that went on into the sunset, an' hair that went with 'em. I don't know if we were in love, but it wasn't about body parts yet, that's fo' sure. That might a been the last time I lied next to a naked girl an' she didn't move to cover anything up. She didn't hide a thing. All I wanted to do was paint her, an' lie naked next to her. I'd close my eyes an' pretend I was blind an' feel her body. She made it all seem so clean.

Emanuel   I had a thing for my neighbor. They lived right across the street. They had a pool just like ours. We'd sit down next to the pool, 'cause it had a wooden fence around it, an' you couldn't see us if we were sittin' in the grass right beside it with our backs up to it. Yeah, she was sort of a bigger girl, on the pleasantly plump side, but sorta cute. We'd sit there an' talk, an' then we got into this game, see. The game went like this: If I could guess what she had for dinner, I'd get to make out with her for five minutes.

Hector   Hey—*he gets up to fetch a beer*—what a bargain.

Emanuel   Oh, she was a fabulous kisser, man. Oh, geez. Real good with the tongue—sorta flicked it around like a outta water goldfish.

Doans   Man, like if she was a North Hill chick it'd a been a piece a cake: Pasta. . . pasta. . . pasta. . . okay—you got me— meatball sandwich.

Emanuel   They were Polish, man. It was one a three things: Polish sausage an' sauerkraut, hotdogs an' sauerkraut, or a frozen pizza with sausage an' peppers. It was real easy, 'cause she never brushed her teeth after dinner, even when it was gonna be a while till our rendezvous. . . Sometimes when I'm sittin' at work dreamin' a some other life, I'll think a her sauerkraut breath an' the smell a chlorine. I spent hours at a time with her tongue in my mouth an' a soggy ass from sittin' in cold pool water.

Doans   Suburbia love at it's finest.

Emanuel   Sometimes she'd undress in front a her window an' I'd be like—where's my jerk-off sock? She gave me a pair a her panties an' I sniffed every molecule outta those things. They were great till mom found 'em an' stuck 'em in the trash compactor. She pushed the button like ten times.

Doans   You ever do her, man?

Emanuel   Hell no. . . we were just a couple a kids learnin' how to back outta the driveway.

Doans   Man, the first time I was with a chick—I mean really with a chick—was at the seminary. She was at the nunnery a mile away.

Hector   Nothin' like puttin' raw meat outside the bear's cage, man—*he laughs.*

Doans   Yeah, well maybe they got a two-for-one deal on the masonry; I don't know. Naturally, we'd cut over to the woods an' wait for 'em every chance we could. Saturdays mostly. There was a little swimmin' hole there too, man. Just a small pool. Naw, more like a marsh—ice cold 'cause it was spring-fed.

Hector   You go skinny-dippin', man?

Doans   Naw—they were too shy. So were we, really. We'd do
the swimmin' thing, then pair off. I liked to take my little virgin to
this old log cabin. A real log cabin out in the middle a nowhere. It
was barely standin', but nobody messed with it. We'd sit by the
hearth an' light the smallest fire—just for the sake a lightin' a fire.
One day we were sittin' there, our engines revved like dragsters,
just makin' out. . . an' she says somethin' like so, are you gonna
wait your whole life to do it or what?

Hector   You put the pedal to the metal?

Doans   Man, I was scared!

Hector   Scared a what?—*snickering.*

Doans   What do you think?

Hector   So what'd you do?

Doans   What'd I *do*? . . . Aw, I think I just kept on kissin' her.
·I·figured, if I'm kissin' her, she can't say nothin'. I was about to
explode, but I felt embarrassed in front of her, an' so I wouldn't
allow our bodies to touch—only our hot little Valentino lips.
She'd pull back every so often an' just give me this look, an' I was
so fuckin' scared I just couldn't.

Hector   I thought you said this was your first real-live
encounter.

Doans   Take it easy, I'm gettin' there. So like in the fall, I
don't know how, but somebody got hold of a car. Maybe it was
the dude in town who had the car. We hooked up with a few a the
locals, just to keep ourselves connected with the planet makeover
happenin' durin' that time, an' maybe one a those guys had the
car. Well, me an' this dude went on a double date, an' we ended
up down this dirt road surrounded by nothin' but corn fields. I was
in the back seat with my little nun, an' my buddy, Henry Miller
Junior, was in front with Anais Nin. Henry an' Anais were makin'
pretty good progress, while I was caught in round two a stage
fright with Sally Fields. . . She was so sweet. She just reached
down an' whipped it out an' jerked me off. I didn't have time to
. put up a fight. She was nice. There was nothin' in it for her, except
the satisfaction a semi-deflowerin' me.

Emanuel   Pretty nice, Doansy.

Doans   Yeah, man. I went back to base camp an' my balls felt like somebody took a sledge hammer to 'em. I thought I got VD!

Emanuel   From doin' what?

Doans   Fuck—I don't know. Like, I was one step up from the stork story. I thought it jumped outta her lap onto my balls. I laid there all night long worried shitless, wonderin' how I was gonna tell the priests. It went away in a day or two, an' from then on she didn't have to pry them blue jeans open.

Hector   Nothin' like bein' downstream when some Catholic chick's dam bursts.

Doans   Yeah, but she was just a normal girl. Well, she was in the convent, so she wasn't normal exactly. But she wasn't too whacked out.

The corn cooks slowly, and the glorious star known by laymen as The Sun, the only known mother to a whole rat's nest of incorrigible little beasts, goes from overhead to askance, shifting shadows and mood alike. Hector serves ears on paper plates, which he twirls over a stick of butter. Beers go down quickly. Primed with alcohol, the air unmoved from its sticky entrenchment, they eat corn only—three, four, five, six ears each—a full meal here in these parts when late summer shows off and makes the other seasons gasp in amazement. It is here, before twilight's transition, that humanity's questions are most often asked, and are sometimes answered.

Hector   *He lay with his hands behind his head against the log, his stomach packed, sweating from the meal, watching the sky through the dog feet patches made by the canopy.* Listen, Doans. Listen to this: A few nights ago I was lyin' in bed. I just could not get comfortable. I was sweatin' up a storm. I kept movin' around. I went downstairs an' tried to watch TV. But nothin' I did helped. I went outside an' laid in a lawn chair. The chair was wet from dew, but I didn't care. Pretty soon that made me cold—so I went in an' took a hot shower. When I finished dryin' off, the heat hit me again an' I was burnin' up. I ended up on the floor with my face shoved in front a the fan.

Doans   Man, that sounds real bad. Maybe you should see a doc.

Hector   No, I'm all right. Listen. Just listen: You know, when I was lyin' there I started thinkin' about dad. I think about both of 'em all the time. I wonder if they're doin' okay.

Doans   They're doin' okay, man. I just seen 'em.

Hector   Yeah. . . sure. . . Mostly I thought about dad an' how he can't ever get comfortable. He's lived over half his life in that wheel chair, an' most a the time he's uncomfortable. You know, he'll go to bed an' won't be able to go to sleep for two hours sometimes. He can barely turn himself over. Can you imagine? . . . One night I can't get comfortable, I can't sleep, an' that's how he is every night. His legs are sore. He's got those burns on his shins. He just lies there. . . What does he think about?

Doans   He thinks about what he's gonna accomplish the next day, man. I know that for a fact.

Hector   He keeps goin'. He never stops. I can only remember one time when he showed the slightest chink in his armor. We were sittin' in the shop. He had this funny look, like a sick animal. His eyes were slow. He said—you know my quality a life isn't very good. My hands are goin'. I can't hear. My eyes. . . Doans—I couldn't do anything to help. I didn't know what to say to 'em. How was I gonna put a positive spin on *that*? He was right. All I could do was shrug my shoulders. I wanted to reach out, but I didn't want 'em to lose it. I knew if he lost it, I would too. I kept the distance. I had to. . . *He twists his head up to look at his brother.* Isn't that sad?

Doans   It's one big fat crapper—*he flicks a cigarette butt across the mud.*

Hector   Every day he gets himself up—an' for what? His life's in the details a what he makes with his hands—*his own hands go all cyclone, up and down an invisible Trajan's Column.* He has to create. The day he loses that, he won't get outta bed.

Doans   He ain't never gonna lose that, man. Not him.

Hector   I hope to God he doesn't.

Doans   You forgot the most important piece, man.

Hector   What's that?

Doans   You forgot to mention *them*.

Hector   I know, man. But they're both fadin' so fast. . .

Doans   The romance never died, man. That love affair between 'em is still there. Mom could hack dad up with a butcher knife, an' he'd still love her. I don't know what they did in their previous lives to deserve what this life dished out to 'em, but they took every bullet fired their way an' kept on a marchin'. People don't know. They met when they were teenagers, an' they still got it bad for each other. Man, our dad clung to his woman like a barnacle. Yeah, he did always tell us mom was more important than we were. That ain't cool. You don't tell your kid somethin' like that. But the way he saw it, he didn't have a choice. He was desperate. Maybe he saw the flood right in his face, an' he knew his only chance—*our* only chance—was to cling to the one person he knew he could count on. Maybe the only chance for all of us to survive was for him to partially shut us out. He worshipped mom, man. I saw that more than I felt 'em pushin' me outta the way.

Hector   They don't make 'em like them anymore, Doans.

Doans   Well, they do, but it's awful hard to plow through all the slop this post-modern limbo dishes out.

Hector   Today they'd be on welfare. Mom would a fucked around, or just left. We would a been sent off to different places.

Doans   Maybe. That sounds like a pretty likely scenario.

Hector   An' they wouldn't a gotten the kind a help they got. You don't see friends stoppin' by the house to drop off blank checks too much these days.

Doans   No, that kind a help is fadin' fast, man. As the last Depression Era soldiers fade, so fades some real square notions.

Hector   Their set a rules looked real archaic when we were growin' up.

Doans   They were, man. They came from survival school. That looks pretty whacked out in the middle a hippieville.

Hector   All I ever had to worry about was track practice an' algebra. Pax Americana, man. They fought for it. The sixties bulldozed it. We pissed on it. An' now. . . now what?

The wind blows in chaotic spurts and sprints—lifting the lulled

*low branches of the trees. There comes the unaccounted for stench
of some dead creature, possibly a large fish, more likely a small
land animal. From up on the road comes a strange, dull thud that
keeps going and going; each of them silently tries to discern its
source, but to no avail.*

Hector   I remember one time I rode down to Aunt Ruby's with
dad. We stopped at her department store an' dad told me to go in
an' get her. He said she worked in the lingerie department. I
said—what's that? He said—you don't know what lingerie is? I
was like ten. He told me it was women's underwear. So I go inside
an' ask the first person I saw where the lingerie department was,
an' before you know it I'm standin' eye-to-eye with big old
watermelon bra cups an' beige panties, an' then Aunt Ruby's
lookin' down at me with that long, sad face. It was the only time I
ever thought she was gonna bust out laughin'. . . . *He rolls onto his
side, hands under his head.*

Doans   Wasn't it great how dad used to send us in to fetch
some real oddball lunatic? . . . Did I tell you about the time he told
me to tell the kike he wanted to see 'em?

Hector   Dad?

Doans   Oh, sure. Dad was a real Jew lover.

Hector   I never noticed.

Doans   Listen, man, dad was like any other Catholic monkey
wrench durin' that time. It wasn't like he was this big-time anti-
Semite. He just had an easier time dealin' with labels than he did
any particular guy who happened to be of a certain ethnic group.
Mostly when he was mad.

Hector   So tell me. He told you to go fetch the kike.

Doans   Well, yeah. We were sittin' in the parkin' lot outside
this camera shop an' he's goin' off on this guy—who ain't there, a
course—'cause he's not payin' up. He told me to go in an' tell that
son of a bitch kike that if he didn't give 'em his money, he's
gonna have the cops all over the place. So, bein' the half-robot
half-smartass that I was, that's what I did. I went in an' told the
guy pretty much verbatim. The guy comes out an' says somethin'
like—you lookin' for the son of a bitch kike that won't pay up?

Let the record show, we didn't stop at Swenson's that day.

Hector   Hey—that's what you get when you send a wise-crackin' ten-year-old into a camera shop as your bill collector.

Doans   There were some scary dudes. Man, you didn't go on deliveries too much, did you?

Hector   Just sometimes. Mostly in Akron an' Canton.

Doans   Yeah, we went all over the state, man. Cleveland. Columbus. Canton. Massillon. Youngstown. Toledo. Didn't go as far as Cincinnati. All those camera dudes, man. . . there were some sly jokers. It's amazin' we weren't kidnapped or sodomized every week. The old man was cool, though. We always stopped somewhere good to eat. When I think a all the hours I logged sittin' in that front seat, flickin' the doorknob, chattin' with the old man. I'll tell you somethin'. It gave me a real good picture a the way people are. I got to see first hand, early on, what sort a glue holds this here world together.

Hector   You ever work in the shop?

Doans   No way, man. That was mostly for the girls. Junior an' Adam might a helped 'em move shit around sometimes, but they never worked behind the counter.

Hector   I remember when Deuce stole money from the shop.

Doans   Yeah—that was a real bad scene, man. He didn't exactly steal it. What he did was, he was takin' in business on the sly, without runnin' it through the shop.

Hector   He was lucky he found Harold, man.

Doans   Harold was a good guy. Harold was a great guy.

Hector   What's the story on him?

Doans   He walked into the shop one day an' asked for a job. He said he was mechanically inclined, an' he just wanted to learn the trade. I'm sure dad was struck by the dude's overall clean-cut, Ritchie Cunningham presentation. The fact that he couldn't see two feet in front of 'em might a made dad think twice. It took Harold a while to catch on 'cause a his blindness, but once he learned somethin', that was it. He didn't make mistakes. The fucker was slow, but the best repairman dad had. Not too many re-do's with Harold.

Hector   Sometimes I think about that. How dad took the time to teach a blind guy how to fix cameras, an' he had like zero patience with us about *anything*.

Doans   Two cripples, man. Like two dogs, or two guinea pigs, or two anything.

Hector   He still fixin' shit, man?

Doans   As far as I know. Livin' in the same house he was in like forty years ago.

Hector   Jesus.

Doans   What's a matter?

Hector   No, it's pretty cool. Just wild.

Doans   He had to go into other things. He fixes VCR's an' shit now. Not sure if he does TV's. His kids are just about grown up. . .

Hector   *Changing channels in his head*—You do any more casts with Wolfy?

Doans   Naw, man. Well, yeah, I did that one test cast I told you about. It looks good, man. No bubbles at-tall.

Hector   You think you'll be able to do some next week?

Doans   Hmm. . . that looks like quite a stretch, bro'. I'm in deep with the dove sculpture now. I gots to keep chuggin' away on that or the mailman don't bring me no paycheck.

Hector   I know, man, but it's been a few weeks—*he leans up on an elbow, propping his head with his hand.* We gotta move on it while I'm not workin'.

Doans   I hear you, man I do hear you. Maybe I can find some time this week an' I can cast a couple.

Hector   They have to be clean, Doans. You know, without any cracks or bubbles. People won't buy 'em.

Doans   Like, I think I been through this meat grinder before, man—*his head cocks to look at his dragon.*

Hector   I'm just sayin'.

Doans   I dig what you're sayin'. I'll see what I can do.

Hector   I can't go around to the galleries without somethin' to show 'em.

Doans   Yeah. Okay.

Hector   I still think Wal-Mart, man. You could sell millions of 'em.

Doans   Wal-Mart. . . hmmm. . . yeah. . . I don't know. . .

Hector   You get into Wal-Mart with even one piece an' that's it, man. You're gonna be in bathrooms an' foyers all over the fuckin' country.

Doans   I don't know, man—*he pulls out a cigarette from his shirt pocket and lights it, then sets his elbow on his knee and takes a drag.*

Hector   You don't know what?

Doans   I don't know if that sculpture is Wal-Mart material.

Hector   We can tone it down if we have to. Bring her tits down a cup size, make it a little less threatenin'.

Doans   The threatenin' part is kind a instrumental to the whole thing, man.

Hector   Hey, man, everybody has to compromise somethin'. Even Michelangelo or Norman Rockwell.

Doans   I'll see what I can do, man. I'll keep you posted.

Hector   We're runnin' outta time. As soon as we get this bar goin', I'll be tied up.

Doans   I'll eat my Wheaties. I'll try, man.

As Emanuel hauls in more bottom feeders, Gabriel stands over Doans, who cleans up his carving with the tip of his dull blade. He's dissatisfied with it and decides to toss it in the night's fire. Gabriel believes it to be pretty darn good and thinks he'll take up soap carving again and surprise Abby with an owl. Hector, having drifted off, rouses from a black dream and starts talking to the dead wood and black earth.

Hector   Hollywood's taken the place a church. New York an' L.A— they got this country by the balls. It all runs through those two cities. They define what people do, an' what people want. You .wanna know why people are zombied out? 'Cause they got no fuckin' sense a identity, man. People feel like they're a nothin'. Why the hell do you think all these so-called reality TV shows are so popular? People are graspin'. There's no sense a belongin' anymore. Even the village idiot had a role to play, but in the modern global village we're all fed dummied-down graham crackers merely to keep us starin'. . .

Doans   Yeah, I know, man; but like a country's gotta have some central cog—you know?

Hector   Why?

Doans   Why?

Hector   Yeah, why?

Doans   'Cause, man, that's just the way it is. It's not *why*, it's just *it is*.

Hector   Well, I say fuck that.

Doans   Say it, man. But it ain't gonna roll over for you.

Hector   You're right—what can we do? They're tearin' *down* moral standards! This is entertain-me-world. Morals—*anti-morals*—come from the one-upsmanship a rebel upon rebel. Indecency upon indecency. . . Meanwhile, our brains are bein' shut off 'cause we don't need 'em anymore. Oh, our brains are *busy*—but they're not ponderin' anything. Religion, critical analysis, an' social involvement—they're old school, man. Fossils. Today, if a kid's not in front a the TV, he's in front a the computer. An' if he's not in front a the computer, he's in front a the X-Box. When was the last time you drove by an empty lot, in the dead a summer, an' saw a bunch a kids playin' a pickup game a baseball or football? Man, we gobbled up any empty space as quick as we could so nobody else'd get there first. There was competition, man. . . People are *surprised* when some punk takes a gun into school an' blows away the teacher 'cause he's flunkin' social studies? Man—the parents aren't home, the sexual predators *are*, an' we're supposed to believe in the lie that civilization is on this upward march. I'm sorry, but I dissent! One a those steps had a hole in it an' we're in a free-fall! . . . We live in a country where violence isn't deemed offensive, but sex is. We can't talk to our kids about it, but it's everywhere—plastered everywhere! . . . Violence, that's another story. I mean, guns are like this symbolic thing we don't wanna give up. They sell computer games to kids where the purpose is to kill as many people as you can, be the biggest thug on the block. This shit's bein' played in millions an' millions a homes across America! Dad's think it's *funny*. Mothers think it's *harmless*. That's fuckin' insane! You think that has no affect on our kids? Do you really? How fuckin' stupid can you be? How much disrespect can you heap on the human species? We got the president a The United States advocatin' a new war against Iraq. Is Iraq a real threat right now? Is it? Is it worth those body bags comin' off those planes?—'cause to get 'em this time won't be so clean. It won't be a video game. There's gonna be street fightin'. Hand-to-hand shit. He can't find Bin Laden, so let's do *somethin'*. Why not another war? Let's finish my daddy's war. Let's alienate Europe—our only friend. Let's flex our muscle. We don't need anybody tellin' us what to do. This is what the *president* is teachin' our kids!

Doans   It is insane, man. Where've you been?

Hector   Capitalism is a dead end.

Doans   Yeah, well, show me a better way. I'll be there.

Hector   In this country, the system says there'll be only two political parties of any consequence. Everybody else, go home. We don't want your ideas. We don't *value* your ideas. You are a direct threat to our power base, an' we don't want you around. We set the rules. The rules aren't fair. Too bad. . . That's not democracy, man! That's a two-headed oligarchy. A two-pronged aristocracy.

Doans   You dig communism, man? I don't think so.

Hector   How the fuck would I know? Look—all I'm sayin' is more isn't necessarily better. Faster isn't always better. Bigger isn't always better. That's what cancer is, man. Too much of a good thing. No control. Unrestrained growth. You know, in the 20's and 30's socialism an' communism weren't four-letter words. That wasn't galvanized until McCarthy. An' why? 'Cause people could see for themselves the abuses takin' place in factories an' docks an' canneries an' wheat fields all over. They had two eyes. It was still okay to care about your fellow man. . . Here was a different system, one that said you know, maybe there should be restrictions on this here free enterprise. Maybe there should be a more equitable distribution a wealth. Maybe every child deserves at least some minimal level a health care. Okay—so it was a knee-jerk philosophy in reaction to unchecked free markets, an' it busted holes in its own house. But the intentions were honorable. Man, there used to be a real voice other than this current Democrat-Republican monopoly megaphone brain-washin' crap. New, different, non-majority ideas used to have a real chance. At least a chance to influence, if not to win.

Doans   Blacklist singin' in the dead of *niiiiiight*. . .

Hector   Yeah—I mean, what the hell is *that*? You call that a free country?

Doans   The ultimate freedom—hell yeah. You're free to fuck your neighbor, to rig the system, if you can—

Hector   'Cause that doesn't sound like a democracy to me. It's like they wear that flag, drape themselves with these words, an' they got nothin' to do with democratic ideals. Freedom, in this country, has become predatory in nature. *That's* where it's comin' from. But that's not where it should be comin' from. That's not what the Constitutional Convention had in mind. They've bastardized it! Sodomized it! An' then wrapped themselves in red, white, an' blue!

Doans   Yeah, an' they'll keep doin' it until enough folks've had enough.

Hector   Fuck 'em.

Doans   Sure. *Here-here!*

Hector   Fuck their spy satellites. Fuck their nuclear bombs. Fuck their non-existent energy policy. Fuck their greed. Fuck their phoniness. Fuck their perpetuation a crises. Fuck their energy wars. Fuck their New Crusades. Fuck their redneck-an'-proud-of-it, dip-shit Harrison Bergeron act. It's the fuckin' Twilight Zone—I'm tellin' you! Hideousness is beauty! We're all obsolete!

The Buffalo Skull

He had first spotted the point of the left horn glimmering dully in

*the sun as he rummaged through the brush looking for wood.
Without thinking, he went down for closer inspection. He began to
scrape the mud around it with the stiffened rims of his hands; his
motions were awkward and frantic. As the horns revealed
themselves, he wondered where the skull had come from, if it had
been nailed to somebody's door, fallen off, and moved downriver;
or, had it been lying here all this time—hundreds or even
thousands of years? Having lost track of time, afraid that the
others might come looking for him, he covered the skull with brush
and then immersed his arms in the slowly flowing water and
rubbed them clean. Lastly, he removed his sandals and waded up
to his knees and cleaned them. He flicked his hands, stepped into
his sandals, and hurried back. . . Now, for the second time, he sits
forward on his knees in the soothing river mud, exhuming the past.
Using a long stick he pries it up, and the sudden release makes a
sticky gushing groan. Repeatedly, he dips the skull into the water
and then, as compacted hunks of sediment fall away and the murky
water pulls down smaller granules of soot and humus, the skull,
completely entact, stares back at him, perched on his fingertips.
The sun, jabbing down in ice pick slithers, mottles the skull and
penetrates the breezy undercurrents there beneath the long arms
of the willows and sycamores like the bold pivot of a marching
phalanx. The boy, weeping sponge for a missed date with destiny,
a Renaissance man born twenty years too late, alone to the
gathering flood's warning spray, weeping for the dead, for the
wounded and forgotten, for the calluses upon calluses layered
upon the imaginations of men—anachronism of flesh and blood—
bleeding from the daily carnage inflicted on his person. . .*
Emanuel   So, is this the end; the heart of a nation reduced to
rolling fossils after the slash and burn of freedom's march? Were
we, four-hundred years ago, predetermined to be standing on these
banks, after the song and dance, the infertile egg of senseless
cross-breeding? It appears so. The world waits, while we wait for
nothing and no one. All that is mankind, we embody manically.
All his essentials, are our commandments. The guilt I do have,
Doans, isn't the guilt of our Catholic upbringing; it's from the

horrific visions I see in my head. The people not yet born—
women, children, men, who will receive our wasted planet, staring
blankly and wonderingly at their father's father's fathers. The life
of a man surely must be lived without the weight of either
forefather or progeny pinching down on him; yet, how can so
many of us do so little for loved ones we don't yet know? . . . Is it
our collective bigotry? Is it the racism? Is it too old rituals
slathered on too thin daily bread? Information overload? What's to
become of this land when those who see the heat turning up, turn
away from the flashpoints and take up arms instead for propa-
ganda machines—imposters of the worst order—to protect,
fearfully, mummified lives not worth living? What's next when
lies are manufactured in assembly lines, and executioners grin at
you as though you were today's booby prize? I feel so impotent.
What can I do that hasn't already been tried before? What good
are my tears, when no one around here seems to care? Why forfeit
days with my own child trying to help children unborn who I don't
know? . . . I must believe there's something out there—some kind
of hope—else I would have ended it already. Could it be that hope
itself stands as the footer for sound logic, a logic that might lead us
out of not just this immediate labyrinth—but from our infancy as
civilizations and on towards new and lasting peace and prosperity?
My eyes tell me no. My ears hear laughter. And my mind can
barely muster a smug scowl. But I do know this: I, the father of a
child, a child I love greater than all things on earth, can't turn
away from my post. Her life yet lived will be the springtime
blossoms of my life's diligence and duty. And her child, no less
than mine, will be *her* bursting bud of nurturing love so that this
human chain, though we might lose the sweetness of taste from
here to there, nevertheless links generation to generation. . . I want
to know what to do. I'll do anything—as an ant on the march—if it
would push back the tide mounting for a charge against this
blessed planet. We've been good at conquering; can we be equally
adept at learning from it?

PART THREE

Pseudoman

I am constant turmoil coiled around perpetual truth-mining. I can't sit still, watching the world in its billion spinning tops scoring histories of love and betrayal and jealousy; I am, or was, no mere observer—but one of the iconoclastic catalysts that stood out among the multitudes. In youth, I yearned for order. Middle-age carved away my expectations, of others, but mostly of myself. In old age, I lamented what I knew I should have done differently, especially the loves close at hand I forsook for the sake of a bronze posterity. The agendas of men have, through the ages, reshaped my reality so that I recognize only a few habitual ticks and some general principles to which I did at one time share with those super heroes henceforth born from my life. . . . As the days spin into years and then decades, as truth for a whole cast of reasons has become something bartered and manipulated, Pseudoman, lurking beneath the lampposts of technological breakthrough, has emerged into daylight, no longer a mere mythological fear—no nightmare of writers and poets—but the humdrum reality of a yawning species. It is upon this empire falling that he thrives most. Here, where freedom writhes in agony from the lash of the master's whip, where crass meets religion to produce a new tragic irony, the ground is fertile for it. This new breed of man is real, is visible at this very moment. You must only look into the nearest pool of water or bathroom mirror. . . I am

*leading you to the trough. It is up to you, reader, to drink or
shuffle on.*

*On a baseball field of this dusty, blistered island stand boys of
summer's dreaming—Icarus, Leonardo, The Wright Brothers,
Charles Lindbergh and Amelia Earhart, the men of Apollo—
brothers in desire, separated only by the limits of science. The
time has come for Gabriel to spread his wings and fly.*
Emanuel . Gabe! What's that tied to your back—an attic fan? I
thought you were goin' up in some kind a airplane?—*Standing
skeptically beside the adventurer, he wants to see him do what no
man—at least in this group—has done before. . . and yet, he wants
to see the train wreck. The quirky inconsistencies of man's love for
fellow man are never more verbose than on a competitive field of
grass.*
Gabriel   This is it. It's not really an airplane.
Emanuel   It's not really an airplane? You ain't a shittin', Gabe.
You gotta be pullin' our legs. Doansy, tell me he's pullin' our
legs.
Doans   Nothin' doin', man. This here be the said contraption—*he gives the machine a friendly tap.*
Emanuel   How the hell you get airborne, man? Like, I don't see a
cliff in sight. ·
Doans   He starts a runnin', man, back an' forth like a
chipmunk until the wind's just right an' the parachute fills up like
Goliath's condom. . . then wah-lah! The man's aloft!
Emanuel   This I gotta see. I mean *this* I gotta see.
*As the others stand, deferentially, in the midst of this post modern
re-run, Doans and Gabriel go over the game plan one last time.
Doans, for all his conscious effort not to, can't help thinking about
the drill press in Gabriel's basement and how useful it would be.*
Doans   Gabe, my boy, you about ready to get started?
Gabriel   I'm ready.
Emanuel   Good luck, man—*stepping aside, amazed at what he's
seeing.*
Doans   The wind all right?

Gabriel   Fine.

Doans   Hector—come here an' pull this cord. You're the closest thing to Paul Bunyan we got.

Hector   *Trotting up, sweating and red, the affable Benny Hill Bunyan of brute wit*—Tell me when.

Doans   Tell 'em when, Gabe.

Gabriel   *He makes a final check of straps, goggles, and— tapping his toes into the dirt—his shoes.* Okay. He can do it now.

Doans   Okay, Hector. Give that thing a pull. Give 'em room, everybody!

Hector gives that lawn mower cord a yank. It engages on the first macho try. Doans waves them back, back, as the propulsion of the blade sends dust—not as winged waifs, but as grumpy, sleep-interrupted mongrels—into the air. . . The quiet lad begins to run. For a man who pursues no physical exertion other than lowering the handle on the aforementioned, enviable drill press, often for the simple pleasure of seeing holes created one after another in a scrap piece of lumber, he's got the build of a still-formidable bull on the mend.

Doans   He's gotta run into the wind!—*shouting with funneled hands.* It might take 'em a few tries! Stay behind 'em an' if he don't make it we'll help carry the parachute while he walks back! He can only try it a few times before he gets tired! That monstrosity weighs fifty fuckin' pounds! . . .

And then across the field he did go, against plausibility, into the teeth of stagnation, trampling the bland clover of his pre-fab days.

Emanuel   Would you look at 'em run. . . Go, man!

Doans   It's lookin' good!—the chute's fillin' up! . . .

Emanuel   Gabe!

Doans   He might have it!

Emanuel   Gabe!

Hector   Yeeeeee—ha!

Emanuel   Look at 'em. . . He got it! . . . He made it!

Through the membrane—a destroyer, a fertilizer, the new Hermes—aloft, he is indeed, above the trees and erectile broken chimneys standing stiff. Away he goes, gaining slow altitude, a

shrinking phantom stealing their own plumage quietly. Then back
around he comes, buzzing straight for them, dipping a bit so they
might wave and jump; and he might give the thumbs up and grit
his teeth and howl against the beat of the battering fan-blade.

Emanuel   Can he control that thing?

Doans   Once he's up there, man, it's like no problem.

Emanuel   He looks like he's just floatin' up there.

Doans   He can really boogie in that thing—you'd be surprised.

Emanuel   What's he do when he wants to come down?

Doans   I think he just slows it down, then cuts the engine.

When they were boys they watched blimps, as common as the
circling buzzard, float across the gray industrial skies—gray in
sound, gray in motion, gray in soul, proudly gray, before the first
hint of layoffs or plant closings, when the city was still on-the-go,
Midwest industrialism with virility still in its portfolio. The low,
reverberating drone of Gabriel in flight takes each of them back to
those days, but none more so than Gabriel himself. He reflected so
little on life's powder cake foibles, until now, that he remained
wooden in physical features, inner conflict, and mental examina-
tions of the rugs, one after another, being swept from beneath his
feet. But then something happened. Perhaps a sudden fear—a
glimpse at his own mortality through the ashen, closed lids of a
passing uncle. Or a desire in cold storage thawed by some
painfully common event—this desire coming back to life amidst
mummified death all around—death he had neglected to see for an
entire generation—death with teeth and itching claws—death in
full, rounding home gallop—and so to this death he stood with all
that pent-up disuse and began pummeling back, without mercy,
landing blow after blow, with precision, square on the kisser of
Pseudoman's smarmy mug. His appearance did not change. He
spoke little of the blitzkrieg being carried out, if only in perfect
mental warfare inside his own head, to Abby or even to Doans.
The only hint of protest came with the purchase of his flying
machine. With it, if only for himself, he wept great tear trails
across the sky, scored pornographic, vitriolic graffiti upon pastel
clouds, and shot in cold blood those he saw as genocidal criminals

in the guise of new world liberators. . . Gabriel, the reticent.
Gabriel, the stoic. The passed-over sphinx in Sears jeans and
flannel.

Emanuel   Beautiful. . . way to go, Gabe. . .

Doans   Yeah. Ain't that somethin' else. I'm so happy for 'em.

Emanuel   Doans—you bring your skull?

Doans   Well, let me see. . . *padding his ribs and then pants*
pockets. . . I think I did. You wanna give it a hit?

Emanuel   The thought crossed my mind. How long is Boris
gonna keep us Bull Winkle's holdin' the bomb?

Doans   Till he wants to come down. Maybe a half-hour.
Maybe an hour—*he produces skull and bag, holding them up.*

Hector   *Placing his large hands over his brother's*—Uh. . .
why don't we get off the field, man. You know, stand in a slightly
less conspicuous location.

Doans   Like over by them trees, you mean? Good idea, bro'.

Hector   I'd hate to get busted in a baseball field in broad
daylight.

Emanuel   Yeah, not shit, man. My wife doesn't need any more
reason to think I'm some a-hole.

They head toward the aqua blue cement outhouse, dying under the
heat on a summer's flaring nostrils day.

Doans   How about right here, just inside the john? Man, I ain't
smoked a doobie in a bathroom since high school. Where's Mrs.
Benson? Good ol' Mrs. Benson always found some reason to stick
her fat nose inside the john. I guess lack a dick will make you do
funny things—even teachers.

Emanuel   You smoked pot in school, man? Bold.

Doans   What am I talkin' about? I didn't smoke pot in high
school. Nobody smoked pot until they hit college, man. Am I
thinkin' a high school or college, or some other life maybe Jules
told me about last week whilst paintin' the blessed stars on the
canvas of rebirth? . . . *He lights the skull and passes it over to*
Emanuel for a first hit. . . Here you go. . .

Emanuel   Thanks, bro'.

Doans   *Receiving it back*—Hey, you guys remember that old

Corvair I used to have?—*he takes a hit, holds it, then coughs and his bugged eyes bug more.*

Hector   Sure, man.

Doans   Yeah—*in a Jim Bowie, shot in the heart a million times by those lyin', cheatin', yellow-bellied Mexicans voice*—it had all those buttons an' round displays. The chicks loved that thing, man. *He offers the joint to the big man.*

Hector   Aunt Sophie had a Corvair—*he teases. Though he gripped a cigarette like a hotdog, he holds the small skull on his fat fingertips like the last egg on earth. He remembers the Corvair, and her Cat in the Hat pillbox hat that brushed the roof of the car whenever she turned her head to say something refreshingly odd— product of never having been hooked by the crook of children.* You an' Aunt Sophie, Doans.

Emanuel   My first car was Sissy's '69 Volkswagon. Me an' dad tore that engine apart an' rebuilt the whole thing. *Yes, you did, son. You were his last set of hands for the well-greased mind of the former most likely to excel at everything. You were his hands, his mirror, his torment, and his proof in God's unexpected barnstorming. All winter long, on the floor of the garage, you dismantled the engine for him, then reassembled it as he explained nothing and you recoiled into your recumbent posture of the misplaced soul. How you wanted it, the father-son duet. And all you ever got were jars filled with urine. Ah, well. You were too young and too over- the-top to recognize his peace pipe.*

Doans   I remember that car. . . Man, I probably had ten Volkswagon's in my life.

Emanuel   Ann-Marie bought it new, then sold it to Sissy who proceeded to burn a hole in one a the pistons. I mean a hole you could put your finger through.

Hector   Sissy an' her cars. She never changed the oil, man.

Doans   Bless her heart.

Emanuel   Me an' Darlene took that thing to White Rock for a trial run. First time outside the neighborhood. The heater box was locked open, man. Hot air blasted on our feet the whole way.

Doans, re-lighting the half-spent charred remains and then, while still glowing, offering to Emanuel, who takes it and sucks on it like a real pro. The dust bowl ball field flicks a memory; the weed fans the flames and turns the memory on—from black and white to Magic Bus color.

Doans   My first wife took the 60's literally, man. I came home an' found her humpin' some jock from the football team . . . *No regrets—just something too alive with acid-tentacles around his youth-in-yonder-direction to keep to himself.*

Hector   Is that right?

Doans   Yeah, man! We supposedly had this open marriage, you know? I didn't mean it like you can open your legs for any easy-ridin' midnight cowboy who comes draggin' his boner—thump, thump, thump—through the front door an' up those steps a Nirvana.

Emanuel   You caught her, man?

Doans   Yeah. I caught her.

Emanuel   What'd you do?

Doans   What'd I do? . . . What'd I do? . . . What do you think I did? I set her cheatin' hippie ass a walkin'—that's what I did.

Emanuel   Good for you, man. Good for you.

Doans   *He starts chuckling*—Man, like this chick read too many Timothy Leary diatribes. She was privileged East Coast white bread all the way.

Hector   What was she doin' at Kent?

Doans   Dabblin'. She was a big-time dabbler. Ain't that what the privileged soft behinds in this world do? They dabble in the real world for kicks.

Emanuel   Man, I remember your wedding.

Doans   Which one?

Emanuel   I think that one. It was at some park.

Doans   Yeah, man, that was it. Goodyear Park.

Emanuel   Everybody was standin' around in a circle. Flowers—I remember all the flowers. That was the first time I felt ecstasy an' terror in the same brain-breath. I think I was lookin' at some bridesmaid standin' in backlightin'. . . . *Was it the anti-pollution commercial earlier in the day with the teary-eyed Indian? The girl down the street blowing her mind asking Alice for some pill-popping advice? The body bags floating across dinner air space? The mind travel each night—triggered by the music—to places where your burgeoning insanity could be conquered by the need to defend all that's right and good?. . . Which cocktail of Christ vs. anti-Christ was it on that particular day that sent you running for the nearest vomitorium?*

Doans   It was groovy, man.

Emanuel   An' passin' the cup around. . . *The circle, on dewy over-grown afternoon grass, stillness in the air linked with children soldiers, children prophets, and nauseous parents.*

Hector   You remember mom an' dad?

Emanuel   No, but I can imagine.

Doans   They were pretty cool about it, man.

Hector   Yeah?

Doans   Well, yeah. Are you kiddin' me? Yeah, they were cool. Devout Roman Catholic American Gothic meets Sonny an' Cher, an' not one beep from the Pope mobile. They were real dignified about it.

Emanuel   I remember some dirty lake, pickin' up snails along the water. *Logan's Run and all those breasts; The female bosom is your source of unrequited, romantic masochism, my boy.*

Hector   Then why'd they get so bent outta shape about Abby's wedding?

Doans   Her first wedding? Like, I missed that one, man; where was it?

Hector   St. Mark's.

Doans   St. Mark's? Catholic?

Hector   Episcopalian.

Doans   Mom an' dad gave her a hard time?

Hector   Brutal. I think they were gonna boycott it for a while.

Doans   Yeah, mom was always harder on the girls. I stopped tryin' to figure out where those ICBM silos were buried a long time ago.

Hector   Poor Abby—*shaking his head.*

Doans   She took the brunt of a lot a metal-to-metal gearcrunchin'. Had that mom robe thrown over her shoulders way before her time. Nobody asked *her*. God bless her.

There is sudden pause as cyclones rip and discard and transplant, the chaos of unresolved childhood anxieties. The result is a collage of themselves, cloaked as a parody of the old man.

Hector	Tap-tap-tap. . . it's good ol' Saaaa—tur—daaaaaay. . .
Doans	Noooooooo! . . . Aaaaaaaaa! . . .
Emanuel	Go away—*batting his hands at something.*
Doans	Back!—Back, you filthy, one-eyed beast! Back to the Labyrinth, back to the center a the earth from where you came. . .
Hector	Jesus *Christ*! . . . Good. . . ol'. . . *Saturdays.*
Doans	Man—*shaking his head*—I'd be lyin' in bed, like at 7:00 a.m., an' I'd hear it.
Emanuel	Squeak. . . squeak. . . squeak. . .
Hector	*Feigning, with hand to ear*—A mouse?
Doans	Here he comes, walkin' down the hall on his crutches. He gets to your door. Man, you're like all cozy an' warm in your little nest away from the family, the only time a the day you can get any real peace an' quiet. . . *tap-tap-tap.* . .
Hector	*Switching hand and ear*—What's that?
Doans	It's good ol' Saaaaaa—tur—daaaaaaay. . .
Hector	The dishwasher's broke. The fence needs fixin'.
Emanuel	Clean the garage. Scrub the floors. Scrub the walls. Rotate the tires.
Hector	Paint some rooms. There's a leak in the bathtub.
Emanuel	While we're at it, why don't we re-grout the tub.
Hector	Clean the basement.
Doans	Deliveries, man—every fuckin' weekend.
Hector	Clean the shop.
Emanuel	Pick up mulberries from the blacktop.
Hector	Mow the next-door-neighbor lady's yard.
Doans	Dig weeds.
Hector	Only two real dandelion diggers; the rest a you can use butter knives.
Emanuel	Wash the car, edge the drive.
Hector	Hold this, hold that.

Emanuel	Stand *here*, not *there*.
Hector	Don't move. Don't even *blink*.
Emanuel	Yesssssss—*sssir!*
Hector	Good ol' *Saaaaa—*
Emanuel	*tuuuuuur—*
Doans	*daaaaaaay.* . . . The bedpan of our miserable existence. I

do believe we were one a the chosen few—a special group
indeed—who had the honor a partakin' in this here Satanic
weekend ritual.

Hector	What would he a done without our hands, man?
Doans	Walked around the earth five times.
Hector	He was micro-managin' before micro-managin' had a

name.

Emanuel	Sundays were almost as bad.
Doans	Sundays? Naw, man. Sundays were a piece a cake.
Emanuel	Not for me.
Hector	Brother here hated church like nobody else—*he starts*

laughing.

Doans	You did, little bro'?
Emanuel	God. I used to pray for snow.
Doans	How about summer?
Emanuel	I don't know. I guess I just prayed for a miracle.
Hector	There were some pretty rough Sunday mornings.
Doans	You too, man?
Hector	I wasn't like the Scarecrow here—afraid a the fire. I

mean rough like havin' the worse fuckin' hangover you can
imagine.

Doans	I hear you there, man. I gagged on more than one Body

a Christ in my day, that's for damn sure.

Hector	That reminds me a the Suzie Solinski episode.
Emanuel	Oh yeah? Suzie Solinski? I remember her.
Doans	Not the dreaded Suzie *Solinski.*
Hector	Shut up, man. Listen. We were out Saturday night in

the station wagon.

Doans	You an' the Suze.
Hector	We went to this Todd Rundgren concert at Blossom.

Man, she had like a bottle an' a half a wine.

Doans   Uh-oh. No-no-*noooooo*. . . Mad Dog?

Hector   Boone's Farm.

Emanuel   Holy crapoly.

Hector   I thought she was all right. She was, until the last half bottle. Then, right in the middle a makin' out, with her big warm tit in my hand, she pulls away an' pukes all over the door.

Doans   Nice.

Hector   Wait—it gets better.

Emanuel   You continue with the mammary massage?

Hector   Sure. After we wiped up the door an' she ran into the Sunoco bathroom to rinse out her mouth.

Emanuel   Good man—*he nods.*

Hector   The next mornin'—Sunday—we're in the car gettin' ready to leave for church an' mom rolls down the window for some air. She's puffin' on a Benson-Hedges, maybe havin' some drive-by orphanage drop-off fantasy. . . Man, just as we're pullin' outta the drive, she rolls the window back up. . . an' guess what happens?

Doans   The Virgin Mary appeared on the dashboard.

Hector   This puke chunk on the window, man—

Emanuel   Aw, that's gross. . .

Hector   Like, this piece a ground beef or ham ball or somethin' is clingin' to the window. I'm sittin' in the back seat dyin'.

Emanuel   I don't remember that, man. She say anything?

Hector   She didn't see it. After Mass, before church let out, I asked dad for the keys. I told 'em I felt sick an' wanted to go out to the car. I rolled that window up an' down, but the chunk never came back. It was a long time before I felt comfortable when that window went up or down. I thought it was gonna reappear when I least expected it.

Doans   The sweet regurgitations a cheap backseat love.

Hector   Front seat.

Doans   Front seat, back seat—it's still the same tongues an' greedy let-me-have-them-biscuits hands.

Emanuel   Ever try doin' it in a Honda, man? Try doin' it in a

Honda.

Doans   Like, Springsteen always said love was bigger than a Subaru.

Emanuel   It was like sittin' in a refrigerator—impossible to have sex, other than havin' her sit on your lap an' bouncin' her up an' down. An' even then her legs were pinned one against the door an' the other against the gearshift. You just sorta squeezed your ass cheeks real hard an' hoped that would move you a little.

Doans   Man, dad never let me take the car out on a date. Maybe like once a month. But I didn't really have a steady girlfriend in high school, so it didn't put no crimp in my love life.

Hector   I remember when you an' Darlene broke up—*turning to the younger.* I was back at Kent.

Doans   You take it pretty hard, man?

Emanuel   Sure. . . sure, I did. I always fell hard. Man, that was real young love—as real as it gets. I thought those Saturday nights with my head in her lap watchin' Paradise Island an' Love Boat were gonna last forever.

Doans   So, like what happened?

Emanuel   Her parents, man. They were caught up in that whole 70's no-strings-on-me scene. They sorta nudged me out, an' the squirrelly son a their country club pals in. They were two smiley happy people for never spendin' more than thirty minutes a day together. That was my first knife in the heart. My first experience with betrayal.

Doans   It changes you, man—*holding in a big, long hit and then passing it back to Hector.* It really does.

Emanuel   I went crazy for about a week. I wanted to die. I had no life perspective to tell me it was gonna be all right. I had no experience in pickin' up the pieces an' movin' on. The only person that meant anything to me turned her back on me an' said she never loved me.

Doans   She told you that?

Emanuel   Yeah, she told me that.

Doans   She ever tell you she loved you?

Emanuel   Only a million times. Overnight—she turned it off like

that—*snapping his fingers.*
Hector   You think she did love you, Manny—*speaking softly*—
or do you think she was lyin' all the time?
Emanuel   I think—
Doans   Man, a course she did. There ain't nothin' to understand where the female ego's concerned.
Emanuel   *Tossing and turning it inside*—Yeah, but then how
could she do that?
Doans   How could she do that? . . . You wanna know how she
could do that? . . . I'll tell you how she could do that. A chick's all
about feelin' good about herself, you dig? The same juice that
pushes their little bods around—chop-chop-chop—doin'
housework, dollin' themselves up, blabbin' out compliments to
complete strangers, is the same juice that sends 'em in the about-
face away from the wall a truth when the cookie crumbles. Man, a
chick ain't about truth-seekin'—she's about validation. There ain't
no governor on her heart when the breakup comes. She'll cry more
than you—oh yeah. Ball her eyes out. An' then twenty minutes
later she's on the phone with five friends linin' up the next John.
Validation seekers, man—they'll rob, cheat, steal, lie, deny, an'
wrap it all in a weepy, slobbery pity party denial sandwich.
Emanuel   I don't know—*swinging his leg along the wall. He puts
his head back and rolls it from side to side.*
Doans   But that's cool, you know? Look—it's just a matter a
the juice faucet. When it's flowin', it's a goin', an' when she shuts
it off, well, you ain't gettin' a drop. It's that simple. Don't mess
with the blueprint. The blueprint ain't gonna change. Just
understand that once she shuts it off, more than likely it's off for
good. You're only ever on this side a the line or the other.
Worshipped like Pharaoh himself, or viewed like some scumbag
criminal sniffin' for crumbs a her holy bread.
*Oh, the skies of dust-blue in rail yard wait; watcher, winker,
fellow vagabond with nothing but knapsack and belly fire, holding
the sun, allowing the birds their precision flight, meddling not in
men's small ambitions. Across the field trees, gray-green, arch to
feel the latent streams of wind currents.*

*Emanuel   He squints, flicks his head, and then scratches his
nose*—You think Gabe's all right up there?
*Far off, near the shallow and slippery clouds, Gabriel scratches
his mark in the sky. They watch, silent, wondering if they are
witnessing a gambit of middle-age, or the needle of courage
finally hitting the groove of reasonable manifestation.*
Doans   Oh, yeah. He's all right.
Emanuel   What's he doin'?
Doans   He's just cuttin' cords an' hot wirin' the new mind
meld machine. He's off in another time, another vortex. Like, he's
re-inventin' the photons a mankind, an' here we are, the grovelin'
dogs a Pythias, rollin' in our own fecal energy. . .
Emanuel   Yeah?—*craning his neck.* Yeah? . . . An' I thought he
was just flyin'.
Hector   Manny—anything left in that skull?
Emanuel   The skull is dry, brother. Doansy—you got any more
oregano?
Doans   Yeah. . . *fetching the plastic bag from his pocket.* . .
Here. . .
Emanuel   After my divorce, you know what the highlight a my
week was? Sittin' in the laundry room a my apartment Thursday
evenin' washin' my clothes.
Doans   I can dig that. You mean the routine?
Emanuel   Yeah, I guess it was the routine. Just rubbin' elbows
with other people who gotta wash their clothes too. Like fetchin'
water at the local well. Mostly I was alone. Sometimes other
people, they'd come in, but I didn't talk to 'em much. I didn't
mind 'em, but on the other hand, I didn't feel like talkin' either.
I'd just sit there an' stare at the wall an' listen to the machines.
Doans   Man, I know what you mean. I still like doin' laundry.
Hector   Chelsea vouch for you on that?
Doans   I do! I'm serious. It keeps my mind jumpin'.
Emanuel   After the divorce, I became a money makin' machine.
Now that I wasn't married, I didn't mind overtime. When I was
married, even when things weren't so hot, overtime killed me. The
thought a givin' more than nine hours to somebody an' havin' it

push into my personal time—that just ate me up. All that changed. I was datin' Mazz. I'd give myself to the job durin' the week, an' then give myself to her on the weekend. I loved the structure. The new freedom after my marriage, the freedom a livin' on my own in that little apartment, the freedom of a new girlfriend. It was probably the best time a my life. I put no promises on her, an' made it clear where I was comin' from. That I needed time. That it might not last. I think that kept her interested. We knew it might just be a transitional thing; we weren't tryin' to push it toward somethin' permanent. For probably the only time in my life I lived without any great expectations. It was beautiful. We had somethin' really rare. . . I'm not sayin' our marriage ain't good, but. . . After my divorce, I was startin' over in every sense. I had no money. I got that apartment an' didn't even have a mattress for over a month—I slept on the floor. I had nothin', you know? I did a lot a thinkin'. I mean a ton. I didn't wanna be bitter. I'd seen enough people turn bitter. I wanted to learn from it. I faced myself. I knew I was as much to blame as her. Maybe more. I told Mazz all about it. I never tried to hide my ugly parts—I laid it all out there.

Doans   Man, like you never wanna show 'em *all* your cards.

Emanuel   I wasn't gonna deceive her in any way—*he says*. Not that I was deceitful before. But I told myself this time I was gonna lay it all out. Take me or leave me, but this is who I am. There were times she probably would a rather had me not be so honest. At every step I went outta my way to shine the light on my warts. She responded. She never knew that kind a honesty. . . *It comes across only as his mouth absently chewing at nothing. Inside, he feels the cauterized hole of lost love. He had been for many years trying to retrieve it from the abyss of a closed heart. This anguish he felt daily, with each unreturned kiss, with every warm gaze dropped on the floor*. . . Things are different now. She still feels threatened by my ex; I don't know why. She doesn't like the fact that I don't hate her. She wants me to hate her. She doesn't want me to hate anything else—but she wants me to hate her. I won't. I can't.

Doans   I remember, man. You had a real clarity about you. I remember those phone conversations. I hope you wrote it all down. Clarity like that comes maybe once in a lifetime.

Emanuel   I was an ascetic, except for the weekend when I was an absolute sensualist. I wanted to shoot outta that pit I'd fallen into. I wanted to use the time to better myself.

Doans   So, what's the final score, bro'? You think you're better for it?

Emanuel   I think. . . how do I say this; I think it's easier to find purity when you have nothin' to lose. I had no money. I had a job, but I didn't care if lost it. I had only a few personal belongings. I ate when I was hungry an' rode my bike a lot. I was datin' Mazz, but I hardly saw her durin' the week. I ate, read, an' thought. I saw things clearly. Things were black an' white. I *was* an ascetic. . . It was beautiful, just a beautiful time a my life. I couldn't understand the way people ran around like scared chickens, makin' one bad decision after another. . . Man, I had no moral dilemmas, about *anything*. . . Do you understand? Do you understand what I'm sayin'?—*he touches Doans on the arm.*

Doans   *Not knowing where to put his eyes*—I don't think so, man.

Emanuel   ·What I'm tryin' to say is, I became like Jesus.

Doans   Yeah, Manny?—*he says softly.*

Emanuel   Jesus Christ, the man.

Doans   Yeah? . . . Yeah? . . . I dig.

Emanuel   *Moving back, letting go*—But you know what I found out? I found out that how close you get to Godliness is directly related to how much you distance yourself from the real world. I had no wife, no kids. No insomnia from gettin' up four times a night. No stress from a mortgage payment. No worries about how I was gonna pay for my kid's college. No parent with dementia or second-hand smoke emphysema. . . I was as pure as snow, an' now, lookin' back, though I sometimes wish for that kind a freedom again, I see it as. . . Look, I don't wanna offend any-body—especially you, Doans.

Doans   You're not gonna offend me, man.

Emanuel   I'm just speakin' for myself here. . . but I don't need

Jesus. Take away the church an' all a those rituals; take away second an' third hand interpretations a His words, an' it's just this man. A good man. A really good man. But to me just a nice clean voice without the baritone of experience. Why would I look to Jesus, when I got our own dad to look at not two milliseconds from my last thought?

Doans   I don't know, man. . . there ain't no reason to. . .

Emanuel   I wish for that ascetic, monastic way a livin' again, but I know the only way to find it is to not have the very thing that's most real—Mazzy, my daughter, an' our life together. The world's monks aren't involved in the real world, man. They're unblemished 'cause they don't put themselves in a position to lose anything. How can you love without emotional investment?—without the real possibility a losin' what your whole world sits on? . . . They're completely irrelevant.

Doans   You mean like priests, man? You mean they're irrelevant?

Emanuel   Whatever sorta standard or image or whatever they're tryin' to project—that's irrelevant. I got this Bible freak friend, an' she thinks these celibate freaks are the cat's meow. A real priest hag. An' I'm sayin'—No, no, no, *no!* It's where ideal an' reality meet, an' guess what? They don't jive. Not 'cause people got Original Sin, man, but 'cause the model is flawed. You know, like I could sit here an' say all you need is love, man. Peace, brother. Just *love* one another. Sure, that'd be great. But that ain't real—unless you got nothin' to lose, or don't *care* about losin' what you got. So what good does it do to go around slingin' slogans a some fantasy, utopian bullshit? It's a dream, a Disney World. How about let's look at things straight on. Get out from behind that velvet curtain—drop them drawers—let's see you for what *you* are—not what you're associated with. I'm not advocatin' hedonism. I'm not sayin' we oughtta give up, just 'cause Oz don't exist. The opposite. I'm sayin', Oz doesn't exist, okay, where do we go from here?

Hector   You mean Oz, like heaven? Like, God doesn't exist? I don't know if I can swallow that sword, little brother. I think I just choked on the lack a pussy it's gonna get me.

Emanuel   I'm sayin' Oz—Oz, whatever fantasy you're currently usin' as some crutch to avoid your own personal reality.

Doans   Like, I dig what you're sayin', man. Yeah! Cool interpretation a yo' life transition resonatin' at high frequency. But you know sometimes clingin' to that slogan, that Oz as you call it, ain't such a bad thing. Sometimes you gotta look just to the right to see Alexandria's Lighthouse.

Emanuel   Sure, man. All I'm sayin' is, shoot for that Lighthouse, but don't be surprised if you don't make it. An' don't hang no guilt bullshit on your struggle to get there. Don't hang no guilt on your *fellow man*, either, if he drowns along the way.

Doans   Assumin' you're not whackin' off when the rest a the slave ship is row-row-row-your-boatin'.

Emanuel   Yeah. This whole discussion assumes that your intentions are genuine, man.

Doans   Hmm. . . like, bravo, brother. I think you got some real TNT in that birthday cake. . . Yeah, well, you wanna hear my after-the-fall story?

Emanuel   Let it roll, man.

Doans   Yeah, well, I pretty much wanted to kill myself after me an' Dee called it quits. I was real suicidal. I wanted to drive my car into a brick wall.

Emanuel   Seriously?

Doans   Yeah. I did.

Emanuel   How come?

Doans   How come? . . . Man, like at the time I didn't know. My hull was torpedoed. I was sinkin' fast. How come? . . . I went to a shrink. This shrink was for real. He says—you're fuckin' crazy for worryin' about *her*. Why are you worried about her? She's not worried about *you*. You wanna do *what*? You wanna drive yourself into a brick wall? You got it all wrong, man. You need to start worryin' about you. Forget about her. She doesn't exist. Erase that notion. I says, man—but, I can't. Oh, yes you can—he says. You wanna survive? You wanna stay in one piece? That's what we're talkin' about here. You don't wanna hit that

brick wall. Ain't gonna help nobody if you hit that brick wall.
Man, like don't even drive for a month. You want me to take your
keys? Maybe you get a friend to take your keys for a month. Why
you care so much about her? That's what got you here to begin
with. Why don't you care about yourself? There ain't nothin'
wrong with you, man. You think there is? You seem like a nice
enough dude. You ain't no dummy. You're all right. Don't you
think you deserve somethin' outta this world? A course you do.
Don't listen to that voice. How long you had that voice whisperin'
in your ear? I bet since you were a boy. The voice is your problem,
man. You're all right. You're a good man. You work hard. You
don't fuck around. Anybody can see that. Why couldn't she see
that? . . . He saved my life, that shrink. I couldn't pay 'em. Had no
cash. That angel in Bermuda shorts—he got my gears goin' again.
It took time. No overnight fixes. I started thinkin'. My brain was
dusty. I fumigated the carpetin'. I scrubbed them toilets. The pipes
started poppin'. I woke *up!*

Emanuel   To what, man?

Doans   I busted outta that egg. I breathed the air! I looked in
the mirror an' there weren't no demons in there—just little ol'
Doansy. The dude was right! There wasn't nothin' wrong with me.
When I got farther away from Monkey Island, I wanted to cry!
Like, how could I let somebody reassemble my pieces an' parts,
like I was some flea market erector set? Doans!—I said. *Doans!
Hey!* . . . But, like the man said—that's water over the dam. You
wanna survive?—he asked me. Uh. . . yeah. Then forget about it.
Drop it. Let go. Goooo—bye. . . I was livin' on my own for the
first time in my adult life. No panties hangin' from the shower rod.
No trash bag sittin' at the front door. You know what I did, man?
You'll never guess. I went down the celibacy highway.

Emanuel   Get out.

Doans   No, I did.

Emanuel   For how long?

Doans   A year.

Emanuel   A year? Yeah?

Doans   It was beautiful, man.

Emanuel   Wow.

Doans   After a while you don't even miss it. I think that part a your space station shuts down, goes into suspended animation after a certain amount a disuse. I had these great girlfriends. They knew where I was at. There were no hurt feelin's, just lots a coffee shop dialogue. . . Yeah. Celibacy, man. The colon cleanser a the soul.

Emanuel   I'd a been sneakin' out at night to farmer Jones' flock, man. *Come baaaaaaaaaaaaaaaaaaaaaaaack. . .*

Doans   No, man. I didn't need it. Like when you ain't hungry. Like when you ain't tired. It was only a year. A year's nothin'. After a year I went through this thing where I wouldn't let myself stay over at a chick's place. I was off the celibacy train, but like I was no way gonna jump back on the same old gray mare in a different saddle. I'd tell 'em right up front, before we headed home—Uhhhh. . . I ain't gonna stay over, you know. No matter what. It ain't nothin' personal. Just some bad habit I'm tryin' to kick. . . Mostly, they were cool with it. I mean, there were a few quick exits, an' some almost-sleepovers. I took Dracula's creed: gotta be in my own casket by sun-up. As long as I was home by sun-up, it was cool. No reee-lay-shun-*ships*. My key to the city. Let me drop my heel in that baby pool 'fore I back myself into the deep end. Let me re-evolve sos I know what to do with this Paleolithic lily pad, this spongy ton a fun thang called woman.

Tapping the skull against the corner of the building, Doans nods quietly. Hector, then Emanuel shuffle out from the shadows of the outhouse and take positions against the wall, which offers their bodies to the harshest angle of the sun.

Hector   Man, I went celibate for a year, an' I wasn't even tryin'.

Doans   . Oh yeah, man?

Hector   Moondog had me sleepin' on the couch for over a year. From just after Thanksgiving to the following Christmas. Every night on that fuckin' couch. Wakin' up with a sore back every day. Great. . . It was really fuckin' great. That *bitch*. Why work on your marriage when you're gettin' everything you need? Just cut 'em

off. It's all perfectly legal. The laws *encourage* it. You can cut a
guy's balls off, but you can't cut a woman's cash flow—isn't that
somethin' else. You know why? 'Cause all the laws now target the
true deadbeat, asshole dads. They use a sledgehammer to swat the
fly. Make sure you get that fly! Don't let *him* get away. But guess
what? Every other divorced father gets steam-rolled in the process.
Go ahead—*lifting up his shackled wrists*—take my child. My life.
My reason for livin'. . . How come when you get a girl pregnant,
it's fifty-fifty; how come when you're married, it's fifty-fifty; but
when you get divorced, suddenly the man's a second-class citizen?
I'd like to know. Nobody marries a woman because a her
economic status. But for a man, to attract another woman, that's a
big deal to have half your wages garnished. What if you wanna
have a new family a your own? You only got half your income to
work with. Your child gets fucked 'cause your ex-wife—who was
three months pregnant when you got divorced—not by you, by the
way—is either stoned or detached, an' isn't really there when
she's there. Her new husband makes three times what you do, but
his income for some reason doesn't figure into the equation. An'
the dumb bitch listens to her daddy's lawyer friend who says go
for the absolute maximum, go for the jugular, fuck *him* an' *his* life.
In a roundabout way—your own daughter's life. . . Tell me—how
is that fair? Does that make any sense? . . . Moondog's a nutcase,
but she automatically gets custody. Okay. Sure. There's no
incentive for women to try anymore. What recourse do I have?
Why don't you just turn me upside-down, shake out all my money,
an' divvy it up among the state, the lawyers, an' the carpetbagger
in high heels? Then hack out my heart an' toss it on the floor.
Doans   So, man, what'd you do after you an' Moondog split?
What was your thing?
Hector   What was my thing? Uh. . . well, I got a lot more
pussy, for one thing.
Doans   I bet you did.
Hector   Got to tug on my first belly button ring an' pierced
nipple—*biting loudly, the air; pinching painfully, the wind.*
Emanuel   How about tongue, man; you date any chicks with a

pierced tongue?

Hector   Nope. I drew the line at pierced tongues, eyebrows, an' lips.

Emanuel   I think it's cool. I think it's real sexy.

Hector   I fucked a chick with a moustache once. That was different. An' one chick had a wooden leg.

Emanuel   For real?

Hector   Well, plastic. She took it off in the bathroom before hoppin' over to bed.

Emanuel   You know she had a peg leg before you got her in the sack, man?

Hector   Nope. I just thought she maybe got fucked hard up the ass the night before, you know, with that stiff, stick-up-the-ass walk.

Doans   Surprise, surprise! Ain't no stick up the ass, but a *peg leg.*

Hector   She was great.

Doans   You lived the high life for a while, didn't you, man?

Hector   Yeah, it was all right—*wincing a face of indifference.* I put the cut-off at around 30. You get much below 30 an' what you get out of it isn't worth what you gotta deal with. . . I did this twenty-four-year-old dental assistant. She starts talkin' relation-ship after the second date. She starts talkin' movin' in after a month. Whack!—I cut her off, man. I said—relationship? . . . *Relationship? . . . Don't you get it? I thought you were old enough I didn't have to splain it to you, Lucy. The only relationship we have is this kosher foot long with those soft white buns.*

Doans   Maybe you should a strung it out a little longer, man. You know, don't close the door too tight. Get another two months a prime yo-yo.

Hector   I tried, man, but she didn't listen. She heard what she wanted to hear. I don't know if she thought I'd come around, or if she was just a horndog.

Emanuel   She was probably lookin' for her sugar daddy.

Doans   Well, that's obvious.

Emanuel   Those are the kind you gotta watch out for. Sharks in skirts, is what they are.

Hector   *Wincing, rolling his head around on the concrete wall*—It got old. I hate goin' to bars. At my age, the only people hangin' out at bars are storytellers. Drunk, lonely storytellers. An' all the stories are tragedies. It's like you gotta pass through all that shit. Like you can't help yourself. What else do you do on Friday nights? Sit alone at home an' think about your daughter that you can't see? Think about your ex-wife buyin' lingerie with the child support money you send her every month? Friday is a real brain-deadener. Meaningless sex is the best thing goin'.

Twilight

It appears as some gaudy hotel lobby art show—with its heart on its sleeve—the evening sky in longitudinal fans of violet. . . They watch the belly crawl. . . The river burns retinas with its dazzling reflection dance. . . Doans and Gabriel and Emanuel on backs facing the southwest, Hector a few yards away reclined in a washed up plastic chair facing right into the lap of the river.

Hector   Look at that sky. . . God, I love this time a night.

Gabriel   Beautiful. . .

Hector   That's a strange color a blue for the sky to be.

Gabriel   Isn't it though? It looks like an autumn sky.

Emanuel   It better not be.

Doans   You know what stars them are, Hector?

Hector   Nope. . . Can't really say. . .

Emanuel   Hope the clouds stay away. . . Doans?

Doans   Yeah, man?

Emanuel   You think there's some sorta absolute set a ethics?

Doans   Naw, man. . . Do you?

Emanuel   I'm not sure. It sorta puts a wrinkle in the whole deity question, doesn't it.

Doans   Not at all. Why would it?

Emanuel   'Cause then morality isn't fixed. It's a movin' target.

Doans   Okay. Don't you think that reflects what you see with your own two eyes? It might ruffle your security feathers, but isn't that how things really are? Don't you think God would also reflect reality, given that our intellect has any hope a comprehendin' the meanin', purpose, or designs a this deity?

Emanuel   It's hard to say.

Doans   Well, yeah, it is hard to say. I think God allows for all kinds a perceived inconsistencies. 'Cause they're not really inconsistencies. They're human attempts at categorization. You gotta categorize, man. It's how our minds work. But the minute you do, you move away from the truth. Maybe what *you* call *ultimate* truth.

Emanuel   Then how do you know which moral compass to buy? How do you ever find your way anywhere?

Doans   Look, man. You ain't gonna be judged by what your *country* does, by what your *times* do. Like, you can't choose your motif. You're gonna be judged by what *you* do. You ain't got much say in the terrain you was plunked down in. An' they ain't all the same. They're different as different can be. Now, within that terrain, how do you behave? There's the moral question.

Emanuel   I don't know, man. What about dissenters? Me? You? Are you good, as long as you go along with current moral codes a behavior? That absolves a whole mess a Nazis, man. An' I guess people like us are goin' straight to hell.

Doans   Hey—like, I don't even know if I believe in heaven an' hell, man—you know? Like, heaven an' hell—the one in the Bible? . . . It's just symbolism, man. Allegories. God: symbolism. Allegory. Hal: symbolism. Allegory. *I think. I believe*: symbolism. Allegory. Absolve Nazis? Why not, man? Jesus would a. You got to, if you're Christian to the core. Well, you an' me, we can't absolve 'em; we can *forgive* 'em. But what does that mean? Let 'em do it some more? No, no , *no*. . . Let 'em do it again? I don't think so. Free 'em all? No way. What does it mean to forgive somebody's soul, man? I think it means you're lookin' ahead instead a behind, that's all. An' in general, people who look ahead go farther than people who look behind.

Emanuel   You think God's a symbol?

Doans   Sure.

Emanuel   Wow.

Doans   I didn't know you believed, man.

Emanuel   I wanna.

Doans   Great. Groovy.

Emanuel   I don't know if I can swallow that God's a symbol, man.

Hector   What about your Oz theory?

Emanuel   *He shrugs, his eyes moving sluggishly in the sky.*

Doans   Well, don't you think that's what He was to Mr. Hunter an' Gatherer? He symbolized the energy responsible for the rains. For the sun. For safety from disease an' famine an' war. Civilization progressed. He codified it. Refined it. Trimmed away what didn't fit. Molded it to suit his needs.

Emanuel   So God's some made up utility? I've been down that logic path, man.

Doans   I'm sayin' it's all just a name for *everything*. The term *God* is just the part we think aids our meager human designs—you dig? The term *Satan* is the part responsible for the part a the intersection that we'd rather toss out with the coffee grounds. They're subsets. Well, not really. That's the label *we* put on 'em. They're just there all around us, part a the environment, which some lab technician, some dude called a medicine man, or oracle, or priest, or TV evangelist breaks down into different Petri dishes. Our minds handle Petri dishes. We're quantifiers, generally speaking—not abstractionists. Quantify it, label it, sell it to the belly a the slave ship. That's cool. That's okay, man. Just remember once in a while where all them dishes come from, an' why.

Emanuel   What for?—*the elder can't see the easy grin.*

Doans   What for?

Emanuel   What good is it to know things; I mean, if you can't do anything to change events?

Gabriel   Doesn't do any good at all, Manny—*he says, lifting his head*. It's just one more thing to argue about over your slice of peace and quiet before Wheel of Fortune.

Emanuel   You'd think, with all the knowledge we now possess, we'd be crashin' through that attic to those stars up there. . . Why aren't we? . . . I can't remember when things looked darker.

Gabriel   Everybody's gonna have a bomb, and then it's good-bye Middle East.

Emanuel   Knowledge is just a mirage, man.

Doans   A mirage?

Emanuel   A mirage.

Doans   A mirage a what?

Emanuel   A mirage a progress. A mirage a peace. A mirage a some better way. . . Where's knowledge gotten us?

Hector   To the moon, man.

Emanuel   To the moon. . . if you believe it.

Doans   Don't you believe it, man?

Emanuel   I don't know what to believe anymore, Doans.

Doans   Yeah, but can you blame knowledge on the current lack a peace in the Middle East?

Emanuel   Maybe I can't blame it, but I can ask why it stands by an' lets it happen.

Doans   It's just a headless horseman, bro'. You know that.

Emanuel   It's a mirage.

Doans   It's a mirage. . . you keep sayin' that.

Emanuel   'Cause it keeps standin' there, like God Himself, expressionless, a bag a empty promises. . . Doans—*he turns his head, knowing he can't see his brother directly, but wanting to direct his voice*—you went celibate.

Doans   Yeah, man. You gonna try it?

Emanuel   Somethin' else. I closed my eyes to it all. I walked away from the White Rabbit.

Doans   Groovy.

Emanuel   I haven't read a book in over a year. I haven't read a paper or magazine—I haven't turned on the news. I don't know who the Secretary a State is anymore, an' I'm tryin' like hell to forget about Alfred E. Newman.

Hector   *In his mocking pterodactyl voice*—You know what we do with criminals? We kill 'em—*and then, in Beavis and Butthead homage*—He-he-he. . . He-he-he-he-he. . . I saw it with my own two eyes. I thought it was his Charlie Brown moment. . . an' then he won the fuckin' election—*shaking his head in defeat.*
Doans   Man, like if I couldn't read or listen to the radio, I'd go nuts.
Emanuel   You ain't missin' a thing.
Doans   Hey—like, I stepped away from the jaws a Modern Times, I got myself a little shack in the middle a nowhere next to the howlin' dogs a Deliverance; but that don't mean I turned off an' dropped out a civilization.
Emanuel   I don't know—*he says to himself.* You know how many things I've ever read that I can honestly say changed me, fundamentally, inside? *He raises his right hand for his own benefit.* I can count 'em on one hand. Okay, maybe two. Everything else is fiber, at best. The brain wants to know, man. It wants to learn, an' it wants to create, an' organize. By the time you're all grown up an' on auto-pilot day after day, there's not much out there that's gonna flip your polarity. It gives you a sense a control, which a course you don't have. It satisfies those mental taste buds. But mostly it just eats up your time, stuffs your brain with crap, an' turns you into a neurotic.
Doans   Well. . . okay, but what are you gonna talk about with the spouse, man? After the lovin' an' the cigs've been lit; where's the wit an' wisdom?
Emanuel   Man—everywhere. In the beads a sweat on her nose. In the sweet milk oozin' outta her nipples. In the leaf shadows on the cement outside the library. In the first time your daughter swims the width a the pool. . . You know how many parents miss it, man? They're readin', or on cell phones, or goin' through mail—an' hey—I'm not knockin' the fact that we all have like zero time to get shit done, an' I recognize people need to feed their own personal solar systems. But I was right there with her, man. I saw her take that giant step for girlkind. I watched, I felt, an' I *learned.* Through the silent observation a my daughter, in this last year,

I've learned more about this life on earth than I've gotten from any book. . . I feel like the luckiest, most blessed guy alive 'cause I'm able to see what others maybe miss. It's a privilege to bear witness, to *assist*, in my daughter's metamorphosis.

At times it becomes too painful to watch, these wandering Jews of the soul, a biosphere of questions, but welcome nowhere. Nearing the end of this journey, I wonder what it has accomplished, what my purpose has been? Why have I shined light on these four men, men of nowhere, men hapless as they come, men who seemingly offer nothing to the beehive of humanity other than what little pleasures they might dole out to themselves—slivers really— between the megalithic slabs of state, religion, and popular beliefs? Why do I gravitate toward the underbelly of the beast, when it's so much easier to massage the shimmering flanks? My explanation is simple, though to you, weary reader, perhaps a little disappointing: I love these men. I am of their earth and wood. Their failings are my own failings. I have but the benefit of hindsight—the accumulation of more history is all—to keep me on the opposite shore, but certainly nothing inherently better. My hope is that you will see them as I do, that you will accept their inconsistencies and prejudices just as you accept your own. You will connect what should be connected, and leave dangling the stray hairs from the bust of reason. Then, just maybe, you may understand the voices of the past—those howling dogs of humanism—what they were trying to say, and how they were shot down.

Emanuel   No?

Doans   Naw, man. I never minded bein' seen with 'em.

Emanuel   I don't like believin' it, but it's true. I'm not gonna lie about it.

Doans   Don't sweat it, man. You were just a little kid.

Emanuel   Maybe. I hate myself for it. But I couldn't help it. I didn't feel bad about it then. I only felt bad about it later.

Doans   Every kid's embarrassed to be seen with his parents. You ain't no monster, man.

Emanuel But every kid's dad isn't in a wheel chair. . . I'd go with 'em to the mall. I was maybe twelve or thirteen. He never bought much, he just liked to get out an' see what was goin' on. Like everybody else. Whenever I'd see a girl my age, I couldn't look at her. It was like his handicap was my handicap. I was sure they thought I was diseased or somethin'. So, I couldn't look 'em in the eyes. In some ways it's true; I did feel his handicap. Pushin' 'em, it's like you're invisible. You see what it's like for 'em. The stares from people. The itchy salespeople. . . I wonder if he knew.

Doans Knew what?

Emanuel That I was embarrassed to be with 'em.

Doans Probably. I mean, he probably knew you felt consti-pated around 'em. But that kind a shit never bothered 'em. He's got a heart as big as anybody.

Emanuel I resented 'em. There he was with broken legs, an' I resented 'em for it.

Doans Yeah, I know.

Emanuel Do you?

Doans Man, like you wanted to fly. You didn't want nothin' holdin' you down.

Emanuel I think I'm the only one. I don't think anybody else felt that way.

Doans We all dealt with it in different ways. Man, not everybody had this other throbbin' orb pullin' 'em toward some other place. I did. Hector did. Maybe Jessie. You did.

Emanuel I'm the only one who condemned 'em for his curse.

Doans You're also the only one who treated 'em like he didn't have it—which is a good thing, man. Think about that one for a while. Don't you think he got tired a people treatin' 'em like some nine-month-old baby? Man, you saw 'em without no sad face. He probably dug the shit outta that. . . Wow—like, here's somebody who's gonna be square with me. Who don't take my shit. Who ain't gonna let my wheel chair get in the way a his own ambition. I think I like this guy. I think he reminds me a myself. Yeah. Dig it.

Emanuel Maybe.

Doans There's no maybe about it. Nobody likes to be

patronized. He's a big boy. He knows what it's like to be thirteen.
Emanuel I wanna stop time, Doans. He's goin' fast, my insides
are unravelin' from the pain. Where's God? I wanna have Him
explain a few things.

Shooting Stars

Emanuel Great fire, man—*talking to Hector, looking over at
his brother, and just as he had wanted to tell his father everything,
he wanted to tell Hector everything.*
Doans Yeah. Like, what a bonfire. The orange-blue wings a
earth's locked frictions heapin' back toward the flecks a starlight.
Real groovy.
Gabriel I haven't seen a fire like this since Boy Scouts. Cub
Scouts maybe.
Emanuel Who's got the hot dogs? You bring any, Gabe-man?
Gabriel I didn't know I was supposed to. *He sits up, leaning
forward*—You want me to go get some?
Emanuel Naw, Gabe, stay put. Pretty soon we'll be fryin' up
some catfish.
Gabriel But we only got a few.
Emanuel I know, Gabe. Haven't you ever heard a divine
intervention? I got this feelin', see. I got this notion that somethin'
real big's gonna happen real soon, an' it's got somethin' to do
with those four lines. Better not go anywhere, 'cause pretty soon
we're gonna be yankin' an' crankin' like four invisible teenagers
in a sorority bathhouse. We're gonna be haulin' in catfish hand-
over-fist.
Doans Gabe, if you wanna, yeah, go get some. I need a pack a
cigarettes too.
Emanuel You're gonna miss the show, man. I'm tellin' you.
Gabriel I'll go—*he stands, brushing himself off, dutiful.* I'll
only be gone half an hour. Want me to buy some oil for the

catfish?

Emanuel   Hell no! Man, don't do that. It's bad luck. You want it to rain, you gotta forget your umbrella. Anyhow, I think there's a few drops up in the cabin. Gabe, how about you get me a pack a beef jerky?—*turning up on an elbow, he reaches into his back pocket, takes out his wallet, and hands him a ten.* Here. . . go to town, man.

Gabriel   Anything else?

Hector   See if they got any sparklers.

Doans   Sparklers? What do you want sparklers for, man?

Hector   Don't you like sparklers?

Doans   Do I look like I don't like sparklers?

Gabriel   How many do you want?

Hector   Get a bunch—*he opens his wallet and hands Gabriel the only bill he has—a fifty.*

Gabriel   Fifty dollars worth?

Hector   That's all I got. Maybe ten bucks worth.

Doans   Buns! We almost forgot buns.

Gabriel   I didn't forget.

Doans   Yeah. Good man, Gabe. Like, I can always count on you. *Gabriel recedes into the black night, and they hear him move up the wooden stairs.*

Emanuel   *Raising up to a seated position, his back in protest, his stomach muscles taking offense*—Hector. Toss me a beer, would you?

Doans   Wait a minute—*though still more or less on his back, he cowers, putting his hands above his face.* I'm in the line a fire. Let me at least duck into my shell.

Hector   Here you go, brother—*he tosses low and Emanuel makes a nice save.*

Emanuel   *From the cosmic Wailing Wall everywhere he looked— he pounds his head with questions about his brother, his father, his wife, and the air we breathe. The stars give him answers with silent winks. He hears what he always heard—the wake-up bells giving him courage for another morning.* It gonna get any cooler tonight?

Hector   Maybe. If the clouds stay away.

Emanuel   They better, man. I wanna see those meteors.

Doans   Man, you all right?

Emanuel   I'm okay.

Doans   Yeah? You sound scared.

Emanuel   I was just thinkin' about this dream I had last night.

Doans   Yeah? What was it about?

Emanuel   It was about dad.

Doans   I think about 'em every night before I go sto sleep.

Hector   Me too.

Emanuel   Yeah. . . Dad went off somewhere in his van. Junior came by an' Doansy, you asked 'em what was up, an' he said dad was dead. The way he said it, I didn't know if he was kiddin'. I asked 'em, but he wouldn't look at me. He just kept lookin' at you, Doansy, an' wouldn't say anything. Finally, I told 'em if he didn't tell me I'd kill 'em. He said yeah, dad was dead. He died in a car crash. . . I just broke down. The floodgates let loose. I cried like I never cried before. . . But then, in the middle a cryin', I realized he hadn't suffered. No amputated legs, no wastin' away in a nursin' home. An' I pointed to the sky an' said thank you, thank you, thank you. . . his terrestrial sufferin' is finally over. . . I just wandered off. All of us scattered into different directions. Everybody turned into who they really were without the restraints a the cage that's been around us all our lives. One of us got whacked out an' became a street preacher. Somebody else went back in time an' became a beatnik. A few of use became hermits. We were no longer a family. The reasons for stayin' together were gone, man. Gone.

Doans   You think that's what's gonna happen?

Emanuel   You mean that we'll all go off our separate ways? Yeah I do. Which is really okay with me.

Doans   Don't you wonder about dad's real dad; what's his story, man? Maybe that's where this whole freak show got off the ground.

Hector   Different realities, man. There's more than one reality. We all got our own reality to feed.

Doans   You better believe it, man. Yeah.

Emanuel   Why you think *we're* together, man? What's the tie that binds *us*?

Doans   Us?

Emanuel   Yeah. What the hell is it?

Doans   Like, we're all tryin' to control our own lives, which are way outta control. That's all, man. That's what artists do. That's what any free-thinkin' creative minds eventually do— where the confluence a the desire an' the real form the bittersweet estuary.

Emanuel   It's painful. It's all a lot a bullshit.

Doans   Naw, man, it ain't all bullshit.

Emanuel   We keep goin' over the same shit all the time.

Doans   You think eatin' food's bullshit, man? You think sleepin's bullshit? Some people gotta comb over the mess every day, an' if they don't, the mess gets messier.

Emanuel   But we can't do anything about it. Where's it get us?

Doans   It gets you to another day, man. It gets us to this beautiful night. It gets us together. It keeps our wives from wantin' to throw us out the window. You think that's bullshit?

Emanuel   But don't you wish we could just get together an' sit around an' talk about other things, man, without all this skippin' record, middle-aged angst?

Doans   Talk about what? What do you wanna chat about, man? I'll talk about anything.

Emanuel   I don't know.

Doans   You wanna be somebody else, man? You don't wanna be nobody else. You think you do, but that's just that insomnia justifyin' his existence again. Here! Off with his nuts!

Emanuel   It's miserable.

Doans   What's miserable?

Emanuel   Look at us. We're like river rats.

Doans   A course we are. So what?

Emanuel   So, maybe I don't wanna be.

Doans   Sure. Okay. Good luck, man.

The stars can be connected any way you want them to be.

*Everything imaginable is up there, in those white pinpricks of
possibilities. . . The river heaves, moans, and lets out a deep
satisfying sigh. Without a clock ticking, time seems on the other
side of the globe. That's the fallacy of hope. It's what makes
success out of failure; it's what makes beauty out of tragedy.*

Emanuel   Hector?

Hector   Yeah, Manny?

Emanuel   I got some old records in my attic. We can take some
over to MacTear's.

Hector   Yeah? Who do you have?

Emanuel   Bowie. . . Dylan. . . some live Joe Walsh. . . Buddy
Holly. . . James Brown. . . The Beatles. . . The Beach Boys. . . I
got a whole bunch.

Hector   That's great, little brother. That's really great.

Emanuel   I don't want it to be some kind a museum, you know?
That's not it.

Hector   It'll be all right.

Emanuel   More like an oasis. It'll be real alive. We'll have
Mazzy's sister come in an' clean once a week. There won't be any
dust anywhere.

Hector   Don't worry. We won't let it be a sad place.

Emanuel   Doansy, we wanna put some a your pictures up.

Doans   Yeah?

Emanuel   We can sell 'em, or just hang 'em. Whatever you want.

Doans   You sell 'em, an' I'll give you ten percent, man.

Emanuel   No. It's all yours.

Doans   Thanks, man. I appreciate it.

Emanuel   It'll have the best Guinness in town. The only
Guinness in town that's poured properly. You don't wanna wait—
go some place else. We don't want you here. We don't want your
stinkin' money.

Doans   That's groovy, man. A place that don't cut no corners.
Groovy.

*Across the river moonlight dips its elbow all along the shoreline
and it seems as if—for only a brief instant—it was the side to be
on, and their side was dead and cold. They hadn't played music.*

Tomorrow, under the heat of the sun, they would jam.

Emanuel	Anybody see anything yet?
Doans	I saw somethin' a minute ago.
Emanuel	What was it?
Doans	I don't know. It sorta fluttered up there, then went away.
Gabriel	Maybe it was a plane.
Doans	I don't think so.
Emanuel	They should be startin' pretty soon.
Hector	If I fall asleep, an' they start, somebody wake me up.
Emanuel	I got you, Hector. Don't worry. I got you.
Hector	Thanks, man. Okay. I'm gonna close my eyes now. Just for a few minutes. Don't forget. . .
Emanuel	I won't forget. You don't have to worry.
Hector	When is Gabe gonna get back with those sparklers? . . .
Gabriel	I'm back.
Hector	You're back? . . . When did you get back?
Gabriel	About an hour ago.
Emanuel	Doans? I never know what to say. I think your paintings are really cool.
Doans	You don't gotta say nothin'.
Emanuel	I'm not verbal that way.
Doans	Naw, man. The more somebody gabs about 'em, the less they say.
Emanuel	I don't have the right vocabulary. I'm too busy lookin'.
Doans	That's all right, man.
Emanuel	Yeah? Really?
Doans	I love you, little brother.
Emanuel	Yeah, man. Me too. . . Gabe, you still awake?
Gabriel	Sure.
Emanuel	You think you could show me how to fly that contraption a yours? I wanna see what this river looks like to God.
Gabriel	I can show you. But you're better off taking lessons.
Emanuel	Yeah, maybe I'll take some lessons. . . You know what'd be real cool? Think about this: Some Friday night, I'll tell Mazzy I'll be home late. I'll tell her to get a little fire goin' outside

an' wait for me. I'll tell her to put the speakers in the windows an' have maybe the Scott Joplin record playin', an' put on the dress she wears every time I'm not there an' she wants to pretend like she's havin' dinner with Gatsby himself. . . An' then, like this angel she's never seen before, reborn into the man she's always wanted me to be, I'll come floatin' down in my flyin' machine, as white as the clouds.